APOSTLE RISING

Richard Godwin is a crime and horror writer as well as a produced playwright.

He was born in London and obtained a BA and MA in English and American Literature from King's College London. He has travelled the world extensively and lectured and worked in property.

Many of his stories have appeared in magazines. His works in print include 'Chemical', published in the Anthology *Back In 5 Minutes*, released by LITTLE EPISODES PUBLISHING (2010), and 'Doll', published in *Howl: Tales Of The Feral And Infernal*, LAME GOAT PRESS (2010), and 'Face Off', published in *Crime Factory* Issue #5, CREATESPACE (2010)'.

His *Chin Wags At The Slaughterhouse* are interviews he has conducted with writers and can be found at the blog on his website here http://richardgodwin.net/ where you can also find a full list of his works.

Apostle Rising is his first crime novel.

He divides his time between London and the US.

APOSTLE RISING

RICHARD GODWIN

BLACK
JACKAL
BOOKS

A Black Jackal Books Paperback

First published in Great Britain in 2011 by Black Jackal Books

Copyright © Richard Godwin 2011

ISBN 978-0-9567113-0-4

Book and cover design by Matt Swann
mattswanncreative.blogspot.com

Printed by CPI Group UK

Black Jackal Books Ltd, Suite 106, 143 Kingston Road, London SW19 1LJ
www.blackjackalbooks.com

For Page

1

The woods are cast deep in folded meadow shade, hues of blackness tinged with the heavy odours of autumn, rotting to nothing in the scattered leaves where insects scurry and blind slugs creep and grope their way to mulch.

The trees are perfectly silent now. The light is like some vermilion bleed.

An unbridled moon hangs overhead, a watchful eye casting the frozen promise of winter across the hushed landscape. The deer nose their way deeper into the soft warm fur of their sleep, feeling the hot pulse of their heartbeat regular as a jackhammer.

A path stretches and tilts into the woods, lost in thick shadows.

The sound of tearing.

A flash of steel. A figure lands heavily on the dense carpet of leaves. They rise and fall like spent currency as small nocturnal animals scurry away. A shadow leans over him now arcing the blade.

The leaves, russet in the autumn chill are flecked with red. Deep drops like wax. He struggles, thrashing his arms into the darkness. The other figure is faster and stronger and leans his will into him. Soon the body lies there hacked like butcher's meat. Then he tends to his work assisted by the watchful eye of the moon.

He alters the body and positions it precisely below a tree which by moonlight casts the shadow of a cross. Soon the woods are empty again, filled only by the heavy smell of rotting and nature's turning, and this still and butchered Christ.

2

Frank Castle tried to avoid waking, the stinging morning light an abrasion of his soul.

The scars he bore from the encounter told him it was finished, and he fingered their dead skin lovingly.

The case was buried and it wouldn't rest.

He lay in the dark and felt it move inside him kicking like a foetus, the images flooding his mind. He reminded himself that the file was closed, a tangible object untouched by time.

But it was not the tangible world he walked in. And it was time that ruined him.

It returned as he knew it would and it unwrapped his better efforts like rotting stitches on an infected wound.

3

'Cold cases remain unsolved because some detail needed by the police is missing, we reopen them to insert new DNA evidence or new information in the hope that it will shed light into areas previously inaccessible to us.'

The voice was like gravel.

Castle paused to take a sip of water wishing it was whisky.

He looked down at the sea of faces, wondering how many of them would make it through the long bloody corridor of homicide.

He held them in his stare, his eyes like gunmetal, his face like warped granite. The lights and the audience were getting on his nerves, as was the endless speculation. Yet beneath his hardness lay some wound, a flickering at the edge of his face which held a key to him.

He glanced at his watch and one young clean-cut Rookie in the front row caught his eye and saw something bleed beneath the reinforced steel.

Castle had wanted answers on this one for years and decided to ad lib.

He pushed his notes aside and looked intently at the new recruits.

'The Woodland Killings, as they became known, were the work of one man in my opinion, and they remain unsolved because the techniques for detection we have today were not available then and we cannot now get enough information to find out who was guilty of them.'

He could feel the officer in the front row watching him and now his hand went up.

'Chief Inspector Castle, the arrest of Samuel Walsh led to a dead end, despite much evidence that he could have been responsible. Do you think he was the killer?'

'No I don't. He was the best we had at the time, but there were other parties who may well have been responsible for those killings.'

'Ten killings, Chief Inspector, that makes whoever committed them a major serial killer.'

Castle looked down at the young officer and saw himself many years before.

'Inspector?'

'Excuse me. Mike Nash.'

'OK, Inspector Nash, you're right. This was the work of a major serial killer, and he's still out there. We didn't get him. He was very smart and very sophisticated in the way he treated the police and his victims, and there was a level of taunting which gave the investigation an edge which on retrospect I might even say undermined our ability to do our jobs properly. Nowadays we wouldn't rise to some of those baits. We have far more of an arsenal at our disposal in the form of DNA and psychological profiling, but we never caught him. We haven't got any further on this case.'

'You said other parties may have committed the crimes?'

'Yes.'

'Who?'

'Unfortunately, we do not have the time to discuss that here.'

'The killings, the manner in which they were committed, there is still a major psychopath on the loose.'

'Gentlemen, we're out of time.'

He switched off the power point and collected his papers.

Nash waited by the door. He knew of Castle's reputation as an obsessive, a great detective who'd been involved in one of the biggest manhunts England had ever seen.

His fellow officers respected him and also saw him as a warning of what can happen when you get too bogged down in a case. They admired him and pitied him. Nash looked over at him and could feel the pull of the man, there was something old world and solid about him, as if he was made of some material that was no longer used.

'That was great, Chief Inspector Castle, really interesting, it's what I've always wanted to do as a police officer, get involved in.'

'Then you're in the right place.'

Castle patted him on the back and headed to his car.

Fumbling for his keys he dropped them and as he leant down to pick them up saw a pair of police regulation shoes appear.

He rose slowly, taking in the slim legs realising he was not about to get jumped.

'Inspector Stone.'

'I owe you a drink.'

'That's a song I love to hear.'

'Hard day at the office?'

'Just reliving the Woodland Killings in one of my cold case talks, nothing a whisky wouldn't fix.'

'Or two.'

'Now, you wouldn't be encouraging me would you?'

'As a police officer or a drinker?'

'Both.'

She laughed and they walked round to the Crooked Key, where they sat in their usual corner.

She brought him over a double and watched as he knocked it back and went in search of another.

Jacki Stone had just finished taking her kickboxing class.

She was proud of her black belt and found it hard to get adequate combat partners, having humiliated just about every male peer in the area. No one wanted to fight her.

Still, she persisted and kept herself so fit the other officers watched her with a secret lust that was kept well enclosed beneath a politically correct veneer.

In a dress, she was a knockout.

As many men found out to their embarrassment.

Her martial prowess did not undercut her feminine allure, although she would pack a punch as readily in a ball gown as in a pair of combat fatigues.

The first officer who'd tried it on with her received such a hard slap he didn't speak to her for a week, while the second found himself on his arse before he could finish his sentence.

She stood about five eight in her police regulation shoes. Her legs were rarely seen outside uniform and could deliver a lethal kick.

She opted for a professional austerity, wearing her hair scraped back.

At home she would untie it, allowing her husband the sight of its hazel lustre. At work she kept her sparkling brown eyes on the job.

Castle sat down, nursing the single malt.

'So, Frank? What's up?'

'A young inspector was asking a few questions about the old case, good questions, got me thinking.'

'The last time we spoke you said you'd never catch him.'

'I know.'

'So, why can't you let go of it? There are plenty of other murders out there waiting to be solved.'

'The killer played a game with us, and won.'

'And you still think it's the same man?'

'Can I get you another one?'

'I'm OK.'

'Keeping fit.'

'Frank, you didn't answer.'

'I didn't realise I was being interviewed.'

'I've watched this case eat you up.'

'It was before your time, Jacki.'

'It's still here. It's here when we go out on a new investigation. I can touch it.'

'Yeah, I still think it's him.'

'Why?'

'Karl Black had all the ability to do those killings.'

'But there was no evidence.'

'No.'

'And what was his motive?'

Castle swigged his malt and looked at his partner a long time before answering.

'What motivates any psycho?'

'There's no link between him and the victims that gives a motive.'

'Yeah, he's brilliant.'

'Why are you so convinced that it's Black? Apart from the fact that he pissed you off?'

'Call it a hunch.'

Stone didn't say anything.

She'd seen Castle solve many a case on a hunch alone.

4

Traffic passing through Bushy Park had been stopped, and outside the gates a queue of red lights shone into the night time like haloed eyes. The scene was a grim wound in the heart of the pleasant landscape. The first officers at the crime scene stood in the rain, water splashing off the tent and cascading down their waterproofs as they looked for evidence and the pathologist began his examination.

It wasn't long before Castle and Stone arrived and when they did she noticed her partner stop by the tree.

He looked haunted.

Inside the tent the body was falling apart into strips.

The flesh was ribboned, the cuts ritualistic.

'What've we got?', Castle said.

Alan Marker stood up and Castle looked into the tired eyes of this reassuringly consistent actor in the drama of his career.

'Hi Frank, multiple stab wounds, lacerating the carotid artery first and then a pattern of wounds to the upper body.'

'Unusual pattern.'

'Yes. I'm looking at it.'

'The flesh looks furrowed.'

'The killer's deliberately inflicted a shape on the victim, although what, I don't know- Are you all right, Frank? You look jaded.'

'It's nothing.'

'This can't be affecting the detective who's seen more bloodshed than a film critic.'

Marker glanced across at Stone.

'Was this a frenzied attack, Alan?', she said.

'I see why you ask that, but, no. The wounds are very controlled and very precise, which is why I'd say the killer had a clear idea of what he was going to do before he did it. Multiple wounds don't always indicate frenzy.'

'You're saying he had a clear idea of what he wanted to do before he attacked the victim?'

'I am. Wounds leave very little information about the weapon, but there's something unusual here. And there's great deliberation in the way he's been placed.'

'By this tree, whatever it is', Stone said.

'Fraxinus. It's an ash tree.'

'Frank?'

Stone cast a worried look at her partner, who was standing there staring down at the body like a rookie on a murder scene.

'And this is Ash Walk. I know this place.'

He stared at the vista of trees, his face harrowed, wandering.

'I'll send you the report back from the lab.'

Stone followed Castle back to the car in the rain, the smell of damp and rotting leaves heavy in the air.

He switched on the ignition and turned his eyes to her, but they were looking at something else.

'Seen it before. Twenty-eight years ago. Same position, same tree, same woods, same wounds. And you ask me why I can't let go of the case?'

Alan Marker's report revealed little, just as Castle expected.

There was no DNA, and beyond the general detail of the wounds and approximate time of death, it said nothing that could help with the investigation.

The only thing it did pick up on was the ribboned effect of the wounding.

Stone remembered it.

'According to Alan', Castle said, 'the weapon has an unusual cutting edge, the killer's dragging downward with it, trying to lodge furrows in the flesh.'

'Any idea why?'

He shook his head.

'It's the old case again', he said as he thumped a copy of the file down on Stone's desk. 'Get reading.'

And as she did, she saw why the Woodland Killings had obsessed her partner all these years. It was the work of an accomplished killer, and the similarities to the present case summoned disturbing echoes from the past.

As with the previous killings, the body had been placed beneath an ash tree.

This was a copy cat killing, but by the same man? And the wounding was the work of someone who took pride in the lacerations, as if each rending of the flesh was some aesthetic statement. Page after page showed deliberation in the act of killing, some method that went beyond mere organisation, as if some specific, aberrational belief system was driving the killer. Stone lost herself in the pages, unaware of time.

She looked up to see Castle standing there.

'There's design in the wounding. Do you know what I'm saying?'

'I do.'

'Where is Karl Black now?', she said.

'The last I knew he'd gone into a monastery.'

'This murder is identical to the first one.'

'Yes.'

'I mean it's a replica.'

'Do we know who the victim is?'

'Terence Smythe, junior minister for justice.'

'Why doesn't that surprise me?'

'Frank, you're one step ahead of everyone on this, doesn't that mean something to you after all these years?'

'Only if I get to catch him this time.'

'And what if it isn't the same man?'

'Could kill two birds with one stone.'

'That's why I'm here.'

'Very funny.'

'But why politicians?'

'I don't know. Black never gave any clues at all as to what motivated him. He worked on some other level, some impenetrable level we just couldn't reach. He wasn't motivated by anything we as police officers could recognise or fathom.'

'Things have moved on Frank. Offender profiling, our training in crime investigation.'

'Training's one thing, and then there's a whole other thing. The thing you start to see and taste if you stay in this job long enough, the shadow that falls between you and the real extreme criminals, the darkest side of crime. Stick around and you'll see what I'm talking about.'

'Black, like everyone else, can be subjected to analysis.'

'He's not like everyone else.'

'He's not beyond crime detection.'

'You've read some of that file, keep reading.'

'I can see he played games with you.'

'Not just me.'

'The police. But he wouldn't get away with a lot of that today. Like anyone else he can be drawn out.'

'Wait till you meet him.'

'One thing's for sure, I wouldn't want to be one right now.'

'What?'

'A politician.'

5

Karl Black stood in the huge oak-panelled library that creaked with age and history. A sense of carved time filled the air as he moved among his books, first editions, mostly of a religious nature. The Lindisfarne Gospels stood next to the Psalter of Christina of Markyate, neighbours from another era. The leather spines and mere presence of the man exuded a sense of retreat from the twenty-first century.

The panelling glanced off the sunlit windows sending layered facades of the library bookcases scattering and dancing down the well-manicured lawns.

Their verdancy belied the austere lifestyle of the building and its history.

It existed in the middle ages, bereft of technology.

The room housed neither phone nor computer and the light itself was dim, hung as if with difficulty there and involved in a struggle to remain alive.

Black stood lowering over the room, his shadow cast out onto the lawn.

Hands behind his back, thumbs interlaced, he walked with the posture of someone keeping a hierarchy in check.

He stared out at the grounds of the order he had founded and built up.

There was a knock at the door.

He turned, the face half-masked by a full black beard both kempt and subtly stylised, the eyes deep-set and unreadable.

A small man entered. His face was pallid and contemplative. He moved slowly and his entire manner positioned him in another era.

He wore a jerkin and bowed his head slightly as he spoke to Black who loomed above him, a good few feet taller.

'What is it Jonas?'

The voice was deep and he spoke with a command, despite asking a question.

'We have visitors.'

'Of what kind?'

'Novices.'

'Show them through into the ante-chamber and I will join you shortly.'

'Very well.'

'How ready are they?'

'Believers, although needing work to strengthen their belief.'

'Do you have prior knowledge of them?'

'I do. I have been inculcating them into the ways of the Brotherhood.'

'Good.'

As he left, Black turned and looked again at the tranquil grounds.

He stood well over six feet with a powerful physique. His broad shoulders might have belonged to someone who carried out heavy manual labour, although there was a sophistication to him that contradicted this. There was no spare flesh on him and he moved with total economy, as if preserving energy.

Outside clouds darkened the sun and the distant sound of thunder rolled across the land.

In the antechamber, Wilkes questioned the novices about their understanding of the Brotherhood. He sat extremely still and held sway over them.

A young woman with mousey hair sat next to her brother who kept looking at his feet, while a jovial woman with a bob kept interrupting Wilkes until he said 'Imogen, you will listen and remain silent, for the new role of woman kind is not part of the Brotherhood.'

She blushed.

'I didn't realise I was talking so much, the new role of womankind? Oh, you mean, feminism, no I'm not a feminist, please carry on.'

Wilkes looked at her and watched as the brother looked to his sister.

He waited for them to speak, a native menace shadowing his face.

'Sheila?'

'Yes?'

'Did you want to say something?'

'No. Not at all.'

She looked away.

'Believers all I know you are, but this step will alter the nature of your belief. Consider coming here as arriving at the True Church, all others mere fabricated representations of the teachings of Christ. Yes we share the same beliefs, but we are here teaching the inner mysteries of Christianity, we are here showing what the real meaning of Christ's teachings are, and that means casting off your worldly shackles and your worldly roles.'

He paused to take in their reaction. He looked at Sheila's brother, who seemed to be struggling with what he'd said.

'Malcolm?'

He was a pale young man with greasy hair, and paused a long time before speaking, searching for the right words.

'What is the difference between what you teach here and what the church teaches?', he said.

'Consider it not so much a difference as an extra dimension to what you already know.'

'And what is the role of woman in the Brotherhood?', Imogen said.

'The very role she was meant to play, which is nothing to do with the unshackled Jezebel modernity has given licence to.'

He allowed the silence of the building to take hold.

In the corridor Black's steps were heard.

He would finish their induction and they would leave with a little more mystery and a little more intrigue.

Castle shut the folder with annoyance.

There was nothing there he didn't already know, nothing he hadn't read a hundred times or more.

At her desk Jacki Stone was poring over it, lost in the world that had taken the best part of her partner's career and life. Previously his only refuge had been whisky, now he felt he had an ally.

He watched her, recognising the absorption, the sinking into the clouded depths.

'Anything?', he said.

She looked up at him, a hundred miles away.

'Interesting.'

'So?'

'Black's got a lot of questions he's never answered.'

'Tell me about it.'

'I know you've said this Frank, but how he got away with some of the statements he made is unbelievable.'

'Hardest guy I ever interviewed. He showed nothing, gave nothing away and I felt that no matter how long I held him, no matter how long I questioned him or gave him the nice cop to my seriously nasty I want to bite your head off one, he wouldn't crack.'

'Psychopaths rarely do.'

'Except when we've got something on them and tell me now, Jacki, we did didn't we?'

'Yeah, we did, Frank.'

'All the links to a killer we needed, except-'.

'DNA and motive.'

'Right.'

'We need to re-interview him.'

'I'm ready.'

'I checked out the monastery he entered, and he's not there any more.'

'That was twenty-six years ago.'

'PC Smart's trying a trace right now.'

'Good, I fancy getting my dusters out of the drawer.'

'Steady, Frank. And by the way, sorry.'

'What for?'

'Not understanding sooner.'

'I know from the outside I looked like just another jaded cop hung up on failure. But I knew Black was hiding something. If he didn't do those killings, he knew something and was protecting whoever did.'

'He was in the right place at the right time for us, but there was too much missing, perhaps now we might have him.'

'Let's hope.'

'The thing that undoes people like him in the end is arrogance, the feeling of invincibility. Say he did it and got away with it, he's performing a re-run. Whatever motivated him to kill all those years ago has resurfaced. But this time, we can catch him.'

'If he's anywhere near this, I'm gonna hook him and I'm gonna stick the barb so deep into him that he'll need to cut out his soul to remove it.'

Castle returned to his desk to make some calls and disappeared to the pub for an hour.

A few whiskies later he found PC Kevin Smart cracking a joke in the corridor.

Another officer was laughing and Castle knew it was something blue and something old.

Smart was a private sexist. Polite to the women PC's, especially Stone, dirty as they come when they turned their backs.

He straightened up as he saw Castle approach.

'So, Smart?'

'I have what you need, Sir.'

He waved a folder.

'Good.'

'Would you like me to give it to Inspector Stone?'

Castle walked off with the folder, hearing schoolboy tittering as the door swung shut behind him.

It made interesting reading.

Despite his indiscretions, Smart had done his job.

He found Stone in the same position at her desk as when he'd gone out.

'Karl Back left the monastery a few years ago, when he founded The Last Brotherhood.'

'The what?', she said, looking up.

'His new order, cult, I don't know what to call it. It's a Christian outfit he runs, set in some old monastic grounds in Hertfordshire. He owns the land, he owns the organisation, and that's where we're going to find him.'

'What are we waiting for?'

'You drive', he said, tossing her the keys.

Darkness fell and a few hours later their unmarked car crunched the gravel on the winding drive.

Their Flesh, like a jacket of Blood,
Lies deep beyond the tidal Moon,
Whose gradient of light licks this Wounding Time
Into some Sepulchre of Dawn
These solemn Branches
That lacerate so its eldritch face
Fetter and Uncoil the Sick Souls
And So the Alteration Begins
I merge with his Penumbral movements
A Tracing of his Fate
Now his shadow moves on the ground like the fallen leaves of summer
The righteous laugh and chatter in their House of Power
The fools listen to the words of the False Preachers
While I live in a Place of echoes and dawns
So silent their tongues patter not their timeless resonance away
They are untuned and seek now verily for history's wheel
As it turns upon its axis where they will hang
They bore the nails
But I am commissioned with fresh ones and will hammer them home
Out here the folds of nature encircle them and render their flesh complete
They move in history without knowledge or thought
As leaves fall
And the light is lacerated in the sky
When the time comes, the moon, this Commissioner of nighttime, will stiffen like a blade
The dawn of the new era is here and the cries of the weary can be heard in every street
They travel in Filth, the Silent Breeders of Disease, vomiting forth in a toxic stream
Like rats from a sewer, copulating and chattering and climbing on one another's backs

Now the woodlands return us to where we were before the laughter of the Corrupt
I see him now
Time lays his heavy hand upon his shoulder

As Castle and Stone walked to the huge embossed door that enclosed The Last Brotherhood, a blade sliced the air in the woods.

Beneath an ash tree where the light broke to cast a crucifix, a man held his bleeding face as another stood over him and slashed him to ribbons, laying him beneath its branches.

The strokes were swift and regular and gave no indication of the killer's mood.

He left him there, lying in the dense carpet of leaves, disappearing silently into the night.

6

He kept them waiting.

Castle knew he would, recalling the way he'd been all those years ago when he'd tried to snare him.

Black took the news of their arrival without reaction and stood looking out at the blackened grounds of the Brotherhood, while they waited in an office in a wing that felt colder than the rest of the building.

There was no central heating at the Brotherhood, and only a few fires adorned the rooms.

Stone started to pace as Castle sat and waited. He looked as immobile as a statue.

Finally, as the cold of the place began to work its way into Stone's bones, a door opened and Black walked in.

For a moment she was unnerved by his presence. He was so self-possessed, she felt disoriented. He moved as if everything about him had been controlled for years.

'How can I help you?', Black said, the voice steady and unemotional.

Castle stood up.

'A body's been found in Bushy Park near where the original killings took place', he said.

'The original killings - you make it sound like Genesis.'

His lips moved after he had finished speaking, as if a smirk was starting to crawl across his face, then it seemed to erase itself.

Stone could feel her hard professional persona kicking in.

'We're investigating a serious homicide, Mr Black', she said.

'And you are?'

'Inspector Jacki Stone.'

'Nice to see a woman on the job. Of course I know you Mr Castle, I know you all too well, with your feeble accusations, all evidence of course, evidence of your complete inability to solve a crime. Sick of hassling motorists? Got something juicy to sink those whisky sodden teeth of yours into? Now, let me see. Police thinking. We interviewed Karl Black before, why don't we do it again? And we wonder why there are so many criminals on the streets. Can't do it yourself? Get a woman to do it.'

Stone started to move forward and Castle put a hand on her shoulder.

'I'm not rising to that', he said, 'and besides, we can always do this down at the police station.'

'You find my surroundings too intimidating, do you? Not enough of a whiff of corruption? Perhaps you need to go out and shoot an innocent man. Perhaps a traveller on a train with no guilt whatsoever, so that you can boost your flagging career, but then again, it always was flagging, wasn't it, Chief Inspector Castle?'

'You haven't changed, Mr Black.'

'I have nothing to change, unlike you. It's a pity you're not like the chess piece you're named after, you're more of a pawn.'

Out of the corner of his eye Castle could see a look pass across Stone's face. He'd seen it before when she was about to deck a fellow officer for sexism.

He got in between her and Black, knowing his game and ignoring his comment.

'We're here on police business.'

'Another misnomer, for what do you police? The streets aren't safe and you're patently not interested in apprehending criminals, especially when most of them walk your corridors, so what should you be called?'

'Now just a minute, Mr Black-'.

'It's OK, Inspector Stone.'

'She spoke. How novel.'

'A murder has been committed. It bears a striking resemblance to the first of the killings which I interviewed you about', Castle said.

'Which you mis-interviewed me about. You know, I'm getting pretty tired of your time-wasting. You never linked me to those killings and the best you can do now is reel me in. You're a sorry pair. Need a drink Frank? I can see the whisky hanging off your lips. And as for you, Inspector Stone, your femininity cries out for a little male attention. You look like someone who's all on her own. What's the matter, hubby run off with someone else?'

'I look forward to interviewing you Mr Black', she said.

'I look forward to showing you up for the cretin you are. A double failure: as a woman and as a police officer. The name inspector should not be uttered in the same breath as a mediocre inadequate such as yourself.'

'Where were you on Tuesday night?'

'Now, let me see, two nights ago, I was here holding a conference of the Brotherhood, easily verified with witnesses.' He reached into a drawer and handed Castle a sheet with names, addresses and phone numbers. 'You see, my movements are accounted for. But who would account for you in your private life, in those moments when you're not playing cop? Who watches you, or is it yourself keeping vigil on your nightmares?'

'We'll have more questions to ask you.'

'Well you do that, while you avoid who you really are, you know it's you who's being hunted, Chief Inspector.'

Black opened the door and held it as they moved into the darkened corridor.

He closed it, leaving them standing in the dark. They found the front door with difficulty and left the grounds in silence.

In the car Stone said 'When he walked in everything I planned to say swam away.'

Castle nodded.

'Feel like you were fighting a tide?'

'Yes. Like I was part of a rehearsal.'

'That's what he does Jacki, it's his skill, making everything seem unreal, getting in your head.'

As their lights swept the drive they illuminated the front of the building.

Over the huge double door ran the name 'Rondelo'.

Stone turned to Castle.

'I didn't notice that before.'

'Too dark.'

After a few miles she said:'That's some son of a bitch.'

'He hasn't even got going yet.'

'Of course, if these names check out, we've got nothing to question him about.'

'No.'

'I can't get the chill of the place out of me, fancy a drink?'

'I could do with a bottle.'

Kevin Smart came back to them the next day with the news that the names on the list Black had given them checked out.

'He was at The Brotherhood while the murder was being committed.'

Castle looked at Stone as her phone rang.

'Thank you, Kevin.'

He waited as she took the call, noticing the tension creep into her face.

The Woodlands files had taken over her desk.

'We've got another body', she said.

7

The crime scene was an echo of the first one. Stone felt as though she was stepping into a prism, as if the space of the murder and its grim imagery represented some fragmented shape from the killer's mind. The symmetry that existed between the past and the present, the flashbacks it induced of the earlier killings locked their investigation in a mirror.

She looked across at Castle and saw the haunting in his face. He stood staring down at the corpse through a time tunnel, cut off, as if a curtain had fallen around him, and his life had been claimed by another man's actions.

She began to look for clues, signs of what was driving the killer and felt a wash of unreality loosen her grip on what it was she was looking at. It looked like a forgery of a murder, some black mockery of their attempts to pin crime's shadow on the wall. She felt as though she was digging in a psyche for a flesh wound.

She thought of the files clogging up her desk at the station. The images of laceration and punctured flesh raced through her mind as she looked down at the body in front of her, its wounding a snapshot of the original killings.

The sense of deja vu was disorienting, as if some part of the process she would ordinarily follow as an officer was being scrambled. She searched for a point of orientation, looking for differences to the first murder, and even the trees began to look unreal.

Her own footsteps seemed predictable and she felt placed, like a prop in a costume drama.

Although the bodies were in a different section of the wood, it might have been the same spot. The ash loomed over the corpse, its branches bending down in a gesture of accusation. There was a shape here, and it held a key. The cruciform branches were a distraction from something else.

The victim had been placed in the same position as the first one. Bushy Park, pleasant walk for couples and families was now darkened and obscure, the receptacle of something black beyond comprehension and the horizon tilted beneath the bloodshed.

'Do you think he's done this deliberately?', she said.

Castle's eyes seemed to float up out of some depth and she waited for them to show acknowledgement of who she was.

'Jacki?'

'I mean, it's like an echo chamber. Do you think it's deliberate, that he wants to mess with our procedure, so we don't get a reading on him?'

'Been here before.'

'So it must be doubly unnerving to you, Frank.'

'He did it the first time, he's doing it again.'

'Who?'

Castle shrugged.

'The first time, all those years ago, I kept getting deja vu. It was all part of it. The killer was very adept at getting under the skin of the investigation and peeling it away until we felt raw. Now this. It's an echo until you hear another sound. He does that. Drums at a different beat. Like someone tapping their finger on a window. You check the evidence, ask yourself did you hear it? It's like being snow-blind. And then it changes. He's trying to unsettle us all right.'

'He's recreating the old murder scenes. This could only be done by someone who had access to police files.'

'Or the killer.'

'And whoever's doing this is forcing the investigation back to where it was all those years ago.'

'And where it stalled.'

'If we stick with what we know, his motive, to kill-'.

'I think he has more than one. There's the killing and the pleasure he gets from the torture and for what it's worth I don't think it's sexual. And there's getting at the police too.'

'Just a way of him remaining free.'

Castle shook his head.

'More than that. He wants to enter us. Same way a rapist likes to get inside a woman uninvited, claim her, he wants to get inside our heads with this. If the victim gets killed, it's us he wants to penetrate.'

Stone pulled her coat round her.

'You saw the first killings Frank. How similar are these?'

'The last twenty-eight years might not exist. I'm there again.'

'So is it the same man? If we start from the premise that only someone with inside knowledge could be doing this, then surely that narrows the field?'

'Yes.'

'What does that leave us with?'

'Pathologists.'

'Police officers.'

'Or the same killer.'

'As I look at this I see that there are the murders, and then there is the game.'

'You see why this case took so much of my time.'

Castle looked through the moonlit trees at the distant vista of grass and undulating hill, feeling a million miles away from sanity.

'I need to solve this case, Jacki.'

'I know.'

They saw Alan Marker walk through the police tape and start his examination.

Meanwhile Stone conducted a tour of the area, finding nothing except the usual woodland activity. The killer hadn't strayed from the path, which indicated he hadn't hidden. Or had hidden in such a way so as not to disturb the undergrowth.

She examined the path. There was a footprint at its mouth, then nothing.

The lack of crime scene information indicated the killer had a good working knowledge of DNA evidence and police information gathering.

A PC saw her looking at the footprint.

'Want me to dust that for you, Inspector?'

'Yes and send it to forensics.'

'Sure.'   •

'We're not just looking for shoe size or type, but any anomalies, anything unusual, such as tread patterns or weight distribution. We need to dig a little harder on this one.'

'I'll do that.'

She saw Alan Marker take off his gloves.

'Same ID', he said. 'I'll give you more when I've got the body at the lab, but this killer has a very particular way of conducting his business.'

'Multiple lacerations resulting in a ribboned effect and tears to the body area', Castle said.

'Right.'

'The carotid artery severed first?'

'You can write my report if you like, Frank.'

On the way back Castle remembered the hours he'd spent at the original scenes finding nothing, while the killer made plans for the next victim.

'We focus on catching him before he strikes. We try to identify who the next victim will be, we draw up a list and we wait. We get as much man power as we can, we lay traps.'

'What's the criteria?'

'If the last victim was a politician that narrows the field.'

'We need to find out more about Terence Smythe.'

The second victim was identified before they got the lab report: Malcolm Pont, shadow minister for health.

Stone started to chase up their backgrounds, looking for anything in their policies or careers that could link them and give a theory as to what was motivating the killer.

And Castle started to lay traps, all the while seeing Karl Black's face laughing at him out of the choking fog of the past.

8

The pull on Stone was monumental.

The strange interlocking of the two murders and the previous homicide sent an eerie echo across time, and she felt something dragging her deeper into the whole sequence of events as it unfolded all those years ago.

The night she returned from the second crime scene, she couldn't shake off the image of the body lying beneath the tree. The murder was so controlled as to be beyond the realm of anything she'd encountered or been trained to encounter. She wondered what the significance of Bushy Park was, looking for a doorway into the killer's mind, as if logic could find a soul, as if there was a geography for the darkness in the world.

The file and the pictures it contained of the first set of murders seemed to be coming to life in front of her and she felt connected to Castle in a way she never had till now.

A hot bath, some Occitane, a glass of red wine, did nothing to shake off the resident sense of menace, a menace she'd experienced all too often, but there was something else here, something else entirely.

She sat on the sofa with the file, going over the original investigation.

Castle's notes lay scattered across the inserted pages like the desperate jottings of a man obsessed, and she began to share his obsession.

An hour passed and she looked at her watch.

Don wasn't home yet.

They'd been married two years and recently he'd been staying out later.

She hated nagging, so the few times she'd wondered what he was up to, she'd let it go, but she was beginning to get suspicious.

A mailer from a florist raised her concerns, but she'd dismissed it too.

Now she stood at the window looking out at the dark street lashed by rain and wanted her husband home.

She tried his mobile and got his voicemail, hanging up in irritation, and spent the evening moving between the bottle of wine and the file.

When he finally returned she was asleep on the sofa and too tired to ask him anything.

The next morning he came down clean-shaven and smelling of cologne. As she watched him get ready to go to work, she felt comforted by his presence and afraid of losing the constant he represented in her life, as if the case could impinge on her private world and unsettle it. Everything still seemed unreal to her, as if in just the last few days some unnerving presence had entered her world. She searched for tangibles in her mind.

The moment she first met Don flashed before her eyes.

He'd always been exactly her type, and that was the problem.

Outside her life as a policewoman she couldn't imagine things without him.

'Good evening, darling?', she said, checking for any note of alarm in her voice.

'Yes, found you sprawled out with more police work.'

'What did you get up to?'

She gave him a squeeze as he made some toast.

'Couple of drinks with the guys, I thought you could do with the space, you know with this new case.'

'Thanks.'

But as he left she noticed he was taking a jacket into the dry cleaners, one which he only had cleaned a few days before, and the suspicion returned. There were days like this when she wondered if her work jaded her, as if she couldn't find the off switch to looking for clues when it came to her private life.

As she watched him drive away, Karl Black's face flickered past the window, laughing.

She replayed the film of her meeting with him.

The same evasive and knowing presence lurked behind every page and jotting in the file.

As it was, the file would be taken out of her hands. For a while. She and Castle were about to get really busy.

That morning the mutilated body of a prostitute was found in the basement of some flats in Roehampton.

They got the alert and went to the scene to find a half naked woman with stab wounds disfiguring her neck and legs. Entire sections of her flesh hung off her like pieces of steak. Some of the lacerations met at cross-sections and the flesh had fallen away, revealing lurid red patches as if she'd been skinned alive.

Pieces of her own flesh lay scattered by her side as if in some ritualistic offering to an insane god.

Her bra had been removed and her skirt was ripped, and she decorated the urine-stained floor like a piece of human debris.

Marker was there before them.

'She was killed somewhere else and moved here', he said to Castle.

'You sure?'

'Insufficient blood spatter for this to be the scene of her murder. If it had been here she would have leaked enough blood to carpet the floor. The body's been dragged, as the horizontal creases on her skirt indicate. Although there's dirt around them, if you look in the folds, they're clean. She was then lifted at some point. There are grip marks on her clothing. I'd say she was hoisted into a car and brought here.'

'Do we know who she was?'

The young PC who admitted them held up the sample bag holding her purse.

'Sandra Jakes, a working girl. Soho patch, she's a long way from Roehampton.'

'Did she live here?'

'No.'

'Could've been visiting a client.'

'One thing's for sure. If he didn't use a body bag, his boot's going to be full of her blood', Marker said.

'We need to get the girls on her patch interviewed, get as much info as possible on their customers as well as her background', Castle said to Stone. He turned to the PC. 'I'll contact your DI to let him know I want everyone in these flats visited. Someone may have seen or heard something, seen a car coming or going.'

The PC nodded.

'Anything else Chief Inspector?'

'Tell them to look for a boot full of blood.'

Back at the station there were no leads on the case that was really preoccupying both of them, and they spent the afternoon making calls about the dead prostitute.

The feedback filtering through from the officers at Soho was that there were no customers anyone suspected, and Sandra's private life had been shared with a partner for the last two years. A female partner.

There was nothing to go on, and the dead end led Castle straight to the Crooked Key where Stone found him at the end of the day. He sat in their recess staring through the malt into the woodlands that they both knew was sneaking into their lives like a poisoned shadow.

'Buy you one?', Stone said.

Castle emptied his glass and handed it to her.

'Thanks.'

Knowing they hadn't eaten since the morning, she ordered some food and they sat and shared some chicken wings while avoiding the topic they were both thinking about. She sipped her wine, tasting apricot.

They talked about Stone's husband, Castle's life, what there was of it, tossing these themes around like cushions, until she snapped.

'We both know what's eating us, and I think we need to talk about it Frank.'

'I couldn't agree more.'

'What do we do?'

'Nothing. Nothing we can do at the moment, except draw up a list of probable targets.'

'Do you know how long that list is likely to be? Are we talking ministers or anyone involved in politics?'

'Welcome to the world of Karl Black.'

'He can't be that good.'

'Did I ever tell you about my predecessor?'

'DI Rover?'

'Yeah. A good officer, a very good detective.'

'No you didn't.'

'Then listen as if your life depended on it because you've entered a very strange and murky world, and things won't be the same for you again, Jacki.' She took a sip of her wine which tasted of metal suddenly. 'When I started, I learnt everything from Rover. He was old school, but a natural when it came to piecing together a case and tricking the suspect. He didn't waste time and although some of his methods would be frowned upon by modern standards and the spotlight that shines on all of us, he got things done. When the first body was discovered, I'd just started with him and followed his method on the case. He did everything right, and soon we were on Black's scent. I'd seen Rover interview hundreds of suspects and he could break people down better than any cop I've known. He could read people and get them to the point where they gave it away, but Black was too good for him. And he started to get inside Rover's head.'

'Get inside how?'

Castle took a deep swig of malt, letting it caress his mouth and warm him.

'Rover started to say that Black was finding out about him personally. Getting information on his private life and using it against him. He'd bring it up in the interviews. Some officers thought it was the pressure of the job getting to him, police paranoia, but I saw it for myself and didn't think so. Black had some knack for getting into your mind. He sniffed out others' weakness as easily as one of our dogs can smell drugs and he articulated it and undermined Rover. He might have had some personal source of information, I've never worked that one out, but over the months Rover became unhinged by it all and had to take early retirement. I took over and he started to do the same to me.'

'How?'

'He picks up on you, probably subconscious verbal clues we all give out. He's very good at reading people. And you can't tell what's going on with him, whether you're getting to him or not. You begin to feel that he knows about your private life and he starts to enter your world.'

Black's comment about her marriage flickered into Stone's mind and her suspicions about Don returned. She wondered briefly if she was a failure as a woman, then dismissed it.

'Frank we all feel the pressures of this job sometimes. After a hard day I wonder why I got into this, and I see Don come home from selling houses and wish I'd been an estate agent.'

'But you don't.'

'No.'

'What I'm trying to tell you is be careful. You're involved in an investigation that's going to change your life and career. Black is not the run of the mill killer.'

'If he is a killer.'

Castle paused and stared into his glass and then at Stone.

'We need a line between ourselves and the criminals, otherwise, what are we? We keep that line in place for a reason. Rover was as tough as concrete and Black cracked him. Somehow he crosses your line without you knowing it.'

'I hear you Frank.'

'You're reading the old file. The victims were all variously tortured and mutilated. We knew we had a psychopath on our hands, one who shifted and turned every time we got close to catching his scent. The first time I met Black I knew. You'll get your hunches and when you do listen to them. He was too energised around the case, too involved in the interviews I conducted and I stand by what I said. The fact that my career was torn to rags by the press as a result of the failure to catch the killer doesn't mean I got it wrong. There's something different about him, something else I never really got the hook into, and he's still got it. In the same way as good cops have some extra sense, he has something else on top of it, as if he's reading the way you're reading him. It's like chasing someone in a hall of mirrors. Walking into that place the other day was like stepping back twenty-eight years and I felt like a rookie again. That's what he does, that's what he's expert at, making people feel inadequate and vulnerable.'

'You vulnerable Frank?'

'He'll play games with your head Jacki, so be prepared.'

'I will.'

They finished their drinks and left.

Outside the rain swept the street as they hurried to their cars.

As they drove away, Karl Black looked out at the dark landscape of The Last Brotherhood, the water flooding across the lawns.

Once home Stone stared out of the window wondering where Don was.

The downpour lasted all night, washing the spot where the politicians' bodies had been found, thinning their blood on the leaves, and as it hammered against Castle's window panes, he saw Black's face staring at him out of a void.

He reached out to cuff him to find he wasn't there.

9

Terence Smythe, ex-minister for justice courtesy of the knife wounds that cut short his career, had been a big campaigner for gay marital rights.

Stone had researched his background and come up with this thread that ran through his career like a pink banner.

He'd started off with it heavily on his agenda and run with it. And it seemed he was genuine, not another politician trying to offload a popular theme onto the public.

Heterosexual himself and happily married, he was committed to the cause, which made his policies all the more interesting.

He'd worked hard to come up through the ranks of the Labour party and was now shining like a new star in their firmament.

He was above board and there didn't seem to be any skeletons in his closet, and he was to all accounts popular with his colleagues.

Stone's research on Malcolm Pont took longer.

He was more typically an all-rounder who excelled in front of an audience, but the one thing Stone came up with that struck her as significant was his pro-abortion campaigning.

She and Castle were already chasing the tail of a religiously motivated killer and although this was back in the ground of the investigative process that had been used without bearing fruit in The Woodlands Killings, they felt it was their best approach. Anything that could exacerbate the mind of a religiously inflamed psychopath was deemed to be significant.

Pont experienced repeated run-ins with pro-life campaigners, even receiving death threats at one stage, which was in a police report.

The two themes of gay marriage and abortion provided sufficient grounds for the investigation to begin and she and Castle drew up a list of ministers who had expressed views likely to annoy the religious, and got the details of the suspects of the death threats against Pont.

The two names that came up were Laurence Steele and Hilary Game.

He was a lay preacher with a Christian sect called The Ramblers, so named because of their emphasis on the right to roam freely in the teachings of the Bible and break free of the interpretations of the mainstream church. Their particular emphasis was on sex as the Bible taught it.

She was a mother of eight whose husbands had all deserted her, some of whose children had been taken into care and who was a member of a Christian group called The New Order, which followed the Old Testament's teachings.

In a ramshackle flat on a Notting Hill housing estate, he sat amid Bibles and banners.

He let them in without demur and waited for them to explain the nature of their visit.

Dressed in a track suit and unshaven, he stared evenly at Castle.

'Mr Steele, we know that you were behind some death threats against Terence Smythe.'

'A long time ago, Officer, as you can see.'

He waved a hand at the walls, on which were emblazoned 'Love', 'Peace', 'Forgiveness', and 'Hate is the Beginning of Sin'.

Castle ignored the demotional taunt.

'We're conducting an investigation and we need to talk to you', Stone said.

'I've made my peace with Mr Smythe, he is no longer significant. We live in a world where the fallen triumph, but I have my faith and I have found peace and contentment with my brotherhood.'

Stone noticed the last word with interest.

'You belong to a group?'

'We are all part of the wider fellowship of man.'

He was beginning to irritate her. She wasn't going to waste any more time playing games with a zealot.

'The Ramblers, I believe is your group.'

'Yes.'

'What do you believe in?'

'The lilies of the valley. You know the sermon on the mount, I'm sure, Officer, no matter how irreligious and preoccupied you may be. The Bible uses many metaphors of growth and freedom, and we advocate the right of the religious to open up the interpretation of the Bible, away shall we say from some of the mainstream teachings of the church which we are in no way at odds with, but we see another message, one which shows us the way forward if this planet is to be saved.'

'Why did you make death threats against Terence Smythe, Mr Steele?'

'It depends how your interpret it.'

'We're not here to play games and we can do this down at the station', Castle said.

'I was fiercely opposed to his views on marriage.'

'You have something against gays?', Stone said. 'I can see you're not married.'

'You're jumping to conclusions, Officer.'

She looked around her at the dirty carpet and total unkempt masculinity of the place.

'No woman would put up with a place like this.'

'It is not your place to come here and cast aspersions on the way I live.'

'I'm here to ask questions, and I suggest you start answering them.'

'What are you asking?'

'What were you so opposed to in what Terence Smythe was saying?'

'To the religious, marriage is a sacred institution. Are you married, Officer?'

'I'm asking the questions here.'

'A man marrying another man is sacrilege. I believe in a Christian society and I was offended by what he was preaching. I was young and a little hot-headed.'

'Have you had any contact with Mr Smythe since the occasion

two years ago when you were arrested for making the calls?'

'No.'

'How far would you take your religious beliefs?', Castle said.

'As far as is necessary.'

'Including breaking the law?'

'I've done that once and learned from my mistake. Really, I left Smythe alone after that incident.'

'Where were you last Tuesday?', Castle said.

'Why?'

'Just answer the question.'

'At what time?'

'During the evening.'

'I was at a meeting of The Ramblers. We meet every Tuesday at the church of St Thomas down the road.'

'Then you'll have witnesses.'

'Yes.'

'We need names.'

He went into the address book in his phone and gave them some numbers.

'What is this all about?'

'Terrence Smythe was found murdered last Tuesday.'

'Check the information I've given you. Is that all?'

'For the moment', Stone said.

They left and stepped out into the curtain of rain.

Hilary Game weighed about twenty-four stone and sat puffing while they questioned her.

She lived in a pebble dashed house in the Bedford Hill area of Streatham, surrounded by toys, nappies, clothes and graffiti that lined her wall in lipstick and which had obviously been put there by her kids, who seemed to be running the household.

Stone interviewed her, giving Castle a chance to look around.

The kitchen was full of discount tins of baked beans and cheap cider. A wire hung out of the wall, slightly too high for a child to reach. A plasma screen took up most of one wall in the living room. A girl of no more than ten carted around a screaming baby, while a red-faced boy puled and threw toys about. In the corner another baby slept, and upstairs the sound of running feet indicated an army of kids left unattended.

'What's this all about?', Game said.

'We wanted to ask you some questions about Malcolm Pont.'

'Oh him.'

'You were interviewed by the police a few years ago in connection with some threats against him.'

'That was all sorted.'

'Why did you threaten him?'

'I don't agree with his views on abortion. Look, the police said they'd drop the charges.'

'You think that if someone expresses an opinion you don't like you can threaten them?'

'Look around you, I like kids. I think abortion is murder and I think a human who commits it or encourages it is a murderer and should be dealt with by the law. I believe in the death penalty. I believe we should reproduce. I believe that the police are not doing their job. I believe that the law is wrong.'

'And you obviously believe in breaking the law. What does your group The New Order believe in?'

'We're part of the church. We believe the Old Testament is just as important as the New Testament and that it is the way.'

'The new way?'

'The only way. We call it the new way because all the other ways are the old ways and we need change.'

'Why not just go to church along with everyone else? Why start up some special group?'

'Look', she said, standing up, 'I haven't got time to have you question me about something that happened two years ago. If you don't mind, I've got children to attend to.'

'You had some children taken into care, didn't you, Mrs Game?'

'That's got nothing to do with this.'

'No it hasn't, but you stand there preaching about other people and aren't doing a particularly good job as a mother.'

She might as well have shot her.

She stood there speechless while Stone said 'Have you had any contact with Malcolm Pont since the incident?'

'No.'

'Where were you two nights ago?'

'Why?'

'Answer the question.'

'I was busy.'

'Doing what?'

'Working.'

'OK, we need the name and address of your employer.'

She hesitated.

'John Stakes. He runs a shop round the corner. '

'We'll speak to him.'

'Do you have to?'

'Yes.'

'What's this all about?'

'Malcolm Pont was found murdered two nights ago.'

'Can't say I'm surprised.'

Stone looked across at Castle.

'We'll be in touch if this doesn't pan out', she said.

Outside the rain continued to pour as if the skies had opened and couldn't close again.

As it was, their alibis panned out.

Every name that Steele gave them backed up his story of being at a meeting of The Ramblers the night Terence Smythe had been killed.

Hilary Game's claim to have been working the night Malcolm Pont was butchered was also substantiated, although Stone was convinced she was hiding something.

'Like what?', Castle said.

'She looked uncomfortable, like she didn't want us to talk to her boss.'

'She's off the hook, though.'

'Maybe.'

He could see her getting her teeth into this and knew what that was like, all those years of obsessing over the Woodland Killings to the point where colleagues and friends had all warned him he was heading for a breakdown, and still he couldn't stop.

He let her get on with it.

As it was, she was right, but it didn't help the investigation.

Hilary Game was claiming benefits and working at the same time.

Stone shelved it, neither having the time nor the inclination to chase it up.

She thought she'd save it in case Game's name came up again.

At the other end of the office she could see Castle put down the phone.

'Jacki, we've got another body.'

10

In a back lane near Wimbledon Common, between the two parks, in a swathe of land where darkness seemed to settle more easily than light, where animals scurried by day and other animals by night, another half-naked women lay amidst used syringes and condoms.

The bruising and lacerations were extensive and showed like a panorama of reds and crimsons. The rain had started to fall again adding misery and stress to their ongoing difficulties, and she was drenched and discarded like a piece of rubbish.

Castle and Stone approached, the beams of their torches scanning the undergrowth.

The victim's skirt had been pulled up, exposing her buttocks and a blue tattoo of a butterfly. She wore nothing else, lying naked and bloody in the garbage that had been dumped there. A beer can lay next to a half-eaten hamburger, an oily rag clung to the side of a tyre. Castle tramped down some of the weeds, their thick stems snapping in the cool air. A rat scurried away from the swinging arc of his torchlight.

They heard footsteps behind them.

Alan Marker's face was becoming a fixture in their days and they watched as the grey head bent unemotionally to the latest victim.

'It's the work of the same man. The patterns of wounding are identical.'

'Same as Sandra Jakes?', Stone said.

'Oh yes. Not your other killer. This one lacks his sophistication.'

'Sophistication?'

'There's rage in this attack, the flesh wounds are ragged. Look. One moment he's cutting horizontally across the flesh, then the next downwards, as if he's dragging his rage across her body. He's

46

lacerating the fibres of elastic tissue, so her wounds gape. A mess. The other killer is directed, cold when he kills.' He stood up and stepped away from the body, took off his gloves and ran his hand through the thick grey shock of his hair. 'Yes, you've got one very advanced psychopath and another preying on prostitutes again.'

Castle turned to Stone.

'That's all we need, another Jack the Ripper.'

'I'll put out an ID and find out where she worked.'

They made their way back in the rain.

11

Castle was telling Stone about the significance of the ash tree.

'Cropped up in the original Woodland Killings, in case you hadn't noticed.'

'How could I miss it?', she said.

'There's a lot of mythology around it. In Norse mythology, the first man, Ask, was made from the branches and flesh of an ash. There are loads of myths and rituals surrounding it.'

'Like?'

'It's thought to be curative. In one belief when Christianity entered Northern Europe, the Scandinavian gods were transformed into witches and ash became their favourite tree.'

'Some sort of conflict between paganism and Christianity?'

'That's one way of looking at it. In Norse mythology it was the World Tree and it reached up into the Heavens, while its roots reached down into the Underworld.'

'So to a modern mind, what does that mean? It connects good and evil?'

Castle shrugged.

'The roots of the tree were believed to be connected to the Rivers of the Past, the Present and the Future.'

'It's as if the killer is bringing the past back to life by re-enacting the original killings.'

'It's also very strong. The joint of an ash tree is said to be able to bear more weight than any other wood. The killer chose this particular tree not just because of the crucifix it cast, obviously an important symbol to him, but also because of its mythological significance.'

'As if he wants to be Adam.'

'Ask.'

'The first man. Like he's getting rid of the rest of the race', Stone said.

'Part of it.'

At Rondelo Black was talking to Jonas Wilkes.

He looked like a troubadour, some misfit from another era and was wrapt by Black's words, standing in silence, his head slightly to the left.

Occasionally he interjected a comment that was veiled in mystery.

'Jonas, we live in troubled times', Black said. 'The unfaithful walk among us and we need to be prepared. I have great works in mind, as you know, and you are indeed a trusted confidant.'

'The Last Brotherhood is the only refuge I know where the outside world and its attendant sickness may be shut out.'

'Very good.'

He paused, his eye following the line of the stone flagging as it crossed the floor stopping at the wood panelled walls.

'The police were asking questions.'

'They are nothing except the useless servants of the corrupt, Jonas.'

'What did they want?'

'No matter of concern to you, brother. What I need to talk to you about is far more pressing and far more important. We need numbers. We need to build up a body of the faithful so that we are prepared to do battle.'

'We need spearmen to conduct our fight. Where be the aketons or brigadines amid the sorry cloth we see worn today?'

'Christ the Vanquisher is risen and the lamb has fled. The wolf is alive and the unholy are but carrion to the Great Plan.'

'Where be the kettle hats? There be none sporting a great helm. The sword within our heart is the symbol of the one we carry to bear our Righteous Arms against the Fallen.'

'Jonas, you know the teachings well. I need you to take over the recruitment of the new, I need you to ensure they are ready. I will be busy now, and need someone I can rely on, and it is you I choose.'

A glow lit up the pale face, like a dying coal in the snow.

'I will recruit as many as we need and keep the unworthy away.'

'You have been with the Brotherhood from its genesis and I can think of no better man to lead the newcomers.'

'I am the Captain of the Rant, and no mere antinomian.'

'Then rant against them, rant against the lies, rant against the Corrupt, rant against the officers of the law who uphold a false idol and leader. I vouchsafe you.'

'Do you have any particular instructions beyond those already in force?'

'Yes. Make sure you get the best and most worthy. Those who know the scriptures and are ready to receive our secret teachings, those who will fight, those who will work. Those who will be loyal to the Brotherhood.'

'You need warriors to lead the fight.'

'Exactly.'

'I will do it.'

'And make sure they are ready. Make sure they will stand against the Corrupt.'

Wilkes left the room and travelled down the darkened corridor to begin the work at once.

Castle and Stone weren't making much advance on what they now called the second Woodland Killings.

The only suspects they had were out of the frame, and the list of potential victims was growing by the hour.

At the end of a long day Castle said 'we're going to have to narrow this down, or he'll be running rings around us.'

'Like Black you mean?'

'Do we have an ID on the second woman?'

'Sandy Honner.'

'Soho patch?'

'Yeah.'

'Whoever's killing these women doesn't care about us finding out who they were.'

'He has an obsession with taking them to a particular area. Any news from Roehampton?'

'The DI there says his officers have done the rounds, but no one saw or heard anything.'

'Nothing?'

'That's what he's saying.'

'Either that, or they're not talking.'

'Do we have a background on Sandy Honner?'

'Once again, there are no stories of her being hassled, no recent reports of attacks on her. All the girls say they're baffled.'

'And afraid.'

Castle stared out of the window.

'It seems like it's been raining for days', he said.

'It has.'

I see them moving among the spectral shadows on the lawn, swanlike but not made of dove

They change and lie, the summons to the Truth eluding them, a language that they miss

Pretenders to a throne they do not know, servants of the world, the hour is upon them, the Summons has been made and drawn up on paper from above

Every offence to The Work, every slander against The Work will be found out and as they embroider their Lies with money and power, they fall

I see him there, the False Christ, the sinner with no knowledge of The Cross

He will find out

He has played the part but does not know the language

The words dry in his mouth like leaves

The Cross knows him, but he doesn't know The Cross

He struts

I watch

He is alone

He is learning new words

He is the man of parts and nothing

The rain falls against his windows, the rain cannot wash him clean

Only the right death can wash him clean

And I am the cleanser

Into his house, through the open window, I hear him talk learning his lines

There through the open doorway I see him and The Cross's shadow on the wall

He will know

They will all know

12

In a large Victorian house with high ceilings an elegant man with a few days' growth of beard sat learning lines on a sofa surrounded by throw cushions and candles.

He held a script and mumbled the words, stopping and starting again.

Occasionally he made a note.

He looked at the window, sheeted with rain.

The glass held his image for a moment, and the flow of rain gave it the appearance of melting.

His face was open, mystical and he seemed to be contemplating something.

As he stood up, he did not see the figure behind him.

It had been standing there for a while, and now it reached from behind with a blade in its hand and carved his neck open easily with a neat, elegant gesture, that was almost balletic.

The man reeled, staggered, fell back, looking upwards at his attacker who moved into the shadows.

He stood in the middle of the room, his beard dripping blood. His head tilted against the deep wound, rolling and splitting against the rent flesh.

He tried to stem the tide of blood with his hands which turned the flow into a shower, sending a spray of it outwards from his neck.

It reached the cream curtains and the magnolia wallpaper and the other came before him and impaled him with the knife many times until he lay there surrounded by the cushions and the rain.

Outside in the empty streets the figure moved into the shadows.

13

Alan Marker stood beneath the lab strip lights, his hair a halo of white.

He looked into the blue fire of Castle's eyes, knowing he needed something from him.

'Sorry, Frank.'

'Nothing?'

He shook his head.

'The killer's been gifted the rain. There's no DNA.'

Castle returned to his office with Stone.

They were whittling down the list of potential victims and when they got the news about the third victim put it straight in the bin.

Stone took the call. Castle could tell from her face that the investigation was about to duck down a side street.

'An actor's been murdered in Hampstead.'

For a brief moment everything in Castle's mind sped up, as if someone had pressed the fast forward button.

'Which case is this?'

'The Woodlands copycat.'

'You sure? It feels like there's an army of killers out there.'

'Same MO.'

'And the victim?'

'Lewis Montelle. He's acted in some big films.'

Castle shrugged.

'When was the last time I went to the cinema?'

As they made their way to the crime scene Stone said 'he's shifting his ground.'

Castle said little as he drove, watching the streets flash by like the backdrop in a silent film, unreal, divorced by normality from the black world he moved in. He thought of what self-belief was driving these men, what darkness or insanity gave them such conviction that they neither feared nor cared about the police. He felt affronted and angry. And deep inside his anger lay such impotence all he could think of was drink.

The house was in a prime location.

'Flask Walk, very nice', Stone said. 'He'd obviously done well, living in one of the wealthiest spots in Hampstead.'

'That's actors for you.'

They looked at the large, immaculate Victorian house, and as they crossed the police cordon they felt a shift of perspective at visiting an indoor murder scene. So far the woodland scenery had imbued each killing with its own flavour, and now this felt like a different killer.

Surrounded by ornate statues and some tastefully selected art a man lay in a black pool of his own blood.

'No trees, no leaves', Castle said.

But there was something about the position of the body that Stone connected with the others she'd seen and the pictures of the victims of the original killings.

He lay in the middle of the room, the rest of which looked totally undisturbed.

'There was no struggle', she said.

She analysed the position, kneeling and walking round the room, looking at it from different angles.

Castle watched her.

'What are you doing?'

'There's something about the way he's leaving them, some pattern.'

'They're not in identical postures.'

'No. It's not that', she said, straining against the window to see the corpse from afar, then walking back towards it. 'It's not the position.'

'What then?'

'Have you noticed their hands?'

'What about them?'

'Smythe's index finger was raised, so was Pont's. Look.' She pointed at Lewis Montelle's hand.

It was resting unnaturally on one of the throw cushions as if it had been placed there, and the fingers had been straightened by the killer to face the far wall.

'This cushion's been taken off the sofa. The others are positioned. That's how he would have placed them. But his hand wouldn't have landed like that. It's pointing at something.'

'What?'

'The killer's leaving us a message.'

The far wall was hung with a number of paintings, classical landscapes, a Graham Sutherland, a couple of portraits, a Pollock print.

They began to turn the paintings round.

Behind one of the portraits something had been written on the wall.

Castle removed it.

Written in neat Old English script the message read:

'The False Prophets Shall be Brought to Heel.'

'He had time to kill him and write this', Stone said.

'All through the last case I felt I was turning up at a scene which the killer controlled. And here it is again, the sense that he's confident and organised, not in any hurry. Like someone in charge of a set in a theatre.'

'What does it mean?'

'What it means is that we've missed something at the first two scenes.'

They took pictures and left.

The woods were dry now and the light better than when they had been there the previous week.

They drove straight to the spot and inspected the area.

'Nothing on the tree', Stone said.

'He wouldn't be that obvious. Can you remember which way Smythe's finger was pointing?'

'That way, I think.'

She pointed into the undergrowth.

They walked towards it, stopping at intervals and checking the barks.

Some graffiti emblazoned a branch, someone had carved initials into another tree.

They went deeper. Logs and fallen branches cluttered the ground and the light faded.

Castle found it first.

Carved into the stump of an oak was the first message.

Neat. Old English.

'The Corrupt are Discovered.'

He examined the bark, the edges of the letters neatly grooved, as if an engraver had been at work.

Over by the second crime scene they pictured the position in which they'd found Malcolm Pont.

Stone thought he'd been pointing one way, Castle said another.

They walked separately round the scene until she came across a disused toilet in some trees.

The door bore the message skilfully rendered in the same style.

'The Rapists of the Land are Apprehended.'

She called Castle, who lumbered through the undergrowth.

'Mean anything to you?', she said.

It means something, but not to me.'

'Is it Biblical?'

'Sounds it. We better get one of our boys onto it. Dredge the net for references.'

'Notice the capitals?'

'He's trying to draw our attention to something.'

They took shots and left.

14

When Don didn't come home until two o'clock the next morning, all her suspicions came back.

The case had been preoccupying her and she'd not been paying attention to his hours, often falling asleep with the file and leaving early the following morning. But that night she'd lain there and heard him creep up the stairs and come into the bedroom smelling of another woman. Cheap perfume clashing with his aftershave. She knew Don's odour, it was a secret comforter she didn't talk about. Sometimes as he slept she would lie so close to him she was almost touching him and breathe him in like an expensive wine. Now this other odour entered the room with him, summoning some predatory rage deep from inside her. She wanted to lash out and had to remind herself she was a cop.

She flicked the light on.

'Sorry, didn't mean to wake you', he said.

She looked over at the man who'd always been able to talk her round, his masculine jaw, his blue eyes, and the anger rocketed accompanied by the huge doses of stress that were already in her system.

'Where have you been?', she said, hearing a frost creep into her voice.

'Having a few drinks.'

'At this time? Level with me Don.'

He took his jacket off and put it on the back of the chair.

'What's there to level?'

'You don't come in at this time from a few drinks.'

'I do.'

She sat up.

'Stop lying to me, Don.'

'I don't need this. Ever since you've taken on this last case, you've been impossible. Why do you think I stay away? Where is my wife? Mrs Castle.'

'Don't give me that, I know when you're lying, Don.'

'When do I quiz you about your long hours? I have a few drinks with some friends, because you're never home, and I married you Jacki, not the Met, and you start this.'

'Are you saying you're not seeing another woman?'

'You know what, I don't know why I bothered coming back.'

He slammed the bedroom door and she could hear him making up the sofa downstairs.

She lay there wondering if the case wasn't getting to her, replaying Frank's words about how Black gets into people's heads, thinking what if it isn't Black? Just stress?

But when she picked up his discarded jacket and smelled it, she knew.

The next morning as she sat alone over breakfast, knowing she would be returning to an empty house, Black's face loomed at her out of some darkness that had entered her life a week ago.

His words echoed in her head all morning.

'Hubby run off with someone else?'

His image hovered at the threshold of her mind, like a rapist's hand tapping at a window pane.

Castle had also started to be troubled in the old way again.

When he'd cracked under the pressure of the Woodland Killings, and hidden at the bottom of a whisky bottle while his wife left and many of his friends gave up, he'd seen Black at every twist and turn in his life as the case gripped it.

He felt Black was watching him, gathering information on his private life, using it against him.

His superior had bottom lined it:

'Either you go and see the police psychiatrist or I'm taking you off this case, Frank.'

The idea of not getting the chance to solve it had been life-threatening to him and he'd gone.

The report had diagnosed the early stages of paranoia and PTSD.

Now it was happening all over again.

He dreamed of Black every night, as if the man had some special key to his psyche and was unlocking it at will. Cases he'd solved reopened again, fleshed with ambiguities he wondered how he'd missed.

Men he'd put away shadow danced into his mind pleading innocence.

He looked at his face, a ruined cop staring back at him with sullen resentment.

And he thought of all he'd learned in his long and troubled career.

Dipping into his past was like dragging his hand through sand and withdrawing nothing. He watched it run through his fingers and wondered where all the time he'd set aside to do other things had gone.

He tried to catch himself and felt he was falling.

He steadied his shaking hand on the bottle, now almost empty and poured it slowly, the deep golden malt the only sunshine left on his bloodshot horizon.

He knew it.

Black had got in.

In his dreams, he was followed by him, led up dark alleys where victims lay in pools of blood surrounded by shredded police documents, walled in by the laughter of his nemesis.

He knew if he questioned Black again he'd get in more.

15

Reviewing the careers and lives of Smythe and Pont made interesting reading.

Both had been involved in early scams that hadn't shown up at first.

Smythe had almost been arrested over fraud charges when he worked for a small constituency in the North of England. Apparently, some charity funds had gone missing.

It was obvious from the evidence he knew or had something to do with it, but it was going to be hard to press fraud charges and the police let the thing go. Later in his career an internal auditor had raised the alarm about his account keeping and been promptly fired. It seemed the pro-gay rights lobbyist was not the squeaky clean politically correct minister he liked to portray himself as.

But neither was Pont.

Before he became a politician he'd been on the board of a small company called 'Safe Choices'.

They ran health workshops and had a private clinic specialising in abortions. Pont made a lot of money from it, protected as he was by his position on the board when a scandal broke. For maximum profit they'd hired some doctors with dubious qualifications. Two women died as a result of badly administered terminations and although the clinic was shut down, Pont waltzed right into politics.

It wasn't long before he made his stand on his favourite turf.

A family man, he had an affair with a secretary that ended bitterly when she found herself pregnant. She claimed he drugged her and woke to find someone had performed an abortion without her consent.

A bruised and angry woman threatened press exposure.

A few lawyers' letters and a few grand later and the whole thing was dropped, Pont establishing himself as a leading shadow minister.

Stone studied the links and handed the file to Castle who read it with interest.

He took a sip of water. Since the case started his voice had thickened into a gravel drive. Now when he spoke it sounded like he'd been gargling with rocks, an aspect of his personal presentation he wished to soften.

'They're both hypocrites', he said.

'And they're both encroaching on traditionally religious territory.'

'Christian territory.'

'But Lewis Montelle wasn't a politician, so that link breaks down. Any theory we had's already blown out of the water.'

'He recently acted the role of Christ in a film fundamentalist Christian groups are clamouring to have banned. It hasn't been released yet, but he has sex with Mary Magdalene in it.'

'OK, so Christianity's the best we've got to go on.'

'The killer's attacking their veneers.'

That night Castle dreamed he was chasing a masked killer along a weathered track. He could see his face in a small stream that ran alongside him, and all the life seemed to be there in his reflection, as if he stared at some self alongside whom he had merely coexisted all these empty years.

He watched himself give chase, seeing the figure flee. The scene broke and parted, returning him to some landscape he knew. Trees creaked and dripped. He ached.

A deep resonance of him and all he'd hoped to be hung in their branches like some burnt offering. He caught hold of the tails of the fleeing figure and clenching his fist, pulled.

He stood there looking down at his fist, tense beneath a swollen moon. As he opened his hand he saw a fragment of newspaper with his name on it, yellowed with time.

A light wind caught it and it turned to dust.

Suddenly the figure was there again. He stood waiting. Castle gave chase.

Then he turned and changed direction, but Castle was at his heels and could smell him.

He remembered the smell of freshly baked bread and sitting at the kitchen table as a child. The odour soured to the acrid stench of mould, of decay.

Just as he reached out to grab him, the track changed and he found himself in the middle of darkness.

The next morning Stone was waiting for him as he got in.

Since Don had moved out, she'd been getting in earlier and earlier.

'Coffee?', he said.

'We haven't got time. The body of another woman's been found.'

16

They knew before they got there that this was the second killer, as they'd begun to think of him.

Off a stretch of the A3 beyond Richmond Park, in some overgrown land a body lay. They stood examining the desecration while cars bombed past a few metres away.

'Who found her?', Castle said.

'Some kids came here before school for a smoke. One of them put the call through on a mobile.'

The body lay open like a half-eaten steak and was partially covered in leaves which were golden and turning to the sludge that signalled winter's firm grip on the land.

Slugs and beetles scuttled among them, sliding blindly across the wasted flesh. The leaves on her stuck to her wounds.

She stared up from the ground with opaque eyes, like some nightmare decorated growth, a violated weed in a ruined garden.

This time, the wounds were deeper.

The lacerations on her leg showed bone.

Overhead a weak and sickly sun struggled with the clouds. Beneath its afflicted light the curve of leg bone showed like some strange white carving, an attempt at sculpture beneath the physical violation.

'He wants them exposed', Stone said. 'Leaving them like this out in the open.'

'This is not a sexually motivated killer.'

'No. These women offer sex for cash, they're already exposed sexually. We're not looking for a rapist, Frank. I can guarantee you he won't have touched them.'

'What then?'

'He wants their humanity exposed. Their insides. He wants these women rendered down to organ and bone.'

'For all to see.'

'For all to see.'

'And in doing so he dehumanises them.'

'Yes. They've offered their flesh, he's offering the rest of them.'

'Their only secret places.'

'He wants them opened up.'

'Makes you wonder.'

'What?'

'What's he offering them to?'

'Whatever sick god he serves.'

They toured the area looking for clues, but found none, waiting for Marker to arrive. It was just a chunk of wild and rarely traversed land. The absence of litter testified to this, telling them the killer knew the spot was derelict.

Castle was feeling the strain again, thinking of whisky, realising many shops weren't even open yet. He needed a release.

Even Marker's humour, his buffer against the attendant horrors of his job, irritated him.

'I think I'll put in for overtime. Do you think this killer will take a break for Christmas?', he said, putting on his gloves.

Castle ignored the comment and waited.

'Why do you think he's picking this area?', Stone said.

'No idea. We need extra manpower with these two cases running alongside each other. There's gotta be a clue here, but right now I can't see what.'

'Someone who either lives locally or has some grievance against something round here.'

'Richmond Park laps at over eight miles and the surrounding area's pretty big, that doesn't narrow it down enough.'

'And in the meantime we're no nearer to figuring out who's behind the other killings.'

'We need to call Tom Spinner.'

'This one's a little different', Marker said, peeling off his gloves. 'The wounding as you can probably see is much deeper and there's a reason for that. She's had her liver removed.'

'A latter day Jack the Ripper', Castle said. 'Great.'

———•———

Back at the station he made the call. Tom Spinner said he'd come in that afternoon.

He was a first rate offender profiler with a first rate ability to piss Castle off. Although he'd helped him on countless cases and Castle recognised and respected his ability, he found his hackles rising within minutes of Spinner entering the room.

He and Stone went over what they had and threw around ideas like abandoned toys.

They knew they were stuck and thought of Black so often that if they'd talked about him they'd both have reached for a drink.

As it was, after an hour of frustration Castle went out and popped into the Crooked Key.

The barman was glad to see him.

The barman was always glad to see him.

'What'll it be Frank, orange juice?'

'Training to be a stand-up?'

'I've got some nice Johnny Walker, Black label.'

'Just give me the Glenmorangie', he said with a snarl.

'What did I say?'

'You don't want to know.'

He retreated to his corner and waited for Spinner to arrive at the station.

At Rondelo, Black and Wilkes were discussing the new recruits.

'The number is almost there and then we have the unit', Wilkes said.

'Good. Then marshal these troops, Jonas, and harness them to the Will of the Brotherhood, for all will fall under it.'

'I am working them in the manner you have taught.'

'The women within their role, the men within theirs.'

'Yes. And drawing on our teachings.'

'Explain to them the mystery of the Gospels that they be ready.'

'They will know the commission from God.'

'Make them knowledgeable, Jonas.'

'They will enter and leave the belly of the whale with much they never had before.'

'With everything there is and everything that will be left.'

'And of the two natures?'

'Let them learn that they be ready to understand this matter.'

'And the monastery within will keep the world without, so that they may remain purified of their Sins.'

'Their journey to Rondelo has brought them to this point. Yet they have much to learn still.'

'I will make them ready.'

'So that they know to reject the law, for there is only one.'

Wilkes left and travelled down the darkened passage to his acolytes.

17

During those dark years Castle had teetered on the edge of psychosis. The police psychiatrist had advised termination of police duties for a period long enough to stabilise him.

His notes read:

'Conviction, while a useful tool to a detective, becomes pathological when failure causes a breakdown.

The breakdown of the Woodland Killings case and Chief Inspector's Castle's subsequent fragmentation has left him in a defensive and paranoid ego state. He is also suffering from PTSD.

His conviction that he knows the identity of the real killer is dangerous. It is a defence against mental illness.

While he has undoubtedly been the target of press intrusion, he fails to see this is merely an extension of the press's wider role in this country. His personal sense of outrage coupled with his rage at his own failure to solve the case make for a man who is in a narcissistic frame of mind and in a powerful position.

As such, he is both a danger and a liability to the police force.

I recommend intensive psychotherapy and a period of rest. In therapy he can confront his breakdown and evident alcohol dependency. By taking time off he can hopefully gain some perspective on the situation while being prevented from doing the Metropolitan police force any damage.

Frank Castle is at the same time a hard-working detective with a deep need to see justice done. The wrongful arrest of Samuel Walsh and failure to catch the real killer have no doubt triggered his breakdown, which is acute.'

Castle took a month off, tried fishing and got habitually drunk.

He turned up at the therapy sessions and went through the motions.

He kept Karl Black's picture in a pocket in his mind and saw his face swim up from the bottom of his glass.

At the end of the month he persuaded his commanding officer that he was fit to return to work and did so, with the full support of his fellow officers.

Stone asked Kevin Smart to come up with some information and it was late in coming.

She wanted everything on Lewis Montelle's career to date that might add to what they already had. She hated the idea of standing there with nothing more than a few sketchy ideas when Spinner arrived. She'd heard about him and knew his reputation for being razor sharp and given to sarcasm.

When she found him cracking a joke in the corridor, she barked at him.

'PC Smart, where's the information I asked for?'

'I'm working on it.'

'Do you call cracking your cheap sexist jokes work? If you had a woman in your life you might act like a mature adult not a teenager.'

He turned his back as she walked off and she caught the words 'Old man's run off.'

Before she knew it she'd thundered back down the corridor and was standing inches away from him.

'What did you say?'

'What is your problem?'

'Sexist pricks like you.'

'What's sexist?'

'Get me the information I asked for.'

She turned to leave and heard him say 'I don't blame him, who'd stay with her?'

The stress kicked in and she swung round, slapping him hard across the face.

He stood there with a bright red mark burning his cheek.

She turned and walked away.

An hour later as Castle returned from the pub, she regretted her action and went to look for Smart, but couldn't find him.

Spinner arrived and she gave up on the information, deciding they'd just have to grin and bear it.

As it was, she got Spinner at his best.

She didn't know what to expect, but somehow was thrown by the neat, business-like man who walked through the door.

He wore a pin-striped suit, a floral tie, and loafers, an easing of the professional image, she felt.

He was even-featured without being attractive and wore his thick hair in a short crop.

He moved quickly with a nervous energy that reminded Stone of a squirrel.

He'd read the information they'd e-mailed him and listened carefully now, making notes and then transferring them to the flip chart that was empty apart from a few of her jottings.

'OK if I wipe these?', he said.

'Sure', she said, nonchalantly.

Every time Spinner walked past her she got a whiff of overpowering aftershave that smelt like a throwback to the seventies.

'OK', he said. 'Let's stick with the first case. We've got a highly organised psychopath possibly suffering from schizoid delusions about the crucifixion murdering those he sees as corrupt. Frank, your original analysis that he would pursue politicians was not that far off, except he's now killed an actor. An actor who impersonated Christ. I use that word because that's the way the killer would see it. This is a man who feels deeply angry with the way the world has turned its back on religion. Politicians are important, but this is not the only group he's targeting. You're reliving scenes from the Woodland Killings, Frank, and that may not help too much. We need to keep an open mind while keeping track of what this man's about and right now what he's about is murdering those he sees as responsible for betraying Christianity.'

'Who is he? A priest? A religious nutter?', Stone said.

'Define nutter. He's someone who inhabits a particular belief structure and I suspect the more we go into this investigation, the more we'll find out about that.'

'How far do you want to go? We've already got three dead on this case alone', Castle said.

'Forgive me, Chief Inspector, but I've only just arrived. What have you got? Zilch. Let me piece this together. Drawing up lists of likely targets at the moment is a waste of time, I want to get into this guy's mind and figure out exactly what it is he believes and that's going to take time.'

Castle loosened his collar.

'We'll give you what you need, but we need to make some advance here.'

'I'll take the files away and come in tomorrow with what I've got.'

They gave him copies of the files on both cases and then he left.

'So, a religious killer. I figured that earlier', Stone said.

'He is good. Give him till tomorrow.'

'He wasn't that sarcastic.'

'As I said, give him till tomorrow.'

'And what's that he was wearing? Hai Karate?'

'Don't even ask.'

Stone opened a window and got back to her desk.

'Did the information on Montelle come through?', Castle said.

'No. Still waiting.'

'Where's Smart?'

'No one's seen him.'

'Meantime our killer's still out there.'

18

Power will burn their little hands
The House of Power is packed with obese gorgers on its meat
The tides of time will wash their imprints away
As they strut, the Corrupt, in their Uniform of tatters and rags
The beggar on the street has more honour than these
There he is crippled in his blue Uniform
Ant man
Walk away with your house upon your back
He sees me not
He serves the Law of Liars
I serve the one and only Law

As PC Kevin Smart walked home that night, he did not see the man step from the shadows.

He did not hear the blade come from behind him and slice his carotid artery so deeply that the blood showered two metres across the pavement.

In the darkened alley that ran behind his house, he clutched at nothingness, falling into the blackness as the killer hacked the living life out of him, reducing him to a body twitching uselessly and clutching for his police radio.

His stab wounds were so deep blood flowed from the alley running into a gutter. He looked like something in an abattoir.

As his life ebbed from him and his radio crackled into the night air, the figure disappeared into the night.

19

The third prostitute murdered was Rachel Thomas.

Once again, the women who knew her said she'd never mentioned anyone hassling her.

They were a tight group according to the officers who questioned them and they were angry about what was happening.

Also, they were demanding an arrest and Castle and Stone both knew they were no nearer to making one.

The next morning Tom Spinner arrived bright and early and stinking of aftershave.

He started writing on the flip chart.

'I've looked through everything you've got and we're looking for a man who has either been snubbed by a career in politics or a psychopath who is using religion for his own ends, as yet not apparent. I hope for everyone's sake, it's the first.'

'What would the second entail?', Castle said.

'A killer who's going to take a lot longer to arrest. A man who's using religion as a cover for something else.'

'And the first? Someone who wanted to get into politics?', Stone said.

'He either wanted to get into politics and didn't, or was in politics and his career ended in scandal, it could be a family member, a grandfather who'd been in politics and some scandal had occurred that changed this man's family as he was growing up, or someone with a real axe to grind against the political system.'

Castle looked at the flip chart.

'That's a pretty wide canvas.'

'Yes, but not as wide as the second profile.'

'What do you suggest?'

'We lay a trap. Even if it fails to snare him, we find out more about him from it.'

'What do you have in mind?'

'Let's go back to the original case. Whoever is doing this is using it as a model. What was it that drove you to a breakdown Frank?'

Stone saw him flush.

'Look, I want this guy caught.'

'It's all right, no need to go on the defensive, breakdowns can be positive.'

'Stress', Castle said, 'the guy was playing games with me.'

'Exactly. The guy was playing games with you. You weren't in charge, you felt like a dumb cop and this guy served out the match. He had you running round the court and served you nothing but aces.'

Stone remembered the time Castle had hit a psychologist for saying less.

'What is this, Tom?', she said, 'have a go at the police?'

'I'm not having a go at anyone. I know you're both on the defensive. You look like a bunch of schmucks to the public and no one has any faith in you, even yourselves. No. I'm here to help and you'll only catch this guy if you learn from your mistakes because he hammered you. He played you for suckers and he won.'

Stone could see Castle bristle.

'How exactly is this helping us?', she said.

'You never caught the original killer. And this killer is using his energy, using his power to help him get away with it.'

'It's not the same man?'

'The original killer was one step ahead of you at every turn, if DNA had been around and if modern psychological profiling had existed I'd say you had a fair chance of catching him, but you didn't. The man who's committing these murders has studied the old case. He's also studied you, Frank, and that's why he started the killings in the same style, but now he's changed it because he wants to disorient you. There's too much here. He's applied close scrutiny to the original case, to what happened to you and he's using it for his own ends. He's playing you. Getting at you is as important to him as killing his victims.'

'And the religious theme?'

'We don't know enough yet about how he's using it. But one thing's for sure, if you rise to my bait, you'll rise to his and you'll fail all over again.'

'Right now you're not giving us a lot', Stone said.

'Right now I'm giving you all you've got, which a few hours ago was nothing.'

'OK, the killer. What do we have on the type, the background?'

'He's educated, physically powerful, around six foot, as the angle and depth of the wounds show. Don't be fooled by the religious messages, this is not some indoctrinated whacko, there's careful thought in the way he's executing these killings. He's young enough to have the energy to carry this out, but not a young man and never was.'

'What does that mean?', Stone said.

'Something aged him when he was young, some early formative experience that's scarred his soul, that's left him lacerated in his psyche, hence the deep lacerations he needs to make physical in his victims, those he sees as deserving of the kind of pain he's been carrying all his life.'

'How do you work that out?', Castle said.

'The killer is trying to express something. No matter how deranged it may seem, he's communicating something lost inside him and only accessible to him through the act of killing. There are many ways of killing people and he's using deep cuts. He's been cut deeply. He's externalising it through the act of murder which is his only way of release.'

'How do we trap him?', Stone said.

'You were played. All the time the first killer was murdering he was ahead of you, he had the power and he expressed that power through the killings. You need to make this man feel you have something on him.'

'But we don't', Castle said.

'As yet. But you trick him. You make him think he's given something away. He's not given you any real forensics of any value. He knows a lot about murder and feels he knows more than you. It's almost as if there's a contest here. He believes he's a better student of murder and its dark places than you are, he's saying come and join me out here, if you dare. If you make him believe you've got something he didn't think of, you'll undermine him and throw him off balance and once he's off balance he'll make a mistake, one that could help you catch him. And who knows, maybe even catch the original killer.'

'You said you didn't think this was the same man', Castle said.

'I don't. But there is a link. He's a game player. And the best way of getting to him, of undermining him, is to make him think you're playing him at his own game. His game, whatever that is, whatever it represents to him, is his sense of power, which is all he's got. Make him feel you've got your own strategy, stand deep behind the base line and return serve. It'll throw him. We need to understand his game. If you unlock this process, then you might just unlock the first one. They're mapping into each other and there is a key here.'

'What's the process?', Stone said.

'Killing. Killing is a process, Jacki. It is a way of expressing something from within. The only way left to men who have run out of other options because for whatever reasons their lives have taken them away and brutalised them at the same time.'

'I'd always thought of killing as a pretty final act. Maybe that's the cop in me, too many corpses, they don't walk again.'

'What I mean, Jacki, is serial killing forms a process. The taking of someone's life, the power involved in that, is part of the killer's process of transformation.'

'So, how do we trap him?'

'So far there's been very little press coverage of the murders.'

'Right.'

'We change that. We put out a lot of misinformation and the idea that we know who he is. We put out a profile on the kind of man he'd hate.'

'Which is?'

'A politician. He'll get angry. He doesn't want to be linked to politicians, he wants them rubbed out. We say this is an embittered ex-politician with a grudge and we have leads. We sexualise his motives, se we screw up the image he's presenting. We force him to lose control.'

'And what if he is an embittered ex-politician with a grudge?', Stone said.

'Even if he is, he won't see himself in that light. He's killed off the part of him that led to that experience whether through politics or something he's connected to politics. It'll throw him. And in the process, we'll get an insight into his game.'

Castle nodded. 'I'll contact the press officer.'

'And what do you have on the other killings?', Stone said.

'Not much. This took most of my time. But with the prostitute killer, we're not looking for a Jack the Ripper. He hates prostitutes all right. But there's something here that doesn't sit right for me and I need to look at it more deeply.'

'Sit right how?', Castle said.

'If I knew that I'd tell you. But this isn't as straightforward as it looks.'

He left and they put the story in motion.

Then the news of another killing came through and they raced to the alley where they found their colleague's body.

20

PC Smart lay in a pool of blood with his neck open staring up at the sky.

As Stone looked down at him she recalled the slap she'd administered to him, the sharp taste of bile in her mouth. Castle's face tensed with the sense of personal wounding.

'This fucking bastard's a cop killer now', he said.

'All our theories are being blown apart. Kevin was no politician. What is going on here?'

'I'll tell you what's going on. There's someone out there with a death list which makes sense to no one except him. How do we link Kevin to the others?'

As they waited for Alan Marker to arrive Stone once again studied the position of the body. Nothing in the hands. One gripped his police radio, the other lay uselessly by his side. She walked back, and saw that his left foot was angled away from him. It pointed out of the ally towards a fence.

There in front of a crumbling house, were the words:

'The Scurvy Servants of Worldly Power are Seized.'

They were written in paint across the fence. Same script.

'He did this after the murder?', Castle said.

'Or before.'

Alan Marker was stepping out of his car.

'This guy's busy', he said, walking past them.

They watched as he knelt and started his on scene examination. He looked intently at the neck wound.

'An inch deeper and he'd have removed Smart's head.'

Castle turned to Stone.

'I want Spinner to look at the messages.'

21

Smart's murder stung Castle and Stone like vitriol in an open sore.

The death of a fellow cop felt like a piece of barbed wire caught under their skin, and the case took on a new urgency.

At their third meeting with Spinner, they handed him the information with anger.

'I guess this blows your theory out of the water', Stone said, watching for a reaction and getting nothing.

'Not necessarily. The links may still be there.'

'How? Kevin was no politician.'

'Pursuing the theory, have you put out the profile I gave you?'

'It's hitting the press tomorrow', Castle said.

'I've looked at the other killer and can tell you now that the way you're going to catch him is through the area he's using.'

'Richmond Park?'

'Yes. There may be links to Soho.'

'So we look at anything that connects the locations to past killings, also the backgrounds of anyone with previous living in a ten-mile radius of the park.'

'What's his motive?', Stone said.

'Removal.'

'What?'

'He wants to remove them. He's taking them off the streets like litter and leaving them in a natural surrounding, which symbolically to him will absorb them. They're an eyesore to him, hence the removal of the last victim's liver which by the way, will get worse.'

'So who are we looking for?'

'A younger man than the other killer. Someone with a real grievance against prostitutes and a strong sense of his own morality and moral superiority to them.'

The officers given the task of dredging the internet for anything in the backgrounds of the victims came back with one piece of information Castle and Stone didn't have: before he became a police officer, Kevin Smart had been involved in the Communist party. He'd actively campaigned against capitalism and briefly considered a career in politics.

'The killer knew more about one of my colleagues than I did', Castle said to Stone.

'He's researching them very carefully. Like you've said all along, Frank, there's something totally controlled about all of this.'

'At least Spinner's profile's holding up.'

'OK so it's politics, but a cop's still been killed.'

22

None of the victims had been sexually assaulted.

The story they gave the press of an embittered politician did the rounds. The Sun ran the line: 'loser minister hacks colleagues to feel better about himself', while The Times was more articulate and more devastating: 'police believe the current serial killer is a failed politician with deep-seated sexual problems. Apparently he is sexually assaulting his victims after killing them, revealing an acute necrophiliac personality type. The police cannot give further information, but do have a very good profile of the killer.'

Castle read the coverage with interest.

'He won't like the public to think he's screwing corpses', he said, handing Stone the papers.

'Let's see if it topples him from his perch.'

They sat back and waited for the line to twitch.

At Rondelo, Black was pleased with the new recruits. Wilkes had found men and women he could use and he calculated how he could turn their unshaped metal into the hard cutting edge he needed.

As a child he had stood at the open doorway of his blacksmith father's workshop, the red and angry sparks rising from the great fire within. A dweller on the threshold, he had passed what seemed to him half his boyhood watching those huge scarred hands lift and turn the metal, the clang of steel on stone resonant in the twilight air of his after-school visits.

The smell of burning metal rose now on the static air like a watchful ghost reminding him of something he knew then.

From time to time his father would look over the anvil at him, never speaking, his eyes like fire, his head bent to his work so that they merged with his singed eyebrows. He was telling him something without words. There were no words between his father and him.

Inside the house his mother would be reading from the Bible. She would chide him for lateness, she would chide him for uncleanliness, and each day without fail she would sit him down after supper and read the scriptures to him, her thin and wizened frame like barbed wire inside the tattered grey cardigan she wore. His mute father would sit and listen, dozing behind her shrunken head.

It was her house.

Yet in his workshop he was a giant and forged the metal to his will, bearing burns and scars to his grave.

Karl would watch him in the dying light, see the light of his fire take over in the watchful dark, and follow his work.

It seemed to him his father was forging souls there in the smithy, and he could hear the screams of the sinful as the fire engulfed them.

'Have you taught them of the two seeds yet Jonas?'

'Not yet.'

'Then make them ready. They must be fertile soil to receive the teachings.'

'They know there is only one Law.'

'Cut the cloth and tailor them so that they be serviceable.'

'And keep them outside the Secret Work?'

'That is only for a chosen few.'

'Shall I usher in the guest?'

'Do so. I have been expecting him.'

Wilkes retired to the corridor and a few seconds later an inner door opened into the room where Black had been speaking to him.

Wilkes returned to the recruits.

At the station Castle and Stone went over everything they had and knew that for now they needed Spinner.

The double killings were straining their resources to breaking point. The streets were full of Christmas shoppers and he noticed as the holiday drew nearer Stone was working longer hours, pushing her life away like a bad memory. Castle could see the isolation and stress already etched into her face deepening, the lines getting harder, and the festivities and enforced celebrations made the darkness of the woods blacker to him, as if something beyond his reach were mapping out the precise coordinates of his despair and wandering from himself into the unmapped terrain of his nightmares.

23

Bella Torte was a clever, abrasive minister who came on as a feminist and liked to win arguments. She'd won every debate she'd been involved in at university and enjoyed it most when she beat a male opponent. Friends accused her of being a secret sexist, saying she believed men were a greater challenge, and women were inferior opponents, but she always rebuffed this.

Her agenda was science. As minister for education, she'd rammed science down everyone's throats until they were sick of it. It was her particular god.

She lived in a neat house in Kensington and enjoyed her lunches, where she liked to boast of the humiliation her fellow MP's had suffered at her hands. She kept her hair short and shunned make-up. Neither attractive nor ugly, she was as unremarkable as a copy of an unfashionable work. She wore Hermes scarves to lunches and dressed down for the cameras.

She was popular with scientists. She'd raised their profile, got them massive increases in funding and stressed the importance of their subject on the school syllabus.

'We need scientists in this country', she said so often it sounded like a catch phrase.

She'd recently campaigned against creationist teaching, calling it the workings of a backward mind.

The shadow minister for education harangued her in parliament, calling her a despot.

Her response was swift and devastating:

'The right honourable gentleman is as deluded as what he is preaching, and would turn us all into medieval dunces. What he promotes is based on ignorance and encourages stupidity, he is as medieval and obsolete as his own beliefs.'

The cheers roared round the house and she promptly sat down as her opponent floundered.

The streets of Soho were becoming a cluster of paranoid prostitutes.

They watched each other's backs, vigilant of how long one of them took to buy a pack of cigarettes, wary of new punters, wary of strange requests. Preferring to stick with clients they knew, regulars from passing business or the houses of parliament, they turned down work and consequently put up their prices. An air of guarded vigilance knitted them together and hardened their commercial approach.

Sally Nash had only been working Greek street for a few months.

Although she'd picked up a few regulars, she relied heavily on passing trade to feed her crack habit, and took a few more risks than the other women.

She'd heard what had happened, but felt she could handle any weirdos, taking on as many men as she could.

One evening that winter, a passing blue Ford slowed as she stood at the edge of the road.

She leaned in the open window.

A few seconds later and she got in, lighting up as she did.

She directed the car round the block while she fumbled with the guy's zip, figuring on a quick job, and as she did, felt a hand grip her head and place something over her mouth. A sweet taste ushered in the shadowland of dreams.

When finally she roused from the deep sleep of the chloroform, she found herself staring up at some trees, her dress hoisted around her waist, her jacket and top removed.

She felt a coldness moving inside her, as if some elemental presence had crept beneath her skin, and she searched for a human face below the dark carving of the trees.

A shadow moved, became a hand, and reached down from the darkness to clutch her throat. Her scream died and she felt something popping in her neck, her legs kicking out into the naked night as if they belonged to someone else.

She clawed at him, her hands waving blindly in the dark.

She was held fast to the cold ground, pinioned and broken, losing air in her lungs, the few visible shapes fragmenting and shading into blackness, a warmth flooding down her legs.

Clouds scudded overhead, while beneath the ebony branches of the trees he reached down and slit the soft skin of her breast, a slight tearing noise the only audible thing. She felt the cold metal enter her and tried to remember some words from long ago, the distant image of a key turning in a door unfolding in her mind.

He was pressing in deeper, puncturing her, and the intense cold was replaced by a warmth that spread through her, flooding her and passing like some black tide.

She could hear voices and remembered lying on soiled sheets as a child while an unseen hand hit her.

The words 'dirty bitch!' echoed on the air like a threnody, sonorous and resonant of all the hatred her body had ever known.

Laughing faces passed before her in some fairground parade.

Something dug inside her, turned and moved again.

She felt herself being removed, the place and who she once had been ebbing from her like a memory that flees from the mind.

She tried to clutch at herself like a passing stranger, a familiar face in a busy street.

She thought she could smell woodland berries and grass, and a lawn opened in her mind on which picnickers sat waving and she heard the tinkle of an ice cream van in the night air.

When Castle and Stone inspected the scene the next morning they knew immediately which killer they were dealing with.

Her body was so altered and violated in its essence it was a desecration of nature.

Her breast lay tangled in some undergrowth a few metres away and the memory of her first murder case flashed through Jacki's mind like a repeat of food poisoning. She'd puked that first time and vowed never to do so again. She held good to her word, swallowing bile.

'If this guy keeps up at this rate, there'll be no hookers left', Castle said.

'Two serial killers on the loose at the same time. Ever happened before?'

They looked at each other and returned to the station where Castle rang Spinner.

24

Flo Lane was the bright star of the opposition. With her Pre-Raphaelite hair that cascaded down her shoulders and caught the camera lights, and her warm personality, she appealed to the public.

She had all the characteristics of the party they wanted to overthrow, the party that had been in power for too long, and that's why they wanted her. Branding. Sell the same product back to the public from another store, in this case the opposition party.

Self-opinionated and argumentative, she was the shadow home secretary. Mother of four kids by different fathers she was ardently anti-marriage, claiming it was the last shackle that bound women to the patriarchy they needed to finally topple, and she shouted it from the rooftops.

From her speeches in parliament to her policies, she campaigned for single rights, denying there were any benefits to children in having two parents to bring them up.

She was outraged by the murders recently committed against the working girls as she referred to them.

One evening as Castle sat at home with a bottle of whisky, her voice pitched out of the TV at him.

'What are the police doing about this? Nothing. Women are being killed. Women are being tortured. And they do nothing. Men don't care. Men want wives at home cooking their dinners. The police are far too busy to deal with this. This must be stopped. These are honest working women servicing husbands usually, who go home to their enslaved wives.'

Castle got up and turned the set off.

He was tired of people interfering with police business, people who didn't understand, like politicians who wanted to promote themselves at every opportunity.

He stood looking out at the darkness of the street searching for form in the blackness.

He felt his certainty fragmenting like desiccated rock, his solid world collapsing beneath his fingertips. He was losing his balance and falling, his doubts about himself surfacing from his mind like his predatory self grown hungry for his own blood.

She threw his jacket on the floor.

'Hey!'

'Get your stuff off my sofa.'

Don stood glaring at her. Jacki had been upstairs when she heard the front door shut and when she came down to find Don there some deep territorial instinct took over.

He picked his jacket up, dusting off the fluff.

'I came to get some things.'

'I suppose it doesn't occur to you to call?'

'Forget it.'

He moved towards the door.

'Get them while you're here.'

'You know, it wasn't easy living with you.'

'Oh really?'

'You're married to the job, not committed to me.'

'My philandering husband.'

'Why do you think this happened Jacki?'

'You tell me Don. You knew I was a cop when you married me.'

'You spend more time with Castle than me.'

'You're going to throw this marriage away just like that?'

'Daisy's-.'

'So that's her name? Finally we know!'

'She understands.'

'What?'

'What it's been like.'

'It never occurred to you to talk to me.'

'You're never there!'

'So you pick up some tart.'

'She's a client.'

'Your boss know that?'

'What is that, a threat?'

'You sneak back here for a few things when you think I won't be around?'

'You threw me out.'

'What did you expect me to say? Oh, Don that's OK, fuck whoever you want, just stay here.'

'You know, this didn't just happen overnight.'

'That's why I'm saying we need to talk.'

'I'll call you.'

She watched as he left, turning to the scattered files that filled the room.

For a moment she got a glimpse into Don's world: police reports, late meetings, her tired, him on his own.

25

Jonas Wilkes was holding a meeting in the Round Room at Rondelo. Grotesque and pious carvings shaped the space that creaked with time and the world of lost belief.

The recruits were gathered and listened wrapt in the sermon. One by one, their distinction was fading in the common purpose that united them. Their faces blended in the pews.

'There are two seeds, or two natures which are in Man and Woman. You all have a devil and an angel', he said, looking out at them. 'Cain is still alive in the power players of this world. Cain's Brood are the oppressors we see walk among us today. We are free and this dual seeding now will be taught to you as you take your place among the righteous, for verily I say unto you, you must wage war with this society that has fallen. Corruption is among us. Plague walks the streets. Divided man is lost and at war with himself, like the pelican that drinks its own blood. He nourishes himself with sin and copulates with lepers, breeding a crew of catamites like some sick offering to a false and sullen god. He is divided, but I can teach you unity. I can make you one. Follow me in these teachings. We have Holy Work to do.'

They bowed their heads as Black watched from a hidden gallery. He held the measure of them in his mind, like some gradient of potential energy.

At the same time Bella Torte was delivering an address to an audience of about a thousand.

She hammered home her points with gusto.

'We need more scientists. This country was once great, what are we going to be? I will tell you: great again. How is that going to come about? Through ensuring every child in every school across the country is taught and excels at science. We do not want mediocrity, we want greatness, and this is the way to achieve it.'

She paused to look across her audience, measuring their response.

Composed mainly of scientists and the numerous bureaucrats who managed education budgets, they were following closely.

'I propose withdrawing a section of grants allocated to the humanities. I propose backing science with the largest single amount of money ever given by any government in the history of this country so that it can once again call itself great. We will have leading scientists who will be the envy of the world.'

There was a round of applause.

'Money. That is what you will have. The departments of every school will have the latest technology so that we can give our kids a chance. We will be the envy of other nations.'

Cheering from the back.

'Science will lead this country forward. Science will make us world leaders.'

At the back of the hall a figure slipped out, having heard all it needed to hear.

Flo Lane sat at home dealing with e-mails and preparing her budget, while her kids ran amok and raised merry havoc.

From time to time she would deliver a sharp retort.

This did little, the children holding her in no better regard than some hired help they saw irregularly and had no respect for. She dredged through her e-mails and sent off a few, lost in the chaos that was her life, trying to promote her latest ideas.

There were times like these when she thought politics was no more than selling. Hide your ideas behind jargon, pitch that jargon at the people whose votes you want to win, and package it. Push the package out as far as you can.

As she was working the phone went. The daughter of a friend had been calling her, showing interest in a career in politics. Flo had listened and now decided to put her off once and for all.

'Hi Mandy', she said, weighing up how hard to hit her with the bleak reality of the political world.

'Flo, just wanted to continue our chat.'

'Any time.'

'I've been thinking about something you said last time about politics.'

'Are you really serious about this?'

'Yes.'

'Serious enough to hear the truth?'

'What truth?'

'That the success of any party's policies is dependent on the gullibility and ignorance of its voters.'

She was dismayed to hear laughter travel down the line.

'When did you figure that out?', Mandy said.

'When I was at Oxford.'

'As long ago as that?'

'Most voters don't analyse policy. Most peoples' lives are constrained by the ties and demands of children and mortgages. We inhabit a tightly run economic prison. And gullibility lies in this trap: the uneducated don't understand what the political media machine pitches at them, they get hooked on catchphrases which, when you put them alongside the economic state of the nation, are meaningless at best, lies at worst.'

'Flo.'

'Meanwhile those who do understand what lies behind a manifesto don't dig deeply enough: their lives are an enclosure of debt and consumerism and they want all of society's broken hinges fixed. People vote on their anger and their prejudice.'

'What are you saying?'

'People don't want to look at their lives and take responsibility for them. I recognised this early on in my career as a basic form of ignorance. Their self-delusions are endless, as is the capacity it engenders for their scarcely covert manipulation by the machine. This is about lack of knowledge Mandy, it's about the lack of desire for knowledge, because it takes effort to gain it and with it comes enormous responsibility, responsibility most people don't want.' There was a gasp at the other end of the line. 'Easier to blame the politicians', Flo said.

'I'd always seen you as an idealist.'

'My idealism died somewhere at the point I left Oxford thinking the voting public get what they deserve.'

'But you're a brilliant politician.'

'I'm a good saleswoman and a good manipulator and the mirror my public life holds up to me flatters me.'

'I've obviously called at a bad time.'

She felt guilty and mean and the conversation didn't last much longer, having nowhere to run.

She hung up and as she stared at the row of figures before her she saw a way of getting what she wanted through the back door.

'You don't just have to fool the public, you have to fool your fellow MP's as well', she said out loud as one of her children entered the room, asking for something. His voice was far away and it didn't register with her. She held a hand up and gestured to him to go away. Then she massaged the figures.

That afternoon at Rondelo the new recruits left with a deeper understanding of the beliefs they were being inculcated with. The atmosphere of the ancient monastery was registering its mark on them. They felt part of the old order, when abstinence and service ruled the inhabitants' days.

Their sessions were changing them. They held their heads like the devout, their faces shining with belief, and waited for their next meeting with Wilkes.

In his library Karl Black read the papers, paying particular attention to the latest developments in the twin killings that were flooding the news.

Meanwhile, Wilkes slipped out at the back of Rondelo into the orchard at its end and passing through the fields that boundaried the land went on an errand.

Alan Marker's report on the murder of Sally Nash revealed that her spleen had been removed.

Castle pondered the significance of the body parts the killer was removing while he waited for Tom Spinner to arrive.

He and Stone had spent the morning looking at both cases and focusing on the significance of Richmond Park to the prostitute killer. As yet they'd found nothing.

A whiff of aftershave announced Spinner's arrival. He threw the papers he was carrying onto Stone's desk, marched up to the flipchart and started writing.

Castle and Stone watched with secret relief. The four messages the killer had left at the crime scenes loomed at them like warnings from a by-gone era.

'Read this as communication' Spinner said. 'This is his voice. This killer wants to get his point across. He wants our attention.'

'He's got it', Stone said.

'These are his themes, the things that are preoccupying him. His first message states "The Corrupt are Discovered". Something has failed him. Someone. The theme of corruption represents something rotten in his state, in the world as he sees it, this empire he wants to see overthrown. That's the fuel to his anger. The emphasis on discovered shows he wants to expose someone or something.'

'What?', Castle said.

'It could be symbolic and at this moment in time cloaked in layers of symbolism which only make sense to some psychosis. But people who go around exposing others usually end up exposing themselves and that is what we need to look for in our killer's messages, signs of him.'

Castle and Stone nodded.

'So, following the thread, we move on to the second message. "The Rapists of the Land are Apprehended." What does this mean to him? This is about power, and for him a reversal in power play. He wants justice, his own brand of lawless justice. The law has let him down, hence his easy killing of a police officer. He moves without difficulty from politician to cop. They both represent a law he wants to see smashed. Then we move onto lies. Very important to our killer. He writes "The False Prophets Shall be brought to Heel".'

'He's attacking some lie as he sees it', Castle said.

'Yes. Again he wants justice. He wants the liars brought to

account. False prophecy could represent the misuse of religion or something he sees as usurping the rightful place of religion.'

'Rightful how?', Stone said.

'Again, we're entering the maze of his psychosis, so let's leave it. For now. Next he talks about power. Now why doesn't that surprise me? His last message reads "The Scurvy Servants of Worldly Power Are Seized". There's a group of people this killer wants removed, they represent some betrayal of a truth he serves.'

'Serves?', Castle said.

'He could be involved in an organisation with extreme views. They may not be aware of what he is doing, but their belief system could be feeding his pathology.'

'How can this help us catch him?' Stone said.

'The profile we've put out on him should be reaching him now and hopefully angering him. We need to gather information about any existing groups, whether religious or secular that express opinions relating to the political order as it stands, needing to be brought down, being corrupt, being responsible in some way for the worldly woes we suffer, any organisation with an axe to grind against politics.'

'How big do you want the net?', Castle said.

Spinner looked at him.

'Until a couple of days ago you didn't have a net Chief Inspector.'

26

A huge moon hung in the sky over London. It cast elongated shadows on the littered pavements and shed an eerie glow into rooms where curtains had not yet been drawn.

Bella Torte noticed its light fall across her carpet, lending a surreal air to her fiscal proceedings. She was putting through her budget proposal that evening, a huge claim on the country's resources and a huge long-term burden on the taxpayer.

The figures wriggled away from any culpability should her enterprise fail and the kids just not be bright enough to turn into Nobel winning scientists or not be interested.

She had her vision and everything fitted into it.

From the children she saw and mentally quantified as useful material as she sat on the board of governors of the schools she dealt with, to the parents she secretly rated as having potential or being too mediocre to justify capital investment, she had her game plan of England's educational future securely mapped out.

Confident and brooking no criticism, she forged ahead with her ideas, which she clamped on waverers in her camp as if her proposals were a chastity belt and she was protecting the honour of those less fortunate than her and not sufficiently endowed with the intelligence to discern where the country's best interests lay.

She worked most of the evening, popping out only to the off licence.

In nearby Parson's Green the lights in The White Horse cast their electric glow over the moonlit shadows outside as customers entered the pub. It was a busy evening, and Flo Lane sat in the corner waiting for her date.

She watched the hordes of commuters pass by the windows, scurrying to their homes, some popping in for a drink on the way.

Her life seemed to be passing her by in a series of meaningless dates. She hardly ever had time off from her political career and looking after her children on her own proved a burden in itself.

But a friend had offered to give her the evening off and she waited with a second glass of wine, wondering what was holding him up. A glimpse of herself in the mirror told her all she needed to know: the full face and tired eyes, the shapeless figure.

A text message later confirmed it. She'd been stood up, and she made her way home wobbling along the back alleys.

Journeying through the dark, navigating his way by the moon, Wilkes returned late to Rondelo, entering by the back and going straight upstairs to his chambers.

He went into his monastic room, bare of everything expect the trappings of the teachings of The Last Brotherhood and laid a package on his bed.

Beneath the same swollen moon, Castle stared out of his window.

The darkness showed only the face of Karl Black and he went over in his mind how he could interview him again. As he stood there he noticed a plastic bag move rapidly down the street. A wind was kicking up.

The wind raised Stone's head, as she read through her notes on both cases, avoiding the emptiness of the house and angry at Don.

And as Bella Torte returned home, she noticed a light on in her house.

She decided she must have forgotten to switch it off and turned her key in the door.

27

This night swallows light, but theirs has been extinguished
A lamp guttered by their fetid souls
The only light shining now is Blade
He Ploughs them, their Furrowed Flesh folding away to Blood
His quick reckoning of Justice flickers on her Flesh
And she is ready
A fruit I pluck
A field I tread
A poisoned apple rotten with worms which crawl across her tired tongue
For I have waited in the corridors of time and sought them out
The huntsman draws his bow
She moves among her things seeking refuge from herself
She stands in the room, her back to me
Corruption leaks from her like blood

As Stone put the files away and drained her glass, Don's picture caught her eye. A still shot of a frozen smile, a moment claiming happiness from the hollow passageway of time.

The picture tugged her backwards into memories of her early married years and she felt tricked. She remembered the first time when as a child she'd entered the sea's surge, the buoyant joy of reaching her feet out beyond the coastal shelf turning to anxiety and nausea as a wave washed over her tilting her backwards, her mouth filling with saltwater in the sudden somersault.

The picture stared back at her like a forgery.

She picked it up, cradling the frame, her other hand reaching for the receiver.

Anger stopped her dialling the number. She went over her last conversation with him and suddenly heard Karl Black's voice instead of Don's, as if he was superimposing himself.

She knew she had to fight him taking over and went to bed, away from all the police paperwork. She lay there listening to a soft wind howl at the crack in the window.

The wind gathered speed and intensity that night. It swept the litter across London, blowing dust into the eyes of those caught out late in it. It howled down alleyways and under eaves like some lost lamenting banshee. Perhaps its noise helped the killer in the house.

His tread was undetected and left no trace, as if he was a part of this place he had invaded, as if he knew more of his victims' domain than they did.

And he was unseen.

Bella Torte was knocked unconscious as she stepped into her living room.

When she came to, she found herself gagged and tied into a chair.

She could not see his face, but the man holding her cut her repeatedly and for hours while she bled. Slow, deliberate lacerations moving across her body in some pattern she detected but could not fathom, the intervals between them long and arduous.

She felt her body no longer belonged to her and in the intervals he allowed between the cutting she fell backwards into memories she had carefully concealed behind what seemed suddenly now nothing more than a work facade. Each time he penetrated her, each time she felt the sharp breaking of her skin, its rending by the polished metal whose glint was the constant image in her torture, she felt a conflict of cold and warmth as the weapon entered her, summoning the rush of bodily fluids from her.

He would then retreat and stand in the shadows watching her, as if all of this amounted to some instruction she was receiving.

She remembered giving birth the first time, the indignity of her waters breaking.

She'd been out to dinner with colleagues, ignoring her pregnancy like an inconvenience.

When she stared down at her wet dress she felt angry, exposed.

He came again. So did the opening of her and the strange warmth it unfolded.

The faces of lovers fled across her mind like supplicant spirits, their bodies' warmth leaving her now, her feeling of them deserting her like a wasted limb. Her husband lay across her, a solid weight she wanted to throw off and she looked down seeing her body held less fluid than the carpet, thinking how do we hold so much of it as the tide of her life slowed, her heart aware of its own redundancy.

Pictures of her working life on the coffee table seemed an elaborate con she had perpetrated on herself, since what she held were nightmares and all she'd done to lock the cellar door was no more than some obsessive ritual carried out by a sick child alone in the house.

She saw the killer's hand clutch the weapon's handle, and as he clenched it she saw her public life pop like a shell.

She tried to look around, but the light was dimming. The carpet was soaked, pooled with blood it could not absorb, the overhead lights reflecting in the carmine mirror of its bubbled surface, and as he moved towards her again the shower sprayed her wallpaper and pictures of her with smirking politicians.

She felt as if he was absorbing her and she watched him as he tortured her casually and she looked into his face, a knowledge there between them as if she had contracted him to violate her soul.

What deep and buried guilt, she wondered, had caused her to commission this act?

He seemed to become someone else then, someone she had known a long time ago. She longed to hear his voice, searching for an entrance to this man, and she cried out into silence, the sound of frothing in her lungs ending the startled cry.

At the end as she tried to speak, he opened her mouth with a simple, delicate gesture, holding her lips softly in his warm hand. And he gazed into her, the gaze loosing her from the person she thought that she had been, something moving beneath the veiled surface of his eyes.

He ran his finger along the inside of her lips, rubbing her saliva into her gums, and then removing his hand and watching the thin strand of saliva stretch and break into small pink drops.

She stared up, her lips parted and stretched across her face as he calmly reached into his pocket and withdrew an instrument whose sharpened blade removed her tongue.

He cut right back to her throat in a steady motion, his grip firm, and pulled it out whole and laid it against the wall next to the picture of her with the prime minister, where it seemed to curl, as if in some final effort to speak. Beside it he wrote something, taking his time, before puncturing Bella's heart.

28

Castle woke on the sofa from a dream about Karl Black.

He'd gone into work only to find him seated at Stone's desk.

As he entered the room Black started laughing and said:

'I've been here all along, Chief Inspector, and you think you can catch me?'

He handed him an elaborately wrapped box, Christmas baubles cheering it, and waited as Castle unwrapped the paper, its crinkling surreally loud in the silent police station.

He fixed him intently with a stare as alien as the watchful eyes of another species.

'A little present for you Chief Inspector, it will show you the direction your case is headed.'

Inside was another box.

Beneath the lid was a pile of newspaper which he unravelled to stare at Detective Rover's head.

Black's laughter woke him.

Getting up he noticed it was the small hours.

The darkness outside seemed interminable and woven of some blackness that was dense and tangible, absorbing any attempts to light the way through the night time. The street lights shone feebly and as he staggered upstairs all he could see was his tormentor's face.

Stone lay alone in the darkened house thinking of Don.

She'd twice been on the verge of calling him and stopped herself.

Even the twin cases couldn't take her mind off her marriage now that night had settled and she longed for the morning and the station.

Tom Spinner thought of them both as he worked late into the night, feeling himself on the edge of breakthroughs that never came.

His phoney profile of the Woodlands Killer was doing the rounds in the press.

The Mail ran an article that read:

'Failed politician scythes down his own.

An ex-minister with sexual problems is destroying politicians in our midst. While the police struggle to arrest this latest evil serial killer, one of their own has been taken from them.'

The Independent was a little more articulate.

'An Offender Profiler is helping the Met catch the man known as the Woodlands Killer, owing to his similarity to a serial killer twenty-eight years ago who escaped justice.

According to the profiler the murderer is obsessed with politics and is almost certainly a man whose own career in politics foundered. Embittered and delusional, he is taking revenge on the political establishment. An amoral misfit with low self-esteem, he is almost certainly a loner with sexual dysfunction.'

He read the articles with interest, hoping the taunts would trip him up.

Aware he needed to deliver more, he dug as deeply as he could into the profile, only to find the list of types expanding beneath his fingertips like some free-running oil.

He sensed he was working on the biggest case of his career and was both tempted by the mind of this murderer and challenged by its complexity.

He knew the patterns were there yet when he analysed them he found something else, an evasion and a refutation of his theory. As if the killer was challenging him on his own and hallowed soil.

29

The city sleeps like a lost animal shackled by the hand that moves the chain
The unseen Hand that binds its neck will fetch it to the halter
The Path is dark that leads them to that Door
Yet the briars at the roadside Burn in the wind
The smell is familiar
They have known it before
They attempt to light their way
Now the leaves have fallen and the bare trees carve their message into the chill skies
Their summer's growth falls like Ash from a Fire
She staggers, working her way towards her children, orphans of another world
Yes, she has served her Foul Master and now her bill is rendered unto her
She has Chattered and lived in woven words
And now she will face the Law

The tall buildings blocked the moon's light as Flo Lane struggled through the darkened alleyway. She struggled out at its mouth into the empty street to find her breath smothered. Her lips were pressed tight against her teeth and she tasted blood like rust turning in her saliva.

She couldn't move her head and tried to scream, the sound stifled in her throat.

She swallowed and brought up some of the wine, the cheep Soave burning like acid.

She tried to push into the street but was pulled back into the alley where she fell.

Gagged and frozen by fear she felt her clothes being torn and before she knew it her skirt was lifted from her.

She thought of her date, the evening promise of a liaison that never came, the lost opportunities of her career flashing through her mind like train stations in the rain.

He inserted something between her legs. She was distant now from the scene and felt herself give to it and the accompanying pain.

Something hot ran down the inside of her thigh.

At home her children would be sleeping now, the children that had come out of her into the world like burnt offerings. She remembered tucking them in, folding the sheets down until they were secure in their beds. And she lay on her back in the alley yielding again, as he removed her womb.

She remembered a face from long ago, a voice consoling as a warm embrace offering advice which fled from her now like a retreating tide.

Light ebbed from her as it drained into the sky like the slow leeching of some fluid.

30

Karen Jones hadn't been working the Soho lanes for long. After a few weeks waitressing, her Northern ambitions foundered on the rocks of her damp flat and the demands of her dope-smoking boyfriend, and she realised there had to be more to London than this.

A meeting with a friend and a few drinks had lured her to a one off meeting with a punter and a few minutes later she'd made more than she could in a week of waiting tables.

She liked the easy cash and the power it offered over these sad men, and quickly learned how to make the transaction quicker.

As a newcomer she found the other women helpful, given the recent killings, but protective of their own patch. Muscling in on the market was difficult, but with her knee length boots she made it.

There was another newcomer on the block and she teamed up with her.

Tracy Fletcher had come from the Midlands and ended up on the street after losing her job.

Before losing her looks she decided there had to be a way to make money in the city and was soon turning tricks.

She had a studio in Soho and she and Karen watched each others' backs. Young enough not to care about the threat that was prowling their streets, they carried on making as much as they could.

To them the sounds and smells of Soho were still new enough to register. Their ears caught the textured layers of traffic, sexual trade, tourism and crime. They smelt the stew of fast food, sex, pollution and money, ignoring the tension the other women were feeling. To them the police were a necessary inconvenience.

The build-up of the case was creating more stress for Castle and Stone.

They needed more manpower and they got it.

Extra PC's were assigned roles on their division, carrying out background checks on men living in the area of Richmond Park who had been convicted of sexual assaults and violent attacks, while they got on with what they were good at.

They also got a new officer on their team.

When Mike Nash walked through the door, Castle remembered him from his talk a few weeks earlier.

It seemed like a few years.

The steel blue eyes and clean look took him back to his talk and everything that had subsequently happened loomed out of that brief period of time like an iceberg.

'Morning Chief Inspector Castle.'

'Good to see you. We could use your help round here. I guess you heard what happened.'

'Yes. I didn't know Kevin Smart personally, but the death of a fellow officer is always a blow.'

Castle introduced him to Stone and they set about briefing him.

He spent the morning gathering as much information as he could, the picture of an eager young detective.

When Bella Torte's husband returned from his business trip, he was hit by a nauseating smell as soon as he set foot through the front door.

There in the living room sat some blackened ghoul, a carving of blood and mutilation, its black and hollow mouth open as if delivering a message.

He raced to the phone before pouring a large brandy.

31

The press were having a field day with the Met.

While Spinner's trap lay without twitching in their pages and the killer continued to strike seemingly unmoved by their best efforts to throw him off balance, the tabloids were full of headlines that gave a less than flattering picture of the professional skills of Castle and Stone.

'What are the police doing?' said one headline, while the front page of The Sun read:

'Crack-up cop cocks up again', and gave a lengthy account of Castle's breakdown and the Woodland Killings.

The second paragraph went for broke.

'Twenty-eight years ago Frank Castle failed to apprehend one of the most vicious serial killers this nation's ever seen.

An alcoholic whose wife left him, abandoned by his friends, it was rumoured that he was in collusion with the killer.

He'd interviewed and arrested Karl Black more times than is usual and each time let him go.

Reports that he was somehow under Black's spell led many to believe they were witnessing the public crack-up of a cop who was drawn to the darkness he was meant to be policing.

It is understandable when men who work closely with the sickest minds of humanity become attracted to the darkness, understandable that policemen like Frank Castle crack under the pressure.

He failed.

The case is still unsolved.

He is still in post and heading the present investigation into this second wave of killings which seems to be modelled on the first.

Could the same killer be striking twice?

Does Frank Castle know something the rest of us don't?

And should he be in charge of this investigation when he failed so badly in the first?

Does a man who had to see the police psychiatrist because he was deemed unfit to work have what it takes to see this job through?'

As Castle read the article he felt as though someone had attached the ship's anchor to his leg and thrown it overboard.

Owing to the press mauling he was paying more and more frequent visits to the pub and he was beginning to look frayed round the edges.

When the call came through about a fifth victim, he and Stone drove round to the Torte Kensington address in tired silence.

Inside Mr Torte was pacing the kitchen. His lip was bleeding and Stone noticed he kept biting it while they were there, seemingly unaware of the pain.

A bottle of brandy stood on the kitchen table and his glass always seemed to be full.

He stared at them with bloodshot eyes.

'What kind of animal would do this?'

'We intend to find out and catch this man', Stone said.

'It's a pity you haven't already done so. How many more has he got to kill?'

'We're working on this case as hard as we can, Mr Torte', Castle said. 'Only today we've taken on more manpower.'

'Why Bella?'

'That's what we intend to find out.'

He closed the living room door and spoke to Marker, leaving Stone with Mr Torte.

'Your killer is upping the wounding and now going for mutilation. She was stabbed repeatedly and slowly, probably with the same weapon as on the previous killings, then something particularly nasty occurred. He removed her tongue with an extremely sharp implement.'

'What?'

'A guess. I'd say a rose pruning knife. And you have another message.'

He pointed at the wall behind Castle.

'The System's Brokers are Silenced' stretched across the wallpaper like some mad banner.

On their way back to the station they received a call on their radio.

'Looks like we've got two murders today', Castle said. 'Call Alan.'

In a quiet road in Ealing neighbours twitched their curtains as the flashing lights bombed up the street.

The police cordon had already created a stir and now as Castle and Stone got out all eyes were on them.

The alley was awash with the red tide of Flo Lane's body. Her belly lay open like a botched operation and she stared up at an empty sky.

They waited for Marker.

It didn't take him long to make the connection.

'This is a double killing.'

'You're saying it's the work of the same man who killed Bella Torte?'

'Yes. It's the same weapon. I'd say there are even traces of Bella's blood inside her, I'll know once I've carried out my full report. This guy certainly doesn't believe in wasting time. They were killed within hours of each other.'

The smell in the alley was nauseating and Stone retreated into the street.

'Injuries? Dismemberment?', Castle said.

'He's removed her womb.'

'He took it with him?'

'Oh no. Hew took it out and left it.'

'Where?'

'Behind you.'

There stretched between two nails in the wall lay what had been Flo Lane's womb, beside it the message:

'The False Order is Fallen'.

'He nails the first one's tongue to the wall and this one's womb', Castle said. 'There's a real monster in our midst and we haven't the slightest clue who he is.'

'Well, the sooner you catch him the better. Don't read the papers.'

They sped away and Stone called Spinner who informed them he was already on his way over.

32

Karen and Tracy were busy.

An influx of tourists brought some good trade from husbands bored with sightseeing.

While wives shopped, they popped out for a little light relief and the two newcomers enjoyed a rise in their earnings.

There'd been no sightings of any strange men and the killings seemed to have stopped.

The other women dropped their guard a little and took on customers who a few weeks ago they would have turned away. Only the veterans of the game stuck to what they knew would keep them safe.

Alan Marker's lab report showed that the killer hadn't even cleaned the weapon.

'He left Bella Torte', Castle said to Stone, 'and butchered Flo Lane in the alley. Bella's blood made its way into Flo's womb.'

'He must have known their movements', she said.

'He seems to know an awful lot.'

The image of her butchered womb contaminated with the other victim's blood stirred a sense of black obscenity from Castle's troubled soul and he wondered from what distant reach of the human psyche this killer had wandered to violate the world he knew.

The door swung open.

'Morning Tom', he said.

'I've been looking at the messages. He doesn't just want to destroy the people he sees as responsible for a system he hates, he wants to destroy anyone who adheres to that system, anyone who serves it. "The System's Brokers are Silenced." Bella Torte served the system. Her budget figures lay spread out in front of her corpse. Politicians are his number one target. But it might not just be them, as the murders of PC Smart and Lewis Montelle testify.'

'Could the brokers refer to more than just politicians?', Stone said.

'Yes. They're the wielders of power. The money men, but in this sense it could be those high up the ladder.'

'So he removes her tongue', Castle said. 'Any clues as to his psychology there?'

'He's censorial. He didn't like what she was saying, but his whole controlled manner of carrying out these executions stems from someone who is operating from a system, his belief structure governs him, regulates his thinking. He is removing statements, utterances that for him do not belong in his world view.'

'And Flo Lane's womb?'

'She didn't believe in marriage, and all those children. She shouldn't have a womb. This is a killer with a medieval sense of religion.'

'OK so we narrow down the list of politicians who may have offended him, we watch them.'

'Not enough.'

'What else have we got?', Castle said.

'I'm not saying don't do it, I'm saying he might change track again and kill someone who isn't a politician who's offended him just to keep you guessing.'

'A gameplayer.'

'Oh he's a gameplayer all right, and one who is going to increase the level of violence he uses against his victims.'

'That's reassuring.'

'I'm just warning you, Frank. This killer is feeding from his sense of power. The blood's scarcely dry in his mouth when he's hungering for more.'

'And the other killer?'

'I'm still looking.'

'I was thinking about his mutilations, Tom. Any thoughts on the body parts he's removing from the prostitutes?'

'Liver, spleen. One secretes bile, detoxifies poisons. The other filters bacteria and produces antibodies. He's removing their defence systems.'

'Rendering them defenceless.'

'I thought killing them did that', Stone said.

'No, Frank's right. He's rendering everything they represent defenceless.'

'You mean, he's dismantling the system?'

'Yes.'

'And now our other killer's taken to mutilation too.'

Every officer spent the day compiling the list and by the end of it they had over a hundred names.

PC's were dispatched to warn the relevant parties while Castle and Stone read through Marker's reports.

In the meantime, the internet research yielded over a million hits on religious beliefs which might motivate the killer.

They wandered in darkness waiting for him to strike again.

And Castle felt himself back in the woods once more.

33

The recruits were assembled in the round room.

The Imogen of a few days ago, the bobbed and loquacious woman with life and enthusiasm had faded to a cipher. She sat, her hair hanging across her shoulders in limp strands, her white hands placed on her lap. She seemed the picture of religious devotion and self-denial and rarely spoke.

She sat next to Sheila, who slumped her shoulders and sat so still it was as if she did not want to be noticed. From time to time she would twitch nervously, as if someone behind her was prodding her.

Separate from them and sitting with their backs erect, were the line of men.

Malcolm, his hair luminous with oil, sat pale-faced staring up at the vacant gallery, while next to him sat a black-haired man with a sculpted beard that ended in a sharp point on his jutting chin.

They had been waiting for a long time in the frozen room.

'Do you know what time it is?', Malcolm said, turning to Rodrigo.

He smiled.

'There is no time here, Brother.'

'It seems as though we've been waiting for a long time.'

'No watches, for we dwell in timelessness now, as advised. For what is there to wait for, except these teachings?'

His eyes sparkled as he spoke and his appearance was as remote from the twenty-first century as Rondelo itself.

He had a certain confidence about him and he sat perfectly still and at ease with himself.

The door swung open and Wilkes entered noiselessly.

He passed them, going straight to the front.

'We are here because the Bible commands us to reproduce.

Man is Holy and we are at war with the beast, the animal within that walks among us and pays its way with the lies we hear every day', he said.

He looked around at the assembled company, catching Rodrigo's eyes.

'The ways that modern society has used sexuality is the reason we live within the Fall. Corruption lies everywhere like a rank plant that has grown fetid with disease, and that disease is sexuality as it stands. Purity is needed. We are the Purifiers. We must cleanse society of its sickness. We have work to do and The Last Brotherhood is commanded to carry it out.'

Malcolm looked across at his sister, who held her eyes fastened to the stone floor. Behind him he heard the door shut as one of the other recruits left the room.

From the gallery Karl Black disappeared without a sound.

As he entered his library the inner door swung open.

'Welcome', he said. 'Jonas's work is making good progress.'

Every available police officer was on the case.

Politicians that fitted in any way the background Castle had given out were placed under police surveillance, and they watched and waited for the unknown faceless killer to make his next move.

Unmarked cars zoned the area around the Houses of Parliament and armed officers sat in cafes near to the homes and workplaces of ministers for all parties.

Stone was thinking of Don, feeling angry as revenge whipped its tail inside her.

She and Castle met with the Prime Minister to explain the matter.

The meeting was brief and businesslike.

'I understand we have a killer targeting ministers and that you have stepped up security, Chief Inspector Castle', the PM said.

'That's right, Sir. We're offering extra twenty-four hour protection to anyone we think is at risk and we hope to catch this man before another murder is committed.'

'This is shocking. Do you have any idea who is carrying this out?'

'We have a top psychological profiler working with us and we're making good headway, but the killer is clever and doesn't match anyone we have previous on.'

'I've read through some of the material you sent me. The name Karl Black certainly sticks out, especially with the similarity to the Woodland Killings. Have you interviewed him?'

'We have and he has an alibi.'

'I see. Any other suspects?'

'We're working on it.'

'I respect what you do enormously, it must be a tremendously hard job.' He looked at his watch. 'Well, good luck. Anything more I can do for you?'

'Yes. It's a long shot, but he may attempt a killing here. Would it be possible to get an idea of security?'

'Yes of course. I'll get someone to show you around.'

'Thank you, Sir.'

He extended a warm handshake.

'Good luck.'

As Castle turned to leave the room, he caught the glare of his own reflection in the window, a sad and troubled face not even his own staring back at him and no distinguishable features of a cop there at all.

The Chief of Security gave them a tour, and things were tight enough to put their minds at rest, apart from a few holes which could be filled in.

They toured the offices and ended up at the library.

'So far so good', Castle said.

'We're pretty vigilant', the guard said. 'Have to be.'

Castle looked at the guard's uniform. It defined him. He stood out.

He swung open the library doors where huge bundles of papers and documents were being carried and stacked.

'What goes on here?'

'MP's need access to records, so the librarians get what they need and they're taken up to them.'

'Easy for someone to get in here? Get access to the documents and take them up to an MP?'

'Not without a pass. Also, it's a tight crew and they'd know. Here, let me introduce you to Mary. Can you spare a moment?'

A flushed woman carrying papers walked over to them.

A badge with the Houses of Parliament crest showed her to be Mary Clarke, head librarian.

'Yes?', she said, looking at the officers.

'Mary, this is Chief Inspector Castle and DI Stone. They're checking our security, could you spare a minute to tell them how things run here so they can figure out if there are any areas which need tightening up?'

'I'm extremely busy, but my assistant can help you. Adam, have you got a moment?'

A young man with long hair and blue eyes emerged from behind some book cases. He set down the papers he was holding and walked over to them. Stone briefly acknowledged a flicker of attraction, pushing the thought of Don away.

'How can I help?', he said.

The guard explained.

'Yes, of course', he said, 'let me show you around. We all know each other, so if anyone appeared who was an impostor we'd immediately contact security. Also, it's very hard to find any files here without having a background in archives. I'd say security in this section of the house was pretty tight.'

'Thank you', Castle said, 'you've been very helpful.'

He and Stone left feeling satisfied that the killer would find it hard to hit one of his targets there.

On the way back to the station Stone thought about her marriage. She felt as though her time and reality were governed by the actions of someone who shouldn't be free to roam society like some killing playground. Her private life had been chipped away to the point of violation and she felt herself clinging to the job. This job of detecting someone they couldn't even make a sketch of. Meanwhile, her time became a prison while she pursued justice.

She pushed this realisation away, connecting it to some of the things Don had said to her.

34

Jonas Wilkes walked out of Rondelo, disappeared into the woods and went to a derelict farm building on the outskirts of a nearby town. He wore a gambeson and looked like a historical exile.

He closed the door and lit one of the oil burning lamps he kept there.

Cobwebs hung from the wooden corners of the building like some tapestry of devotion spun by ascetic withdrawal from the world. The place had a bareness and isolation about it that testified to a nature more at home in worldly retreat than engagement with fellow man.

He sat there and the focus of his eyes turned inward. He would not return until much later, travelling in the dark through unlit woods.

And then he journeyed as some shadow merged with the layers of nighttime, an unseen messenger who knew his way in nature as no light was needed to guide him and he was steered by the watchful eye of the dark.

Castle and Stone were grateful for the extra manpower.

Some of the research was paying off.

A sect called The Preachers of the New Dawn held some beliefs that leapt out at Mike Nash, who promptly took what he'd got to Stone.

'These guys believe some things that match your brief', he said, handing her his downloads.

She glanced down at the pages and the sections he'd highlighted.

A paragraph berating the sins of the world and the order "the guilty must be persecuted". There followed a tirade against the hidden criminality of the political system and the line "the wrongful must be brought to justice". She read on, noting the Biblical terminology and came to the next highlighted line "the political system is diseased". The last section Mike had picked out read "the leaders of our country are blasphemers". For the first time she felt a glimmer of hope.

'Good work', she said. 'Any idea how long they've been around?'

'About ten years and their leader Maxwell Ravener was arrested on sexual assault charges before he formed the group. Apparently, he'd been involved in the mainstream church, taken a disliking to a parish councillor, tied her up and raped her.'

'Was he charged?'

'No. She dropped the charges. The police thought this was because of ongoing harassment by some of his friends, a group of people he'd convinced he had some special insight and who now form part of the main body of The Preachers of the New Dawn.'

'They seem to hate the political system we've got, so this matches what we're looking for.'

'Also, a couple of them have minor charges for violence.'

'Nice group.'

She showed it to Castle.

'I think we need to pay them a visit', he said. 'Where they based?'

'Sutton.'

'What are we waiting for?'

As Castle and Stone drove there, Karen and Tracy watched a blue Ford circle and stop in Greek street.

As they walked towards it a police car drove by and the Ford sped away.

Most clients were nervous of police interference but they made a mental note of the car, despite missing its reg number.

The headquarters of the Preachers of the New Dawn was a crumbing pebble dashed house which announced 'The New Jerusalem is Here' as you walked up the path.

The banner hanging in the window was the only colour in the grey building.

Stone rang the bell and Castle looked around at the overgrown garden, the gate hanging off its hinges, and the peeling paint.

A woman in a stained vest opened the door.

Stone flashed her badge at her.

'We're looking for Maxwell Ravener.'

'He's not here.'

'Can you tell us where he is?'

'What's it about?'

'We have a few questions to ask him.'

'Hold on.'

She returned a few moments later with an address scrawled on a piece of paper.

It was a better address and it didn't take them long to find it.

A satellite dish sat proudly on a newly painted wall and the garden was a colour shot of plants.

Stone rang the bell and after a few seconds the door opened.

A man sporting a monocle and wearing a colourful cravat peered at them.

'Yes?'

'Maxwell Ravener?'

'Yes.'

She flashed her badge at him.

'We'd like to ask you a few questions.'

'About what?'

'Can we come in?'

'If you must.'

He let them into the hall and showed them through to the living room.

Plush carpets, plasma screen, all the trappings of a comfortable lifestyle, certainly no worldly self-denials.

'We're investigating some murders.'

'The murders of the politicians?'

'Yes.'

'And what has it got to do with me?'

'The killer shares some of your beliefs', Castle said. 'He's motivated by some hatred of the political system that we notice your group promotes.'

'We don't promote hatred, officer. And there are many groups who share our beliefs.'

'Would you mind telling us where you were last Friday?'

'Mind, yes. I'll tell you. I was holding a meeting at our headquarters which I'm sure you've visited. There were about twenty-six people in attendance and you can have their names and addresses if you wish.'

'That would be helpful', Stone said.

Ravener got up and left the room, returning a few minutes later with a print out of names and addresses.

'Can you explain why your group preaches so much anti-political sentiment?'

'We live in a democracy, officer, in case you hadn't noticed, and that allows free debate. Politicians criticise each other all the time. We're not saying anything out of the ordinary. There are many people who hate politics, which, when you analyse modern warfare and all the innocent bloodshed, is understandable. You can't go round arresting everyone who falls into that camp, or you really would turn into a laughing stock.'

'We'll check out your story', Castle said, getting up.

On the way back, he turned to Stone.

'You get the sense that was just a nutter?'

'Yeah. He's not our man.'

The story checked out and they kept The Preachers of the New Dawn up their sleeve just in case.

35

Karen was drinking in a pub when she spotted custom.

She'd had a quiet day and always recognised a punter.

He was sitting watching her and she walked over to him. He held her eyes as if he was controlling this situation and she thought what suckers men were, how pliant just for the easy thing she was offering. She'd let him feel he was holding the bridle, male delusions only needed their tired heads rubbing for a few seconds and the exchange was easy.

The notes stacked up, the heavy smell of money the odour she held onto in her mind when she gargled them all away at the end of a long day.

Sometimes the notes would scroll into her mind saturated with stains. She caught her reflection in the mirror and realised she was a long way from home.

'Got a cigarette?', she said.

He reached into his pocket and flipped open his pack.

She looked into his eyes, checking him out, as she inhaled.

She couldn't read anything there in his face, which was untroubled by emotion or doubt.

So he knew what he wanted.

So did she.

She took a deep drag on the cigarette, holding his eyes, the red tip burning in the air. She could hear the paper crackle around the tobacco.

'Thanks. Join me?'

He nodded.

'I'll be out in a minute. My car's round the corner.'

The shorthand didn't bother her. This would be a quick one.

She walked outside into the cool night and smoked until he came out. He moved slowly and deliberately, wrapping his hands in the deep pockets of his charcoal grey coat.

'You got cash?'

'Yeah.'

He tapped his pocket.

'It'll be a hundred.'

He opened his wallet and showed a bulge of notes.

She looked at him.

It seemed to her that he wore anonymity like a uniform and she thought of what hidden lives these men led, and how betrayed their wives must be.

'What are we waiting for?', he said, holding her face.

Most punters would have checked out her cleavage, her legs by now, maybe he had problems. Problems were good. They cost extra.

'Nothing', she said.

As she walked towards his car none of the other women saw her because she was off her patch.

She got in and he started driving and she asked where they were going.

'You'll see.'

She reached down to undo his zip, thinking why waste time, help him with his problem and she saw how unmoving his face was, not a flicker of anything she recognised there in the half-light of the car, the shadows from outside strobing past the window.

She saw his hand reach up from the gear stick and hold the back of her head and she braced her neck, pulling away. His zip was jamming and she wanted to see it before she did anything to it.

She tugged on the catch, her nail catching in it and felt him pull her hair back and slip something under her nose.

A dreamless sleep held her for a few hours.

When she awoke the first thing she felt was something sharp against her cheek.

The imprint of a twig there.

She moved her aching head, feeling saliva drip from her mouth.

She was staring at a large tree.

A swollen moon was impaled on its branches and she felt cold.

She reached for her pocket and felt skin, realising she was naked.

A hooded figure stood over her wielding something heavy in his hand.

The next thing she knew he clubbed her and she passed out.

She drifted on the pain.

The blackness eased and she passed into consciousness to witness him cutting her belly apart, the knife travelling up her like some living thing she had stirred from a troubled dream to find there on her like some succubus. It dragged her flesh apart moving upwards to her neck and she felt something heavy being dragged from her.

Her body was fleeing from her and she was transported back to the pains of the labour table, the stirrups cold against her ankles. A breeze passed across her, lifting the tiny hairs on her skin. She felt a dragging pain and lay there in the nighttime shedding what was left of her into a pool that settled on the grass like some unholy lunar mirror.

It was almost morning now and a few clouds promised light.

She wondered if deer could smell human blood and lay there with all sense fading as the stags bellowed like sirens in the nearby park.

The Christmas lights were giving Castle a headache. It was late and he began to resent the long shopping hours.

He manoeuvred the cramped and over-priced aisles, wary of shoppers, watchful of paparazzi hiding among the assorted special offers.

The gaudy tree winked menacingly at him, its baubles shining in lurid reds and golds, inducing a wave of nausea in him.

He thought of his wife, trying to sketch her face back into his mind, seeing the lines blur and fade to a distant memory on his horizon. He didn't even know where she lived any more.

This falling into the shadow of his past was like slipping into quicksand. Her leaving him had taken some part of his life with it and he had walked ever since on a cauterized wound. As if that surgery she applied had left him with only the world of crime. As if by hunting in that twilit world he could find himself and what it was he had lost.

Around him women clutched children and dragged them away from the temptations placed there by store managers, while people with a tortured look on their faces queued at the clanging ringing tills. He watched them, getting a glimpse of himself in another life having a family Christmas. A wash of unreality swept across him.

He'd forgotten what he came in for.

Outside a Father Christmas ho hoed and passed presents among the crowd. He stood like a troll among the cloned shoppers. Parents stopped and waited impatiently while he administered to their offspring's needs, like some fiscal priest in a pantomime.

Beyond him, Castle saw a door opening at the corner of an alleyway. The lights of a pub yawned in the gap and he slipped from the store into the street.

He passed from them, to the faces familiar to any bar.

He sat in a corner clutching his whisky.

Presents, Christmas, celebrations, families were as alien to him as a foreign tongue and he became aware that he stood on the killer's soil listening for a heartbeat. The throng outside, made up of men and women he served, were another species and as he knocked back the malt he realised that beneath the whisky's taste lay a sweet and sanguine tang. The upturned bottles reflected in the mirror administered his forgetting like a vein dripping blood.

The life out there, the purpose that inspired it, lay at the edge of impenetrable woods, a world he could not reach. The blackness pulled him back.

He walked to the bar and ordered another.

Once he had paid, he found his seat taken by a couple whose bags of shopping were strewn across the floor.

He looked at them in revulsion and downed it in one and headed out into the street again, remembering that feeling of landing in a foreign country, these family habits as alien as an exotic smell.

The crowds had thickened and he headed down the alley away from the noise, away from this life which he was too marked to be a part of. His life in CID had cut him away from all this, and he walked with the criminal like an exile with no passport.

Two street lamps cast a funereal glow. One was broken. It flickered like a twitching eye.

He couldn't see what lay at the alley's end and pushed through the darkness, welcoming the fading noise.

He stopped, adjusting to the lack of light. There seemed to be a series of connecting alleyways running off the one he was in and he turned into the first one, seeing only the blurred haze of its outline.

As he did, he heard a noise at his shoulder.

He turned and was struck in the face.

He fell and got to his feet, feeling for his badge, realising it would be useless, punching out in the darkness and losing his balance as he struck air.

The figure hit him from the side now and he tasted blood.

He was falling and was hit again and again, the blows strong and well-aimed.

He reached up and grabbed the man's clothes, feeling a thick spongy material.

His assailant was over him now. The smell of stage costumes. Castle reached for his face and pulled something away. As he staggered to his feet he heard him running down one of the connecting alleys and he walked back to the street lights, holding a blur of white in his tensed fist.

As he stood there, a lost figure in the crowd, he stared down at what he was holding.

The Father Christmas beard lay there with all the menace of a shard of glass in the birthday jelly.

Tom Spinner was going over the original paperwork on the Woodland Killings.

He assiduously studied the profiles of every suspect the police had at the time.

He'd spent hours looking at the profile of Karl Black, but another name jumped out at him now: Samuel Walsh.

He'd had the motive, since he'd known many of the victims and lived in the area, and been arrested at the time.

That evening Tamara Klein worked the group of businessmen assembled to hear her speech.

She was a natural performer and always thought politics and acting bedfellows.

With a strong background in business and a gift for working the media, the government had snatched her up and incorporated her into the cabinet as soon as they could.

There were no indiscretions in her past, no skeletons in her closet.

She liked the media and cultivated its attention. On TV her thick curly hair and round face appealed. She looked average and trustworthy.

She was also an ardent feminist, having strategically upset many men over the years.

Her beliefs were useful to the party, since she was aimed like an exocet missile in the direction of opponents who she saw off in as humiliating a way as possible.

Many confident movers and shakers had come away worse off from doing battle with her and while she had nothing to hide, she certainly had enemies.

'You've got to embrace the new era', she said to the audience. 'Men are no longer calling the shots in the workplace, women are getting equality and where they're not getting it, they're demanding it. As an employer, it is your job, your duty, your future and your livelihood to ensure that this deal is delivered. It's on the table, gentlemen.'

There was a round of applause as she wrapped up.

'Women are your personnel. Survive in the new climate.'

Every businessman in the audience watched her carefully as she prepared to take questions, but one figure at the back watched her more closely before slipping out unseen.

As she wrapped up, her colleague Mary Plover was giving a TV interview.

The presenter was trying unsuccessfully to rile her.

She remained composed as the religious members of the audience rose to the bait.

Her theme was the need to legalise prostitution, something she had pursued down every political corridor she strode.

'There is nothing wrong with it', she said. 'There are men here in this audience who will probably put their hands up and complain about what I am saying because they want to impress their wives, they want to retain the trust of their wives, but go off and use a prostitute. What I am saying is that we need an open debate and until we get rid of the shame and lies we cannot have one.'

'OK, let's hear what our audience thinks', the presenter said.

'I think it is wrong what you are saying', a man in the back row said. 'I am a Muslim and I cannot believe that as a politician you would promote prostitution when these women are being exploited and abused.'

'They are being exploited and abused because it has been driven underground by our absurd laws. When you create a black market in something, you open the doors to exploitation. If we let these women operate as valid businesswomen, they wouldn't need pimps, they would have above board businesses and would be serving the community without being subject to crime.'

'But it is immoral.'

'According to who? You?'

'Let's hear from this lady over here', the presenter said.

'I think the fact that as a woman you are promoting prostitution is shocking. How any woman can sell herself like that and not be on crack or drugs is beyond me and I think you shouldn't be a politician with those kinds of views.'

'Why? What I am proposing would clean up prostitution as we know it. Your moral stance is one-sided. Prostitution has always existed and always will, I am sure you have known a man, perhaps your husband who's used one.'

As the woman was about to say something, she was cut off.

'I'm sorry, but that's all we have time for today.'

The credits rolled as Mary Plover disappeared to the back of the studios and returned to parliament.

36

Once he'd cleaned himself up, he didn't look too bad. His skin didn't bruise easily and there was nothing broken. He'd been hit harder. He faced himself in the stained bathroom mirror, feeling the thick and calloused edges of his skin as his fingers puckered and stretched his cheeks.

The deeply encrusted layers of grime and dirt that clung to the edges of the cabinet depressed him, and his private world felt as tarnished as rusted metal.

He knew what would happen when he got to the station, and it did.

Stone's brief morning glance in his direction as the door swung open lingered and became a stare he felt follow him as he crossed the floor to his desk.

'What happened to you?'

'Don't even ask.'

'I am.'

'I got jumped and before you ask, no, I'm not pursuing it.'

'Where?'

'A common. Bunch of em.'

'Any description?'

'No.'

'Frank, it's assault.'

'I know. Leave it.'

She did, understanding what it meant to this cop, seeing a long line of ranks closing somewhere in the distance.

Castle turned his back to her, leaned over the coffee dispenser and poured some whisky in from his flask, thinking of the white beard lying in his wastepaper bin at home together with his shame.

As he sat down Stone said 'how about we talk to Karl Black again?'

He nodded.

'As soon as I finish this coffee.'

Watchful of themselves, their lives lie trapped in the surface of the Mirror
They haunt the idle days of their Dreams
Unseeing they are Seen
Their Flesh the Fruit upon the Branch which bends to my Hand

Castle and Stone pulled into the drive at Rondelo and walked to the door.

On the way they'd discussed the best way of finding out if Black had anything to do with the killings. They felt that renewed pressure and the fabrication of the basis for an arrest might yield the fruit of breakthrough.

'Let's hope we spot something that can give us the excuse we need', Castle said as they waited for the door to open.

They expected Wilkes to open it but instead saw Black's face appear.

'Ah, the two plods return. Unable to solve a crime? I'm your man.'

He moved aside and watched them as they walked into the hallway.

He walked ahead of them and they followed him to the library.

'Now, what is it this time?', he said, sitting and leaving them standing.

'We're still investigating a particularly brutal series of murders that bear a correlation to the original Woodland Killings', Castle said.

'I had nothing to do with those killings as you know.'

'Why do you think someone would choose to copy them?', Stone said.

'You can't do your job and you want me to do it.'

'We're pursuing every possible angle.'

'You don't have an angle. Every time I see you, Inspector Stone, you look unhappy, can't you detect what's wrong with your private life?'

Castle cut in.

'We have a job to do.'

'Then do it', Black said, standing up. 'Because it is obvious to me that you haven't got a clue who it is you're looking for. You checked my list?'

'Yes', Castle said.

'And you will see that I have an alibi, or have you come to check where I was every night since this killer has been carving up the politicians you're failing to protect and laughing at you?'

'We could find a reason to arrest you', Castle said.

'Then do it, in the meantime.'

He held the door open.

As they drove back Stone thought of Don and she tried him that afternoon, only to get his voicemail.

37

Richmond Park was beginning to look like a butcher's workshop. They drove past the parade of trees, the tranquil green expanse, and walked to the bloodbath.

Alan Marker was finishing up.

'This one's been tortured. The violence is escalating', he said.

Castle saw the body as it was zipped into the bag.

It reminded him of the victims of bomb blasts, ragged flesh and guts spilled like a hyenas' feast.

'What did he remove?'

'The entire contents.'

Marker gestured towards a tree.

Its bark was splattered with what had been Karen Jones. Mangled flesh, skin and tissue hung there attached to vein and wood, an unnatural fruit that had no place there.

Stone toured the area looking for clues.

The killer was moving through the undergrowth like a ghost.

'There's nothing, no indication of how he got here or how he got away. He must have parked somewhere nearby, but I can't find any areas of particular depression in the grass.'

'We need to speak to everyone who knew her and everyone who worked with her. This has to stop before the press destroy our reputation.'

'What's left of it.'

That afternoon Tom Spinner came in.

'I've been looking at both cases', he said.

Stone looked at him.

'Another prostitute's been killed.'

'Let me start with that case then. The killer is motivated by someone or something else.'

'You mean he's working with someone?', Castle said.

'It's not as clear cut as that. His methods aren't those of a hardened serial killer, there is a level to the violence which suggests he is exorcising some of his own demons, something that may have happened to him when visiting a prostitute or some association

with a prostitute, yet at the same time there is a pattern to the killings which is not connected to his personality and suggests to me that someone may be leading him.'

'How?'

'It may be a mentor figure, someone who wants these women killed and who is directing the way he is doing it, aware of the man's need to kill and exploiting it.'

'Who are we looking for?'

'Someone with a connection either to a group with a strong leader figure or with a connection to another single male who is directing his movements.'

'Such as a family member?'

'Possibly.'

'Which means we interview more religious groups', Castle said.

'It might not necessarily lead you to him. He might not be religious.'

'What else do we have?'

'You don't. Right now you're dealing with two very enigmatic killers.'

'And the other case?', Stone said.

'I've been looking through the original files, and the name Samuel Walsh stands out.'

Castle remembered well the arrest and the lack of evidence.

'He was never guilty', he said.

'I know, but there may be a link. Apart from Karl Black, he is the main character in the original drama as it stands in these files, and the only other angle you have.'

'What do you suggest?'

'Dig around him and see what comes up. There is a link to the original killings and someone out there has formed their own pathological viewpoint on it.'

38

Castle and Stone paid another visit to Soho. Cars that stopped to cruise for available flesh vanished.

The prostitutes were angry at loss of custom, but they talked, scared that another of their number had been killed.

Stone spoke to a group of women who described the blue Ford that had taken Karen Jones from the pub, while Castle interviewed a few of the older women, who were taciturn and annoyed the police hadn't done more.

He knew from experience that they were on tricky ground. Despite the fact that these women wanted their help, they also wanted them to disappear without their clients seeing them talk to them.

Stone was talking to Tracy Fletcher when he joined her.

She was very affected by Karen's death and had opened up.

'She never said anyone had been hassling her.'

'Have you seen anyone suspicious hanging around?'

'What, beyond the usual clients?'

'Anyone who you think might have a motive for killing five prostitutes.'

'Sex workers. No. Look, we're vigilant. We stick together since this has started.'

'Did Karen have any ex-boyfriends who might have a grudge?'

'Karen didn't do boyfriends.'

'Any ex-clients with a grudge?'

'She never mentioned anyone and neither did any of the other girls who were killed.'

'We're putting extra police officers on patrol round here. Many of them will look like civilians.'

'They'll probably want a free fuck.'

'Call me if you see anyone out of the ordinary', Stone said, handing her a card.

'What, other than the police?'

'This man will strike again.'

'What got you into this? A good looking woman like you could make a lot turning tricks.'

'Call me.'

They walked back to their car.

'At least they spoke to you', Castle said.

'Only just.'

'I knew we wouldn't make an advance here.'

They drove back to the station, where they found Tom Spinner waiting for them.

He was animated, his papers covering Stone's desk.

'The significant thing about the prostitute killings', he said, 'is that none of them were sexually assaulted. But he's choosing sex workers. He's going into an area where sex is readily available, abducting women and torturing them before killing them, but not touching them or using them in any sexual way. He's saying I don't need you sexually, I'm going to ignore what you do, what you are, and kill you.'

'So what does that tell us about him?', Stone said.

'His need to reject what they do and control them to the point of murder indicates previous exposure to them. He's used prostitutes before. The need to humiliate is deeply tied up with revenge, with reclaiming some sense of lost power. The reason he's killing them is elaborately connected with something in his own psyche and then there's Richmond Park.'

'We've got a list of names of men living in the area who've committed sexual crimes.'

'You're wasting your time. The park's not significant because he lives near it. It represents something to him. We need to look at the park's history, symbolism, because this man is motivated by the symbolic. That's the borderland of the psyche he inhabits and moves within. That's what the prostitutes are. Symbols. They represent some sort of disease, something he's uneasy with. Killing emerges at the threshold of his struggle with this symbolic terrain. It is something symbolic, a purge for him, he doesn't even see it as murder, but getting rid of something that is a plague on society. This killer thinks he's doing society a favour. And the park where he takes them to kill them is symbolic.'

'So we check the park's history?', Castle said.

'One thing that is a big part of its history is hunting. The deer there go back to Henry the Eighth who used to hunt there. It's full of deer.'

'He sees himself as a hunter.'

'Yes. In one sense he's hunting these women down. It's a possible explanation. We need to look at the positions these women were found in, and see if they relate to any key historical parts of the park.'

'Sounds like a long shot', Stone said.

'Well right now, Inspector you're shooting in the dark and it's all you've got.'

39

Tamara Klein picked her kids up from school and went home to prepare a meeting.

They rowed in the back of the car and she yelled at them, before sitting them down to supper.

By the time her husband came in she was angry as hell. She still had an evening's work ahead of her and all she wanted was a glass of wine.

'Why the fuck can't you look after the kids for once?', she said as he walked through the door.

'That's a nice welcome.'

'You sexist bastard. You still think it's the little woman's job. I'm a fucking MP.'

'Or an MP who's a lousy fuck', he said under his breath.

She hurled one of her shoes at him.

He ducked.

'And you wonder why I stay out late? I do my share of child rearing and I work also.'

'But because you're a man your job's more important.'

'I didn't say that.'

'If you think I'm cooking you dinner, you've got another thing coming.'

'Don't worry, I'm going out.'

As the door slammed, Tamara returned to her papers.

Mary Plover wanted to speak to the police about the prostitute killings.

She was angry and felt this was a good vehicle for publicity.

She phoned the station and left messages for Castle but got no response and that evening drove round to try to see him, but arriving late was told he'd left for the day.

She was going to make sure that no more prostitutes were killed. She'd get it on the agenda.

Castle sat in the Crooked Key nursing a whisky while she drove away.

Returning home, she didn't see the car in her tail-lights.

It followed her right to her house and turned and passed her as she put her key in the door.

She turned on all the lights and sat down to deal with her e-mails.

40

Frank Castle's breakdown was brought on by a mixture of stress and his publicly exposed failure to solve the case.

The press appetite for blood was fed by the outcry when the case fell apart. And the key name in its implosion was that of Samuel Walsh.

Castle had arrested Walsh on the grounds that he knew many of the victims personally.

As a social worker he had paid their families visits and met them professionally.

He also had a history of mental health problems, a theme the tabloids made mincemeat out of. The fact that a social worker with a history of depression could have had access to so many vulnerable people gave them headlines for months, as did Castle's professional failings and private behaviour.

The twin stories were juxtaposed like a two-way bet on the public's appetite. The front pages were dominated by headlines like:

'Crazy cop loses it', 'Castle hits the bottle', 'Police Force? What Police Force?', 'What are we paying them for?'

When they felt the need for some variety, they went for Walsh.

'Social worker nutter in the frame', 'Samuel Walsh, the nation's serial killer', 'Would you let this man visit you?', 'Walsh the Ripper.'

Although Walsh's name was cleared, the press continued to intrude on his private life, digging up his mental health history and isolating him.

Castle hit the bottle in a big way and never really crawled out of it.

The paparazzi waited for him outside pubs and snapped him swaying home.

On one occasion, he lashed out and hit a photographer and was hauled over the coals for this and suspended.

He remembered saying to his wife 'I fail to catch a serial killer and the press turn me into public enemy number one.' He also remembered sitting on his hands so as not to hit the police psychiatrist who labelled him paranoid with a retarded emotional vocabulary and rage problems.

Justice, that's what all this was about, and he could no more get any for the victims than he could for himself.

Karl Black continued to taunt him, using the press as a podium which he used effectively to publicise his own innocence and religious beliefs.

One leading Sunday newspaper gave him an in-depth interview in which he said:

'I have been harassed by the police over crimes they know full well I am completely innocent of. The police in this country persecute anyone with strong religious views because they are corrupt and this is what has happened to me. Another innocent man has been arrested and I think it is high time we asked ourselves whether they know what they are doing. I know what I think and Frank Castle should be sacked on the spot without pay. He is a menace and a threat to law and order in this country. He has no understanding of the workings of justice.'

Black's taunts pursued him for years until he disappeared out of the public radar when he joined a monastery.

By then he had convinced everyone he was a religious man who, like Walsh, had fallen prey to the Met's incompetence.

Castle was put on low-publicity cases while The Woodland Killings continued to haunt him.

The effect on Walsh was altogether more dramatic.

The wrongful arrest and negative publicity wrecked his life. He never recovered. The press continued to hassle him. Some months later he took his own life.

Stone dug around until she found this out and decided that Tom Spinner's angle was leading nowhere.

'Frank, Samuel Walsh killed himself shortly after the original killings.'

He looked up at her reliving the sense of injustice he'd felt towards him at the time.

'I didn't know.'

'It didn't make the headlines, the press were being blamed for the pressure.'

'I think I stopped reading the papers at about that time.'

'The family demanded privacy.'

When Tom Spinner came in that afternoon, she told him what she'd found out.

'We're chasing another red herring', she said.

'Not necessarily. Dig further. Look at his private life. There may still be clues there.'

That afternoon Tamara Klein was interviewed by a journalist about her views on women and the workplace.

She rarely gave interviews, but when she did she made sure it was with a journalist favourable to her cause.

She was handed a question she would have asked herself:

'Do you think that women enjoy equal opportunities in the work place?'

'No. We don't. We struggled too long under the heel of patriarchy. Employers rarely recognise the hardships we put up with and still don't treat maternity sympathetically. We don't get equal pay and we don't get equal rights.'

'And what do you think are the driving forces behind this continued repression?'

'Male dominance and religion.'

'How religion?'

'The Bible portrays women as inferior. Women have been assigned a role by religion, and we're meant to stick to what our given remit is. When we step outside this, we're deemed to be sinful or in the wrong.'

'So you'd say that religion represses women?'

'It has repressed women and it helps the forces of repression in the market place by limiting what we're meant to achieve in our lives.'

She was very satisfied with the interview.

It would have a wide readership.

41

The next morning Tom Spinner turned up at the station bright and early. He wore a tie with setting suns scattered on blue oceans, ran his finger along the inside of his collar, removed the tie and threw it down on Stone's desk.

She wondered if this was some sort of territorial gesture on his part and decided against asking. The conflict between cop and psychologist she'd seen at work between him and Castle had taken time to resolve and she didn't want to start anything that would take their eye off the investigation. She looked at him as he set his papers down on her desk, reams of jottings held together by bright elastic bands and she knew they needed him.

He looked at her, then at Castle.

'Our killer is trying to purify them.'

'How?', she said.

'By killing them in an increasingly ritualised fashion. Ritualistic behaviour is often linked to a purification pattern. Handwashing rituals are commonly known about, but there are many others, bizarre ones in the weird and wonderful world of pathology. Bloodletting is an example. There is a need for cleansing in this man, and he feels contaminated at some level. He wants to remove something, which is why he's started removing parts of their anatomy.'

'You mean dismemberment is connected to cleansing?', Castle said.

Spinner nodded.

'He's trying to clean something out at such a deep internal level he can't even reach it himself. That part of his psyche, whatever scarred it is buried from him and impels him to dip his hands inside the mutilated bodies of others.'

'Can you get any reading on him from this?', Castle said.

'The defilement he feels could be early sexual abuse, it could be something else.'

'And how did you figure this out?', Stone said.

'By reading the killings. Every murderer has his own signature, read that and you get his psyche.'

'Well this guy's still out there killing and we're still here trying to figure out who he is. We're looking at the fact that he takes them from Soho to Richmond Park, we're working on the links, the history, but so far we've come up with nothing that gets us any closer to catching him.'

'There is something else in these killings.'

'Someone directing him?', Castle said.

'Yes.'

'But we don't know who or why', Castle said. 'We need to catch him on his turf.'

'You can put as many men out there as you like, but this killer's clever.'

'Try to catch him in the Park.'

'Or around the park. But then we don't now where he's killing them, so you may not get to the victim in time', Spinner said.

The police on the Soho case noticed the blue Ford cruise, circle and stop.

Two officers watched as it drove away with a girl inside and followed from a distance.

It left the area and headed towards Piccadilly, then passed through Hyde Park.

It finally stopped at an address in Earl's Court.

The man got out with the girl, who was shaking.

He grabbed her arm and she struggled briefly with him before he looked round, then hit her hard across the face.

The officers waited until he went into a flat and followed.

A few seconds later they kicked his front door in.

The girl was on the bed and he was standing over her with a raised fist.

They cuffed him and took him to the station with the girl, who wasn't saying much.

Then they called Castle.

The news of a positive arrest lit him and Stone up and they made their way over to the interview room.

The PC's assigned with finding information on Samuel Walsh were digging into his private life and career.

He had been a well-regarded social worker with a string of successful cases under his belt.

His colleagues remembered him as an affable and professional man, and everyone was shocked when he killed himself.

Privately, he had enjoyed a happy marriage to Mary.

They had been unable to have any children of their own, and had fostered several.

All the kids they'd looked after had been happy with them and they had a reputation as loving and capable foster parents.

Everything that came up about Samuel Walsh made his arrest look like a particularly bad choice.

There was nothing there that indicated anything which might help with the case.

In the interview room, Castle and Stone found the suspect sitting with his brief.

He wasn't saying much. All they had was a name.

'John Fulton', Castle said, 'you were sighted abducting a woman this afternoon.'

He looked at his brief who nodded.

'Yeah? What about it?'

'What were you doing?'

'Business.'

'What business?'

'I don't have to answer your questions.'

'A number of prostitutes have been murdered in recent weeks.'

'That', he said.

'It might seem nothing to you, but you've got a lot of explaining to do.'

'A blue Ford has been seen by the sex workers and you drive a blue Ford', Stone said.

'I drive a blue Ford, that it?', he said.

'What were you doing with the woman? She looked frightened and your officers say you abducted her.'

'She owes me money. She works for me.'

'Are you her pimp?', Stone said.

'Business manager.'

'You're still in trouble', Castle said, 'living off immoral earnings is a crime.'

'It ain't murder', he said.

They checked it out and the woman worked for him.

It seemed they had another false trail.

42

When Tom Spinner got the feedback on the research into Samuel Walsh, he was not convinced.

Mike Nash told him all they were coming up with were glowing credentials.

'The guy was a model social worker and foster parent. There's nothing around him that links in any way to a serial killer.'

'I'm not saying that he's the killer. But there's something there.'

'How do you know?'

'Other than Black, he is the only key name in the file and this killer is a copycat.'

'What are we looking for?'

'A link. And it won't necessarily be in Walsh's character or behaviour, it will be around him.'

'So what do we do?'

'Keep digging.'

A team of police officers scoured Richmond Park.

They searched in the undergrowth for weapons, discarded items that might give clues about the identity of the killer, forensic information, dropped litter, and found nothing.

They searched the surrounding areas of parkland and similarly came up with no information that could help with the case.

Inquiries into men with previous convictions for sexual assault and violent crimes led to a spate of arrests that ended with the cul de sac of alibis.

And meanwhile the press circled Castle and Stone.

One of its instruments for criticising the police was Mary Plover's campaign to save the prostitutes which was making headway and involved the press at every level. She publicly attacked the police for their incompetence and the evils of patriarchy for bearing a fruit as pernicious as prostitution, and meanwhile got great publicity for her party.

She went on TV and said:

'If these were what are called respectable women being killed there would be a public outcry. But we still haven't shed our sexist assumptions about women and the degrading trade prostitutes find themselves ensnared by. They are being slaughtered and the police have done nothing to catch the killer. When we live in a society that treats women as equals in the workplace and does not assign them to this kind of work, then we can look forward. This killer must be apprehended now.'

She used every opportunity to question the Met's efficiency and integrity, getting a lot of press for herself in the process.

Stone met with Don that evening.

The sense of isolation when she lay awake in their bed was gnawing at her and her sense of empathy for Castle's alcoholism growing by the day. She understood him. It was not an insight she wished to bear, and she began to feel as though she were carrying a diseased foetus inside her, the sense that only addiction could ease the feeling of personal laceration caused by the killer's subterfuge.

When six o'clock arrived, the benefit of an early close to her day was wiped out by anxiety.

She hurried about the room, lighting and extinguishing candles, opening windows to remove the smell of sulphur and then feeling furtive and dishonest.

She poured some wine and noticing the bottle was half empty walked quickly to the off licence. Catching a glimpse of herself in the hallway mirror she ran upstairs and changed her top. Something less girly, more serious. She wanted Don to take her seriously.

When the bell rang the bed was scattered with the entire contents of her wardrobe and she fumbled with the buttons on a white blouse.

She descended red-faced to see the front door open.

Don looked up at her.

'I thought you weren't in.'

'I am.'

'I rang and then-.'

'Drink?', she said, walking past him into the kitchen.

'I'll have a beer.'

'There's only wine.'

'Wine then.'

He sat down, looking round the room and noticing the absence of paperwork. They held their glasses in silence for a while.

'Have you been thinking about things?', she said.

'Yes.'

'And?'

'I think you don't realise how much was missing from our marriage and for how long.'

'Well whatever it is, I hope you're getting it from Daisy.'

'Come on, Jacki.'

'What?'

'Let's be reasonable.'

'Do you think you can walk out on me, have a quick screw and wander back?'

'Who said anything about wandering back?'

'So what then?'

'I want you to understand what happened.'

'What, that you were unfaithful?'

'Oh, come on', he said standing up.

He put his glass down on the coffee table. Their coffee table.

She wanted to say something nice and took a sip of wine, but it seemed that ever since he'd arrived her sense of personal hurt and indignation kept overwhelming her better intentions.

She looked at him, she could tell he'd made an effort, not a crease in his shirt. She wanted to enjoy his company again, but all she could see was the man who'd betrayed her.

'Maybe this was a mistake', he said.

'Why?'

'You're not ready.'

She felt cornered, isolated and deceived and for a moment the cornerstone of her pain became Don, the person she was meant to be able to trust, who was meant to be there for her.

'I wonder what I ever saw in a gutless creep like you', she said.

'And you wonder why I left?'

He turned and moved towards the hallway as she smelt the dinner in the kitchen and wanted to reach out and stop him, to bring him back. She opened her mouth as he vanished through the door, but found no words to say before she heard the front door close.

She felt the crack that had been made in her life widen and splinter. Her world was tilting into nothing and she went through to the kitchen where she turned off the oven and opened the other bottle of wine.

43

The worm burrows deep into the Body Politic
Its Flesh decayed and rotten as carrion
Lie chatterers swim like scum to the top of the sewer
Servants deluding us they are our Masters
The Book has it written they are the disease which must be expunged
Their Flesh will a thousand times be cut and hewn like sliced meat
They are an untilled land where nothing grows
A stream of offal food and burnt offerings to the corpse police
Their screams echo unheard along a million galleried walkways
Where their footfalls fade to nothing

Castle thought all cops should have a heart of stone. Beyond the reach of human feeling, where the scars and mutilations mattered not and they moved in some freezing atmosphere of law and order.

He thought of Stone and of how homicide had changed her. Horror had crawled across her face when she stared at the first body.

Of how, day after day, he'd seen that vulnerability chipped away, the softness getting jagged, edges appearing in the place of curves, a veil over the eyes, a muscularity taking over her femininity like a guard dog ever poised to bite.

And now this immersion into these killings. He was seeing her sink week by week, away from something that had once been her anchor as a cop, a raggedness and despair moving behind her eyes.

What price to our humanity this job?, he thought.

He tried to measure the effect of this exposure to the killer's actions on their souls, and weighed his career in the palm of his sweating hand, aware that his life was running away.

A bead of sweat ran down his brow into his eyes and the room danced.

He thought of why he had become a cop, the reasons distant now as a childhood trauma.

And he thought how in all the cases he'd solved the heart of crime seemed closer to his waking dreams than his own shadow and that men killed as easily over the momentary wavering of a perception as they did over the endless torturing of their souls.

Tamara Klein got back to an empty house.

Her husband had left a note attached to the fridge which read: 'Taken the kids out.'

She threw it across the room and sat down with a glass of wine.

It was cold and went down easily and she soon forgot about her resentments and what she wanted to say to her husband.

Instead she tore strips off the cold chicken in the fridge and popped another cork.

The car outside slowed, turned and vanished.

44

Castle left The Moon Under Water pub.

Suspicious of the paparazzi, he'd been avoiding The Crooked Key and this was near enough to the station. And far enough away.

Only a few old men remained at the bar, their stained reflections hung like ghosts in the tarnished mirror where the barman glanced at his watch. Closing time.

Castle walked the block to his car, checking for followers in the street. He felt conspicuous and thought back to the days when the press respected the police.

A vein throbbed at his temple and he touched his hand to the soft tube of blood, feeling a nerve twinge and pain race into his head.

Something sparked in him, some memory he thought a dream.

He walked, remembering his day. Waking drenched in sweat, the taste of failure in his mouth like lead. The flicker of a dream he could not remember, like a face at the window. He got to his car and sat there staring at the last few drunks staggering home, comrades in disease.

Karl Black's voice and the sense of failure.

A dream of a broken shell on a beach, of picking it up and finding entrails inside the cool body, crawling and writhing like worms.

He sat there staring through the glass at the cold street.

Stragglers from an office party leaned on one another trying to summon the notes of a lost song. One of them sported a Father Christmas outfit.

He danced and capered and as his female companions whooped and yelled, Castle thought he saw him wave a switchblade in the air.

The festivity leant on buried hatred.

The celebrations hid poison.

He started to drive home, thinking of the years he had been lost in the woods. Karl Black. The stain of the Woodlands Killings on his skin like some black unchosen tattoo.

Houses and lives passing by his window like the backdrop in a film.

The memory of Karl Black's taunts pulled him up and he stopped the car.

He hadn't spoken to his wife in years.

Her face rose before him conjuring the feeling of a lost limb.

'I hope you and Mr Black are very happy together', she said, her face fleeing before him now, the memory of her tear-stained face fresh as paint.

What was her life now?

What pathway had she opened for herself when she left him?

He got out of the car and walked to a late night shop, noticing the faded white line in the middle of the road, thinking they need to get it fixed, the faces of prisoners rising before him in some tide of ghosts, the line he trod blurring now as he wondered where the boundaries of the law ended.

He went inside to the harsh glare of strip lights, his head throbbing.

He reached down a bottle of Johnny Walker from the shelf.

'Do you sell paracetamol?'

'Yes Sir.'

As he paid he saw the cover of The Evening Standard on the counter.

'This police investigation is just criminal' loomed out at him like an accusing finger and his head pounded as if someone had hit him.

He drove, meandering through the half-deserted and desolate streets, retracing his past, chasing his dreams like fugitives.

He noticed how he was drawn to all the scenes of his investigations.

He turned homeward and lost track, stopping by the side of the road and drinking from the bottle, washing a fistful of pills down and drowning them in his stomach with the warming malt.

He thought of Stone, saw her being dragged down into the dark underbelly of homicide, her face changing, the hope in her eyes dying day by day.

And he drove.

He flicked on the radio, searching for songs he knew, something to distract him.

'I fought the law' taunted him in some slow mockery of his failings and he switched it off, turning from the street he hadn't seen and pulling the car over.

He didn't know where he was and got out and walked as if following some other that walked ahead of him.

The night wrapped around him like a caul.

He knew the door before he got there. The bell, the light in the window all familiar to him, trademarks of a lost location he had seen countless times on the beat.

He rang and entered this house he had never visited before, knowing its smell like all the others, a false promise of an anaesthetic as precise as the prick of a needle. The old acerbic smell of male sexual debris catching him in his throat and merging him with some shadowland where all the lost and the rejected shed a little piece of themselves.

The light overhead cast a distorted shadow of him as he stood in the hallway, recognising where he was.

A door on the next landing opened and he climbed the ruined staircase, his rubber soles squelching on the cheap linoleum.

She let him in and he became faceless again.

He half felt her against him, the tainted skin like some callus pressed close to him, her face distorted as if in some grim comedy he could not fathom.

He looked into her eyes and saw his face there, etched into their dead centres, stretched and gnomish as a gargoyle. He spent himself and watched his futile offering exchanged for what little physical presence she possessed, as if she was conjuring some scarred being from the act, and what was left of him summoned him to leave, called him away like death's shadow at the doorway, pulling his skin away from contact with her body, used and splayed, as if too many had lived there and it was tired of movement.

He finished and paid without looking at her and went to his car and searched for his whisky.

He awoke the next morning in a road he did not know, wondering what lawless events had accompanied the night's passage. A crow maundered on the pavement, pecking at a condom.

The sky overhead was cracking to reveal a pale sun.

She was drowsy and didn't notice his shadow.

She'd put her papers away and was retiring with the bottle when she felt something move behind her.

As she reached out the glass fell, shattering, and she felt a hand encircle her neck, jerking her backwards and then something hot and warm drip down her blouse onto the carpet where thick drops splashed and exploded like bulbs.

She tried to turn but his grip was strong.

She searched for language, her weapon, and stared into another world registering an unreflecting void, something alien she could never reach. She felt herself ebbing from the room.

Light faded and returned and in some strobe flickering of consciousness she glimpsed his face like an intruder in a dream, standing there in her house, like a shard of glass in her food. She struggled to bring his face into focus, seeing a fragmented form, something alien and predestined, feeling the oceanic tug of destiny as she was swallowed by some psychic surge and collapsed in her effort of struggling, his face dim now, her mouth dry as cracked parchment.

She tried to scream but something silenced her.

A body hot and fat, run to fat like the animal she is
Less than human,
Just a servant of the Liars of the Law and the False Prophets and the Anti-Priests
She would have it her way and say her words of filth and opprobrium,
She is the luster after raped sorrows corrupted into joys,
Her face is made of nothing and her body tenses under my grip
Like a beast before its halter
She talks but does not summon words and use them for the services of mankind

She must be cleansed
Blade does so
I remove her skin and peel away her lies
Talk
She screams and shatters the silence where no one hears
No one will stop this act
She falls to the ground
The blood pumps from her lacerated breasts
She is becoming the witness of oblivion
Her mouth moves open, the black hole of nothing from whence she came
And I tug a tooth from her head and its hole, snakes coiling around her throat

She is Filth and Blade enters her now piercing and puncturing her like the body she worships and adores and would have enter her and ride upon her like the mule she is

Her screams give way to her joy at being thus entered for she is the Whore of Liars and all they seek, yet still it comes

Blade sings now and hacks away herself
Peels and empties her
She cannot speak
She does not have words
Her eyes look upwards in startled shock
And she is here alone
With me
And Blade
And he tells her
He teaches her the lesson she needs to learn and must

He punctures her and repeats the entry and she thrusts her hips forward and arches her neck, two drops of sweat glistening on her furrowed brow, the only jewels she wears

She will not see the next Dawn
And all falls still

45

Mary Plover tried again. Another date. Another man.

She was not going to be put off her stride. She was a politician, and she had a lot to offer. She knew her skills and she knew how to work people.

She found him on the net: handsome and businesslike.

She arranged to meet him the following week.

A different pub this time.

She looked at herself in the mirror.

A new hairstyle perhaps?

A change of clothes.

The research on Samuel Walsh was slow.

The latest developments surrounded the children he had fostered: six boys and four girls.

There had been no complaints and the records detailed a successful and responsible foster parent.

Mike Nash headed up the group of officers who dredged through the characters and lives of the children. It was slow work.

When the call came through about the latest victim, Castle and Stone took it like the latest weather report in a hurricane.

The crime scene was more disturbing than the previous ones.

Like some carnival of butchery in an asylum.

Tamara Klein lay on the sofa. The entire contents of her mouth had been removed, so that her face faded to a blackened hole. Her eyelids showed green eye shadow that looked like a painted joke hovering over the mutilation of her lost lips. She looked upwards, her neck stretched to breaking point, staring at the banner on the ceiling.

'The Houses of Politics are Conquered.'

Alan Marker busied himself with the examination.

'What's it written in?', Stone said.

'Her blood.'

Nothing in the room had been disturbed. It was orderly and arranged and Tamara Klein's body unsettled it like a human finger in a pie. There on the coffee table lay her tongue.

Back at the station everyone was working overtime to pursue the research on the prostitute killings.

Mike Nash was put in charge of the section. Castle told him they needed something fast.

They were only just managing to hold the press off and now there was a seventh victim in the other case, they knew the paps would be knocking down their doors.

46

A politician never believes their tongue will be removed
And why shouldn't it?
In the middle ages people had far worse removed
Her long and lying tongue cut by Blade and cast there
Her lying face hacked like a piece of meat
*She obtained great sexual pleasure from her murder, I saw her stains
leaking down her dress like an admission of her desire for rape but that
would not be given to her, no, for she is diseased, not a pure woman, and
like Eve and all followers of Eve she has bitten from the Apple and seeks
corruption and man's downfall*
That is the Sisterhood's trick: provocation and blame
*She takes her pleasure in stolen things and the corruption of her
stinking organs*
*Pitiful girl played in the playground of her Parliament, washing the
members dry with her lust and sick desire, unfolding her self into her
womb while children scuttle forth like sick spiders from her leaking hole
a hole now in her face and hence she goes down like all the others, she
arched her neck so, and thrust her hips the pleasure Blade gave her the
pleasure oh and she coupled with its steel and did issue forth such cries
they were heard in every bedroom on soiled sheets where blood mingles
with the juices that bring such scum forth*
Capricious girl she capered so
*She did cry out oh pleasurable sire do make me scream in pleasure
again for I am wet and open*
She did frolic so
Privy Sir, she said, do you see, how I am?
And opened wide she did for her career to widen
*She said she'd lain with pigs and vermin and they had coupled with her
and she had found great pleasure in their flesh*
She said she had copulated in the Houses where their Lies are told

Oh how she loved it when Blade did what Blade does and tore her living breath from her like twine upon a blighted vine and she thanked me for it saying it was the greatest pleasure she had ever known and they all are like that because it is their desire and it is Written for Thus it Shall Be

47

Jonas Wilkes turned the key, unlocked the door and walked out into the garden at the back of Rondelo.

It had the feeling of an ancient parish, more like an orchard than a garden. The ancient walls of red brick stood half-crumbling at its green perimeter, the borders edged with weeds and tendrils. It was an enclosure in which no other world was known.

The apple trees were gnarled with time, the grass uneven and thick. It was testament to the self-sufficient lives of the monks who had cultivated it.

Wilkes carried a small box.

From a distance it looked like an antique and was indeed very old.

At the end he entered a small outbuilding and went inside.

The last one rubbed the leg of the table furiously as she was penetrated

She grasped it with lecherous hands and wildly tore at it, looking for something, pulling it towards her legs, opening her legs wider in her frenzy like the animal she was

She rubbed it and got not the thing she wanted most for they must be deprived of that which is the tether which they use to bind man to his downfall

She looked up at me with eyes full of desire and subtle craving and asked me to cut her again and again saying privy please Sir push it in deeper for I am full of lust and it has made me want such things whereof I dare not speak

Mary Plover sat in the pub.

Opposite her in the polished mirror was the reflection of a woman newly bobbed and wearing a tight fitting jacket.

She wondered if it suited her.

She sipped her wine. She didn't want him to see an empty glass when he arrived.

Couples talked and laughed and she tried to remember their language.

A man walked in at the far end.

He carried a bunch of roses.

As he approached, she recognised him.

Fatter than in the picture. Older.

'Sally?', he said.

'Yes. Bernard?'

'These are for you.'

'They're lovely.'

He sat down.

'Can I get you another drink?'

'Please.'

She studied him as he ordered and thought he'd do for the moment.

The hours were starting to pay off.

Mike Nash honed in on one of the adopted sons of Samuel Walsh.

Paul Metcalfe had been arrested shortly after leaving his adoptive home.

The Walshes had looked after him for two years and when he left their home, he got a job in a warehouse.

Then he'd got mixed up with the wrong crowd, taken too many drugs and begun a series of violent assaults on various people.

He'd broken a police officer's nose and attacked a priest.

There was something there and he passed it on to Castle.

I know them when I see them, all bottled lace and firm thigh
They sigh in their Parlours and come out looking for the Flesh Barrows
where the sick and sundry offer their wares
And they bring the Country to Ruination with their spread offerings,

while all men may crawl between their legs

Many before me have waged the Holy War against their Sin and hacked and hewn them into other types of Flesh, but I know they must be rent in Certain Ways for the House of Liars to be Brought Down

Mary was laughing when they got out of the restaurant.

She liked this man.

A good dinner and he listened to her, although she did not discuss politics.

Once or twice she caught him looking at her and she wondered if he recognised her.

It had been so long.

'Can I drive you somewhere?', he said.

'It's OK.'

Just then drops of rain burst from the sky and her jacket began to get soaked.

She didn't want him to know where she lived. Not just yet.

'Could you give me a lift round the corner?' she said.

'Of course.'

She got into his car and gave a false address.

She could get home easily from there and have a hot bath.

She watched him drive and thought about meeting him again.

As she gave him directions, she became aware he was not listening to her.

She repeated the directions.

'Left here.'

'All right, Mary, just relax', he said.

Suddenly she felt cold and clutched her new jacket tighter round her.

'Let me out. I said stop!'

He carried on driving.

She tried the handle of the door. It was locked.

'Where are you taking me?'

He drove in silence and turned into a deserted area at the back of some garages.

As he stopped she tried the door handle again.

'Mary, I know you and you know what you want here', he said.

He moved towards her and she tried to pull away but he clamped his hand over her mouth.

Then she felt his other hand push her legs apart and pull at her panty hose, tugging away her knickers and fondling her.

A scream died in her throat.

He ripped her blouse open and pulled one of her breasts out and got on top of her and pushed himself into her and she felt it all happening in a rush and then something hot falling into her as he pulled away and the door opened and she was lying on the ground looking at his car drive off and trying to see the registration number naked there with her skirt hoisted up around her and her breasts bare to the air.

48

Paul Metcalfe lived in an exclusive gated development deep in the green belt of Surrey.

The sun was high in the sky as Castle and Stone waited at the gate to be admitted and winter seemed to be signalling its departure.

'Feels like spring', Stone said.

'Winter's not gone yet.'

The gates swung apart and they drove up the long gravelled drive.

At its end a tall man with a boxer's build stood waiting for them, two Dobermans at his side.

'Mr Metcalfe.'

'Yes. Chief Inspector Castle?'

He extended his hand and gave a strong grip.

'Anywhere we can talk?'

He showed them into the snooker room.

'Drink?'

They shook their heads.

'We wanted to ask you about Samuel Walsh', Castle said.

'So I gathered.'

'You were fostered by him', Stone said.

'That's right. He can't have done anything, the fellow's dead.'

'We're just trying to gather some background information on him in connection with another case.'

'The Woodland Killings. Weren't you involved with the first investigation, Chief Inspector Castle?'

'That's right.'

'So what's Sam got to do with it?'

'He was arrested in connection with the first killings and proven to be innocent.'

'That's right. You cocked that up didn't you? But then the police usually do. Drove the man to suicide. How do you feel about that?'

Stone saw Castle bristle and jumped in.

'We want to know how you found Mr Walsh as an adoptive father.'

'Very good. Caring, a decent bloke, one of the few of them about.'

'Anything unusual about him while you were growing up?'

'No. And while you're at it, before you step all over things with your great big police boots, I've been away on business during all these last murders, so I have an alibi and you're wasting your time. It's got nothing to do with me any more than the original ones had anything to do with Sam.'

'Can you prove your whereabouts?'

He handed Stone a card.

'Speak to my secretary, she'll give you all the information you need. You really are a disgrace, an excuse for a police force, now if you don't mind, I want you to leave.'

He led them out through the hall.

'So why agree to meet with us, Mr Metcalfe?', Stone said.

'A hobby of mine.'

'What?'

'Police baiting. You drove Sam to suicide. You can't even begin to solve this case, and you wonder why the public have no time for you.'

As they stood outside, he shut the door on them and they left the gated grounds.

'What do you think?', Stone said.

'If his alibi holds, then he's just another angry member of the public.'

Jonas Wilkes descended the spiral staircase at the top of Rondelo carrying some antique books.

Their heavy bound leather spines shone as the sunlight caught them.

Entering the library where Black stood facing the grounds, he said: 'These were the ones you asked for.'

Black took them and inspected them.

'Yes.'

'The recruits arrive shortly.'

'I shall be ready for them.'

49

That weekend Castle headed out into the country.

He knew he needed time off from the case and slung a bag in the car and just drove.

It was strange, he thought, how as a cop, as someone who spent every waking hour trying to figure out the motivations and lives of others, his own life remained a mystery to him at some level.

The fact was as he sat at home he felt he didn't have a life outside the job.

He'd sat on the sofa all morning that Saturday and finally snapped.

So, not knowing where he was going, he drove to the A3, stopping at a Shell station to fill up.

As he watched the buildings thin, as the sense of greenery grew, he realised what he was doing.

A few days ago he'd searched for information about his wife's whereabouts. He'd begun to want to see her. There was something he only half knew or understood in this sudden need to talk to her.

He'd found her last known address on the net, a village called Monks Gate in West Sussex. At the time he'd glanced at it and exited the site. Suddenly the address appeared in his mind as if he'd known it all his life: 42 Newells Lane.

He turned off the motorway, stopping at a parade of shops. He bought a sandwich and sat eating it in the car.

Then he logged the address in his Sat Nav and drove there. The scenery seemed to pass him by like the static backdrop in a film, and suddenly he found himself there.

He drove down Newells Lane, turned at the end and stopped outside the house. It was nondescript and anonymous with a tidy tended lawn at the front.

An old woman stood in the front garden next door watering her plants.

Castle got out and rang the bell.

'They've gone away', the woman said.

He turned.

'I'm looking for someone', he said.

'They're on holiday.'

'Do you know how long for?'

'Two weeks. They're a lovely family.'

The word jarred him and his sense of alienation made him want to turn heel and drive away.

'Have you lived here long?'

'I brought up a family in this house.'

'You know them well?'

'The Joneses? Yes. Lovely family. Who is it you're looking for?'

'Katlyn Castle.'

The woman mused over the name.

'Katlyn Castle.'

'I'm sorry to trouble you', he said, and began to move away.

'Now wait a minute. There was a woman who lived there, quiet she was, kept herself to herself, she called herself Kate.'

'Light brown hair?'

'Yes.'

'Speaks with a slight Irish accent?'

'That's her.'

'How long ago did she leave?'

'Now let me think. The Joneses have been here for … they had their son here and he's eighteen, and she was pregnant when they moved in. Yes, she would have left eighteen years ago.'

'I don't suppose you have any idea where she went.'

'No. Sorry.'

He looked around at her garden and her neat life.

'Thank you.'

The woman stared after him as he walked back down the path.

He drove, not seeing where he was going, thinking of Katlyn living there.

A pub swung into view and he stopped and ordered a pint. Then he drove home, buying a bottle of whisky on the way.

50

Tom Spinner was setting the flip chart on fire.

'He removes her tongue. Speech. He doesn't want them to talk. He doesn't want them to say certain things that he finds discomforting, that upset his beliefs. He's into censorship. Censoring something that's been said. It may have been a long time ago, something happened. What? Let's see. He wants to shut it up. Shut her up. What did she say? He's not schizophrenic, the voice is not internal, not some command to kill. We're dealing with a religiously motivated killer, but one who believes in something offbeat, and who feels that politicians are something that must be removed.'

'So where does that leave us?', Castle said. 'Only a few million zealots and nutters.'

'It's significant that none of his victims are sexually assaulted.'

'Neither are the victims of the prostitute killer. We've already established these are not sexually motivated', Stone said.

'There *is* a sexual motive. The killer obtains sexual gratification by killing, but he does not want to sexually assault these women in the traditional sense.'

'And what does that mean?'

'He wants to erase their sexual identity. He wants to remove them as modern women from the society they inhabit. He doesn't want modern, liberated women. He wants their tongues cut out. These women talk too much for his liking, they've got too much to say. This is a sexual assault on their modernity. He wants them removed from history and put back where they were.'

Stone looked over at Castle, who stood staring at Spinner with his arms folded, his face like weathered granite.

All she knew was that this guy was getting more violent and that they were no nearer to knowing who he was.

Mary Plover sat at home clutching a brandy.

She'd cancelled her appointments and drawn the curtains.

She could feel him all over her.

She stood up and caught her own image in the mirror and hurled the glass at it.

'Stupid bitch!'

She had almost called the police but stopped herself.

The date knew who she was and the last thing she needed now was the press having a field day with the fact that she'd used an internet dating service.

She was a politician.

51

In the silent street a car drove past.

It slowed outside her windows, a small illumination from the single lamp visible through the curtains.

It carried on to the end of the street.

Mary didn't hear it.

As Castle got in his car to drive home the empty whisky bottle sparkled at him lodged as it was in the gap between the seats. He remembered staggering out of the Moon Under Water, the surreal meanderings of his drunken journey.

The smell of the room entered his nostrils like the sudden odour of sea water, a stretch of ocean opening on his horizon.

He glanced up at the dying light, watching a half moon struggle in the sky and tried to recall the previous evening's events. Passing out on the kitchen floor, the taste of the past rotting in his mouth like the rusted hinge of a door that led back into some nightmare.

Scenes from nocturnal streets raced through his mind, folding to nothing and he drove home.

He wanted nothing more than a bath and to rest.

Katlyn's face flashed into his mind, something she'd said a long time ago like some foreign anthem ringing in the stale air of the car.

'Times have changed, Frank, women don't play out gender roles any more, waiting for their man while he loses himself in some criminal sickness.'

He tried to hold the contour of her face in his mind, but it was as strange as the carving in a dream.

The lines that held it blurred like a shape in water.

As he drove a car cut him up.

He flashed the driver who two-fingered him as the lights turned red.

Before he knew it he was out of the car.

So was the other guy.

'What's your problem mate?'

'You. Cutting me up.'

'What you gonna do about it?'

Castle looked at him, ten years younger than him maybe, a few inches taller, unshaven, out of shape.

'Don't you know what I'm going to do?'

'No.'

The guy started laughing.

Castle looked round, realising he was not in a squad car, feeling all at once a burden lifting from his shoulders, a relaxation in his chest, a white line fading somewhere in his mind and he looked again at the laughing face of the other driver who turned now and started to get back into his car.

'Wanker', he said.

Castle grabbed him by the collar and pulled him back out and hit him.

It was a good well-aimed punch that brought with it a resounding crack. He hit him again, watching the nose spread over the face like a smeared berry.

He kept hitting him until he wasn't moving and then reached down and checked his pulse and drove away.

When she sees Blade she will know her pleasure fill her
The man could not do that for her
She had the rape and it was not her desire
For I watch them
I know their ways
She wants the dark deep penetrating and the steel to enter her and devour her with its thrust from timeless eras when women were the roles they were assigned and shall keep to for all Eternity since to break with that Commandment will bring Downfall and ruination and this Act ceases that and the Liars will be taken from their House of Filth

She sits alone in the dark and waits

Her legs will part for Blade who will give birth to her laceration while she yields for more and her neck arches in slow burning ecstasy for that is what they want that is what they have worked for with their lies that serve the Corrupt and since they are their servants they must meet Blade

Blade knows all and he will give them their measure

Her date is waiting for her

He does not carry roses

52

The recruits assembled in the Round Room at Rondelo.

Wilkes had prepared them well for their first meeting with Black. He had brought them to the point where their need for a figurehead overrode all other concerns. He had opened their minds so that Black's presence would be felt as some mystical arrival in their lives.

He'd taught them the basics of the teachings of The Last Brotherhood and now they would be immersed in its deeper waters.

Black appeared at the gallery above them, then walked down slowly to where they sat.

He wore the monk's cowl with hood over his face and when he got to them he lifted this and raising his arms, said 'Brothers, know you the two seeds? Know you the task that stands before us now and which we must do?'

The murmur of assent sounded like the ground rumbling and he walked among them and began their teaching.

She sees through glass
Glass woman
Her looks like something broken upon a wheel now turning on its axis
As all things do
I am from
And hence
I am the direction in which they find themselves
She hears nothing
No movement outside for she is lost in her own reflection, a disgust that hangs upon the air of her head and moves nowhere except in the circles of her Lies, her shallow Lies like all of them and their House of

Filth which will be burnt and all before them run into history and down the dark tunnel like rats fleeing from Blade

Blade knows and follows her where she goes and so she speaks forth that Filth

I wait

Wait

Know

Then pull their Destinies from my sleeve

And as of old hack the Filth to their tattered ends

Politics, the old Sin

She is waiting for me and feels soon the rush of air as Blade comes against her

Her skin waits for Blade its caress sinking like a kiss into the white flesh as she pours forth and utters the last statements that she can muster for she has mustered many from her tongue for that is what they pay her to do

53

Stone turned off her usual route into work and cruised the pebble-dashed streets, working east to Don's address.

When she got there, she stopped the car a few doors away and looked for signs of life, wondering what it was she expected to see. Him.

The drive stood empty, the downstairs curtains drawn. Someone else's house where part of her life now lived. The sense of exile from herself was so acute she cut her lip in biting on her own teeth. She sat dabbing her mouth with a tissue, watching the blood smear and fade.

He often left for work early.

Suddenly the thought of seeing the other woman entered her mind and her thoughts raced. She didn't know what she would do if she saw her.

She thought of the case, of the dead bodies and forced herself to drive away.

'What is the Law? A concoction of disease, for they worship the False Idol and they are Corrupt. Seekers, Brothers, you have come here for Counsel and I shall give you Counsel. I say unto Ye, this is the dawn of the end of the Liars, this is the time of their Crucifixion for now it is they who will feel the nails blistering them and tearing apart their skin while those who serve the State laugh and cackle in the undergrowth where they hide like criminals because that is what they are.'

The recruits rose.

He seemed to enter them with his words.

'It is very simple, Brothers. The Crucifiers must be Crucified. They lie and it drips from their tongues like poison. But they will fall.'

A murmur of assent.

'You know the Two Seeds and the mastery of them is now given unto you. For to be a master of your Souls you have to enter the Battle. Are you ready for the Battle Brothers?'

They shouted their affirmation, wrapt by him.

'For verily I say unto Ye "The Law was our schoolmaster to bring us to Christ, that we might be justified by faith, But after the faith is come, we are no longer under a schoolmaster", Galatians, 3. 24-25. Jonas is my General, and you will heed his Commands.'

He swished his robe and disappeared.

Later that day he gave his orders to Jonas.

Transposing it is another matter
Taking it across them by Blade
Blade cuts and he takes them through
It is Written that everywhere the Servants of Lies will be caught and executed
Now the new Dawn breaks upon the horizon in joy
Now the Corrupt shall be found out
For their servants the Officers of the Corrupt Law are impotent
They cannot stop this Act

Tracy Fletcher strutted her stuff. She wore a lime-green skirt that ended at the tops of her buttocks, white ankle boots with a chain hoisted above one, and a top that let her show a good eyeshot of cleavage when she leaned in a car window.

She was sick of the cop cars everywhere and needed to make more money.

Karen's death had shaken her up but not so badly that she was going to give up on the easiest money she'd ever made.

'Cock cash', she called it, and joked about how easy men were.

She'd got close to some of the women, but not as close as she had to Karen.

She liked her.

And while the clients had got fewer, aware as they were of the police presence, she would meet another woman she liked and get together with her.

In the meantime she needed more cash for her crack habit and she was going to go right out and get it.

'Fuck this psycho', she said to one of the women that morning. 'These guys can't do anything with it, they can give it to me and pay me and I'm gonna get my stash and get out.'

She stood in a quiet road at the edge of Soho. No cops.

She could see some guys hanging round and knew the look.

She'd work this corner.

Tracy didn't give in that easily.

54

Mike Nash was onto something. He'd been persistent and now felt as though he'd hit a section of mountain road where he caught a flash of sea. And he could smell it.

He'd collated everything his team had given him and dug a little deeper. And the history of Richmond Park began to open up its vistas into the prostitute killer's psyche.

Castle could see it on his face, remembering the early breakthroughs he'd made in his career and the overwhelming sense of satisfaction they brought.

'Frank, Sawyer's Hill was Henry the Eighth's favourite hunting ground in the Royal Park. The area known as Soho was farmland until 1536 when Henry the Eighth turned it into a Royal Park for the Palace of Whitehall.'

'That's the link', Castle said.

'Also, the word derives from the old hunting call "Soho! There goes the fox".'

'So, Richmond Park and the hunting motif', Stone said. 'It's all adding up.'

Nash trawled police records for ex-offenders with this particular obsession and came up with only a handful of names who were unlikely to be linked to the killings.

He studied the imagery of the victims' wounds and looked for patterns.

He'd got this between his teeth and wasn't going to let go.

Sinclair Mover and Maurice Tweed were sitting in their club. The deep leather chairs creaked comfortably beneath them as they talked.

Whiskies apiece they stared at each other in mutual self-satisfaction and a latent sense of competition that was unabated by the occasional gibes they threw this way and that like so much unwanted litter.

'Still seeing her Maurice?', Mover said, his cheeks flushed, his hands gripping his glass.

'Yes, she's game.'

Tweed eased his thin frame back into the chair.

He held his pallid face before him, away from his shoulders like an advertising board awaiting a slogan.

'Hear you struck lucky in commodities', Mover said, his heavy veined jowls wobbling as he spoke.

'Not bad.'

He tapped ash from his cigar, ignoring it as it fluttered to the floor.

'The cabinet wants some figures.'

'Got them. I don't know what the taxpayer is making all this fuss about, where does he think, whoever he is, that this money comes from?'

Tweed let out a laugh that sounded more like a grunt, as if he was too busy to laugh and stopped it half-way. He swung one long and slender leg over the other one in a gesture that was rendered epicene by his simultaneously puckering his lips to receive his cigar. He inhaled, admiring its red end.

'Business is another game to politics, but they need us', Mover said.

'Ab-solutely.'

Mover poured himself another drink.

A waiter scuttled by.

When he was gone the conversation resumed.

'Some good deals abroad', Mover said. 'Thanks to us, this country's got a good defense system.'

'We don't get thanks for our services. Thanks is in here', Tweed said, patting his breast pocket and producing a leathery thud.

'I set this government up. Funded it.'

'Know you did.'

'How's your anti-church campaign going?'

'Hope to tax them soon.'

'Drink?'

Outside it began to rain, a slow spring descent.

———

The second time it happened, he'd found himself moving in some strange half-world where the present teetered on a precipice up which his past clambered like a leprous visitor that stalked him.

Waking on the sofa and stepping from his front door into the office brought with it some displacement of his reality that day and Castle found himself dogged by a sense of déjà vu as profoundly unsettling as the rerun of a bad day.

Stone's words echoed in his mind as if she stood at the end of a long tunnel and he found himself shuffling papers and then clutching the steering wheel of his car, his knuckles white, the fingers bloodless.

This time it was another street.

He got out and walked seeing the doorway just like the other one.

He had no sense of climbing the stairs, just her sudden unwelcome nakedness and hands upon him and feeling cold, as if someone had opened a window onto his soul.

He looked into her eyes, like two stones and felt himself moving, disconnected from the rocking motion like an anchorless boat.

She said something then and he looked at her, a pliant face mirrored to itself and masking a hardness like flint from which no spark would ever rise.

'What?', he said, the voice of a stranger in the room.

'You got a problem?'

He pulled himself off her and began dressing hurriedly, wanting to get away, seeing a copy of The Sun lying there like some bugging device in his brain.

And he looked again at the cold face and wasted flesh and he wanted fire, seeing the papers burn in some sudden inferno from which no warmth issued, only further freezing snow and he moved before he knew it, lost in some act that momentarily brought life back into his purpose, although he did not know where he was.

As the tide surged in his ears his own hands drew him off, while the other one ceased his blows.

She was bleeding, and had drawn her knees up retreating in the soiled bed, her sex staring at him from this hunched position, the image of an unmasked con trick in all its ugliness.

Crime scenes flashed through his mind in some nauseating sequence of human dismemberment, her unashamed nudity spread before him in some sickening show of sin and gain.

Blood was dripping from her face and she seemed some eldritch ghoul to him, a thing of white and red accusing him.

She got up, her nudity threatening to him now and he could see she knew him.

Her flesh looked rotten, infected with disease and he tasted bile.

The sense of crime hung in the air like smoke and his world shifted on its axis as he fled, her slow mockery ringing in his ears like some playground taunt from long ago.

The street was not even real beneath his feet as he made his car and drove away, driving from his past as a man pursued by some wraith.

55

She waits
Outside he stands
Blade
Her body aches for it
I see her kneel before her false idol and lust for politicians' Lies
Like sugar coated sweetness that endures no more than her pleasure's Flesh
For when she knows that he is here and enters her and rides her thus she is rejoined
With the Forces that govern this Universe for it is Written the Unrighteous will Fall
Like all the others she is unprepared for me
She moves across her room and I watch in her garden
Her face in the mirror
She looks and rejects the image searching for her Fantasy self
No more dates for Mary
As I tread her floor she cannot feel my breath upon her
Blade will teach her
Blade will show her what she needs to know and she will learn her lessons well
For what she has served and the Lies she has spoken must be stopped
She looks like a Walker of the Streets the sorry fallen to the other Killer in our midst
She looks like the women she would but cannot save
She serves the wrong Master
She doesn't know her true Master is now in her house and holds her halter in his hand
She teaches the Legacy of the Crucifiers

When he awoke the next morning, Castle felt as if he didn't fit, his skin like another's. Someone inhabited him, a watchman whose accusations surfaced in the quiet hours as he lay between the lines stifling his own breath.

Castle held his arms, pinioning them to his sides, as if he wished to cuff himself and render some stasis to his own disconnection. A picture of him as a young man, a rookie cop flashed past him as he walked through the living room, all his dead idealism alive there in the fresh unwasted face.

It stared out at him like an image on a gravestone.

He moved around his house as if sleepwalking, the familiar objects beyond arm's reach.

Flashes of the night before entered his brain, a barrage of images of wounds, deep lacerations, skin opening to internal redness, a woman on a bed hunched and exposed like a piece of meat.

He tried to remember what had happened, the slow memory dripping into his waking brain, leeching the morning light of its hope.

His mind felt at the tipping point of some awareness, as if knowledge of who he had become were trying to force its way past an internal barrier he had built.

The bricks that had built him as a Detective coughed dust as he felt some part of him diminish in this day's awakening.

Guilt hovered at the chamber of his heart like the memory of an ache and he saw her soiled face, thinking of the case and the killer of these women his badge said he was meant to protect. The hatred of all of them, of what they did was too brief to draw breath within him.

Some part of him shifted away from himself until he tasted unfamiliar in his own mouth and knew he had a problem he couldn't find the name for.

His sense of separateness as a cop, his familiar perch of law was gone and he felt himself slipping down a long tunnel into a darkness out of which hands reached like the quiet tendrils of some vine that coiled around his beating heart.

He reminded himself of who he was.

And slipped further away from himself.

He thought of the things he wanted to do to the killer, trying to keep Karl Black's face from his mind, and sated some lust there awhile before realising much of this was like the wounds he saw at the crime scenes. He needed to inflict a level of pain on the men responsible for filling his dreams with blood, a level of pain that brought with it the taste he knew they lived with. And as he touched his tongue to his dry lips, he thought how arid his soul had grown and knew that who he was had withered. It seemed to him that he accompanied himself now. As if he quested the lost enterprise he had been.

And he wondered if he were capable of catching this killer. Whether by predetermination or the sick inspired design of some maleficent star he was cursed to fail, rolling forever on the tidal wave of some shadow by which he was stalked.

He held himself by the shoulders, squeezing tightly until the pain came and he thought only of the station.

He toted his badge with him like some scar that gave focus to a wound.

As Mary reached for the phone a blade hacked her carotid artery so neatly and smoothly that the jet of blood hit the wall before she opened her mouth to scream. The only noise in the deadened room was the hum of the dialling tone.

She moved to see him, her head swivelling on the open wound and the laceration widening into a grin that stretched its way across her neck in some Vaudeville appreciation of an offstage joke, the tearing skin like rent silk in the silent house. She stilled herself, fighting to control her twitching muscles, her head refusing to obey the injunction of the brain, her face tilted in some grotesque comedy now at him. She watched her dripping, drenched and soiled in blood, and looked into his eyes seeing something from a world she could not fathom, some elemental resonance of herself and her life.

He moved again. One gesture. And cut her open and placed her neatly upon the rug that adorned her floor before leaving in silence as he came.

Outside the rain continued, gathering momentum.

It ran and trilled down Mary Plover's curtained window panes.

56

Castle woke on his sofa. His arm was numb beneath him and he stretched and flexed his throbbing hand.

He'd dreamt of another body in the woods, the old woods, and his life seemed made of other men's deeds.

The rain gave some background chorus to Stone's efforts that long night as she sat at home surrounded by paperwork and looked at the picture of her and Don, her marriage like a lost memory. She looked out of the window as the water washed down the street gaining in momentum.

They are now within the Latter days of the Judgement of the Fallen

They steel themselves with words bought from the prostitutes they frequent but their Corruption will be their undoing

Politicians fee the Whores who scuttle away to new clients bought on the back of the disease that plagues our country

But the anti-Priests will be tortured and lo they fall with their organs verily revealed as being not Righteous for the Righteous will prevail

I watch as the two move along their stolen moneys and their watchtowers of False Laws

They build the Vale of Filth

Now Blade sings upon his steel

The very metal is Blade arched in hack time

He knows their puncture wounds and heals not the disease but opens them to the World that is his

He enters them making man woman woman see her lowly and Fallen Ways

For it is Written they are diseased

Their Disease will spread no more

Not unto the pure who wage this Battle and Holy War

Not unto the Land of Blade

Not unto Blade's Dictates

57

Mover and Tweed were preparing a particularly good deal.

Mover had poured money into the party and now wanted his interest back. To them politicians were nothing more than high profile salesmen. *They* were the empire builders.

Tweed was building his case against the church and knew how much he could gain from it. The revenue from taxation would be enormous.

They had members of the cabinet cornered and fully intended to pursue their interests.

'We could profit from each other's personal deals', Mover said.

'Do you have something in mind?'

'I promote your case, you promote mine and we take a percentage for our efforts.'

'Sounds like a good plan.'

The streets of Soho were a throng of activity.

Tracy was making good money. She'd found new clients. Men came and went quickly and she was coining it in. She was young enough not to feel the threat, the silent menace that stalked the streets hungry for flesh.

She became less vigilant turning tricks while high and soon looked like just another used street hooker.

The car cruised Soho like a silent shark.

She was sick of the streets and the stained passenger seats and felt safe in her studio.

Her clients came there and she increased her fees. If they got rough she could put up a fight and saw any troublemakers off easily.

She hated them and wanted them out of there as quickly as possible.

Sometimes at night when she was out and needed spare cash she picked one up and got in his car. High on crack she didn't care.

One night the punter paid her and she unzipped his trousers as he stopped the car.

He reached over to lift her skirt and she squeezed him as hard as she could, running off with the cash before he could do anything.

Stone needed to know.

She'd been up all night with the case, lain in the cold bed and found herself reaching across the empty sheets for Don.

The dream had woken her.

Alone on a beach and a hand on her shoulder.

The voice whispered in her ear.

'I know you want to kill him.'

As she turned, she saw Black's face laughing at her.

She'd got up, made tea, wondered what it meant and started thinking about Don.

Then driven round there.

Parked outside her house and waited.

All night.

Feeling alone.

Feeling dirty.

Feeling hatred.

Feeling herself fall while she clutched her badge, turning it over in her sweating hand like some talisman that had the power to anchor her to this unsolid world, the imprint etched into her palm when she removed it.

No light shone for her and she thought of Castle, wondering if this is what it was like, being a CID officer, married to crime, falling apart.

Finally, at daybreak, she saw Don at the window, his face normal, rested, and she felt her stomach convulse.

She drove out of there and to the office, wishing she still wore the uniform.

58

Mary Plover lay spread across her living room like a vivisection.

'Neat work', Alan Marker said. 'Your killer is gaining a taste for this.'

Castle gave him a jaded look.

'Your gallows humour's wearing a little thin.'

He looked over at Stone who was examining the wall, which was emblazoned with the latest message:

'The Papers of the Gaolers are Burned.'

As she snapped it he called Tom Spinner and read him the line.

'What do you make of it Tom?'

'The Gaolers are politicians. The killer wants to destroy their legislation. The Papers represents Law as it stands. He wants to change secular law in favour of some religious law. He wants rule by a religious elite.'

Castle had begun to see religion as a four-lane motorway heading straight to bloodshed, and the scene before him did nothing to change his view.

It was a scene from an abattoir.

He had cut her into shanks and lain them neatly across the rug.

Sections of her lined the floor like sushi at a cannibal's party, her liver placed on the coffee table next to her parliamentary papers.

Greek Street was awash with tourists.

Ruck sacks lined the pavements and coloured hats and jackets bumped and jostled each other as they lazily wended their way past prostitutes and fast food shops, staring at maps, turning, re-routing and generally confusing the police presence.

'How we meant to see through this mob?', one PC said to his colleague as they sat watching in a parked car.

'Don't know, but the girls'll be doing good business.'

They shouted out at the tourists who stopped and stared dumbly, some blushing, some asking what they said.

Phrase books were fetched from pockets and the crowd grew thicker. The police found it impossible to see some of the women they were assigned to watch.

One tourist dropped a book.

The title 'Journey of The Last Brotherhood' flashed the air before he replaced it in his ruck sack.

Tracy was high. She floated along the street away from the pub, the notes bulging in her skirt and turned the corner.

Behind her an engine buzzed.

She turned.

The guy was watching her.

She carried on walking and heard him cruise behind her.

She didn't want to do another job, but was getting tired of being followed.

She decided to get the cash and humiliate him like the last guy.

He rolled down the window.

'How much?'

'Hundred for the lot.'

He flashed a wad at her and she got in.

There was something familiar about this guy and she wondered whether she'd seen him before.

She must have done clients more than once and knew they liked what she offered.

He was driving slowly and she thought she'd do it there and then and get out.

She reached over and started unzipping when a hand clamped down on her.

His grip was like a vice.

'What's the matter? Thought I'd get you up.'

'Wait', he said, the voice distant.

She looked out of the window and felt something pressed hard against her face. She kicked out at the fading light.

When she woke she was staring at some trees and felt cold.

A sound came from her, falling into open space. Above her some crisp stars sprinkled in a huge sky.

Her skirt was being lifted up and she could see her breasts and the man standing over her.

Then pain. Hot wet unbearable pain like some rending, some tearing of her flesh.

The figure leant over her and dragged a metre of barbed wire through Tracy's vagina.

59

The Servants are Captured
Now the Masters will be taken

A deer walked slowly in the undergrowth foraging.

From time to time it raised its nose and sniffed the air.

The sun rose in the sky, heralding a warm spring day and the birds chattered in the trees.

The stretch of Park opened like a vista of England.

As it neared some trees it raised its nose again, sniffing something unfamiliar in the air.

It was not yet rutting season and the scent was unknown.

It moved further.

When it got to some trees it leant and gazed at something unfamiliar in the grass.

Tracy lay like an open wound on the verdant Park. She was violated from crutch to neck, and barbed wire ran out of her vagina like some thread to another world where matters have been settled and left for mundane man to tidy away.

Stone was sitting on her sofa reading through the files on the original Woodland killings.

The pages turned in her hand like the familiar signs of railway stations on a journey she had taken many times before.

Outside a full moon hung with some obscene pregnancy in a black sky, its unreal light piercing her window. Beneath its rays the pages glowed surreally.

She got up and drew the curtains, wondering how long she'd been sitting there, the ticking of a clock somewhere in the distance.

Her life seemed to be passing her by.

She climbed the stairs, feeling the emptiness of the house surround her with a vacuous chill.

She lay in bed trying to see the killer's face, to read beneath the messages, to find him beneath his crimes.

As she turned over she felt a hand on her shoulder.

She reached upwards clawing for a face, the hand pressing her down onto the bed.

His other hand closed around her neck, the fingers gripping her throat, pressing hard onto her windpipe.

She gasped for air, her legs thrashing on the bed furiously.

With one hand she reached for the light expecting to see Karl Black's face.

Instead she saw Don looking down at her and laughing.

'I've always hated you Jacki', he said, his voice like ice.

She struggled and awoke, clutching only the pillow.

60

The whisky haze was sending flashing heat pains through Castle's skull.

He eyed himself in the rearview mirror, the retreating street lights a set of dancing halos behind him.

A vein protruded at the edge of his temple, his skin was drawn and taut. He tried to recall the last time he'd eaten.

He thought of forcing Black's hand, of driving round to Rondelo now on his own while his partner rested, breaking in and beating Black senseless. He kept a balaclava in his boot by the jack in case of emergency.

As he stopped at the lights he saw some PC's arrest two drunken guys who were beating seven shades out of each other.

One of them swung at an officer and was promptly floored.

In the scrap his colleague used what some might deem excessive force, bloodying the guy's face.

Castle watched as the lights turned to green and back to red again, the line between cops and criminals blurring.

The car behind him started hooting and Castle nearly got out to hit the other driver, sweat dripping from him as if he had just stepped out of the shower.

Jonas Wilkes walked slowly.

Careful of being followed and watchful in the extreme, he circled the destination he sought and entered a series of back alleys leading nowhere except to the place he started from.

He stopped and turned.

Only the night air.

He looked along the deserted road and heard nothing.

Then he proceeded along the route he had chosen, stopping at some flats where he climbed the ruinous stairwell to a door.

Castle and Stone got the call early.

Some startled children on a school trip had slid in Tracy's blood and screamed so loudly the deer had fled. The teacher in charge had vomited into some bushes and cleared the area before calling the police on his mobile.

When they got there a confused crowd had gathered and some of the children were crying. Stone assigned some women PC's the task of dealing with the kids while Castle went to investigate.

He stared down at a mess of flesh.

Like the Woodlands Killings, this was an increment of violence that was spiralling to a dark place where he lived in his nightmares.

The edges of the barbed wire glistened red in the sunlight which caught its jagged edge and glowed like some luminous hatred left there by the killer.

Her insides were twisted on the metal and strewn about her thighs and buttocks as she lay dismembered as if by a mad obstetrician who'd just delivered her of some nightmare of childbirth.

The wire coiled about her legs like a snake and ate into her flesh, softly tearing away at her.

'Hello Frank', Alan Marker said behind him.

'This just gets nastier.'

'Let's have a look', he said, donning gloves.

He started his examination while Stone toured the area, finding only the signs of deer foraging and the usual wildlife.

'I'm going to have to remove this', Marker said, 'it'll tear the bag.'

He started pulling the wire from inside her.

Blood oozed from the wound like jam and her innards rent away with it, landing in globules of meat in the plastic matting.

Castle looked on and away, attending intermittently to one of the most gruesome sights he'd witnessed.

Sections of her womb were attached to the wire and it carried them away.

A tearing sound accompanied the excavation, a fraying of her flesh like something caught on a hook.

Attached to the end of the wire was a small object.

Marker had to tug it from her to remove it and held it up to the light.

'What is it?', Castle said.

'I don't know.'

When Wilkes left the grimy building he returned by another route, entering Rondelo by the rear and coming unheard and unseen.

He held a parcel which he carried with care, taking it to the farthest wing where he placed it behind the stage the Brotherhood used for its Communions.

Mover and Tweed had a meeting planned.

They were going to enhance each other's sales pitch and ensure they got the best deals on their backing of the party while selling their businesses to the nation.

They were feeling good. While others toiled, they worked together to line their pockets and place the government in a headlock.

Mover tapped ash from his cigar.

'They'll do what we want.'

'They can't do otherwise, we know too much', Tweed said.

Tom Spinner was standing at the flipchart when the news came through from the lab.

'Alan's ID'd the piece on the end of the wire', Mike Nash said.

Castle turned round.

'What is it?'

'A piece of stag horn.'

'A piece of deer?'

'That's right. Someone's cut a section of horn and placed it on the end of the wire.'

'Any idea where it came from?'

'Richmond Park. It's one of their stags.'

'Thanks, Mike.'

'And it's been done recently.'

'It's hunting', Spinner said. 'The women represent the hunt. And our killer has a sense of poetry about him, he's trying to make his murders creative, to deck his obsession with a rose petal. I'll dredge the era he's lost in for more clues.'

61

Stone's private life had begun to feel an object of suspicion to her. Don's departure had left a hole in her into which fell the assorted fragments of the case and its attendant paranoia.

She saw a light in the window as she came home that evening.

She turned her key slowly and entered without closing the door, expecting an intruder. Don was sitting on the sofa staring at the room they used to share. Papers were strewn everywhere.

'I don't suppose you believe in making an appointment?', she said, tidying up. 'I've tried calling you.'

'Jacki, I want to talk. Neither of us is happy.'

'How's Daisy?'

'I want to make things up with you.'

'She got tired of you leaving your dirty clothes everywhere? Got tired of your moaning about work?'

He stood up.

'I wish I hadn't bothered.'

'I'll put some coffee on', she said.

From the kitchen she looked at him. Still the good-looking Don she'd married. But she couldn't get past her anger at what had happened.

'She's not you, Jacki', he said.

'You think I don't know that?'

'I want to come home.'

'Well, it's not as easy as that. You get tired of your affair and you want to come home, just like that. I'm not ready for that. I need time.'

She wanted to forget the anger, forget the hurt, accept it had happened and have him back in her life. But she knew she would be sacrificing her own emotional integrity by doing so, and that her life was not the same any more.

She looked at Don and blamed him for changing it all, and then thought of Black, of how his presence in her life had brought with it something irreversible.

Don was looking around the room, the overwhelming presence of the Met everywhere.

'Do you mind?', she said.

'All this, where's our marriage, Jacki?'

'You're not here, why does it matter?'

'Enough said.'

As she poured, she heard the door slam and wished she'd said less.

The energy of scrutiny she had placed on the case fell now like a shadow on his other life and she felt hungry for knowledge of him and all she was excluded from, as if carnality could be replaced by detail. Karl Black's face stared at her through bars and suddenly she realised it was she who was on the inside.

At Rondelo the recruits were assembled in the Round Room.

They wore monk's cowls and Wilkes presided over their Communion.

Black stood in the gallery and at the end descended carrying a large crudely made goblet.

Reaching out to each of them, he said 'This is the blood of the newly risen Christ, drink of it that ye may be renewed.'

They dipped their acolytes' faces into the cup and removed from it lips stained as if with woodland berries.

As the cup passed from Malcolm to Rodrigo he immersed his face deep into its bowl, pausing there a while as if breathing its vapours. Then he tilted it and moved it away, his mouth now deeply carmine.

A dark Bacchic stain like some sin.

62

The next day Castle and Stone investigated the sites where the bodies had been found in the Park.

The beauty of the area and its weekend peacefulness was overshadowed by the presence of the killings, an eerie overlay of pain on relaxation, as if something had eased its way through the foliage and lay buried in the undergrowth like a steel trap.

The scenes were stained with the blood of victims. The savagery of their butchering was such that the grass had assumed a hue from the hacked and dismembered corpses which had recently lain there, while the trees themselves seemed smeared with the offshoot of the chiselled handiwork of the man who bore the weapon that cut them so.

As Stone walked around the scene of the last crime, she caught the vista of Sawyer's Hill, its clear promontory and terraced grass, and saw a pattern emerge fleetingly through the geographies of the various places this killer had chosen to lay his victims.

She made a note of the co-ordinates as she guessed them from her understanding of the Park and its surrounding land.

There was a shape there, she was sure of it.

'What are you doing?', Castle said, growing curious.

'There's something here. I don't know yet, but I think there's a clue in the way he's laying the bodies out.'

Back at the station she cross-referenced it with a map of Google Earth and laid it out as closely as she could, then overlaid an image of her co-ordinates once connected.

It was clear: a pair of stag's horns emerged from the points when joined.

She showed it to Castle.

'Like Tom said, the guy's fixated with hunting. Stags, women.'

'Mike's working on this.'

She stared at the horns, entering the killer's mind, angling for his reasons.

Castle put a call through to Mike Nash and asked him to bring up everything he had. He also dialled Spinner, who said 'I've had a breakthrough'.

A few hours later they were looking at poetry, and Castle was scratching his head and feeling angry.

'What's this got to do with catching this guy? If I wanted to take poetry classes I wouldn't be involved in a high-level murder case. In case you hadn't noticed, the bodies are piling up while you talk about Royal Rhyme.'

'Rime Royal. Frank, instead of playing the hard-nosed Detective, try listening', Spinner said. 'I said it was hunting and I said the clue is in the history of the Park. This poetry links into both and also a key figure who might go some way to explaining the killer's psychotic motivation.'

'So, the rhyme?', Stone said.

'Thomas Wyatt wrote poems in Rime Royal. He was a major poet of the sixteenth century who modified the Petrarchan sonnet and some of his most famous poems use the image of the hunted deer.'

'What does the deer represent, a woman?', Castle said.

'This is his eleventh sonnet.'

He switched on the power point.

'Whoso list to hunt, I know where is an hind,

But as for me helas, I may no more.'

'Helas?', Castle said.

'Means alas, Frank. Wyatt's writing about a white deer which disappears. It's a love chase which he abandons.'

'The white deer could represent some sort of unattainable purity in the killer's mind', Nash said.

'OK, so this guy was let down, rejected, but prostitutes and purity? A strange match.'

'It's not so obvious, Frank.'

'The poet's saying he's given up', Stone said.

'Yes. But the poem's also about him wanting something that someone else owns.'

'Like a prostitute?'

'The ownership in the killer's psyche is to do with someone else entirely. The prostitutes are merely actors in his drama.

The vain travail hath wearied me so sore,

I am of them that farthest cometh behind

Yet may I by no means my wearied mind

Draw from the deer, but as she fleeth afore

Fainting I follow. I leave off therefore

Sithens in a net I seek to hold the wind.'

'Holding the wind says something', Castle said.

'You're right Frank, he's reaching for something he feels is unattainable and ends up killing it. Murder is possession, after all.'

'The deer's female.'

'Who list her hunt, I put him out of doubt,

As well as I may spend his time in vain.'

'What does that mean?', Castle said.

'He's saying don't bother chasing her, she'll get away.'

'This guy's hung up on some unattainable female ideal', Nash said.

'You're right Mike', Spinner said. 'And because of that he's picking the lowliest of women as he sees them and as society has traditionally seen them and killing them to regain some of the power he feels he's lost through the experience he went through. This is how the poem ends.

Noli me tangere for Caesar's I am,

And wild for to hold though I seem tame.'

'Latin', Castle said.

'Do not touch me. It may have been written on the collars of Caesar's hinds.'

'So what does it represent?'

'The unattainable. Someone the killer wants or wanted who belongs to someone else, someone the killer feels or felt was powerful and he's turned his attention to the readily available who he wants to kill.'

'He wants to tame them.'

'Right Frank.'

'He's caught up in this history and somehow living it out through his psychosis.'

'And Jacki's discovery about the horns strongly indicates that', Spinner said.

'What else do we know about Thomas Wyatt that may help us catch this killer?'

'There's a lot on him', Nash said, 'but first, he was Sir Thomas Wyatt. He had an affair with Anne Boleyn.'

'He screwed Henry the Eighth's wife?', Castle said.

'Yes. She was pregnant when she married the King. Wyatt was later put in the Tower over his suspected betrayal.'

'What happened?'

'He was pardoned.'

'Even though he screwed Anne Boleyn?'

'Even though he said the king "should be cast out of a cart's arse".'

Castle shook his head.

'The killer may see Wyatt as a figure who stood up to authority and made something out of it', Nash said.

'Like writing poetry?'

'He was also Sheriff of Kent and the King's ambassador.'

'Are we looking for an academic?'

'Not necessarily.'

'Then we look for men with an obsession with hunting, particularly Renaissance hunting.'

'I've started to check Google records of searches in this area and I'll get back to you with what I have', Nash said.

63

The cars still patrolled the Soho streets with a regularity that was becoming burdensome to the working women.

Although they didn't want to run into the killer, they were tired of losing their clients because of the police presence.

For the local plod, a relatively easy task was becoming difficult because of the daily influx of hoards of tourists who blocked their view.

Their faces were becoming familiar.

Too familiar, and some of the policemen suspected that these men and women were not regular tourists.

'Who are they?', one PC said to his colleague as they sat and watched.

'I don't know, but why would the same set of people keep coming here every day?'

'Them', he said, pointing at the women.

'But none of them are paying.'

The crowd thickened, obliterating their view of the women, while from an alley Jonas Wilkes watched them and disappeared.

Stone sat alone in the bar, the polished glasses and mirrors showing her a tired woman who'd spent too many hours at the station.

She felt she had cop written all over her as she sipped her Daiquiri.

The guy at the end of the bar walked over and she pushed the thought of Don away. She'd felt his eyes on her a while and knew as she turned to face him she was tilting the rage of her rejection the other way, feeling suddenly aroused by the reflection of cruel desire staring back at her from her face in the polished mirror.

'Can I get you another one?'

She slid the barman her glass.

'Thanks.'

Without even looking at him, even acknowledging him. His use a given in her world and he would move in her world.

She spoke to him in the mirror, taking him in now he was close, the passenger she carried talking to this other man, sending a shower of sparks into another world.

A few years older than her, business type, kept himself in good shape, probably had done this before. Such a small world in a cop's quick reckoning. What laws lay here?

Anger fought her nausea and she took a deep swig of Daiquiri.

'I'm Mike.'

His hand was warm and firm and she felt cold suddenly.

'Lucy.'

'May I?'

She nodded and he slipped onto the next stool.

'I was meant to be meeting some friends but I ended up here on my own.'

'Some friends.'

'They're more colleagues. Anyway, I'm not disappointed.'

She looked round the almost empty bar and wondered if she could go through with this.

He was attractive enough.

'Why?', she said.

'Why?'

'You said you're not disappointed.'

'Oh, a couple of drinks before heading back to the countryside can be very enjoyable.'

'Oh.'

'In the right company.'

She saw that her drink was almost finished.

'Do you do this often?', she said, hearing the cop in her, hating her dress.

'What, drink?'

He smiled.

'Pick up women in bars.'

'Is that what I'm doing?'

She emptied her glass.

'I hope so.'

His eyes moved. A flicker that gave it away.

She thought of Don and felt angry enough to do it.

After a few more drinks she suggested it, surprising herself.

'Why don't we get a room somewhere?'

'I know a place.'

She was pleased at her own directness, angry and aroused at its crude validation of the act.

She watched him out of the corner of her eye as he drove there, his hands calm on the steering wheel, his face clean shaven. Danger crept across the threshold of the window. The countless stories of casual dates ending in rape crowded her head. She could arrest him and this knowledge gave her deep satisfaction.

Suddenly he was just another stooge in her drama and she was hungry to use him.

She checked her watch.

It wasn't far and he took her up in the lift not touching her, waiting.

She began to feel hot.

She wanted to get it over with and thought about a shower.

Once he closed the door and they were in the room she could suddenly smell him, an odour of aftershave and alcohol.

She sat on the bed.

Then she reached out and unbuckled his belt.

Everything felt strange to her.

Him.

His body.

His hands on her as they travelled up her skirt, surprising her with their sudden hot intrusion on her bare flesh, so used to being covered in trousers.

Then as she lay back she felt angry and alone.

She felt as though she were wrestling with him.

When it was all over she watched him fall asleep, then showered and left, putting her shoes on in the corridor and driving home through the empty streets.

64

The next day the memory felt like a wound.

She could smell him on her, this stranger, and washing did nothing to alleviate the taste of betrayal in her mouth.

It wasn't about Don. The betrayal was self-inflicted.

She'd sold herself into some cheapness, an experience borne of anger and hurt leading her back to the place she was running from.

She stepped from the shower, watching the steam rise and evaporate, wrapping a towel tightly round her.

Looking in the mirror brought only dismay.

The tired eyes, the drawn skin, her resentment of what she'd done. She felt used. Invaded. By her own hand. She touched her skin in a gesture of ownership.

She thought of the rape victims she'd seen, terrible cases of some skinned sexuality who came in bruised and battered and she hated men for what they did.

The memory of him entering her twitched like a raw nerve somewhere inside her.

The image of a dentist's chair, of leaning back and seeing the overhead light, the whirr of the drill and the sharp spine arching pain of it touching a nerve and digging deeper into it. Her belly rumbled as if she'd been hit and in a reflex action her hand reached across and covered her abdomen.

She thought of the other cases, the ones she'd doubted.

Of women returned from a drunken liaison who'd forgotten how they'd ended up in bed with a man they didn't like or know. Who out of anger cried rape. Of course, for the sex to have been fully consensual the man needed to be aware of her level of inebriation and back out.

She remembered at one training session saying 'What, even if she was naked and asking for it?' The other women met her with blank stares and she felt like a traitor, catching the roving eye of one macho prick who tried it on with her later.

She'd slapped his face.

She was married to Don.

Don, the reason for all of this.

And she was still married to him.

The anger whipped inside her like a snake and she punched the mirror.

She'd been trained in modern policing surrounding rape, but had never shaken off a sneaking suspicion that if a man and a woman were both drunk, had sex, and she later regretted it, it wasn't rape. Why should the man be more compos mentis under the influence than the woman? Unless he held her down.

Dealing with murder was easier.

And this? Don had driven her to this.

Had she been held down?

An acrid salty smell entered her nose and she wanted to gag.

Suddenly she understood the appeal of claiming rape. She felt dirty and almost got into the shower again.

Someone she didn't know climbing inside her, evacuating himself into her.

And isn't that what Karl Black had done?

Opened some gateway in her soul and climbed inside, just as Castle said he would.

How did he do it?

Paranoia crept across the threshold of her mind like some deep-set watchful shadow, a brooding depth of malignancy with unutterable secrets to tell.

She changed the bed and took her jacket to the cleaner.

As she did, a business card fell from it and she threw it in the rubbish, knowing what it was.

She remembered the dentist's chair, leaning back, feeling helpless while a masked man poked around inside her, the fingers always too large for her mouth, her jaw stretching as she listened for the sound of the drill.

The sterile smell entered her nose before she saw it: the dentist removing the goggles and Karl Black's face staring down at her.

Her mouth felt dry. As she held the bottle of water to her lips, the slurp and slosh of it against the crinkling plastic brought with it a rush of liquid images: water to semen, whisky to blood, the black tide rising like some shadow of warfare on the horizon.

They are like the new baby caught in the umbilical cord
But the umbilicus is their very Choking their very end

65

Tom Spinner was in his element.

Nash's team had collated a body of information that amounted to the first coherent sense of the prostitute killer.

He flecked the flip chart with ink.

'Wyatt separated from his first wife, charging her with adultery. He went on to have an adulterous relationship with the King's wife Anne Boleyn, whether before or after she was Queen, probably both. He was exiled by Henry the Eighth when he served as High Marshal of Calais. The reason was almost certainly to get him away from Anne.'

'Where's this leading?', Castle said impatiently.

'Watch the theme of adultery. It will recur and almost certainly it acts as a key unlocking our killer's psyche. Exile. The killer is exiling his victims by removing them from their place of work and taking them somewhere where he feels a connection, where he feels powerful.'

'Say you're right', Stone said, 'why does he feel powerful in Richmond Park?'

'It's hard to say and not that important. The point is that he's using it.'

'Could he have a link to it in terms of work?'

'Possibly.'

'Then we look through the records of everyone employed by the Park, say, in the last ten years.'

'It might yield you a name. Might not. It's worth a try, but the point is that's where he's putting them and in terms of understanding him, it represents the exiling of those he wants eliminated.'

'If Richmond Park represents his patch, then we catch him there', Castle said.

'Wyatt was an influential man. He was the High Steward of the abbey of West Malling in Kent. He intimately knew the woman closest to the King at that time. He represents getting close to the source of power and undermining it. That's the killer's psyche. He's killing prostitutes because they have fallen from the seat of power, they are women selling themselves to all and sundry, they are easily available, but the Park represents the killer taking back some power of his own. It is the Royal Park and although no literal King is involved, it is an enactment of the Royalty of his psyche and he's either trying to get at someone he knew who was powerful, or acting on the instructions of someone he sees as powerful.'

'If he worked in the Park that narrows the field, but then we need to find someone under another's sway, and we're looking at a co-conspirator', Castle said.

'Look at everyone who worked as a deer culler in the Park. He's a hunter and the deer are highly symbolic in his psyche.'

As he walked past Stone his aftershave induced a wave of nausea in her.

Mover and Tweed walked side by side like a pair of shadows, crossing the paths of other businessmen, wending their way to the Houses of Parliament, laughing at their own jokes, looking over their shoulders to see if anyone else of note was nearby and dismissing the idea as ridiculous.

'There's money to be made here', Tweed said.

'Yes, and we can run it back through the tax system and let the little man pay for it.'

A soiled sun leaked light onto them as they entered Parliament.

66

Castle decided to re-interview Karl Black.

Stone was sceptical.

'What have we got on him that we didn't before?', she said.

'Nothing.'

'Frank?'

'I want to call his bluff. Say we have DNA linking it to someone in his Brotherhood.'

She looked at him as they drove there, wending their way through a mist that rose like some adumbration of the veil that hung over Black. As they crunched the gravel on the drive, she found herself wondering if her partner knew what he was doing.

Wilkes opened the door.

'You are not expected.'

'Is Mr Black in?', Castle said.

He left them standing in the hallway.

The house sent a shiver through Stone.

'It's spring outside, and winter in here.'

When Wilkes returned he took them along the corridors to the library.

Black was inside.

'Still fumbling for a solution, Detectives?'

'We're still looking into the killings', Castle said.

'And because you are mentally retarded and unable to do anything except vent your frustration and chronic ineptitude as officers of a warped law on the motorist you come here to harass me and see if I can help you do your job for which you shouldn't be paid a penny. Everything you do, every time you open your mouth, you reveal what a sorry excuse for a human you are.'

Stone saw Castle bristle and stepped in.

'Most people co-operate with the police unless they've got

something to hide. Do you have something to hide, Mr Black?'

'I'm not hiding my opinion of you am I Inspector Stone? I'm not hiding the fact that I think you are so sub-humanly unintelligent that you ought to be experimented on, but believe me, it will come, one day the police will be put through what they deserve and have deserved for some time, you will suffer so badly that you will be howling for mercy at the hands of those you deem the criminals. I have nothing to hide, you have to hide your complete inability to solve any crimes.'

'We have the DNA of someone who belongs to your organization linked to the murders.'

'Then prove it. Because, Chief Inspector Castle, I don't believe you.'

'We can take you into the station.'

'Go ahead. My lawyer will destroy you and so will the press. They are already licking your wounds, Chief Inspector, and they say they taste of whisky. You are known across the country as the man who couldn't solve the first case. Now you will be known as the man who botched this one, a perpetual laughing stock, how fitting.'

'Are you refusing to co-operate with a police investigation?', Stone said.

'How can I co-operate with a non-existent investigation? Because that is what this is, a shambles.'

'If we find anything, we'll be back', Castle said.

'You won't.'

They found themselves in the dark corridor walking through the cold.

Castle started the engine and drove back to the station.

Meanwhile Black went in to the recruits.

67

'Every action is caused by the soul. It is decreed. Christ commanded the execution of those serving a corrupt political system. All those who fracture the ten Commandments will be dealt with by this Law.'

Black paused, taking in the wrapt faces, his words acting like hooks which he used to draw them to his message. Rodrigo gazed back at him, his face like the unrippled surface of a lake.

'This Fallen world where women work as prostitutes and masquerade their wares as the politics of liberation, this Fallen world where the diseased and the corrupt govern our body politic must be subjected to the Law. I teach you the Law. I bring you the tablets from the Burning Mountain and I say unto you Rise Up! Damn the system! Unlock the chains! Be free!'

The recruits murmured their assent, and shone with a zealous fire that Black now stoked and watched like an arsonist.

'Your enemies sit in the Houses where your votes placed them. They are the vermin which we must eradicate. They bring disease and fetch forth the very Soul of lust and harbour it like an apple rotten to the core with the promise of rebellion against a higher power but that power will triumph.'

Wilkes watched them from behind Black.

'You are soldiers intent upon bringing down the enemy of mankind. These men and women who serve the State are the Ultimate betrayers of Christianity and the true teachings of Christ.'

Wilkes passed him the cup.

'We take our Communion according to our ways.'

They sipped and sat again.

'Fortify yourselves with our teachings. Use this strength to destroy the enemy.'

After they had left, Wilkes approached him.

'Any news?', he said.

'It is time to bring the final act into play.'

'I will have all in preparedness.'

'The rotten fruit is on the vine, our shears are at the ready.'

Wilkes fetched some plastic sacks from behind the kitchens of Rondelo, red liquid luminous at their shallow surface. He went about his business with the measured pace of an executioner. Black prepared his library, moving books and furniture. When he heard the knock at the door, he said 'the newer Brothers are ready', as it swung open.

'So are the anti-priests.'

Don walked into the restaurant in a crisp suit.

Sky blue shirt and navy tie.

That sparkle in his eye.

Stone pushed her half-empty wine glass away, ushering the memory of the stranger in that bed to the edge of her consciousness.

She looked down, avoiding eye contact, fighting her anger at his lateness as she flicked a crumb to the edge of the tablecloth.

'Hi Jacki.'

He leaned to kiss her and she turned away.

'Drink?'

'I'm all right, thanks', she said.

'So, how are you?'

'I thought we needed to talk.'

The waiter came over.

'I'll have a lager', Don said.

They sat reading menus while the restaurant filled up.

Stone was glad of the noise the extra bodies brought with them.

'Are you going to leave her Don?'

'Is that what this is about?'

'What do you think?'

'Why do you think I strayed, Jacki?'

'Now let me think.' She posed, index finger beneath her chin. 'Is it because you're a cheating bastard?'

'You call this talking?'

'So, come on, Don, you tell me why. There's obviously something you want me to know.'

'I know I've hurt you. And I regret my actions. I don't want her.'

'Getting tired of her now?'

'I left because your life as a cop took over. This case took over. And there were others before.'

'Others!'

'Cases. Arrangements we made, holiday plans cancelled. The cases piling up, Jacki. You too tired to talk. I have a career. I don't let it interfere with my marriage.'

'I'm a cop!', she said, slamming her hand down on the table, her wine glass jumping. 'You knew that when I married you.'

'I didn't marry the Met, Jacki, I didn't marry Frank Castle.'

'You jealous of him?'

'No.'

'You are! You think I want to sleep with Frank?'

'What I'm saying is he's more in your life than I am, and has been for years. This didn't just happen overnight, Jacki.'

'Oh? How long did it take for you to stick your prick in her?'

She'd spoken louder than she intended and was aware of heads turning.

Don shook his head.

'This is why I can't talk to you.'

'So talk.'

'If you can't see how impossible it is being married to a police Inspector, how it takes over every corner of our lives, then you're more lost than I thought. You talk to Frank more than you talk to me, that's what I'm trying to say.'

'So where does that leave us?'

'I don't know.'

The waiter brought their orders and they ate in silence.

Mover and Tweed sat in their club congratulating themselves on their latest venture.

The party was behind them and they knew it.

'We can use this for many deals', Tweed said.

'Yes, the banks are in our power.'

'The ministers we spoke to are fully behind us.'

'They have to be.'

They sat and tapped ash onto the carpet while waiters scurried about them fetching their whiskies.

Outside the sun struggled through the windows of the room, leaking a shallow light onto the leather sofas and armchairs that filled it, while the heavy odour of cigar smoke and self-important conversation hung like a miasma in the air.

Outside someone stood watching, waiting. His awareness of their movements exceeded their own and he watched them walk towards his trap.

68

Stacey Palmer had the habit.

Her body craved crack from the moment she awoke, the crystal lying there in her psyche each morning as she opened her eyes.

When her baby had been taken into care, she'd worked hard to get it back so as to sell it.

She'd gone abroad, done the deal and returned with the money.

It didn't last long and soon she'd started turning tricks.

She knew her looks were going, knew the tired lines around her eyes all too well, felt the change in her skin.

She worked her own patch and didn't need protection by a pimp. She cruised the streets for the quickest tricks, turning them in cars and parks while her habit soared.

Each day she applied the heavy make-up, layering it to sustain the illusion necessary to draw these men in. She wore bright clothes.

The idea that she would ever stop, exchange this life for a better one, was long gone, and she traded as much as she could.

Mike Nash walked into Castle's office and said 'I've got some names. Guys who have over a thousand hits on hunting and Tudor history. Guys who have a background in hunting and two of them who've worked in Richmond Park.'

Castle ran his eye down the list.

'Good work, Mike.'

The two Nash had highlighted lived in London.

That afternoon they drove round to the addresses hoping another body wouldn't materialise before they made the breakthrough.

Wilkes was sitting in the outbuilding at the back of Rondelo.

Outside a fierce spring rain beat down on the orchard, rustling the leaves and dappling the grounds in small unattended pools.

A cloaked figure sat beside him.

'It is time for the final one', Wilkes said.

'I know the method.'

Arthur Blake was a small man with a lisp.

Castle sat in his living room while Stone looked around.

'Mr Blake, why have you made so many hits on hunting?'

'It was an interest of my father's and I guess you could say I inherited it.'

'And the history?'

'Is it a crime to be interested in history? What's all this about?'

Castle was already getting the feeling that this was a waste of time. He knew this guy was no more capable of killing all those prostitutes than a man weighing twenty six stones was of running the London Marathon.

'We're investigating some murders.'

'The Woodland Killings as they're describing them in the press? I've read all about them. The press is a vicious beast and merciless. You must feel as if an animal had your leg between its teeth.'

'No. It's not about the Woodland Killings.'

'The prostitutes? Most unfortunate.'

'Can you account for your movements on these dates?'

He handed him a list of times when the murders had been committed. Blake glanced at them.

'Yes. I was on holiday. In Germany. The Rhine, you see, another of my interests, if you check my Google coverage you'll see that I made as many if not more hits on the Rhine, although there have been no killings of prostitutes in that area during the last months to my knowledge. Here's my ticket.'

He handed him an airline ticket with Lufthansa.

Stone came into the room. She shook her head at Castle.

In the car she said:

'Nothing there.'

'I know.'

69

Nash was looking at the Lewis Montelle murder scene. The portrait at his house had been snapped by the crime scene officers and a shot of it lay in the file with a note Castle had written next to it. 'Who is it?'

Nash stared down at the stiff and enigmatic face looking out of a sepia distance.

He had to be someone.

He waded through various search engines and came up with a match. The third message had been written behind a portrait of Lodowick Muggleton.

He whistles as he slices their flesh like sparrow yield so softly sang the bird and he earthwards dived down upon the Earth carrying the remnants of the food and messages from above where they are written on tablets made of stone not for the hands of men nor the Corrupt

The writing says that this slaughter of the Filth is needed for the cleansing of the Earth etched into the slow memory of dawn, the new dawn in which I rise

Identities shift and vary and the names of many men are forgotten, lying with the debris of their falser selves, several attempts to birth themselves

But I walk among the Chosen and know the bodies of the Corrupt yearn for the entrance of Blade shaft like into their Blood that they clamour for to be drunk at the Altars where the priests and true monks of the Time shall imbibe them forth and spew them out like the hot feast and dance of the New Jerusalem where the Corrupt shall lie in their House slain, cuckolded by their desire

They are the small hole in the wall where things crawl and seek you out in your malice

For it is known
Blade shall triumph
For Blade is
And they do not see me walk among them
They do not know me
They cough their lives away among the shackled
Speak not for the slow hand is turning the handle of the Door

Castle and Stone drove to the second address.

Mark Grange had worked as a deer culler in Richmond Park and seemed to have an obsessional interest in hunting and Henry the Eighth.

'I hope he's a better fit than the last guy' Castle said.

'How many men fit this profile?'

They turned into a council estate with broken lifts and as they climbed the soiled stairwell, Castle said 'This place is familiar.'

'Yeah. We interviewed someone in connection with the Woodland Killings.'

'Laurence Steele?'

'Yes.'

He checked the address.

'He lives with Grange.'

'Or he is Grange.'

The taste of arrest was in his mouth and he took the last two floors at a run.

They knocked and stood outside.

'No answer', he said.

Stone looked around while he kicked the door in.

70

Stacey Palmer reached into the tourist's pocket and pulled his wallet.

In a back alley she flipped it open: just as she had expected, a good wad of cash, over £100.

She discarded the credit cards, knowing she'd be put away this time if she was caught on CCTV camera.

On her way out of the alley she saw a punter.

His car was parked round the corner and she did her first job of the day. She was seeing her dealer later, and she needed a lot of money today.

Nash was reading up on Lodowick Muggleton.

And making the links.

There was enough in the way of strange beliefs that connected well with The Last Brotherhood and he wanted to tell Castle and Stone.

He scented the killer in these teachings.

Castle started to search the flat.

It was the same as the last time they had been there. Strangely unaltered, as if its dweller lived in some zone of changelessness. He looked about him, scenting a hidden clue, some anomaly in the environment.

There was something missing, some quotidian element that normalised every room he stepped into, each crime scene and office that punctuated his days.

And then it struck him. There were no clocks, no timepieces whatsoever in the flat, as if time had died. He went into the kitchen: the microwave flashed a constant zero, and the clock on the cooker had been crudely ripped out, the jagged edges of its grooves testament to its rough removal.

He walked back into the living room. Religious messages adorned the walls and the bareness attested to a life lived for the religion of the man they were seeking.

'I don't think two people live here', Stone said, coming out of the bedroom.

'Unless Blake's using the address.'

'They could be working together.'

'I want a unit put on watch outside for when he returns and I want him brought in for questioning when he does.'

'I'll get onto it.'

Castle started turning the place over. Stone went through the kitchen while he ransacked the drawers in the living room.

At the back of one of them he found a leaflet entitled The Order of the Righteous. In it someone had written:

"You are more deer to me than venison

And more weak and I enter your flesh".'

Castle flipped through a few pages. Meeting dates. The Order's teachings. Then:

"So soft your flesh I saw on Sawyer's Hill

While the King trod your land."

'What was the name of that part of Richmond Park where the king hunted?'

'Sawyer's Hill?'

'Yeah. I think we got our man.'

71

Laurence Steele sat with Wilkes in the outbuilding at the back of Rondelo.

A sharp wind hissed outside.

'You have the weapon ready for the next Whore?', Wilkes said.

'Yes.'

Steele unwrapped from a rag a long blade with an insignia at its edge.

He passed it to Wilkes.

'The Whore shall be taken to the very top of Sawyer's Hill and tortured there.'

'You must cut her to the very womb while she bleeds into the nighttime for there she will merge with the spirit of Wyatt and the King. So Anne Boleyn has been stilled and the tide of history returned unto the point at which this axis turns. The teachings of the Order know that your mission is to do this.'

'The cutting?', Steele said.

'Bleed her into her womb for it is the seat of the Earth's disease. These Whores are the Walkers who breed the corruption that sits throned and will be brought down. Cut her deeply so she sings and then hack her to the places which you have been taught within the Holy Book.'

'Then I lay her out with the horns upon her?'

'You lay her out with the horns inserted into her. Deep within her.'

'They are freshly harvested from an ancient stag.'

He brought out two large antlers.

'Good. The Whore will take them.'

Time is and they creep so
From clubs to Houses where they carry Filth with them like a package
of goods
Talk they do and cost so little charging all
Their skin soft in the air I smell and follow them

Castle and Stone raced back to the station and put out an alert for Laurence Steele.

While Nash waited to tell them about his discovery and as officers everywhere looked for Steele, he walked into the streets of Soho undetected.

Wearing a hood and two weeks' beard, he looked unrecognisable.

He carried his weapon unseen and disappeared into the crowds.

72

Their customers crawl through filth to pay them
These narcissi of deceit lying within the prism of themselves
Reflections cast like broken mirrors
Shuffle and wait
Watching unseen and unheard
Through the darkened streets walk like a shadow
They have lost the path that led them here
Like a slow portrait unfolding
They call it freedom but it is nothing more than the
Issuing of their warrants for sales and debits
Their lifetimes spent in useless avoidance
Clocking the mirrors on the wall
Wandering alone the hallways of their distant lives
Their Sins have found them out
And the knowledge shall undo them
So Blade

Mike Nash tried to talk to Castle as he came in but was put on hold.

'We've got a lead on the prostitute killer', he said and he and Stone left immediately, radioing to the patrol cars in Soho.

None of the cars stationed there had seen any movement.

As Wilkes returned to Rondelo and began to prepare for the next leg of the recruits' teachings, Black, secluded in his library, traced the paths of the ancient knowledge, a lore known to him unfolding like a withered leaf in his palm.

And Laurence Steele walked the shadowed streets.

Hookers rendered quiet by the police presence loitered in doorways awaiting custom and he passed them by.

Finally he turned into a square.

A doorway with a soiled message.

He entered and left a few minutes later followed by a woman in bright garments, gaudy as a new penny coined by a forger's mint.

73

Castle and Stone sat in the unmarked car watching the customers come and go, a steady flow of traffic with one thought on its mind: the swift and ready exchange of flesh, sold at a price which steadied the twitching nerves and days that rolled on in a misery of grey uselessness and accustomed entrapment.

The smell of fried food and cheapened lives hung in the air like a fog and the men passed by wrapping themselves in a cloak of anonymity so obvious that it felt like a stain on the pavement, etching its quiet misery into the paving stones and littered streets.

Hours passed and nothing happened and Castle got the old feeling he knew too well.

'He's not here', he said finally, turning to Stone with slow knowledge seeping across his face like a scar.

Outside the hidden men shuffled away, a little less of them as they departed.

Ruling is an art
These others serve Lies on a plate of sugar coated with warm honeyed vomit for their followers to dine from
Usurpers of the true rulers of the Earth
They are the perpetual crucifiers of Christ

Stacey chewed her gum, idly unzipping her top and exposing a little nipple to the air in the car. Her eyelashes were tipped with gold glitter and her face flashed as she talked.

Steele turned and looked at her as if measuring the growth of a mutation.

'Where we going?', she said.

'You'll see.'

'You got the money?'

'It's all here', he said, tapping his wallet.

She leant forward, letting her tit hang and rub against his shoulder, the soft flesh whining on his jacket, the nipple hardening against the action.

'You can do dirty stuff if you like, it'll cost more.'

'Oh?'

He looked downwards at the hard rubbery tip of her breast, the white skin stretched tight and dry.

'Yeah, what do you like?'

'This', he said, showing her the night.

Wilkes undid one of the plastic sacks and poured the blood into the old cup from which they drank, handing round the goblet until their lips were soiled.

'You know the Law, make sure the others also know of it and follow it', he said.

'We do', Malcolm said, nodding.

'We will enforce it with every ounce of holy power now gained', Rodrigo said.

His eyes looked like flames.

Wilkes sent them forth with fresh knowledge, their faces alive with the teachings of the Brotherhood.

'Know them when ye see them, Brothers', he said, 'and remember they are the Crucifiers of Christ.'

Castle and Stone toured the streets looking for him.

The hope of a sighting was fading fast and they knew the press were ready to eat them if another body turned up on the tables for tomorrow morning's breakfast.

Only the tourists and businessmen shuttling between meetings.

Only the throng empty of the man they sought, like a feast abandoned by a predator.

74

Stacey awoke in a cold room, stone walls stared at her with an empty resolution.

No windows.

Her hands shackled to her sides and a sense of cutting.

A chair.

Stains on the floor.

She heard the door as it opened.

He walked in slowly and she tried to speak, her mouth dry and able only to issue a choked wordless sound.

He approached her and reached for something.

She heard a slicing noise and looked to see her clothes falling away from her in shredded patterns like ribbons she recalled from somewhere in her childhood, a fluttering like birds and heavy memories summoning a fear from her bowels and a flow of liquid as she urinated.

She looked down and saw the yellow stream running down her thigh, her hair standing away from her skin, her nipples cold and hard, his hands running down her body and his strange mumbling.

'The hind is caught and trapped for so it has been written.'

'What do you want?'

Just his hands moving, no words.

She spoke it again.

'What do you want?'

Still only the measured thrumming of his fingers against the saturated flesh, the come of many men hot within her and unfed by any fertile measurement of exchange, just the old place of want and need. She tried to speak but his hands silenced her punching against her throat until she choked and placing themselves against her and inside her.

A cold entering that made her warm. The warmth spreading across her body.

She felt him tweak and open her and insert himself in her, just his hands and then more of it. The feeling familiar, like some quotidian rocking of her sleeping soul, a motion restive and accustomed as a dull ache whose pulsing rhythm lulled its pain away.

The hand moving, entering other parts of her, new openings he'd etched and carved so hollowed out she was he walked his hands into her wounds.

Then something else.

He cut her again.

She looked and saw the sharpened knife go in and felt all the men within her mounted on her astride and running away with their panting and stinking come of soiled sheets and her blood was rushing down her legs splattering the hard stone floor, pooling there like some mystical menstruation and now the Virgin Mary rising in the air, for she knew this was her time, the cutting all the time and then her breasts hacked from her, she could see her own skin unfold within a ribbon of her hope her lost years and the reasons for it against the darkened walls of her years as a prostitute all those men laughing and walking away from her, the notes stacked up and then he pushed like they pushed into her wanting to get inside her deeper into her but with the knife which was cutting her flesh, something else deep inside her and then he spoke.

'I will remove it now', he said.

She seemed to be dripping away on a wash of fluid, her body's tide ebbing into a mist that saw her self-beckoning as some ghost of herself shadowed her and spoke a tongue she could not hear. She saw her blood gathering in a black tide beneath her ankles and the cold swept across her like some wind, chilling her, she searched within this for her sex, her ability to charm men on a word or look and saw again the knife glistening maliciously with her blood, bubbles of it frothing on its surface and edge which descended into her again and started to tear away her flesh in living shanks like a butcher's shop, some window she looked into as a child hungry and on her way home from school.

She moved her mouth in slow desperation asking him why why but he just went on with his work with a measured slowness.

His face assumed the look of all the men she let enter her with their voices slow and anonymous in the sheets where their smells lingered like a stain.

Their faces merging and assuming the face of one man making her shudder as the blade shuddered meeting bone, her bone scraping hard against its steel.

He looked the same and became something else, alien as sin, something she could not understand or work like she worked the others to her end and getting away with what she wanted giving nothing in return only the vacuum of herself as she thought of it.

His face now old and unmoved, a mask of wordless knowledge looking at her and into her as he pushed it deeper inside, she was lying on her bed at the studio with clients waiting in the corridors outside, lining up for her services and paying.

Now she counted the cash as it clinked into her pocket and she saw him move across her and push deep into her chest as the door swung open and she heard voices.

What Castle and Stone saw when they entered the room brought them to a standstill.

The tip-off from the squad car had paid off and they found the cellar, the door at street level locked.

They kicked it in and descended into some hell.

The bare light bulb hung from a veined ceiling, illuminating the naked and mutilated body.

Steele was in the process of cutting her open, slowly, to remove her heart and when he heard them behind him he swung at Castle, who moved away and pulled his gun.

Stone moved in and he caught her with the blade pumping blood from her shoulder as she fell to the ground and Castle rose up and whipped him with the pistol until he lay still.

The prostitute hung from his ropes like an open wound, her chest a red gash in her body, her cunt ripped and torn and leaking like a gashed beast, her face a mute look of horror as if a voyager between worlds and witness of some monstrous sight no words can express.

They unroped her and waited for the ambulance to arrive, the blood from her cuts spreading all the time, Castle's face a mirror of failings and closed files.

'Good press coverage', Tweed said, placing the paper crisply on the table.

Mover glanced at the headlines.

'Always will be when we're doing this sort of deal. The taxpayer loves it, the press don't understand it, money is made and the public are happy.

'Keep the wheels well oiled.'

'You can hardly hear them moving.'

When the ambulance arrived they managed to put Stacey on a life-support machine and get her to hospital while Castle arrested Steele and took him back to the station.

His head wounds needed treating before they could begin the interview, and Castle paced the corridors with all the years' aggravation weighing on him. He felt hemmed in by procedure. He wanted this guy behind bars and suddenly the police force seemed the biggest prison of all.

I know the watchfulness of the Fallen
They chatter blindly, and know not what awaits them now in the dark corridors of Time
Their Corrupt ways have trapped them in a mesh
Their Master summons them

Castle sat opposite Steele with Stone at his side.

He hadn't cut her too badly, and she'd been stitched up.

There was a wall of ice between them and Castle tried to stare through it to reach him, a slow fire burning in his blue eyes.

Steele had asked for a lawyer and he sat in silence.

It was a pose of contemplation, as if years of privation had inured him to this experience.

Beside him Bertrand Nap, a seasoned legal aid solicitor sat staring into space, waiting for the interview to begin.

Castle had run across him many times before. He was competent, sharp, and knew the score.

The years rolled back for Castle. All those years of thinking about Black. His expectation of a major coup fought his disappointment that this was not the Woodlands Copycat sitting opposite him.

'Laurence Steele, we are charging you with the murders of six prostitutes. Do you have anything to say?'

Steele looked at Nap, who sat non-committally.

'What do you want me to say?'

'Why don't you start by telling us why you've done this?'

'Done what?'

'We caught you with a victim. You were mutilating Stacey Palmer and almost killed her. And then there are the others.'

'What others?'

'We know you're the killer', Stone said. 'Why don't you just make it easier for yourself?'

'You mean easier for you?'

'We've got enough on you to put you away for a very long time.'

'You haven't got anything on me.'

'We've got you torturing a woman. We've got you mutilating her. We've got you on abduction. We've got you on assault of a police officer. And once we've matched your DNA to the killings we'll have you. Do you know how long you'll be going down for?'

'My client hasn't been found guilty of any murders', Nap said.

Castle leaned towards Steele.

'Tell us why you did it. Were you working with someone?'

'You understand nothing. And as for your sidekick, she is as lost and hopeless as you are. You sin and lie. You cannot solve this, it is beyond you.'

For the rest of the day Steele refused to say anything.

Later on they nursed their wounds at The Crooked Key.

From time to time Stone's wound hurt but by her second glass of wine she was unaware of any lingering pain.

She noticed Castle seemed to be somewhere else, could see the pressure building in him.

'Frank?'

'Maybe the lawmakers are the most screwed up.'

'How come?'

'When you cross the line to crime you know who you are.'

'Like Black?'

'Like Black, like the killer.'

'It's the pressure of the case, Frank.'

'It's walking into the psyche of something that dark, that horrendous. When these psychopaths kill, they're in some other place, some state of mind that seals them off from the ordinary experience of man, of what binds us together as humans.'

'They're already sealed off.'

'In a way, yes, but they're not killing all the time, Jacki. When they do it, they torture and maim, they don't feel it, they don't experience what has happened to their victims.'

'They can't.'

'What I'm saying is we don't have their psyches, their flaws, and we walk in cold to their mutilated world. What's the effect of that on us, Jacki? What imprint does it leave in us over the years?'

'I think you know the answer to that Frank.'

'Which is why I'm saying, administering law can send you crazy.'

'You crazy Frank?'

She looked at him as he drank his whisky, more golden than the dying sun outside the window.

77

Tweed and Mover were working on another proposal for Parliament.

Their last success had spurred them on and they could see a pot of gold at the end of their well-crafted rainbow.

They worked the media and they hoped to have every senior minister in their pockets before long.

The profit margins were swelling all the time as they joined forces.

They left Steele to figure out that he had no other option than to talk.

'There's a crack there and I'm gonna find it', Castle said to Stone.

'You think?'

'Once I get in there I'll prise it open.'

'So far he's not giving anything away.'

'And in the meantime?'

'We've got one killer.'

Walking back to their office, they saw Mike Nash.

'I hear you've caught a suspect.'

'One down one to go. Anything for us?', Castle said.

'Very much so.'

They went in and he handed them the picture of Lodowick Muggleton.

'The portrait on Lewis Montelle's wall', Castle said.

'Right.'

'Who is he?'

'Lodowick Muggleton. Seventeenth century English sectarian.'

'Mike, be sparing with the history.'

'I'll tell you the salient facts, Frank. He had revelations and decided he and his cousin John Reeve were the two witnesses mentioned in the Book of Revelations.'

'How is this linked to the case?'

'I believe the killer is a follower of Muggleton. Not purely, but partly influenced by him.'

'You mean this guy actually has followers?'

'Very much so. Muggleton believed he and his cousin were on a "commission from God". His followers believed he was the "Voice of the last prophet of God". They also believed that the soul was mortal.'

'That's heretical, isn't it?'

'Yes it is.'

'They had a lot of crazy notions, such as that Heaven was six miles above the earth, and that God was between five and six feet tall.'

Castle stifled a laugh.

'And our killer?', Stone said.

'He chose to place the message at the third killing behind the portrait of Muggleton. He didn't put any other messages behind any other portraits, did he?'

'OK. So, he's giving away the clues that killers very often do, whether through arrogance or a desire to promote his belief structure.'

Castle was looking at the information Nash had compiled.

'There's something here.'

'Muggletonians believe they can damn and bless according to God's will.'

'What does that mean?'

'Taken to its extreme, religious war.'

'Which means if he's following this teaching he's definitely acting from religious motivation and believes what he is doing is not murder but the will of God.'

'Sounds like schizophrenia to me', Stone said.

'The analogy is there', Tom Spinner said, stepping through the door and catching her last words. 'I got the stuff you e-mailed me, Mike.'

'What do you think?', Castle said.

'Backs up my profile and usefully gives a body of beliefs we can use to predict his movements. Schizophrenia and religious hysteria have strong overlaps.'

'What does he do next Tom?', Castle said.

'He doesn't think of it as murder, so the political aspect of it could become warped. He might start to pick people who aren't politicians.'

'Which makes it impossible for us to catch him.'

'His thinking about politics is based on these beliefs. He believes that anyone usurping the direct role of God or religion is a criminal and should be dealt with according to the law as he sees it.'

'Which means chopping them up.'

'We need to look at these beliefs alongside what we've already got and see where his killings have been heading in terms of their route from one politician to another. That will give us an idea of where he may be going next.' All heads were turned on him. 'I'll get on with it then.'

As Spinner left the room, Castle's phone rang.

Stone watched his face, seeing it drop, seeing a look of gravity deepen in it.

He put the receiver down.

'Stacey Palmer died a couple of hours ago. Massive haemorrhaging.'

78

'We are the new Medievalists.'

Black was addressing the recruits who sat and sank into his words which he issued with the sense of steam rising from some enormous fire that had burned for years.

'I teach you the ascendancy of the medieval model. God rules, we follow. Those who usher in another form of government will be killed and tortured, according to God's will, for these teachings belong to an oral tradition that has been passed down and now comes into fruition.'

He looked across at them.

'The new ways of this world are diseased. Like a whore whose syphilis reaches into her genitals and decays there while men too sinful to see what they are entering use her, it is decaying before our eyes and we rush onwards with its lies and political policies and disease. We are the surgeons who will cut away this disease with a knife and replace it with health founded on age-old principles and which I bring you burning down from the mountain.'

The recruits nodded.

'The men and women who have taken government upon themselves are the disease bearers, they have tried to destroy the model of life upon which we founded our teachings, a way of life that led gloriously to the truthful and the rightful ways of God where God was respected as our sole Ruler, and these men and women usurp this rule and must be destroyed.'

They looked at him, their lost lives falling away in the aura of truth he cast like a shadow across them, one face burning more brightly than the others.

'Slaughter them!'

They moved towards him in unison.

'Crucify them!'

They stood and he walked among them.

'It's seven murders now', Castle said.

Steele sat opposite him, stress showing on his face.

'We know there are more', Stone said.

She caught a flicker of uncertainty cross Steele's face. Castle looked at her, knowing the ruse.

'We're investigating the murder of a lot more prostitutes. We've been looking through our files and you'll be going down for a long time.'

He folded his arms.

'You can help us and that may help you', Castle said, 'or you can sit there not saying anything and the jury'll just think the worse of you. We may be able to get to why you did this.'

'You understand betrayal, Laurence', Stone said. 'The man who led you to do this, it's him we want. He's killed many people, a lot more than you know about and he's setting you up to be punished for everything he's done. Do you want to be betrayed like that?'

'Betrayal is a terrible thing', he said.

'How about telling us about Anne Boleyn?'

Bertrand Nap looked over his glasses at them.

'Is this relevant?'

'She was unfaithful', Steele said.

'You don't have to answer.'

But Nap's words were lost on him.

'She betrayed the king, the highest man in the land, don't you think that was sinful?'

Castle and Stone exchanged glances, seeing a crack open in this man's psyche, a crack so deep, he lost touch with what he was saying.

'How did she betray the king?', Stone said.

'She slept with Thomas Wyatt, a great poet. He knew and understood, you see, the powerful always get to keep what's theirs, they don't care for anyone else, they take what they feel belongs to them and they do what they want. But you see, Thomas Wyatt knew better.'

'And what did he know?'

Suddenly, he pulled back and turned again to silence.

79

I see Sin like a leper casting sideways glances through the doorways halfway open and ajar upon the forms that lurk and wander there

A shadowland of political traders

They look for Flesh among the Fallen, a soft due upon their wakening Hour

Their words fall from their hollow mouths like worthless currency

Tideless now they flow

Their voices resonate to the timbre of their Lies and their Houses echo this

They are the concealed ones who wander alone through the forest of their thoughts

They are the stealers of Virtue and the disease bearers

They appoint their ministers with the task of deceit

They put on the garb of Justice and flay the innocent

They are the Rapists of Honour

They are the thieves who judge the people they cannot lead

They walk through the doorways to trade in their stolen Flesh, a little pleasure from their bodies rank with lust and hot for their wives who stay at home lusting after all and sundry, waiting for the men to return that they may lie them upon their beds where they pull infants from between their legs and corrupt their minds

They are a charred and bloody workhorse

A stolen stench so hot and Filthy that they scream for it

They know the Whores upon their husbands' clothes, their buried bodies fleshed into them that they feel and they grope and grasp them forth into them and issue the juices of their poisoned lust, telling them to take them where they can and whoring for them in the homes of harried harlots listening to the voices crackle from the televisions while the

Houses of the Corrupt sell the trade that seals these deals that bear the offspring they may hook and profit from

Mike Nash's team had been looking at the early forensics on the Woodland Killings.

There was a specific shape to many of the wounds the killer inflicted on his victims, and Nash saw it.

He'd instructed them to identify the size of the weapon's blade and see what it matched.

That day, he took what they had and tested it against a match that would yield a positive ID of the weapon.

He had enough to go on, but still the favoured killing tool eluded them.

The search engine threw up a few examples, but one stuck out.

He zoned in on it, and saw that it had all the characteristics of the weapon that would inflict the kind of injuries the Woodland Killer inflicted pre-torture.

It also had a flavour that matched the case.

He printed off a sheet and took it through to Castle and Stone, who sat drinking coffees.

'What've you got, Mike?', Castle said.

'You were saying how slow we've been identifying the weapon on the Woodlands case.'

'Yeah, underfunded and overstretched as usual, but then we're the police, everyone's favourite punchbag, read the papers today?'

He slung him The Sun.

The headline 'Useless police let killers run free', loomed back at him from the desk.

'Well, it's no ordinary weapon and bears similarities to many tools and stabbing implements. The reason it's taken so long has as much to do with its strangeness as our lack of resources.'

'What is it?', Castle said.

'Ever heard of a Rondel dagger?'

'No.'

He passed him the sheet.

Castle stared down at a picture of something that looked like a boring tool.

'This it?'

'Yes. It's a medieval weapon. Used to be used in jousting tournaments or as a side-arm. The blade was long and slim, resembling the weapon used to stab the victims, and it could be twelve inches long. It was made of steel. The blade was normally diamond shaped. Both edges could be sharpened.'

'A perfect killing tool', Castle said. 'And the building that houses The Last Brotherhood is called Rondelo.'

'They were designed for stabbing. They were used to puncture chain mail.'

'Very effective', Stone said.

'There are also four-edged Rondel daggers, so that the blade looks like a crucifix.'

Castle and Stone stared up at him.

'The victim also had other wound marks', Castle said.

'Yes. But they all had puncture wounds. The early victims were killed with one weapon. The later ones he mutilated were wounded first then tortured. He used the same weapon with all of them, but brought in a second for the later victims. I believe he's been using a Rondel dagger throughout. Many of the cuts themselves are cruciform.' He passed them some shots. 'These have been blown up. See the tiny crosses in the skin?'

They ran like needlework through the maimed flesh.

'That's the shape we've spoken about', Castle said.

'It's like we were picking upon it at a subliminal level, but the crosses were too small, buried in those furrows he cut into his victims', Stone said.

'How easy would it be to get one of these?', Castle said to Nash.

'He could have acquired it years ago. It may have been passed down or bought in an antiques shop. But I'd say they're rare. He could have had one made specially.'

'Medieval?', Castle said.

'That's right.'

'I say we interview Black again.'

'There's something else', Nash said. 'Rondel daggers became a knight's weapon, and were used as his last line of defense.'

'You think that's influencing the killer now?'

'Psychologically he may feel what he is doing is his last line of defense.'

'A last resort against annihilation by his psychosis', Castle said.

80

Castle was trying out his smoothest interviewer's voice.

'We have good information that you are the prostitute killer, Laurence', he said.

Unused to playing the good cop, he could feel the years of failure burning inside him like acid and he wanted to reach across, grab Steele and punch him, but restraint got the better of him. He wasn't going to pass up the opportunity of redeeming himself as a police officer, no matter how late and intangible that redemption may be.

'If you have evidence, then use it', Steele said with slow mockery in his eyes.

Stone leant across the vacant space that occupied the middle distance between them.

'Do you know what the sentence for abducting, torturing and attempting to murder a woman is?', she said.

Castle sat back and stared at the suspect.

'Do I have to say any more?', Steele said, looking at Nap.

'No.'

He resumed his silence, his face like an eldritch shadow in a lake.

Castle felt the flicker of the shape he sought, a glimpse of barely defined form as if a veil had risen and the hidden being of twenty-eight years had been laid plain.

Outside Stone said 'It's like he's playing for time.'

'Which reinforces the accomplice theory.'

'Yeah, but who? I don't think he was acting with someone else.'

'Tom said he could be following someone's orders.'

'We need something to take into the next interview.'

'I'll tell Mike to look into his background.'

That afternoon, Nash's team stopped their research into Walsh and trawled through everything they could get on Laurence Steele.

81

Nash found it: a history that led right to the killer in their cell.

He took it through to Castle and Stone.

'I've got what you're looking for, Frank. I went back through everything on Steele. Makes interesting reading.'

'What have you got?'

'He worked as a deer culler in Richmond Park. The reason he stopped was he had a nervous breakdown. His manager said he was getting out of control, killing deer he was not assigned to and acting very strangely.'

'Strange how?'

'He would talk about the deer as Henry the Eighth's possessions.'

'Any mention of Anne Boleyn?'

'Yeah. Wait till you hear the rest. He suffered from a history of schizophrenia as a teenager and was treated privately for it in America, that's why there's no record of it here.'

Castle punched the table.

'Why has no one picked up on this before?'

'When we interviewed him, Frank, he had an alibi. With both cases-', Stone said.

'Yeah, I know. Meanwhile the paps are feasting on us.'

'He was extremely disturbed and given to religious mania. The psychiatrist who treated him in the States noted a historical obsession.'

'Let me guess.'

Nash nodded.

'Anne Boleyn. In his therapy sessions he kept going on about Anne and how she didn't belong to the King and she betrayed him.'

'This all fits with Tom's profile', Stone said.

'The therapist got some background out of his sessions when

Steele was more lucid. He'd been seeing a prostitute when he was a teenager, called Anne. He'd become obsessed by her and been thrown out and beaten up by her pimp. The pimp's name was Henry.'

'You're kidding?', Castle said.

'It's like a map. His psyche overlaid on the killings. You can imagine when he starts reading Wyatt it all fits, makes sense of his pain, keeps his obsession going.'

'We interviewed this guy months ago and he's been out there doing this all along', Castle said, kicking a box of papers across the room. 'If the press find out…'

'He was a good shot', Nash said. 'The deer became symbolic to him. The prostitutes represent Anne and are deer to him. Killing them is a means of taking back his power.'

'We've got him', Stone said.

'One more thing. Tom said he thought he was working with someone else. The therapist who saw Steele in America believed that the root of his breakdown was abandonment by his father, who ran off with another woman. Steele never knew his father, but the therapist treating him believed he had a predisposition to falling under the sway of father figures, which is why the therapy worked, since he was a very masculine paternal type of figure who had success with certain mentally ill people.'

'So who's the accomplice?', Castle said.

'I suggest we check out The Order of the Righteous, since that was the material you found at his flat.'

As Castle and Stone stormed down the corridor to the interview room, he turned to her.

'It's gotta be Black.'

82

'Did you write these lines?', Castle said, passing Steele the couplets they'd found at his flat.

He stared down at them.

'Since when is writing illegal?'

'It's not.'

'What do they mean?', Stone said.

'What do you want them to mean?'

'You're obsessed by Anne Boleyn, aren't you?'

'In the middle ages people led lives of quiet devotion to God. To the modern mind that would seem obsessive.'

'Tell us about your schizophrenia', Castle said.

Nap cast a sideways glance at him.

'You can't catch this guy.'

'We've caught you. You were treated for schizophrenia in America, weren't you? The notes we have say you were obsessed by Anne Boleyn. The killer has been abducting prostitutes, torturing them, killing them, placing them in and around Richmond Park, often near the hunting ground of Henry the Eighth. We think you're influenced by Thomas Wyatt's poetry. The lines you've written make reference to Sawyer's Hill.'

'I used to work there.'

'Tell us about Anne', Stone said. 'She betrayed you, didn't she?'

'You don't know what you're talking about.'

'She was a prostitute. She slept with anyone who would pay her.'

'You don't understand!'

'Understand what?'

'You arrest me for writing poetry?'

'Have you got something wrong with you? Can you make love to a real woman?'

'What do you call a real woman?'

'Can you only feel something for women other men pay to sleep with, and you want to own? That is at the core of your mental illness.'

'You're not a real woman. You're nothing.'

Castle stepped in.

'You're swimming in it. We've got you on one crime and it's only a matter of time before forensics link you to the others, start by talking and you'll be doing yourself a favour.'

'Doing you a favour.'

'Tell us about Anne. Henry took her away didn't he? Henry had her all for himself and you couldn't get to her. Did that happen to you in your life before or only once? Your father ran off and you never knew him, did you, is that why you kill prostitutes?'

There was a pause. Then something happened that reminded Stone of the time she saw a cobra strike at the zoo as a little girl.

Steele launched himself across the table at Castle. Before he knew it he had two hands gripping his throat in a death clinch and he was choking.

Stone and two PC's had to pull him away.

They cuffed him and took him back to his cell.

That evening Don paid a visit to Stone.

As he walked through the door, her relief at seeing him was overshadowed by quick defensive anger that she brought under control.

'Do you want to go out Jacki?'

'I can cook us something here.'

And she did. And they talked.

By the end of the night she felt she'd expressed some of what she'd been going through and heard what things had been like for him these last years, with the job taking over.

For a brief moment that made it all the more painful, she experienced what it used to be like, the two of them. Then the last months intervened.

As he left, she knew the job was still running her life.

83

The recruits flooded Parliament Square.

Waving banners that read 'Corrupt governments must fall', they stopped the traffic and made it impossible for the police to see.

Merging as a mob they got in the way and generally disturbed the order of things. They harried and harassed passing tourists and made sure their message was seen by everyone passing as well as the television cameras which caught the disturbance.

Imogen and Sheila walked side by side like two lost penitents, their natural uncertainty now honed into an anxious aggression as they waved their message in the air.

Malcolm pushed and shoved the bodies that got in his way, startled visitors to London toting cameras and guide books.

Rodrigo separated himself from them, moving down the flanks with force and purpose. He broke up crowds, divided families, jostled businessmen, and placed his banner directly in the faces of passing MP's who were unable to see his, shielded as it was by his message.

Wilkes was not among them. At Rondelo he left by the back and passed through the grounds.

No one saw him leave.

Black was sequestered in his library and the place was otherwise deserted.

He walked slowly and with a cautious air, carrying something heavy. At the end of the drive, he got into a taxi which took him to the outskirts of a neighbouring village, where he caught a train.

When he returned that evening he was empty-handed and quick of step.

He went straight to his chambers, passing down the darkened corridors like a shadow that knew every brick and corner of the building.

Blade knows

Blade's understanding is as relentless as the rain that drives against this window where I see their lies concealed like goods they have purchased for a price of Sin

They walk with airs of self-importance, their days of Fame bought by the corruption they spread like disease

Yet when all is told they are numberless and amount to nothing

Within the teachings that now come true they are as naught and will be taken to the place where they will be put upon the Cross to test their true mettle

For they have none and are but as air that blows through an empty building, making strange noises but resonating only to the structure it invades

They are the Filth that now will be reduced

A parasite on humanity

A walker of diseased actions which are promoted by the servants of Law, these men and women in blue who believe they are upholders of some moral truth

They will know themselves when they are cut and ribboned to a hilt of time

Their lies shuffle away like a pack of cards at a game they no longer know how to play

The leaders are discovered in the House of Filth

They are brought to the halter like cattle and slaughtered

84

Mover and Tweed were leaving Parliament when they got caught up in the deluge of bodies pushing and shoving. A sense of outrage and personal affront passed through them as they tried to navigate the mob.

A half-feral face passed before them in the seething tide of chaos and they turned to one another as points of orientation. A couple of the messages born aloft caught their attention and they sneered. Both saw mounting profit margins in the gullibility of these clones, religion had a massive inbuilt client base they could tax.

They sell themselves like the street walkers
These are the days of the Scouring

'Tell us about your accomplice', Castle said.

He could see Steele had lost some of his assurance, he knew the look of the criminal who was trapped and looking to trade with them.

'What accomplice?'

'We know you've been working with someone else, are you really going to protect them? They'll let you rot and go away for this all by yourself.'

He paused, watching Steele.

'These women are scum', he said. 'They are the spreaders of disease. I know you police officers go to them and they let you fuck them for free. Why don't you solve this yourself if you're so sure you've got the right man?'

'We have got the right man', Stone said. 'So, who is he, Laurence?'

He looked away, avoiding them, dodging their questions, but

they knew he wouldn't last much longer.

Meanwhile Nash's team were putting in the hours.

They knew their research had cornered Steele and they tasted success. They wanted to nail the other guy.

Nash ran a tight ship and they respected him.

While some of them pursued the information surrounding Steele, others returned to Samuel Walsh. They'd dredged data on him and those he worked for looking for clues, anything that might link him to the killer, however indirectly, and come up with nothing.

They now looked again at his adopted children.

Castle and Stone had already interviewed Paul Metcalfe and come away with nothing, so the team knew they had to be careful.

But as they looked again, one name stuck out: Alan Maple.

He'd been adopted by Samuel Walsh shortly before his arrest for the Woodland Killings. He was a sensitive boy with a stutter and would have been in his foster family during the time of Walsh's crisis, so the event could have affected him.

The problem was, there was no history of crime or mental illness they could find on Maple. He was the last to be adopted, and seemed just like another of the children Walsh had taken into his home and taken care of. He'd been placed with another family shortly after Walsh's suicide and nothing had been heard of him since.

Where he was now was another matter.

Nash looked at the information and decided to follow it.

They are walking towards Him
The soft melodies he plays

85

Spinner was onto something. His theory was turning fast into a tangible knowledge of this killer, who he was, how he would act. The fact that his religious theories had been vindicated so far, and his profile on the prostitute killer was now being backed up by the character of Steele, gave him confidence and he developed his profile of the Woodlands Killer as Castle and Stone listened.

'There's a split here', he said. 'He's religiously motivated but he's dissociated.'

'Meaning what?', Castle said.

'He's able to separate himself from the fact that he's committing a crime and see it as something else. He feels he's performing the will of God as he sees him, or has been taught to interpret him.'

'Serial killers don't tend to see what they're doing as a crime.'

'This guy actually sees it as a religious act. His beliefs are so unusual that to him this is part of his religion, hence he can separate himself from these acts and carry on as normal.'

'Without drawing attention to himself.'

'Yes.'

'So we're back to the idea of a mentor.'

'More than that.'

'An older guy who controls him in some way?', Stone said.

'This is more than a mentor relationship.'

'What then?'

'I don't know Jacki, but the pattern of the killings is being matched and informed by something else, some belief structure that if it is being fed to him by another figure is intensifying and changing his character.'

'You mean he's getting more violent?', Castle said.

'I mean he's being transformed from a killer to an incredibly dangerous person who is worse than just a killer, someone with an implacable belief in the rightness of what they're doing and an ability to disguise it.'

'Serial killers have always baffled the police, that's why they go down in history because the regular guy doesn't get how they do these things. I know you specialise in the dark corners of the human psyche, but can't you just cut to the chase, Tom?', Castle said.

'This is a partnership.'

'Are you saying someone is telling him to commit these murders? Someone with power over him.'

'The power could be two way.'

'If he's calling the shots, then there's no one leading him.'

'It doesn't work that way. In a master servant relationship the master depends on the servant. He's modelling himself on someone, we've got the copy cat element, but the relationship he shares with this other figure is something organic that is developing as we speak and follows a system of beliefs we can only begin to guess at.'

'Yeah well, I say we interview Black.'

'And we still need to know who if anyone is behind Steele', Stone said.

The Houses of Corruption are Fallen
The Anti-Priests are overthrown

86

It was Black who opened the door and he stood looking down at them with such purity of contempt it unnerved them.

'The two jokes have returned for more humiliation, I see. Detectives, although I feel that is an insult to the word, what do you want this time? Another crime you can't solve?'

Castle ignored the taunt and started reading him his rights. He put the cuffs on tight and took him to the car.

He said nothing all the way to the station, leaving them in a resonant silence, a watchful presence in the car.

In the same silence that seemed to be carried with him from Rondelo, they took him to an interview room where Castle switched on the recorder.

Black sat absorbing them, a smile flickering at the edge of his lips.

'How's the marriage, Inspector Stone?', he said. 'Does your husband, what is his name, Don, like being with a woman made of rock or prefer something a little softer and more yielding to his need for male affirmation , but then you never could do that could you, affirm a man?'

She refused to consider how he'd found out Don's name.

'Tell us about your Brotherhood', she said.

'What, as opposed to sisterhood? Something you are altogether outside of, moving as you do in this world of men, what are you trying to do? Disguise the smell of your own testosterone by surrounding yourself with men? Or is it more to do with your own insecurity about yourself as a female? Women like you lack something, something other women feel confident enough to give. Too afraid he'd see how masculine you are deep down, just like your partner? My Brotherhood. What do you want to know? Are you religious or just a little lost, a crippled policewoman with no one to love her, stuck with an alcoholic failure who is known as the man who couldn't solve the Woodland Killings? In some quarters, Chief Inspector Castle, you are a joke, someone who is seen as a killer's accomplice.'

Stone resisted the bait.

'Your beliefs are strange, aren't they?'

'Define strange.'

'You're secretive. You believe in the medieval vision of the world.'

Black sat back with no trace of emotion or stress.

'Like all servants, which you are, you have no real intelligence. Strange is also a police force which thinks there is nothing wrong with shooting an innocent tourist who looks nothing like a wanted bomber then covering it up with lies and fabricating evidence, clubbing together and nicking the odd motorist while criminals run free because they're far too smart for the likes of you.'

'The killer's beliefs bear a strong resemblance to the teachings of your Brotherhood', Castle said.

'You could make any connections you care to with your ability to warp the truth and lie.'

'The name Lodowick Muggleton ring any bells?'

'Yes, I know of him. Unlike you, Chief Inspector Castle, I have a wide knowledge of all sorts of things. I know the police think it's strange when someone knows something they don't, but you are so incredibly uninformed that if it weren't a crime, it would be laughable. Do you really think there is any significance in my knowing the name of Muggleton?'

At that moment his lawyer arrived, a city hot shot called Ian Baker who Castle knew all too well.

He slammed a list of dates on the table proving Black's whereabouts at all the times of the murders and said 'I demand you release my client now or I'll slap a suit on you that'll raise your hackles and have the press eating you both for breakfast.'

A few moments later Black was standing in the corridor.

'Soon you will see how useless and inept you really are', he said to them and left.

Mover and Tweed were giving a press interview.

'The government is fully aware of the situation', Mover said.

'That the church as it stands need change?', one journalist at the front, handpicked by them, said.

'Let my colleague answer that.'

'The church is so non-PC, it's become a danger to international relations, to women's rights, to trade, to everything this country needs for the era we are entering', Tweed said.

'And how would you define that era?', a journalist at the back said.

'It is the age of free enterprise, of true liberty, when women can enjoy equality in the workplace and this country can take advantage of the enormous benefits that we can offer. If we still follow some medieval system of beliefs that chains us to a past where we were seen as the colonisers and the subjugators of those we need, of those who can give us the workforce that makes this nation excel, then we are starting from a position that will inevitably bring failure. This is the end of religion as we know it. I am not saying there is no place for it, but it has to change and the government is about to introduce radical reforms that will see that occur. And the people who have been repressed, those who have been brought to heel all these years will be thankful for it.'

Before he was given any further questions, he left with Mover and they got into a chauffeur driven car at the back of the studios.

'That went pretty well', Mover said, turning to him as the car sped away.

'When it hits the papers we'll be on our way to a massive profit.'

Castle and Stone were trying to figure out who Steele's accomplice was when Spinner knocked.

'I've figured out part of the Woodland Killer's warped belief system.'

'Let's have it', Castle said.

'There is an esoteric school of Christian thought that teaches of the Dual Christ. He sees Christ as bearing both good and evil and acting sometimes from his shadow while committing great violence on a fallen world. He is inspired by this and when he kills he believes he is the Dual Christ.'

'How did you reach this Tom?', Castle said.

'It's all there in the beliefs as he's acted them out. If Christ is a killer, then the killer is Christ. This is one hell of a psychosis and makes him a predator on a massive scale since he's not in conflict with what he's doing. Usually when a serial killer is out there, he has low points. This guy doesn't. Christ gives benediction to his acts. In his mind he's purging the world of evil.'

'All the strange religious beliefs and checking through the weird Brotherhoods has got us nowhere so far.'

'I'm onto something.'

87

The era of the Corrupt is ended
The New Jerusalem is being built from the bricks and stones of
Blade's utterances
They will be hacked
Police fall away like corrupt flesh
They have served the False Law and lined their pockets with the
proceeds
Now they are executed
This is the War against Corruption
This is the New Jerusalem

Castle and Stone could see Steele was changing.

The longer he was held the more symptoms of his illness he was starting to show.

There was an edginess to him that hadn't been there when he was arrested and they started to work on it.

'Who's your accomplice?', Castle said.

'I work alone.'

'We know there's someone else', Stone said.

'I fulfil the ways of God.'

'By killing women?' Castle leaned towards him. 'Make it easier on yourself, tell us who he is. With your history of schizophrenia, the court will take another view. Someone has been leading you.'

'Do you really think with all the DNA at our disposal we don't know there's someone else you've been working with, Laurence?', Stone said. 'He's been using your obsession with history and Anne Boleyn. You're here and he's not.'

'You'll never catch him.'

'Who?', Castle said.

But he retreated into silence and began rocking on his chair.
He refused to speak again that afternoon.
'He admitted there's someone else', Stone said afterwards.
'Yes. Who?'

Tweed and Mover were enjoying the press coverage of their interview.

They had enough journalists on their payroll to ensure the stories got out just how they wanted them pitched and they sat with every paper in the country spread out on their desks, admiring themselves in the mirror they offered to their sense of success and prestige.

'Ve-ry good', Tweed said to himself, puffing clouds of blue smoke everywhere and summoning his secretary who stood panting at the door.

'Fetch me a scotch', he said without looking up.

He sank it in one and picked the phone up, punching in Mover's number.

'See them?... Yes... Both of us... You get what you pay for.'

Wilkes left the outbuilding at the back of Rondelo, carrying two large cases.

He lugged them with the air of someone struggling with a weight.

He took them to a rear wing where he placed them within a cupboard.

No one ever went to this part of the building except him.

88

The Woodlands killer was stepping out of the fog and starting to materialise in Tom Spinner's brain.

He knew this stage: the pieces of the jigsaw clicking into place like coins in a slot machine. He just couldn't find the right button.

His success with Steele's case gave him a new lease of confidence, while Castle's plummeted.

The Sun that morning ran the headline 'Cock up cop cracking up again?', with a picture of him stumbling out of the Crooked Key next to it. The pressure was beginning to get to him.

He snapped at Tom Spinner when he came in that day.

'Tom, don't give me more theories without any meat.'

'Frank, I read the tabloids too', Spinner said, calmly placing his papers down on the nearest desk. 'And the best advice I can give you is to ignore them.'

'They'll go away once we've caught him', Castle said.

'Which, so long as this guy thinks he's God, may be hard to do', Stone said.

'As I said before, his ideas about politics are far from normal and he may start killing figures you and I wouldn't see as political', Spinner said.

'Which makes our job harder', Stone said.

'Not unless we predict where he's going, Jacki.'

'And how do we do that Tom?'

'If he strays away from killing ministers, then there's a chance he'll hit the same type twice. Someone he sees as supporting a corrupt political system, say a journalist. He kills one, he may well kill two.'

'So we let another person die and get more bad press', Castle said.

'We could put extra protection on those fitting the profile of his victims and catch him at the next killing where he may be more visible', Stone said.

'Yes', Spinner said.

Castle folded his arms.

'We tried protection earlier and it got us nowhere. I feel this guy's dragging us out to waters we don't know and don't understand.'

'That's because his psychosis is mutating as the murders are ongoing. Which is why I'm sure there's someone else involved here.'

'We've got two killers, both with accomplices', Castle said.

'Not in the traditional sense of the word. They have people behind them who influence them or who they feel are encouraging them to do this, however twisted their interpretation of the words of these other men may be.'

'Religion, psychosis, a homicidal mind and someone behind them', Castle said. 'They've got to be part of some order.'

'It's possible, but it may be two people acting on their own.'

'The media line didn't work', Stone said. 'We ran stories in the papers and the guy's still killing.'

'Maybe he doesn't read the papers', Spinner said. 'He could be so out of touch with the modern world that he's rejected anything to do with it. Which makes him all the harder to catch. If you look at the wording of the messages he leaves, it's Biblical. They refer to an old world view and sense of morality that is far removed from the twenty-first century. He may not use the internet, not own any credit cards, not watch TV, not be aware of or interested in what is going on around him unless it affects his religious outlook and that could be fed to him by someone else.'

'Great', Castle said, 'we've got a guy from another era killing in our midst.'

'You need to tighten up security at Parliament', Spinner said.

'We've done it.'

'Do it more. He could go for a kill on their home turf. Ensure all officers on the beat are aware of what to look for.'

'And in the meantime let him kill again?', Castle said.

'I can draw up a list of possible targets outside the purely political and you can put out security on them.'

'And if this guy proves impossible to read?'

'You already have experience of that, Frank. You've interviewed Black and got nothing out of him.'

'And he got away with it, or he didn't do it.'

'The point is you can't read him, so don't try to. Let's see if we can catch him.'

At Rondelo Black stood in the Round Room before the recruits.

'Man is in conflict with his self and God within him. Man has the seed of Corruption deep within his Flesh. And do you know Brothers how to fight that seed, how to overcome it and do God's will that ye may become nearer to God?'

He looked at them, their eyes on him, waiting for him to continue speaking.

'You make sure you slay the Corrupt, you enter the War. I do not say unto ye go about and kill, for that is a sin and a crime.'

He paused, making sure this message got through.

'I do not say unto ye commit any crimes.'

He looked at each in turn.

'But the War must be fought at all levels of spiritual conduct and that is what we are teaching you here.'

Later that day the recruits travelled to Parliament Square with more banners.

'The government is criminal' was picked up by the TV cameras as they heckled and harassed every passing minister.

They managed to block the traffic and made several ministers late for important meetings.

89

When they next interviewed Steele, he was very different to the man they'd pulled in.

He was unravelling before their eyes and they knew where to press for the information they wanted.

'Laurence', Stone said. 'We know you've killed six prostitutes. What we don't know is why.'

'They spread Corruption.'

'Men pay for their services, but that is not a reason to kill them.'

'It is known that this will befall them.'

She looked at Castle.

'Known?'

'They are part of the disease of the Earth. They must be removed.'

'Who is he?', Castle said.

'The King hunted and his deer fled before him.'

'Tell us about Anne', Stone said.

'She was not his.'

'No, she was yours.'

'Yes. That is why they must be killed.'

'Who?'

'The women of the streets.'

'Why?'

'Because they are responsible. All who own women are responsible for Anne and what happened.'

They could see him skating on the edges of his insanity.

'Are you killing the King's deer?'

'Yes. But they do not belong to him.'

'Is that what he told you, Laurence?'

'He told me they must be slaughtered.'

'Like deer?'

'Like deer.'

'Who is he?'

But he was far away again and they left him.

'I feel we're almost there', she said to Castle outside.

'He's talking from his psychosis and it's only a matter of time before he mentions him.'

Nash's team was working hard at finding out what happened to Alan Maple.

A likeable boy who drew little attention to himself while at the Walsh home, he'd been placed soon after Walsh's suicide with another family who saw him through schooling.

He showed no character problems and left home at eighteen to start a job in the North of England.

The last that was known of him he was working at a metal factory.

Wilkes left Rondelo in the middle of the night.

He carried a small bag and walked swiftly and silently.

He left by the front drive, making no noise.

He disappeared into the streets of London unnoticed, leaving again before daylight.

Black didn't hear him return.

He went straight to his chambers before any lights were lit.

90

The next day Steele was ragged at the edges.

He stared at Castle and Stone without recognition when they walked into the interview room and started talking.

'He was the man who hunted deer for their flesh. They are the seductresses. Did you know when a deer looks at you it thinks of sex? Like the whores, like those women paid for by the businessmen, they are the sex mongers of our era. But the King was found out and it was written down by Wyatt. Wyatt understood the true nature of these things. You two serve the state and are unaware of the essential depravity of these women you seek to protect. But you can't protect them, they are using you and I have seen you Castle fucking them, hot and larey, your arse pumping the air like a figurine joke of you, you curse and enter their insides, wetting the bed while Stone masturbates at home with her dildo, you do own a dildo Stone, you're vagina hard as a sack you filthy slag, you slattern.'

Castle and Stone exchanged glances.

'Who's been working with you?', Castle said.

'You can't stop him.'

'You have a problem, don't you, Laurence?', Stone said.

Steele started rocking.

'Why are you protecting him?', Castle said.

'You do not know the meaning of the hunt.'

'Who's the other hunter?', Stone said.

'He's from the other era.'

'Which era?'

'The other, walks in rounds.'

'Who is he?'

He wouldn't speak again.

Outside Castle said 'pretty soon we're going to have to get a psychiatrist in and he'll get him sectioned.'

'How do we interview him then?'

'Legally it won't count for anything.'

'Does it now?'

'Legally, maybe. But I think he may just give up the other guy.'

Tweed was pushing through his proposals with the grease of huge financial backing and engineered press coverage.

He knew he would shortly be in a position to extract money from churches, and the ministers he needed were complying with his requests.

He put a call through to Mover and told him the good news.

'It's going through with no hitches.'

91

At Rondelo, Black admitted a visitor.

There was evident respect in the way he opened the door to him and led him through to his study.

Wilkes was out and the building was otherwise deserted.

The visitor was young in the sense that he had an air of youth about him, although he might have been anywhere between twenty-eight and forty-six. There was something unworldly and untouched about him, yet at the same time a weight of experience that made his years hard to read. The worries and concerns that stamp themselves on the faces of many men had eluded him whether by accident or design and he stood apart.

Handsome in an anonymous way, clean shaven and athletic of build he carried himself with a distinguished air as if he might be royalty.

His eyes were illumined with a glow.

His voice was low and measured.

They sat down and he said 'The works are happening in the way we discussed they would, Karl.'

'Yes. I follow your methods and see much of my teachings there.'

'I see the ways of the world are not changing.'

'That will take time.'

They remained sepulchered in Black's library for some hours and when the young man left, Black shook him warmly by the hand.

He watched him disappear along the drive, vanishing as if he did not exist.

Black stood for a few moments staring up at the sky.

Huge clouds were looming in the distance while at the front, casting its light across the drive and beyond, the sun shone in all its brilliance, a late spring day.

Rondelo itself backed against this sky like an artefact from another era.

Nash's team were getting a lot on Alan Maple.

Initial searches yielded little, until someone traced him from his first job to employment with a company in the South of England which specialised in making replica swords of old military models.

Scimitar and Scythe shut down a few years ago, but Maple had worked for them for ten years.

After that he'd disappeared from the radar.

The team continued to hunt him.

Meanwhile the press had started to circle the Met again.

The latest headline in The Sun stuck in Castle like rusting barbed wire.

'Is Chief Inspector Frank Castle protecting the Woodlands Killer?'

He glanced at the article.

'The unsolved case all those years ago raised many unanswered questions. And now a copycat killer is getting away with it all again. Or is it a copycat? Perhaps the police are more tainted with crime than we know. Perhaps Castle knows something he would rather we didn't find out.

One thing's for sure: Castle isn't telling us the whole truth.'

He glanced at the journalist's name: Stuart Scott.

92

Wilkes knocked on the door of Black's library and entered.

'Yes, Jonas?'

'The recruits have been given their latest instructions and know what to do. I have told them to continue the disruption of ministers.'

'Good.

'They understand the teachings.'

'You have done a good job.'

Wilkes left, closing the door behind him and went to his chambers.

There he packed up the few possessions he owned and left the building by the rear, passing through the orchard and the outbuilding which led him into the grounds beyond.

Mover and Tweed were unaware of the car which patrolled their roads.

It cruised past them while they journeyed to and from meetings too busy to notice anything except their own interests, and slowed outside their houses at night when they sat inside sipping whisky or puffing cigar smoke at their wives.

They moved in a bubble of their own self-seeking.

The man they had arrested was now only present in moments.

Steele made less and less sense and Castle knew he didn't have much time to find out who his accomplice was.

He sat looking at nothing and talking sporadically as they re-interviewed him.

'The man who was working with you is walking free', Castle said.

'The deer roam free and the King hunts them. The wild beasts copulate and run riot while the armies of the law wait for warrants to seize the guilty.'

'Laurence, tell us who he is', Stone said.

He looked at her.

'He is the husband of Anne Boleyn.'

'Who told you to kill the women?', Castle said.

'The Huntsman, of course.'

'And who is The Huntsman?'

'Don't you know?'

'You said he is from another era. Which era?'

'The middle ages.'

'Where is he?'

'At The Hunt.'

'Why were all the women placed in Richmond Park?'

'King's orders.'

'Which King?'

'Jonas the First.'

Castle and Stone looked at each other.

They left the room.

'Jonas Wilkes', Castle said. 'I knew there was a link to Black somewhere in all this.'

'He might not know. Wilkes could be acting independently.'

'That I don't believe.'

'Looks like we've got our other man.'

'We go to Rondelo and we arrest him.'

But when they got there Black informed them that he had gone. They searched the place and knew he was telling the truth.

'Where is he?', Castle said.

'I thought this was your case Detective, still need my help?'

'Are you refusing to cooperate?'

'I don't know where he is. If you arrest me again my lawyer will start to destroy your life.'

'We'll keep a car outside alerted to arrest him if he turns up. If you see him and fail to let us know you will be breaking the law.'

'Oh dear me.'

Nash managed to find out Alan Maple's movements since leaving Scimitar and Scythe.

A spate of jobs had led him to Liverpool, where he worked first for a shipping factory then a surveillance company. A few years ago he'd disappeared.

Nash couldn't find out any more and decided to pay a visit to his last known address.

Wilkes entered the small hotel and passing through the foyer walked up the stairs to his room.

There was no one in attendance and he went unseen.

Dressed more as a citizen of the twenty-first century, he was a figure who could disappear into a crowd. There were no distinguishing features at all about him and he moved quickly without drawing attention to himself, since he lacked the air of someone who was rushing.

He sat on the bed and looked through some papers.

Then he picked up the phone.

'Rodrigo? Alert the others. Major disruption to the ministers', he said, and hung up.

He removed some objects from a bag.

These he packed into some plastic sacks and placed them inside his coat.

He left and walked into the centre of London, where he deposited the bags in a public waste bin.

Returning by the back roads, he entered the hotel unseen again and made his room.

He switched on the news.

Castle and Stone knew it was going to be hard finding Wilkes.

They also knew Black would give them no help.

Castle sat in the Crooked Key wondering which of the punters was a journalist.

'Frank?', Stone said, sitting opposite him, noticing his wandering eyes.

'One of these bastards could be snapping me on their mobile and I wouldn't even know it.'

'Why would they?'

'The paparazzi are after me.'

'Police paranoia.'

'Easy for you to say, but this guy's run a noose round my life and every so often he tugs at it and laughs when I start to choke.'

'There are no paparazzi in here.'

'What if we don't solve this case?'

'Come on, that's not Frank Castle talking is it?', she said, staring over her shoulder and seeing Don, seeing her life fall away, the paperwork mount and Black at Rondelo.

Two paparazzi waited outside for a snap of Frank lurching away. They wanted to catch him driving.

Mover and Tweed sat in their club sipping whisky.

Clouds of smoke hung between them as if a silent barrier.

'I've found a way of making a bigger profit on our latest venture', Tweed said.

Mover sat forward, dragging intently on his cigar, the red end glowing like an ember.

'Oh yes?'

'We add a spatial tax on church buildings. The bigger they are the more they pay.'

'Ex-cellent', Mover said, sitting back with an air of relaxation.

He tapped his ash on the carpet.

In his cell, Steele rocked back and forth, mumbling incoherently.

When his lunch was brought he threw it across the room.

It was obvious he needed a psychiatrist and Castle knew he couldn't delay the decision much longer. While it would be useful to interview him once more if they caught Wilkes, he might not be making any sense by the time they did.

The next morning, led by Rodrigo, the recruits arrived in Parliament Square bearing a new weapon.

As the crowds surged and the ministers shuffled about importantly, they loosed hawks from various strategic points. They circled and swooped, tearing and devouring pigeons and attacking certain ministers who had been targeted by the well-aimed throwing of lumps of meat which the hawks descended on regardless, in one instance scratching the eyes of a minister so badly he needed hospital treatment. He received a phone call while waiting in casualty, wondering why the queues were so long, forgetting his own policies as health minister a few years ago, which were largely responsible for the situation.

'Hello?'

'It's Sinclair Mover.'

'How can I help?'

'I've sent you an e-mail and want a reply.'

'I'm in-.'

'I don't care what meeting you're in. Do it.'

The line went dead and the minister stared at the queue.

He'd have to approve it and set about doing so via his secretary.

93

He stood in Black's library waiting for him.

When the door opened and Black saw him there he betrayed no surprise, as if he were a native inhabitant of Rondelo.

'Your watching days are almost over', Black said.

'They are easy yield to time. They seek only their own ways and so see not when they are watched, but finding the animals thus and trapping them so has proved an easy snare.'

Their voices were like echoes in a vault.

'They do not know about you.'

'No. Nor ever will, for I am absent from their manner of being.'

For a moment they watched one another, with knowledge that almost leant redundancy to words.

'These Filth are only able to exist within their tight and narrow sphere and when caught outside that, as you have seen, they fall like stray beasts.'

'Our traps are hardy and snare them every time.'

As one moved so did the other, as his shadow.

They talked while outside a summer sun set on the grounds.

Soon darkness fell and he left the building.

The next day Steele entered a comatose state.

Peters, the on-duty sergeant called Castle.

'He hasn't moved from the same position for hours.'

'I'll come and have a look at him.'

When he got to the cell Steele didn't acknowledge his presence.

He left him and returned a few hours later. No movement.

Beside him the cold tray of food.

As Castle was about to leave, he caught a flicker. The merest shade of movement.

'Laurence, do you know who I am?'

He turned his eyes on him, two dead black centres in a face of utter calm.

'You are the King's executioner.'

Castle turned to shut the door and Steele launched himself at him.

He managed to crack his head against the frame before Peters pulled him off.

He and Castle cuffed him and locked him in.

Steele could be heard ranting inside.

'The King's Whore procured the downfall of the Kingdom, blood lusters pump semen into this world, serving the lies and the corrupt.'

Castle retreated down the corridor hearing the noise fade.

He looked at his head in the bathroom mirror.

A two inch gash was leaking blood and he tended it, washing beneath the fold of skin.

Peters brought him the first aid kit.

'Nasty cut', he said. 'What are we going to do about him?'

'He's gone. I'll call the psychiatrist.'

Peters nodded.

Castle covered the wound with a plaster and returned to his office.

Later that day the police psychiatrist called two colleagues. They interviewed Steele and pronounced him mentally unfit for further interview. He was sectioned under the mental health act.

'He's on a section two', Castle said to Stone. 'They'll extend it, and in the meantime we haven't got Wilkes. Not a sighting, not a clue as to his whereabouts.'

Nash continued to hunt Alan Maple.

He discovered his last address in Liverpool, then had difficulty tracing him to London.

He dug and eventually came up with a South London address where it appeared he had boarded for a few months before finally vanishing from the radar a few years ago.

He decided to go to the address and see what he could find out.

Meanwhile the police presence was stepped up in Parliament Square.

When Castle heard about the hawks, he said 'Got to be something to do with Wilkes. I want names and addresses of all those caught on CCTV doing this.'

The officers who'd been patrolling Soho were moved across and waited for the next development, but there wasn't one.

Wilkes had other ideas.

When he emerged from his hotel he was unrecognisable.

Dressed like a rapper, he had dyed his hair and wore sunglasses.

He sauntered down the road, got on a tube, changed stations, did so again and ascertaining he was not being followed, eventually got off and walked until he came to a hotel, where he took out another room.

As the unit was stretched to breaking point, that afternoon a story broke in the evening news.

Castle had been snapped driving drunk.

He was shown stumbling out of the Crooked Fork and getting into his unmarked car.

The headline read:

'Crazy cop shows why he can't solve a case.'

Stone saw it first.

She knew Castle would catch wind of it pretty quickly and decided to break it to him herself.

When she did he hit the table, sending papers flying. A half-drunk coffee spilled upwards in the air.

'Fucking paparazzi! I told you they were after me!'

'Frank, drinking and driving?'

'It's this case.'

'Look, I understand, but from now on, I'll be doing the driving.'

The description given out for Wilkes brought in a few down and outs, guys who looked a little out of date mostly, since they'd got their clothes from dustbins.

The focus on a medieval look in police minds was both confusing to them, since no one matched it, and misleading, since they were really looking for a guy who looked like a white rapper.

Wilkes walked among them.

Talking to no one except occasionally his recruits, he harnessed the police to his own devices and used them as he pleased.

Steele was diagnosed as suffering from schizophrenia.

The doctors dug out his history and soon had him on a heavy dose of medication that gave him the shuffle and garbled speech so easily detectable in heavy duty mental patients. He was placed in high security for the criminally insane.

Castle and Stone knew it would be a waste of time visiting him at the hospital but made sure they were told of anyone who did.

He would visit Rondelo, walking in the grounds and talking to Black. He was like a paring from some antique wood, the grain and hue of which were reflected in their consort and communion.

He knew every room and aspect of the building, as if he had designed it himself and they would often converse of the history and its message to the modern world.

Black looked at him as some men gaze into mirrors.

'The Lovers of Flesh are found out in their Flesh.'

'Yes, they let the Cross enter them easily.'

'The Old Order has risen again and the Fallen world is crushed by the times. We are builders.'

'When I see them strut and talk in their cheap and modern language I cannot help but see how they have led themselves to this pass.'

'These breeders of disease, these politicians always have been the Whores of Lies and the very scum on Filth. They will lay with anyone who pays their price, yea they are worse than the common harlot who sometimes will turn a customer away, but these will bed down with anything, no matter what it is if there is a profit in it for them.'

'Yes, and their ways have found them out.'

Often he would stand at Black's library window looking out, like an ancient visitor come back to the place.

Its past and purpose were etched on his face like some secret sign.

'What's Wilkes's profile?', Castle said.

Spinner looked at him.

'As what?'

'An accomplice, an inciter to murder.'

'We don't know he is that.'

'Say he is.'

'OK. Say he is, then you're asking what motivates someone to encourage another to kill?'

'Why not do it himself?'

'The kind of person you're talking about wants power and he gets it feeling he can control another's movements. He'll find someone with mental health problems, usually, which we know Steele has, and influence his thinking, which is already damaged. He won't go out and kill himself because he is constrained by a fear of the law, of being caught, but he wants someone else to do it. This reinforces his sense of superiority.

He will feel superior and want to preserve that at all costs. So if someone else gets arrested, he remains beyond the law.'

'Would he turn to murder himself?'

'Unlikely.'

'Now that Steele's been caught?'

'Probably not. As I say this is a different character, but say he had plans and they have been interrupted by Steele's arrest then his behaviour is going to alter somehow.

He's not likely to have someone else lined up to do the killings so he may start to draw attention to himself.'

'So far he isn't.'

He and Black would talk about the teachings of the Last Brotherhood.

He knew its lore and there was nothing in the way of instruction in the manner of their conversations.

'The Legacy of the Crucifiers is seen by all now', Black said.

'Christ's shadow walks among us.'

'Their money and their famous faces as presented on the televisions and through the media cannot buy them refuge from the coming storm.'

'Those they pay to protect them are unable to stop this.'

'They always were.'

'They hunt for clues and find none.'

'They are the servants of Filth and can do nothing to stop us.'

Incensed by the latest attacks by the paps, Castle sat in the car park of The Sun and waited.

He'd got a good description of Stuart Scott, but wanted to set his eyes on him.

And he got it.

He walked right past him.

5' 10", skinny, face like a rat.

It was all Castle could do not to get out and deck him. He left finger marks in the steering wheel as he drove away.

94

As Steele sat incarcerated and drugged, mumbling of Thomas Wyatt and the soft flesh of fallow deer, Wilkes removed the long-handled dagger from his bag and ventured into the swarming London streets.

It was a warm summer's day, not yet at its zenith of heat, but full of the promise of reward that those mornings when the gentle rays of the sun remind those too busy to think that colours and long days are on their way.

He moved with resolve as if a man on a mission, dodging the passers-by, the typists and the businessmen harried by debt and fear for their futures. He was not part of this, a traveller from a different era, and he despised them all, seeing their flesh fall away and lance itself upon the spikes he carried deep within his heart.

The dagger was tucked firmly within his coat, warm for a day like this but unnoticed by those too busy to engage with their own lives, and still, it was morning and the heat had not yet reached the height it was to that day.

That day which Castle and Stone would remember for its heat and the change of direction their investigation suddenly took.

He moved swiftly, passing Parliament, not once turning his head to look at the building which even now was surrounded by tourists, flocking there like the pigeons that clucked and scurried about searching for scraps of food.

He walked down river and turned into a series of side streets, stopping outside a disused shop which he entered using a key.

He placed some papers on a table and began to read them.

Nash parked in the rundown street. PC Anne Thomson sat in the passenger seat. She was a hard-working policewoman who had impressed Nash with her attitude, working long hours on the case and presenting him with well collated information when he'd asked for it. But he could tell in his conversations with her that paperwork was not the reason she had joined the Met.

He knew that feeling all too well and could see the change in her now she was getting the chance to get involved with what most policemen and women felt was real detective work.

He cast a brief glance at her as she got out of the car. At 5 foot 4 she looked a pushover, but she worked out at the gym two hours every day and knew how to handle herself.

Still, he hoped they didn't see any trouble.

He looked around at Alan Maple's vanishing point.

The houses were uniformly shabby and looked like something some hand had crumpled and thrown there.

There was a feeling of depression and gloom that hung in the air like old cooking.

He found the door and knocked. Thomson stood behind him, watching, taking it in.

After a while he heard the pad of footsteps on the stairs and a man in a dirty blazer answered.

'Yes?'

'I'm looking for Alan Maple', Nash said, flashing his badge.

The man looked at it and said 'Never heard of him.'

'He lived here a few years ago.'

'No. Doesn't ring any bells.'

'Do you know who might be able to help?'

'You could try asking her', he said, picking up a piece of paper with a number written on it. 'She's the landlady.'

He passed it to Nash, who wrote it down, thanked him and returned to the car with Thomson.

He tried the number and left a message on the landlady's voicemail.

By the statue of Eros, where tourists milled and paused, maps in hand and heads turned seeking destinations recommended and unknown, a flock of recruits descended like strange raptors, bird-like in their movements.

The babble of tongues merged into sound and the recruits moved among them predatory and silent.

The tourists were moving in different directions when it started.

One was struck by something that flew at him.

He raised a hand and smeared blood.

A woman with a small child screamed and someone turned her and ripped clothes from her.

She ran half-naked into the street.

Banners were raised aloft and used to strike the sight-seers who were assaulted with venom and zeal.

At the edge of this, Wilkes watched unseen.

When the sirens screamed round the corner he turned and moved away.

Nash's phone went when he got back to the station.

It was the landlady.

He explained that he was trying to find out the whereabouts of Alan Maple.

'I'd like to know too', she said.

'Oh? Problems?'

'He left debts. Caused me a lot of trouble.'

'Do you have any idea where he might have gone?'

'No I don't. But I do know he got religious. Also, I reckon he changed his name.'

'Why do you say that?'

'Only way he could have got out of his debts if you ask me.'

'Was he involved with any particular religious group?'

'I don't know, but he was always banging on about it.'

'Thank you for your time.'

He hung up and considered. If he'd changed his name it gave a new direction to the hunt.

Something in the figure that walked along the quiet Soho street drew the officer's attention.

The man was acting strangely and he decided to ask him if he was looking for something.

When he approached him, the figure glared at him and as he asked for ID, the man made a run for it.

So the officer gave chase.

He'd heard about the commotion earlier, the random attack on tourists and knew the history of the recent problems in Parliament Square.

He chased him down two streets and into a back passage where the man came up against a fence.

As he tried to climb it, the officer grabbed him and pulled him back and as he did so, the man reached into his pocket, spun round and hacked away a good section of the policeman's neck.

Blood pumped from him in a shower and he fell to the ground clutching his throat.

The man got away, but only as far as another policeman who'd seen his colleague in pursuit and he soon had him in a headlock.

He called for help and they took him to the local station.

Mover was content with the way things were going.

Money rolling in and deals being struck.

He lit a cigar and called his secretary.

'Whisky please', he said, watching her arse as she left the room.

He'd funded this government.

He owned this government, he told himself.

A satisfied grin spread across his face.

He leaned back and puffed smoke at the ceiling.

Castle and Stone heard about the attacks by the Eros statue and were baffled.

Everything seemed connected and nothing made sense.

They were hunting a killer obsessed by politicians and ministers were being disrupted as they went about their work.

'What now? Get the tourists?', Castle said.

'Way of bringing down the economy.'

They were waiting for Spinner to arrive when the call came through about the arrest earlier that day.

'It seems we've got him', Castle said as he put the phone down. 'Wilkes was arrested today after assaulting a police officer. Sounds like he was involved in the attacks. He slashed a PC's throat.'

'Let's bring him in. And our colleague?'

'He'll recover.'

95

At Rondelo Black was expecting his visitor.

He needed no key.

As the inner door to his library opened, he said: 'I know you do not watch the news, but the latest plan has gone ahead.'

'As I knew it would.'

'The police are in disarray.'

The other sat facing him in some mirror like reflection of Black's posture and attitude.

Bearing no physical resemblance to him, his body echoed his at every stage of its posture and defiance of the modern world. Like something that existed a long time ago and had returned and always would, he sat implacable and watchful. Each knew the other and words were unnecessary for a while. After some time Black said 'We are ready for the next stage.'

'It is prepared.'

He left later in the twilight, moving stealthily among the gardens and disappearing into shadow.

Rondelo entered the night unlit with Black its only inhabitant now.

Wilkes sat facing Castle and Stone.

He looked unlike the man they had first seen at Rondelo.

Although he had lost the rapper's outfit and wore clothes more like those he used to, he had the air of someone out of his natural habitat and stared at them without speaking.

'Jonas, we know you're behind the prostitute killings. We've got you for attempted murder. Why don't you start talking?', Castle said.

'You are out of your depth, Chief Inspector.'

'Tell us about your involvement with Steele.'

Wilkes leant forward.

'You can't stop this thing. It's far bigger than you.'

'Stop what?'

'Do you really think I'm going to help you?'

'No, but I think you might help yourself. We can keep you for what we've got on you, and it's only a matter of time that we link you in to far more. You tell us about Black, what he's up to, what he's involved in, we cut a deal. You could get out and still have a future. Otherwise, it's life for you.'

'Do you think that frightens me? In the middle ages monks lived lives far tougher than those offered by your prisons. Working long hours for God. They lived in bare cells and enjoyed no creature comforts.'

'Why did you do it, Jonas?', Stone said.

'Do what?'

'Take advantage of a mentally ill man and influence him to kill prostitutes.'

Wilkes leant back and smiled.

It sent a chill down her.

'You know very little about me, Chief Inspector Castle.'

'Tell me then.'

'You're careless. You see me as the caper man, and caper I can.'

'You co-operate with us-.'

'Remember the alley, Chief Inspector Castle? Remember staggering out of the pub and getting jumped?'

Stone saw Castle's neck flush.

'You.'

'Father Christmas beats up the great Detective. You can't read a situation. You can't recognise the actors in this drama. You can't dig deep enough. You've held a shovel in your hands for twenty-eight years and you lie buried in the woods with the victims who haunt your dreams. Don't you see the joke?'

Stone looked at Castle, his face as tense as tired muscle.

She watched the shadow of pleasure sneak its way across Wilkes's chameleon face.

He didn't speak again that day.

As Mover left his office that evening, he didn't notice the car follow him home.

It was the same car that had been patrolling his life for a week now, like a shark smelling blood from a distance.

He parked and sauntered up his path, unlocked his front door and put his lights on.

His wife was out and he sat down to a whisky.

After a phone call, he heard a noise in the hall and as he went to investigate, he felt a hand at his throat and smelt something that soon sent him into a deep sleep.

When he woke some hours later he was bound and tethered in a dark room.

He adjusted to the light and saw a weak bulb glowing in the corner. At first he didn't know if the room was empty or not.

He tried to understand where he was and how he got there, recalling his movements after leaving work.

Then, as he remembered the smell, he saw someone move in the corner of the room.

Out of the shadows he walked.

His handsome looks belied his design and for a moment Mover was thrown by the stranger's face.

'What do you want?', he said.

'You.'

'I've got money, how much do you want?'

'Do you really think this is about money?'

Mover stared at him.

'What then?'

'I'm calling in a debt.'

'Debt?'

'You have raped this country. You are the politicians' whore and you pay me now.'

He pulled his Rondel dagger from its sheath.

Its blade glinted in the light.

He jabbed Mover twice in the chest, drawing blood and a feeble scream from his lips.

'Name your price.'

'There is no price and this is just a beginning.'

'What do you want?'

'As I said, you have raped this country, you are the merchant of Filth and now it is time you are made to pay.'

'If not money then what?'

'This', he said.

And removing a long blade he opened his shirt and cut away a section of Mover's fat chest and presented it to him.

'See your flesh?', he said, 'see its corruption?'

Mover's screams went unheard in the basement room where he was kept and would remain.

The recruits were arrested.

CCTV footage showed clear enough images of them for the police to identify and pull them in.

Some were handed charges, mainly for assault and causing a disturbance, to be handled under the new anti-terrorism act, while others got away with a caution.

Castle and Stone were informed of these developments, and knew they were marginal to their inquiries.

Having no time to spare, they did not attend the interviews, but got in-depth feedback about the statements that were obtained.

It seemed that they were all tight-lipped and protecting their instructor.

They re-interviewed Wilkes and he sat without a lawyer saying little.

The only thing they did get out of him was an admission.

'Why do you want politics disrupted?', Castle said.

'Because the people running this country are sinful', Wilkes said, using a word they immediately linked to the killings and their messages.

Outside in the corridor, Stone said 'could he be the Woodlands Killer?'

'You mean, carrying out killings in the vein of Black while confusing us by getting a mentally ill man to kill prostitutes? One easy way to find out. If there's another killing while he's in here, it's not him.'

Later that day the recruits went to Rondelo.

Black admitted them and took them to the Round Room where what he said to them took little time.

'Brothers', he said 'you have done well. Now it is time to remain quiet. Do not return here and do not make contact with one another.'

Having disbanded them, he remained at Rondelo alone, receiving only one guest there now.

Alone in the basement Mover hung like a piece of meat.

On the second day the man entered the room.

Mover looked at him, the face recognisable, timeless, like an etching he had seen countless times. He wondered if he were a male prostitute he had used on occasions. There had been so many.

'I can give you money and a guarantee no one will hear of this', he said. 'What can you gain from this?'

'I will show you what I can gain', the other said, moving slowly towards him.

He reached across and removed two of Mover's fingers, the bones cracking like parts of a chicken or some small animal at a feast.

The screams resonated in the empty room like a girl's shrill shrieks.

'You Filth, did you think you could run the country? You are a Sinner and Sinners must be punished.'

Placing the severed fingers in Mover's mouth, he left him gasping and spitting blood.

At lunchtime he returned and cut out his tongue.

As he removed the fleshy fat organ, Mover pleaded and cried, pissing himself.

'You use your tongue to spread contagion into this world. Now it is removed by God's will. You have no use for it. Servant of the Corrupt, the House will be torn down.'

He left him wet and soiled, a black hole at the centre of his head.

Nash stayed on the trail of the elusive Alan Maple.

It seemed from his debt records that he had disappeared owing a lot of money. There was no evidence he had gone bankrupt, which indicated he'd changed his identity. He also had a gambling habit. He'd found his name linked to bad debts with various bookmakers, now written off.

One William Hill manager remembered him.

'It wasn't just us', he said. 'I heard he was playing with some hard hitters. Guys I wouldn't go near. Rumour has it he owed them a lot of money.'

He kept digging. No one by the name of Alan Maple had been registered bankrupt the year he had vanished, and so Nash began to trawl through the records of changes of name.

Mover was getting weaker.

The man entered the basement periodically and removed pieces of him, cutting them away with an alacrity matched only by the glimmering knife he used.

Sections of Mover's flesh were taken and placed before him while he was told the reasons this was happening to him.

'When you decided to buy the government, you took charge of something that was Corrupt. You have crucified Christ and served the Anti-Priests', he said.

Mover's cries were unheard and he languished there without the light of day.

Spinner was adamant the killer wasn't Wilkes.

'How can you be sure?', Castle said.

'He's an inciter. His whole motivation in influencing Steele to commit those murders stems from a character that does not actively kill, but uses others to do it. For him to shift like that would be unaccountable in psychological terms.'

'Let's hope you're right. How do we catch this guy? He's still out there.'

'He'll kill again. We need to start trying to work out who his next target will be and get there before him.'

Mover was drifting in and out of consciousness.

The light was dim, but he felt as though he was living in constant blackness.

He heard the door open.

The man entered the room, some spectral presence with a knife.

He reached across and hacked some of Mover's flesh away.

'Eat yourself, Filth.'

Mover held his head as far away as possible from his now dripping body.

'Eat.'

He stuffed some of it into his mouth, and Mover choked.

'You Corrupter, you talker of Sin. You will now receive the dues owed you by the High and Mighty, you will be hacked by Blade. Say He is your Maker.'

Mover muttered something.

'Say it!'

He struggled with the ropes, burning his fat hands against them.

'Say Blade is your Maker.'

Mover tried to speak, causing blood to flow heavily from his lacerated mouth.

The man reached down and removed his arm.

He held it like some bloody stump.

Then he cut away his ears.

'Hear nothing? Hear now!'

Mover was writhing about half butchered and looked like something in its final moments in an abattoir.

The man was serene in his actions, graceful and balletic as he cut away shanks and sections of his flesh, holding them up for him to see as he passed in and out of consciousness and saw himself being dismembered.

'You have served the Crucifiers and now Christ's Law will teach you.'

He cut away a section of Mover's face.

This he showed him.

'See your Filth?'

Then he lacerated him many times.

He cut into his fat chin, throwing it at him.

'Servant of the Corrupt, this is your ending.'

The man reached into Mover's chest and brought forth his heart which he showed to him before he lost consciousness.

Later that day Castle got a call.

'You have your ninth victim', the voice said, and gave an address.

It was muffled and he could tell the caller was using a voice changer.

He and Stone drove round to the address, a disused warehouse, and made their way down to the dingy basement. The descent into darkness was charged with the tidal pull of murder, the sense of blackness and malignancy as alive as the smell of a predatory animal in its lair.

There was a taste that hung in the air, and both Detectives felt it, some penetration into sense of the spectral presence they sought, and of its world.

They forced the door and saw a sight that even Castle found hard to witness.

Mover hung from a rope, cut into sections.

His heart had been placed in front of him and on the wall beside him ran the words:

'The Falsifiers of the Hidden Gospel are Tangled in Their Lies.'

It was written in his blood.

When Alan Marker arrived and carried out his usual investigation, his face registered a sense of disturbance Castle had never seen there before. He became very still as he carried out his brief examination, and said only: 'This is the greatest level of violence I've ever witnessed. He's been tortured for days.'

Outside Castle said 'Call Spinner, we need to start compiling that list. That was Sinclair Mover, a major businessman with links to the government. Our killer's just moved sideways.'

Nash got the breakthrough he was looking for.

Alan Maple changed his name two years ago to Adam Makepiece.

He now began to see what he could find out about him.

It wasn't easy: Adam Makepiece owned no credit cards, did not use e-mail, and had no address.

96

The latest article was one step too far.

Despite police attempts to speak to The Sun, they still ran it. The headline was like a body blow to Castle.

'Castle and Black: the two killers?'

The article read:

'Chief Inspector Frank Castle has had repeated meetings with Karl Black and failed to bring any charges against him. Meanwhile the Woodlands Killer goes free. It seems that Castle is obsessed by Black and likes letting this man pursue his own ends.

There is a good body of evidence that Black may be the original Woodlands Killer, so what is Castle playing at? Is he conducting an investigation or collaborating with a serial killer?'

Castle noted the journalist's name.

Stuart Scott again.

Tweed sat dumbfounded.

The news of Mover's death had reached him and he could not understand how a man of his importance could have been targeted in this way. Things like this just didn't happen in their world.

He reached for a cigar, his only consolation.

Puffing smoke he tried to realise how he could maintain the profit margins now Mover was gone.

Castle and Stone sat grim-faced waiting for Tom Spinner to arrive.

'This guy's mutating faster than a virus', Castle said.

Stone handed him a latte.

'Try it', she said.

He stared at it wondering why it was the wrong colour, and

took a sip.

'Black put me through it and now this guy's doing the same thing. But we've also got Wilkes.'

'He still won't talk.'

'His torture of the last victim puts anything I've witnessed as a cop in the shade. What have we got out there?'

She motioned to him to wipe the froth from his lip as the door opened.

'Morning Tom', she said.

'I've seen the brief. He's moving into extreme psychosis. He won't be able to keep this up for long.'

'How do you know?', Castle said.

'Everything I know about psychology supports it.'

'Well, so far your psychology hasn't helped us catch this guy, has it?'

'He won't be able to maintain the level of energy required to do this.'

'What if he's on a mission from God? He might have more energy than you realise.'

'I think I can tell you the kind of target he'll pick next.'

'What?'

'Another businessman with links to the government. The chances of it are overwhelming. So far, he's stuck to ministers who've done something he sees as offensive to his religious outlook. I've been checking out Mover and he's given huge amounts of money to the government for ends which our killer will see as anti-religious. We need to find out everyone who fits the came category. Any businessmen with strong government links. We need to watch them twenty-four seven and catch him.'

'You better be right', Castle said, facing him with an icy stare.

'What else have we got?', Stone said.

They began to compile the list.

At Rondelo Black received his guest.

'It is only us now', he said.

'We need no more.'

'When I founded the Brotherhood it was in order to bring together the finest principles of monastic living. The ideas that made Christianity the fighting force it was.'

'And you have succeeded.'

'As much as it is possible in today's Fallen World.'

'We are striking at the very heart of government.'

'It is true the body politic is diseased and needs cutting away and Jonas has helped much with the cause, but the world we live in is so riddled with corruption, we need an entire Army to fight it. What we are doing is only the beginning.'

'We will fight on.'

'The Castles of this World are so easy. Stupid and gullible, he believes himself to be the man he sees in the mirror, the man he portrays to the World around him. He does not know himself and that is why he is a failure as a police officer and a drunk. The press have got hold of him and will continue to go for him. To live the true monastic life in this day and era is hard.'

'I live it.'

'So you do.'

'Each time one of the Corrupt is crucified, I see Christ's power rise.'

'That is the true teaching.'

'And as they fall we rise.'

'You are indeed the Apostle. You have sought me and found out the teachings and that is why I am telling you about my monastic life. The years I spent in the monastery I knew they could not maintain the level of discipline required to achieve God's purpose on this planet.'

'The annihilation of politics.'

'The annihilation and the eternal crucifixion of politicians.'

'The police think they can stop our Work.'

'They cannot.'

'What is your hesitation, Karl?'

'Not hesitation. I see how much there is to do.'

'And we will do it.'

'Yes.'

'We will gather together another Army. Next we will slay the

Police. Burn them, torture them. So that their reign of lies will cease.'

'Once we have destroyed the body politic as it stands and replaced it with religious rule, we will take every police officer to camps where they can be routinely interrogated and tortured. They must be stopped and burned. They must be brought to heel.'

'They have served the Corrupt. Under the New Rule, they will be prisoners. Their torture will last for years while they wail and appeal to their Law, which is nothing to us. They will see how their sinfulness has brought them to this pass. Yes, after the next one, we will turn our attention to the police, a major death in the ranks. A New Army and we could mount an attack on them that would bring them to a standstill.'

'All of this can be achieved.'

'Can you imagine how Castle will squeal when the cuts commence?'

'Blade would ring a true song from him. And Stone that whore in blue.'

'She should be cut so deeply she sings with her partner.'

'She cannot maintain her marriage, her life is a sham.'

'We know much.'

They talked as the light failed outside and Rondelo stayed dark. They did not need light to guide their conversation.

The tangled streets opened now and Castle saw the car.

He tailed it to the junction and fell back behind a van, keeping his distance.

They passed out into the suburbs and he followed him to a set of garages at the back of some flats.

Parking far enough away not to be seen he watched as the driver got out.

It was him all right.

He started unlocking a garage as Castle got out.

He was leaning over some boxes when he came up behind him and he turned.

'You think you can taunt the police like that?', he said, the voice someone else's.

Scott was shaken, looked over Castle's shoulder as he turned around and pulled down the door, leaving their shadows entangled on the stone floor, cast there by the single bulb that dangled from the ceiling, a kink in the middle of the cord.

'Look', Scott said, 'I'm just doing my job, so are you. This is harassment.'

He was about to speak when he hit him.

His fist connected squarely with his mouth and beneath the sound was the noise of teeth breaking.

He watched him fall and continued to hit him on the way down, remorseless solid punches learnt at the boxing gym as a boy, spreading Scott's face apart, until his nose was broken and his eyes half closed.

He lay unconscious and Castle hit him again. And again. Until he became aware of the presence of death in the room.

The bulb overhead hissed.

Scott lay without moving.

'No, I'm just doing my job', Castle said, 'and you're impeding me.'

He left him and drove away.

Nash knew he was onto something.

Alan Maple had to be someone in all of this. The link to Walsh was there, the religion, the mysterious disappearance, someone who was not part of the modern world.

This last fact made Nash's job all the harder.

Without internet traceability and credit cards, he didn't exist.

Except he did.

And the fact that he'd changed his name to Adam Makepiece gave enough evidence to begin the search.

He trawled through everything he could find.

Every transaction he'd carried out since he'd become Makepiece.

Wilkes remained silent. Attempts to interview him proved fruitless. Castle and Stone got on with the job of identifying the killer's next victim, while Spinner developed his profile.

'He's reaching a peak.'

'You mean he's using more violence?', Castle said.

'It's more than that. Serial killers are attempting an act of self-transformation. Their methods match the profile of their traumas and their struggle to overcome them. This killer is heightening his activity so that he may be God. He will step up the violence and keep stepping it up until we catch him.'

Castle thought about Marker's report. The level of the injuries to Mover were horrifying.

'We've got a list of names', he said.

Spinner looked at it.

'Put out protection on all of them.'

'Do you have any idea how quickly he'll strike again?', Stone said.

'The early ones were close together. Then there were gaps. He could strike within days.'

'Why so quickly?'

'Because he's reaching a peak and he wants to maintain it.'

'Is he acting alone?', Castle said.

'There's someone else in here, but he's not killing, he's not present at the killings.'

'How do you know?'

'I don't. For sure. But it's a hunch based on the beliefs he's coming out with.'

'What do you make of the last message?'

'The Falsifiers of the Hidden Gospel are Tangled in Their Lies. Very easy. He believes he has access to some secret religious teachings. They are his inspiration, they are telling him to do this. The men and women he is killing have betrayed that teaching.'

'Or someone has told him this?', Stone said.

'Someone has taught him to read it like that.'

97

Nash traced him to an address in Baron's Court, and he drove there with PC Thomson. Barton road was a broad street composed of tall Victorian houses, slightly decayed. A parade of estate agents' boards lined the road, and it had the feel of a deeply imbued transience.

No one put down roots in a place like this.

He found number 2 and they got out of the car and he buzzed the ground floor flat. 'Yeah?'

'I'm police officer Mike Nash, can I speak to you please?'

A car blasted past him, P Diddy blaring from its open windows. 'Yeah?'

'It's the police, can I speak to you please?'

There was a crackle then nothing. He looked at Thomson who was trying to see through the filthy windows. The curtains were drawn and all she could see were the layers of pollution and grime eating into the paintwork. Then the door opened.

A man looking half-asleep stood there rubbing his eyes.

'That intercom's bust, what were you saying?'

Nash showed him his badge.

'Could I have word with you please?'

'Yeah, sure, come in.'

He led them through the damp and musty hallway into the living room.

A glimpse into the kitchen showed rows of empty beer bottles.

The living room was full of unwashed laundry and overflowing ashtrays. It smelled of male living alone.

'You are?'

'John Wallace.'

'Do you know Adam Makepiece?'

'Who?'

'He used to live at this address.'

He scratched his head.

'Before my time.'

'Anyone who might have known him?'

'You could talk to Mick.'

'Who's he?'

'Lived here for ages. If anyone remembers him, he will.'

'Where can I find him?'

'Works over at the Colton Arms.'

'Where's that?', Thomson said.

'Round the corner.'

He gave them directions and they left.

The pub was empty apart from a couple of toothless old winos sitting in the corner.

Behind the unattended bar they could hear someone lugging barrels around at the back.

A few moments later a tall guy in a dirty grey T-shirt emerged.

'What can I get you?'

Nash flashed his badge at him.

'What's this about?'

'I'm looking for an ex-tenant at the address you live in and I've been told you might know him. Adam Makepiece.'

'Oh, I knew him.'

'Can you tell me anything about him?'

'Kept himself to himself. Didn't get on with the other tenants.'

'Quiet?'

'Yes.'

'Do you think that was to do with his stutter?'

'Stutter? No, he could talk all right when he got going. Most of us wanted to go out and get drunk. He didn't. Kept going on about the Bible. Then one day he left.'

'Any idea where he went?'

'No.'

'Is there anything else you can tell me about him?'

'What do you want him for?'

'I can't tell you that, but this is important.'

'Anything else I can tell you. Like what?'

'Anything that stood out about him. What did he look like? Did he have any particular habits?'

'He was a quiet guy. Short hair. Something about the eyes.'

'What?'

'A piercing quality. Look, I don't really study what guys look like, a pair of tits, maybe, but-.'

'What colour were they?'

'Blue? Dunno.'

He leaned back against the counter and crossed his arms.

'How tall would you say he was?'

'Bout your height.'

'Six foot?'

'I'll tell you if I was him I'd have been out on the pull every night.'

'Why do you say that?'

'Well, he was good-looking, not that I'm into blokes or anything, but women liked him. They were always asking me about him, I could tell they were into him. Except, he wasn't interested in them.'

'Do you think he was gay?', Thomson said.

'No. He was religious, he just didn't like women. Something old-fashioned about him.'

'Did he ever display any violent behaviour?', Nash said.

'Not that I can remember.'

'Do you know where he went?'

'No. I remember him saying once he didn't know his father. He joined up with some weird sect or something and that was the last I saw of him.'

'Can you remember the name of this sect?'

'No.'

'Anything else you can think of, please call me', Nash said.

He handed him his card.

As they were walking to the door they heard Mick call after them.

'Can you wait ten minutes?'

'Sure', Nash said.

'It just occurred to me that I might be able to help you, I mean, this is serious isn't it?'

'It is.'

304

'I'm not promising, because it's ages since I've gone through it, but there might be a photo of him back at the flat. One of the women we used to hang out with had the hots for him and she snapped him. I remember he didn't like it and tried to pull the camera off her. She gave me a copy after he left because I was putting together a bit of memorabilia about the good old years and I think I slotted it in there. If you want to come back to the flat with me in ten minutes when I've finished my shift I'll try to dig it out.'

'That would be a big help.'

'Can I get you anything while you wait?'

Nash ordered an orange juice for himself and a mineral water for Thomson and they sat in the corner until Mike was relieved of his duties.

'What do you think, Anne?', he said.

'I think Adam Makepiece is going to be hard to find.'

'Do you pick anything up about these guys?'

She took a sip of her water.

'No. The guy at the flat's hung over, doesn't know anything. I don't think either of them are lying or withholding anything. Let's see if this picture gives us a lead.'

Back at the flat they watched as Mick manoeuvred his way through the mess.

'John always goes out and leaves this place like a tip', he said. 'He had his mates round last night. I think I'll have to get another flat mate. Now that's one thing I'll say about Adam, he was tidy. Here it is.'

He reached down an album covered with dust from the top of some shelves stacked with CD's and empty beer bottles.

'Now, where is it?'

They waited while he flicked through the pages.

'Got it.'

He pulled back the clear strip and removed the photo.

Nash looked at it: a good-looking young man with short hair, almost cropped. His blue eyes stared through the camera lens into the distance.

'This is definitely him?'

'Oh, that's him all right.'

'Can I take this way?'

'You can have it, I don't know what it's doing in there anyway, he never drank with us.'

Nash thanked him and they returned to the station.

He already had a picture of Alan Maple, but it was out of date. Back at the station he and Thomson compared them. They agreed that it would have been hard to tell they were the same person.

He calculated that there was a ten year gap between the two pictures and thought about himself at that age and how different he looked to his younger self.

Now he had something tangible and he took it into Castle and Stone.

Castle was talking to Spinner and as Nash opened the door he broke off what he was saying.

'Mike? Got something?'

'Samuel Walsh adopted a boy called Alan Maple. He was around at the time of the last case and he would have been in the foster home when Walsh committed suicide.'

'All the adopted kids were checked and nothing came up on any of them.'

'I know Frank, but I decided to have another look. I've been digging and Alan Maple disappeared a few years ago, changing his name.'

'To?'

'Adam Makepiece. Who is not in any way traceable via the internet, owns no credit cards, and has proved a very difficult person to find anything about at all.'

They were all looking at him.

'Who is he?'

'I don't know much. But a few years ago he was living at an address I went to earlier today. According to his flat mate, he was very religious and kept himself to himself.'

'Do we have a description?'

'Better than that, I have a picture.'

Castle stared down at it, feeling his cop's sense that this was the killer. He knew the face.

'Where is he now?'

'In some sect, according to his flat mate. I know it's not much.'

'No, it's a lot', Stone said.

'And he matches what we're looking for', Spinner said.

Castle nodded.

'Someone who was around Walsh and who we overlooked because he changed his name.'

Stone was looking over his shoulder at the picture. 'He familiar to you Frank?'

'Now you mention it.'

'It's the assistant librarian.'

'You're right, Jacki.'

'You've met him?', Spinner said.

'Jacki and I spoke to him at the Houses of Parliament when we were checking their security. That's him.'

'Excellent work, Mike', Stone said.

Castle looked at the clock.

'It's 4.30, we can get there before they close.'

Tweed sat thinking through his losses resulting from the murder of his colleague.

It was an inconvenience and he berated the killer. Savages like that, unfit for civilised society, should be tortured, not honest businessmen.

He totted his figures up and lit one of his best cigars.

The figures were making sense again. He would ensure he got maximum profit from his church reforms.

They got there just before the library was closing.

Mary Clarke saw them through the window in the doors as she made her way over with the key.

'Can I help you, Chief Inspector?'

'Yes, we need to see your assistant.'

'Adam? He's not here.'

'He's gone home already?', Stone said. 'We need his address.'

'No, you don't understand, he left. He just didn't come into work a few weeks ago.'

'Where does he live?'

She shook her head.

'I'll give it to you, but it won't do any good.'

'Why do you say that?'

'Because I already went round there. Adam was, somehow I felt, different. I was concerned about him when he didn't come into work, I couldn't get any response when I rang, just a dead line, and so on my way back from work one day, I went round. You hear about people, you know.'

Castle nodded. 'It was a false address.'

'There was no one there, the front door was boarded up, the place was derelict. Here.'

She handed Stone the card.

'And how long ago was this?', Castle said.

'Probably about a month ago. It's very mysterious, we carry out rigorous checks on our employees. I don't know what's happened to him. Is he in trouble?'

'We can't discuss that', Castle said.

'Don't say you want him in connection with those awful murders.'

'As I say, ma'am.'

'Well, it's an awful shame, really, he was a very good employee and now I'm a member of staff down.'

They heard her lock the door behind them as they walked away.

Stone got them there quickly, a flat over a vacant shop with whitewashed windows in Paddington.

Someone had kicked a hole in the boards on the front door and Castle finished the job.

They entered a cold hallway that smelt of mould.

A flight of stairs and a door with peeling paint.

Castle kicked it in and they entered the flat.

'There's nothing here, Frank.'

'Literally.'

No chairs, no furniture, no hangings, not even a fridge. A bare wire hung from the wall where the phone had been cut.

Bare windows and empty rooms.
'I'll get DNA', Castle said.
'You get the sense he was expecting visitors?'
'Like I said, Jacki, one step ahead.'
'Yeah right.'

98

'Crucify the next one', Black said.

'The Cross is ready.'

'Make sure he hangs there for days, and is tortured according to the manner we discussed.'

'I have the tools and they are sharpened. Blade awaits his sorry flesh, which will fold away like rotten meat from a slaughtered animal.'

'They are all animals, scum who walk the earth, corrupting it.'

'Yet it is our Hour, Karl and the Hour of the Risen Christ.'

'Yes. Everyone who reads the Bible and hears of the Resurrection imagines the gentle lamb returning, but they do not realise after the Crucifixion he will return a Warrior with Blade and he will dismember those who have built this False Empire. Look around ye, it lies in rubble and we will sack this City and all those who manage it. They will be taken to places where we will cut and hack them away till they are nothing and the police will suffer.'

'The police are the very ones who support this False Government. They must be tortured the most once we have built the New Jerusalem.'

'Apostle, you are ready for the next one. He will be crucified and then the next phase of our attack will begin but it will be so bloody that no one will be prepared. We will bring this city down. We will destroy their false laws and put in its place the One True and Righteous Law. I have the secret text, the hidden gospel wherein it states that Christ commanded the execution of politicians and all who fracture the Ten Commandments.'

'All politicians now bleed. Blade is ready for him.'

Castle and Stone were filling Spinner in.

'We had the killer under our noses all along', Castle said.

'If it's him.'

'Tom, he's disappeared and he's got the one thing we didn't have until now: motive.'

'And when we say disappeared, Tom, we mean it', Stone said. 'The flat's passed into receivership together with the shop. The landlord said he didn't know anyone was living there.'

'If he was living there', Spinner said, 'it could have just been an address for his place of work. Ideal for someone who wants to observe politicians.'

'He was only registered as living there a few months', Castle said.

Spinner started writing on the flipchart.

'I've put together everything I've thought about this killer and added the information that we've got about Adam Makepiece. He changes his name, he becomes religious. He does have the motive and say we're looking at our killer, it gives me an insight into his psychology.'

'You mean loss of a father?', Stone said.

'More than that. Alan Maple is adopted by a caring and competent foster father who is put through a gruelling time by the police over a highly publicised nationwide hunt for a serial killer. His life is ruined, his career in tatters once it is over. He is innocent. That is the key here. Although he is innocent and the case is never solved, he commits suicide, letting down everyone who depended on him in the process. The fall out is everywhere: children are re-located, his wife never recovers, becoming a chronic alcoholic. Alan might have needed a father figure more than the other children, he may have clicked with Walsh and the effect of his suicide could have altered his psychology for life.'

'How?', Castle said.

'It would have represented to him the breakdown of what he needed and wanted. What he thought he finally got. The police would symbolise corruption to him, as would the judicial process and the law as such. Think of all the messages the killer's left about corruption and the law. He would want revenge and take it in the form of a copycat killing many years later. He would want you to relive your failure, Frank, he would want the nation to relive the experience of injustice he suffered, feeling the pain and never finding out who the killer is.'

'Who's the father?', Castle said.

'Whoever is behind him.'

'You're convinced there is someone else?'

'If my theory's right, it would be highly unlikely that he is operating on his own. He needs to feel the presence of a father in his life. The father would inspire him enough to give him a feeling of power. The belief structure he's immersed himself in would give him a feeling of invincibility.'

'Karl Black.'

'Not necessarily. There are plenty of people out there with strange religious beliefs who are looking for power over someone else. Wilkes is one. Just because he is linked to the prostitute killings it doesn't mean it's all coming from Rondelo.'

'Pretty big coincidence though. And the way Steele's killings have undermined our ability to get on with this case.'

'It's possible it all stems from Black, but it might not.'

'If he's going to target a businessman then we try to catch him, that's all we've still got', Castle said.

'I'm going to look at the records on Alan Maple when he was a child, before he was adopted by Walsh. I want to see what he was like. Any insight into his character at an early age will be highly useful to us now. He was six when he was adopted. He was almost formed. The event that took place was a final trauma for him.'

'You're saying that if he already had traumas this would have pushed him over the edge?', Stone said.

'Any child who is adopted suffers trauma, whether at the time or later. It would have pushed him over the edge.'

'Yet he didn't do anything to draw attention to himself, didn't commit any crimes, showed no disturbed behaviour.'

'Not then, his process was different. Do you think everyone who is disturbed shows it? As I say, trauma can sometimes occur after the event, when we piece together what has happened to us. It's about the fracturing of our reality, the rending of that veil we use to view the chaos of the world. When our reality breaks down, so do we.

Look at the etymology of it. Trauma. It comes from the German word traum which means dream, so it's deeply connected to the warping of our reality. Adam Makepiece has a hole right at the centre of his identity. He's a work in progress. And if he's got a psychopath as a sculptor, then we've got the psychological make-up of our killer.'

'So we're looking for someone who needed a father?', Castle said.

'We're looking for someone who needed God. God the father and all its attendant symbolism.'

Castle turned to Stone.

'You check his records and we'll start trying to protect his next victim. Meantime, we put out an ID with the picture Mike's come up with.'

'Trying to get one step ahead of this guy is like trying to sprint up a down escalator', she said.

Rondelo stood etched against the sky.

Black clouds gathered overhead, as summer moved into autumn.

Leaves fell slowly from the trees and the building itself merged with the darkness.

Black moved alone in its silent corridors, a watcher in the dark.

He made preparations of his own.

The changing of the seasons marked a full year since the first killing.

Tweed met with the minister he was relying on to ensure everything went as planned.

'You've heard the news?', he said.

'Yes. This madman has got to be caught.'

'Supports my theory about religion entirely. Makes people do criminal things, never been good for society and never will, all the more reason to push these measures through.'

'They should get through.'

'They will get through! I haven't worked this hard to see them fail. Make sure they do, if you know what's good for you.'

He turned his back and lit a cigar.

The minister scuttled away.

Castle heard that Stuart Scott was in hospital.

He had no memory of his attacker.

He felt some relief that he'd survived. It hadn't made a shade of difference to the media pressure the police were experiencing.

Stone was working on the list.

They'd called in Nash's team and he'd briefed everyone on the kind of businessman they were looking for.

Meanwhile, Spinner got copies of Alan Maple's records.

He brought them in to Castle and Stone.

'Makes very interesting reading.'

'Alan Maple's background?', Castle said.

'Yes.'

'What do you get from it?', Stone said.

'Alan was a quiet boy. Adopted from birth. No information about who his real parents might be here.'

'Does it matter?', Castle said.

'Only from a DNA point of view.'

'How would that help?'

'It's more complicated, but it could throw light on his predisposition to become a killer, but that would involve finding out about his parents.'

'Which we haven't got time to do.'

'Right.'

'So what you've got there tells us what?', Stone said.

'As I say, he never knew who his real parents were and went from one home to another. Unsettled childhood.'

Castle nodded.

'As you might expect.'

'Yes. But at the age of six, shortly before going to the Walsh family, two things happened, which are very significant. One, he witnesses his foster mother having sex. Two, he becomes interested in religion.'

'I see where we're heading with the religion, and he's young, but the sex?', Castle said.

'She was having sex. Young Alan came downstairs and saw it

and suddenly something happened.'

'What?'

'First of all, she wasn't having it with her husband. Secondly, her sexual partner starts acting rough.'

'Rough how?', Stone said.

'A report was put together by a senior social worker who believed Alan was disturbed. According to it, she was raped. They were worried about his being with these two adoptive parents and consequently moved him. The woman reported rape to the police and it was a particularly nasty one.'

'Any details?', Castle said.

'She was cut. Held down, raped and beaten up. Alan would have seen it, how much, we don't know, but enough to change his view of sex and in my opinion leave him with a deep trauma.'

'So he gets religious?', Stone said.

'Yes. Shortly after, Alan starts talking about God, God coming to him in a dream, telling him he is his son and that there are secret teachings.'

'Secret teachings?', Castle said.

'Yes.'

'Sounds like a blueprint for someone who'd end up in The Last Brotherhood.'

'There's more than that. He talked about fathers all the time. The social worker who relocated him with the Walshes stressed his need for a strong father figure which is one reason they picked Walsh, he'd had a good success rate with disturbed kids.'

'You're saying he needed a father, that's why he ended up with someone who led him into killing?', Stone said.

'I am. But also, shortly before going to the Walshes, he does two things which are out of character for him, given the fact that he's been a quiet boy until now. He assaults a boy at school for making fun of religion.'

'Playground fight?'

'No, Frank. He badly hurt this kid. He had a bad stutter and often that sort of loss of articulacy can lead to violence. He broke his nose, fractured his head.'

'OK.'

315

'Two, he smashes the TV at the home he's in.'

'Religion too?', Stone said.

'No. He was watching the news and shouted all politicians are liars and threw a table through the TV set.'

'So he has a streak of violence and a religious belief', Castle said.

'He didn't stop with the religion there. All through his time at the Walshes it was noted.'

'How normal is it for a kid under stress to show that kind of violence and then for it to go into abeyance?', Stone said.

'With certain character types, they learn from it, they put it on hold and act it out secretly.'

'You mean they learn they don't want to be punished?', Stone said.

'Yes. They do it furtively.'

'What sort of character type are we talking about?', Castle said.

'A psychopathic one.'

'At that age?'

'Has to start somewhere. It wouldn't be fully developed and it would come and go, but piecing this together we have a disturbed boy who witnessed something traumatic, who had a streak of violence, who got refostered by a man he got on very well with.'

'Who then kills himself', Castle said.

'Yeah. And he already hates politicians, remember. The whole mess surrounding Walsh's treatment at the hands of the police and the press would have deepened that feeling.'

'It's like he was primed to do this', Castle said.

'He was primed to hate the political and legal system and to need a father.'

'And say he ran into Black?'

'If he did, Frank, then we have the killings set up. And if it wasn't Black, then it was someone like him.'

'But he stayed quiet all those years since. No arrests, no reported violence', Stone said.

'Psychopaths are very good at that.'

'He's got to be our man', Castle said.

'He's got the profile and the motivation.'

'Except, we don't have a good likeness of him now, and we don't know where he lives.'

'He disappeared off the radar.'

The first list they compiled was so long they would have needed every police force in Europe involved.

There were so many businessmen with links to the government in terms of past donations and publicity that protecting them all would be impossible.

Castle and Stone reviewed the list, taking out everyone who had not donated money to the government in the past year and narrowed it down.

'It's still too long', Castle said.

'How many names have we got now?'

'Over a hundred.'

'I suggest we remove anyone not living in the London area.'

'Yeah, so far he's struck here.'

They managed to reduce it to sixty.

'We need this a lot smaller if we can manage it.'

'How many are you thinking? Ten?'

'Maximum.'

'We could narrow it down to men only.'

'He's killed two women already.'

'Yeah, but Tom says the pattern he's following indicates a man next.'

'How can he tell?'

'Something about the pathology of the guy and the fact that he wants to differentiate himself from the prostitute killer who's killed only women. You know what these fucking ego-maniacs are like.'

'Mike's come up with an idea. He said look for businessmen with a scandal surrounding corruption and put them at the top.'

'That sounds good.'

Removing the women left them with forty-six.

Nash's idea gave them a list of ten men who had donated large sums of money to the government in the last year, who lived in the London area and who had all had scandals.

'That's manageable', Castle said, looking at the list.

'Can we protect all of them?'

'I suggest what we do now is pick our top two, give them the best round the clock protection we can offer, and then assign the others a secondary level protection.'

'Sit back and wait.'

'That's it.'

Black was preparing something at Rondelo.

Alone, he destroyed documents. The ancient fireplaces crackled and flared as papers turned to ash.

He readied the Brotherhood for its next challenge.

He waited.

99

'Adam Makepiece met Karl Black at the monastery he went to after the Woodland Killings.'

Nash had unearthed more information and Castle looked at him with hunger for detail etched into his face.

'How long ago was this Mike?'

'According to my source they first met ten years ago.'

'Who's your source?'

'Jeremiah Poulter, monk and seriously religious guy.'

'Aren't they all', Stone said.

'He's the real deal. Very serious about his religion, felt the calling to Christianity from childhood, remembers Black well.'

'What does he remember?', Castle said.

'He was there when Black joined the order. Recalls his religious fervour, which, according to Jeremiah, "crackled like firewood".'

'His words.'

'Yes, Frank. He said he always found Black offputting, as if he was serving his will, not God's.'

'How do you tell the difference?', Stone said. 'We've got a killer who thinks he's serving God's will.'

'I guess if you aren't doing anything too whacko or killing people, you can argue you're serving God's will. Jeremiah's very devout and said Black showed a tendency early on to want to take the order over. But its ways are strictly set in place to offset that kind of thing, and he feels that's one of the reasons Black eventually left.'

'What did he say about Adam Makepiece?', Castle said.

'That the monastery held retreats and Adam attended one.'

'Only one?'

'Yes. He gravitated towards Black as if he was the reason he came.'

'He was.'

'He stuck to him like glue. He saw the young man was entranced, spellbound.'

'And then what?'

'He didn't know. He remembers him and the sway Black seemed to have over him.'

'Their meetings must have continued after that', Castle said. 'He mentored him in some way, shaped him to his own ends.'

'They obviously maintained contact. Black left the monastery and founded The Last Brotherhood.'

'The perfect podium to continue his inculcation of Makepiece', Stone said.

'So, Adam Makepiece seeks Karl Black out in the monastery he's read he's gone into. Black finds someone he can mould. He leaves and uses The Last Brotherhood to launch his second wave of killings.'

'With Makepiece as his missile', Stone said.

'Right. He's been gifted a servant killer.'

'Like he's still doing it, but one step removed.'

'Still playing with our heads.'

'It all fits', Nash said.

'Except for one thing which bothers me.'

'What?', Castle said.

'It's been noted that Alan Maple had a stutter.'

'Right.'

'According to his flat mate and provider of the photograph, Adam Makepiece didn't have a stutter. Also, Jeremiah says Adam spoke fluently.'

'Maybe they've forgotten.'

'I could believe that of the flat mate, Frank, but I specifically asked Jeremiah about it and he said Adam most definitely did not have a stutter.'

'People can get treatment for it', Spinner said, 'also religious conversion is a powerful psychological force that can bring about drastic character changes in people. His speech impediment almost certainly resulted from his early traumas. When he met Black he transferred onto him as a father and that could have cured his problem.'

While they were talking Stone was looking through Alan Maple's records.

'Except', she said, 'there's something else that doesn't add up.'

They turned to her.

'What?', Castle said.

'Alan Maple had green eyes.'

'Adam Makepiece's are blue', Nash said.

Castle looked at the file Stone was holding, then back at the photograph.

'Contact lenses?', he said. 'Can we get this photo checked to see if he's wearing them?'

'We can try', Nash said.

I see them moving in their Lies like fish in a slow poison
The men in blue, the shadow of the crucifix on them
Castle and Stone Blade will hack you away hack you away
You will be taken and tortured
You will be placed under our arrest
You will be confined

Tweed sat smoking in his club.

It wasn't the same without Mover.

It wasn't as if his image of himself was fading, it was too strongly entrenched in massive profits for that to happen, and all he needed to do was look at his profits to feel himself. It was that he felt frayed around the edges and the idea that someone like Mover could be got at in this way profoundly unsettled him.

He blew smoke everywhere and saw no one he wished to talk to.

He left, unaware of someone following him.

Tom Spinner felt the coastal shelf of his early profile of the killer slip away beneath his feet, the hardened sand of well-worn paths dissolving into that nothingness - the familiar territory of deep psychosis.

He knew he'd got the right hooks in the right places and was on his scent and gaining ground, knew it from the early stages when he identified the variation on the Messiah complex. But as he'd watched it darken, as the paint dried and he stared into that occluded section of his canvas where the demons lurked, he knew there was an entire world he was missing.

With Mike Nash's unearthing of Adam Makepiece's early obsession with Karl Black came the cavernous descent following the psychological dig. He saw the teeth of cogs meshing and fitting like mechanical conspirators in these homicides and realised how dangerous and exceptional this murderer was.

The scientist in him wondered at this deadly bird of paradise, and he slowed his beating heart to focus on his job.

He felt the abyss of the psychosis, the echo of it immense in his mind, knowing and tasting the depths of this man's pathology and its coupling with a belief system that held it in check as perfectly as a ballerina in a pirouette.

The balance was perfect: the danger more real than ever.

He could smell him. This feral monster bore great sophistication in his knowledge of the art of murder, its slow dissections and unravellings of the human spirit.

The Commandment to kill: what drove him onwards like a juggernaut, an implacable belief in the supreme righteousness of these murders, the inheriting of a tradition buried in time.

He thought of all that had been achieved in the way of service to such credence, from military bloodshed to the widespread slaughter of civilians in the name of ideology.

Only the fact that he was in a minority separated Adam Makepiece's actions from these. When he considered the endless series of war crimes history bore testimony to, which was worse? Operating on the side of law and order was a little like lassoing a horse that had run wild, when it might equally be serviceable within a martial context.

Given the choice between the blessing of politics or the curse of madness, Spinner couldn't call the odds.

What he knew though, and with no uncertainty, was the fact that this man was psychologically the perfect killing machine: stilled in his psychosis and energised beyond belief, blessed by God, allied with a benefactor who lived in darkness, and the inheritor of a tradition that mocked the police.

The law was being undermined, broken, vilified and negated and he sensed the enormity of what still lay out there as a world of massacre.

To stop this man would take the depth that usually only accompanies the kind of psychosis he navigated with ease. And how to find him, when he was as elusive as the creatures who live at those depths.

The lab scanned the picture and came back with the verdict that Adam Makepiece was not wearing contact lenses.

'So if Adam Makepiece isn't Alan Maple, who the hell is he?', Castle said.

'This much is sure, Frank', Nash said. 'Alan Maple had green eyes and a stutter. He was adopted by the Walshes and the rest of the facts we have about him up until the time of his disappearance are right. He had gambling debts. He had heavies after him. He changed his name to Adam Makepiece.'

'But this guy', Castle said, prodding the photograph, 'is not him.'

'OK', Stone said, 'the only difference is he's got blue eyes and no stutter. Tom told us about speech defects and what could have happened there, could the lab be wrong?'

Nash shook his head.

'They said they were certain.'

'Your trail leads us right to Alan Maple changing his name', Castle said, 'and then someone else steps into the frame.'

'So who are we looking for?', Stone said.

'Someone who stole his identity', Nash said. 'The only thing we can do is dig around the gambling syndicate Alan Maple was on the run from.'

'You think they tried to get him killed?'

'Well Frank, if he was on the run from them, maybe he wanted to fake his own death, maybe he and someone else swapped identities.'

'OK, regardless of who he really is, we're hunting Adam Makepiece based on what we've got, which right now amounts to that picture and the profile we've got. We put together a list of likely targets. In the meantime, Jacki, let's speak to this bookmaker. Mike, your help's been invaluable.'

100

The following morning before Castle and Stone left to interview the bookmaker, Spinner came into the office.

'Thinking of the profile', he said, 'I want to tell you how the killer operates when he kills.'

Now he had scent of him the old school cop in Castle was kicking in.

'I don't care who Adam Makepiece is, all I know is it's the guy we interviewed in the library, and we've got enough to know how to track him now', he said.

Spinner ignored the comment.

'Everything he experiences is at a height.'

'Adrenaline rush', Stone said.

'More than that. He believes he's acting out God's will. And in that state he will be extremely strong.'

'The superhuman strength of psychosis', she said.

'Psychologically speaking, he will feel invincible and yes there will be an accompanying physical strength. He will not go away and feel down, because the belief system he has taken on has been too deeply rooted in him for that.'

'How do you know?', Castle said.

'He wouldn't be able to kill if it wasn't.'

'He's split from what he's doing.'

'Which means, Frank, when you catch him he won't go easily. You may have to take him out.'

'If we catch him.'

'The reason it's taken so long is there are so many complicating factors.'

'Like in the original case.'

'Adam Makepiece has a double motive to his homicides', Spinner said.

'Which is what, apart from killing politicians?'
'Getting at the police.'
'Me', Castle said.
'In some way this is personal.'
'Black's influence.'
'Perhaps.'

Castle stared down at the picture that lay on his desk and thought how most guys have photographs of their wife and kids at the office, while his was adorned with the likeness of a serial killer. He felt the face staring back at him had been dogging him all his life.

He walks like an animal
Fat
Lazy Full of money
Coughing Filth
Like Vermin
Servant of Corruption
The air is thin between us
He is at home
But I am here
And Blade is here
I drag him across the hallway
He tries to resist but is weak
I drag him and he screams
I cut away sections of Flesh
I pound him until he stops screaming
He lies there
In his own blood
Blade will do the rest
Blade is ready for him
And so is the Cross
This is the beginning of the Crucifixion of the Crucifiers

101

They went to the William Hill in Thornton Heath.

John Marks was behind the till counting out some winnings to a customer who looked elated. Marks saw them and looked away. It wouldn't be unusual for a bookie not to want the police visiting his premises, but Castle wondered if he had something to hide.

They waited for him to finish, watching the out of work guys lost in the screens.

The customer took his money and walked away from the counter.

'Can we have a word please?', Castle said.

'Look, I'm very busy.'

'This is a serious matter.'

'All right. Sally?' A woman came out from the back office. 'Can you take over?'

They waited while he opened a side door and let them through to his office. His shirt was grimy at the collar and as he sat down Stone noticed the Hammers tattoo on his arm.

He looked like a guy who'd been on the wrong side of the law. He was out of shape, no surprise, Stone thought, as she looked around at the hamburger boxes and chip wrappers falling out of his bin.

Files clogged up what available space there was and various frames showing William Hill accolades lined the walls.

'What's this about?', Marks said.

'One of my officers spoke to you recently about Alan Maple', Castle said.

'Yes.'

Castle could see a barrier coming up.

'We're investigating a series of murders.'

'The Woodland Killings?'

'I can't say any more than that.'

'Na. Alan wouldn't have had anything to do with that.'

'I need information from you.'

'I can tell you right now that I'm a good judge of character. Have to be in this game, I can tell the heavies from the patsies and Alan ain't a killer.'

'Ain't?'

'Wasn't.'

'I need the names of the men he was involved with.'

'What? The gambling syndicate?'

'Yes.'

'Dunno.'

He stood up but Castle and Stone weren't going anywhere.

'Sit down please Mr Marks', Castle said.

'I can't tell you anything.'

Castle could sense fear and waited until Marks was seated again.

'I need names.'

'Look, I didn't know them, all right? Only a couple of 'em ever came in.'

'Did any of them have accounts with you?'

He held Castle's gaze for a moment, a flicker of uncertainty on his face.

'All right.' He stood up. 'But this is strictly in confidence, OK?'

'Yes.'

'One guy, one of the heavies, he had a bad habit. Kept himself afloat by ripping off guys like Alan. He'd see em in here and get them involved in a game or two. His mates are all hustlers, they'd let the patsy ride high, hook him in, and then get him in a shit load of debt. If he didn't pay, well they got heavy.' He was searching through a card index holder. 'I haven't computerized this and it was many years ago, but - here it is. Derek Fletcher.'

He handed Castle the card.

'Is there anything else you can tell us?', Stone said.

'No. I can remember some of the faces of the crowd he hung out with, but no names. No one else had an account. Fletcher was the heavy. If anything happened to Alan, he'd know about it.'

Castle looked at the card. It was six years out of date.

Derek Fletcher's last known know address was in Streatham.

Stone drove to number 2 Wellfield Road, a shabby 20's house with PVC windows.

There were lights on inside and as Castle rang the bell they could hear the sound of a baby crying. He looked up at the first floor window and saw the twitch of a curtain. Finally a woman opened the door.

'Yes?'

'We're looking for Derek Fletcher.'

She looked over Castle's shoulder, her pale face riddled with suspicion.

'What's he done now?'

'Do you know him?'

She folded her arms.

'I ought to. I was married to him.'

'So he doesn't live here any more', Stone said.

'No. And he owes child maintenance.'

'Do you have an address for him?'

'I do.'

She went and wrote it down on a piece of paper. Castle peered into the hall, which was a mess of junk mail and various bags.

She came back with a piece of paper which she handed to Stone.

'Can you do anything about the money he owes me?'

'I'm sorry, but that's a matter for social services madam', Stone said.

They left and drove to the address in Mitcham, 10 Sadler Close, a grey house in a rundown street.

A Norton clogging up the cramped front garden, overflowing with weeds. Castle rang the bell and they stood at the peeling front door. Through the window they could see the flashing light of the TV screen.

Nothing.

He rang again.

A man's voice from inside.

'Who is it?'

'Police.'

There was a pause and the sound of something being dragged across the floor. A cupboard opening and closing.

They'd carried out a criminal records search on Fletcher and knew he'd gone to prison for armed robbery. They also knew he'd acted as a fence in the past.

Castle was about to ring the bell again when the door opened.

'Derek Fletcher?'

'Yeah, what's this about?'

'Can we come in please?'

'All right.'

He showed them through to the living room. The TV was showing a horse race and Fletcher's eyes immediately went to it.

He stood about six four, heavy and overweight in a pair of brown trousers and a white vest. C18 was tattooed into his right bicep.

'Bollocks', he said as the race ended.

He gestured to them to sit down on the sofa and sat opposite them in a chair.

'So?'

'We're investigating a disappearance', Castle said.

'Disappearance?'

'Of Alan Maple.'

'Never 'eard of him.'

'I think you have. He was involved in a gambling racket you were running.'

'No.'

'Look, we can do this down at the station if you prefer. All you need to do is give us the information we need.'

'Depends if I can give it to you.'

'Alan Maple.'

He scratched his head.

'Oh, that Alan, never thought of him by his surname, it was a long time ago.'

'Green eyes, stutter.'

'Don't remember nothing about his eyes. But, yes, the fellow I'm thinking about had a stutter. Nice fellow, what about him?'

'I believe you're one of the last people to have seen him alive.'

'Alive? Now hold on.'

'He disappeared around the time he was gambling with you. Now we're not here to investigate any gambling rackets, we just want to find out what happened to Alan.'

'And why do you think I know?'

'Because I think he owed you money.'

'Na.'

'Look, we know about your record, we haven't come here to make waves in your life, but we can start digging if you want us to. We also know you have some information. Give it to us and we'll leave.'

Fletcher thought for a moment.

'All right. I'll tell you what I can. Alan had a habit. A lot of us do. I was involved in some private games, a lot of money, you know the sort of thing. Alan got involved and owed us. He didn't pay.'

'Who were the other men involved?'

'Two are in prison, two are dead.'

'Do you think any of them could have done anything to Alan?'

'Charlie used to get heavy.'

'Charlie who?'

'Staker. He's inside, doing ten for armed robbery. None of the others would've cared. It was always Charlie who'd want his pound of flesh, but I can tell you we didn't hurt him much.'

'Much?', Stone said.

'He owed us a couple of k.'

'Which you'd hustled him for.'

'I ain't a hustler. Anyway, he was living in a flat round the corner from the bookie's.'

'In Thornton Heath?', Castle said.

'Yeah. He had this flat mate, bloody nutter he was. An we went round there to sort Alan out. He was there on his own. We weren't going to hurt him, just scare him and get our money. If Charlie had never gone over the top I would have stopped him. I've been inside once and don't want to go back. Anyway, we found Alan with all these papers and suitcases.'

'What papers?'

'Deed Poll. He'd changed his name and was about to do a runner.'

'Can you remember the name on the papers?'

'What do you think I am, an encyclopaedia?'

'So what happened?'

'Charlie starts pushing him about. He smacks Alan a couple of times. Nothing more than a black eye, that sort of thing. Anyway he says he'll pay us tomorrow. "Do we look like a couple of mugs?", Charlie says. Alan says they're not his cases and Charlie asks him why he's changed his name. Anyway, right at that moment the front door opens and it's his flat mate standing there with this look in his eyes. I've seen it before, I've seen it inside if you know what I mean and it don't matter how big the bloke is, it's a look that tells you to be careful. He stands there staring us down and says "Let him go now". Now Charlie's a big bloke and he's in one and he marches right over to this guy and says "what are you gonna do about it?" The guy stands there and says "You don't want to know that". Charlie throws a punch and he sidesteps him. I never saw him pull it, but he's got a knife in his hand all of a sudden and he stabs Charlie right in the fist and then slashes his cheek. In those few seconds that it takes Charlie to register what's happened he reaches behind a bookcase and draws a sword.'

'What sort of sword?', Stone said.

'Long handle, looked sharp, very sharp. He starts waving it about, threatening us, and we leave.'

'What did he look like?', Castle said.

'Tall. Six foot. Well built like he worked out. Not someone you would associate with violence. But I tell you, his eyes, I remember them.'

'Can you remember their colour?'

'Yeah. I can as a matter of fact. Blue. Piercing blue. Like they were on fire.'

Castle showed him Adam Makepiece's picture.

'This him?'

'Yeah, that's him all right.'

'Is there anything else you can remember about him?'

'No. But I did notice all these Bibles at the flat.'

'Bibles?'

'Yeah. They were everywhere. Piles of em in the hall. Rows of em in the living room. I didn't think Alan was religious, although

I've known guys trying to give up gambling get into all that stuff, but I always thought it must have had something to do with his flat mate.'

'Is that the last time you saw Alan?'

Fletcher paused for a moment.

'No. Charlie was very angry. Wanted to kill this other bloke, wanted his money. Was not going to let him get away. We went back later that day, Charlie had to have his face stitched up, he's still got the scar. As we turned the corner we saw them getting in a minicab. They were carrying their cases. We was parked round the corner and followed em.'

'Where?'

'An address in Windsor. They obviously wanted to get right out of the area. They went into a house and Charlie was right up for going straight in, but I told him to wait. We needed to check out who was living there.'

'We need the address.'

'It was a long time ago.'

'Even so.'

He shook his head.

'I don't know the house number. Not after two years, but it was the last house.'

He stood up and got a map off the shelf.

They watched as he thumbed through the index.

'Yeah, here it is, Albany road.'

Stone wrote it down.

'So, what happened?', she said.

'We went back the next day. We waited. There was no sign of movement. Nothing. Eventually Charlie got out of the car and just rang the bell.'

'You stayed in the car?', Castle said.

'No. I went with him. What other option did I have? Anyway, we waited, and this woman answered the door. Charlie just bursts past her and starts searching the house. She's about to call the police and I stop her. I always believe in talking to people. Anyway, they're not there. No sign of em. The woman tells me that Alan and her son had stayed the night and left that morning.'

'Her son?'

'Yeah. The flat mate. She'd put em up and didn't seem too happy with her son, kept saying he brought her nothing but trouble. Said she didn't even know Alan, that it was the only time she'd met him, what had they done and good riddance, that sort of thing.'

'Did she mention her son's name?', Stone said.

'Now you mention it. Funny name, something like Lija.'

'Lija?'

'Something like that. That was the last we saw of 'em. We tried making enquiries, we watched the house, but they never went back. Shortly after that we both went inside. Charlie's still in there.'

'Did you get the woman's name?', Castle said.

'No.'

'Is there anything else you can remember about Alan at that time?'

Fletcher thought for a moment.

'When we was making enquiries, we found out from one of the punters at the bookie's that Alan had been working as a sexton.'

'Where?'

'Wimbledon cemetery. We went there but he hadn't been in to work for days. His boss told us the last day he went in, which was a couple of days after we tracked him to that house.'

'There's nothing else you can tell us?'

'No.'

They stepped out into the overgrown front garden and walked to the car.

Black stood in the darkened hallways, cloistered and merged with the building, an offshoot of its medievalism.

Receiving no visitors, he stood at night staring blackly into the winter darkness, willing something he had started long ago towards its end.

Seeing the face of Castle recede like a drowning man, he shook away the twenty-first century and willed something older into being where he could resonate to his own particular form of homicide.

Blood lust and the torture of enemies were on his mind, a refrain from the depths of his psyche rising now and inspiring him. He saw his Apostle's face in the empty building and knew he was executing the final act.

It was for him a prelude to what would follow, what he had planned all these years.

The years of waiting, he called them.

From the time he tainted Castle with his escape from the first Woodland Killings he'd planned something bigger on a scale that would shake up the police force, and he hoped it would continue with the slow crucifixion of Castle.

102

The evening they left Fletcher, Stone dropped Castle at his house.

'You get the sense we're about to come face to face with him?', she said as she pulled up outside.

'No.'

'Me neither. Why is it that although we're on his tail, although we're getting definite leads I have the strong feeling there's something else here, something entirely hidden from us?'

He looked right into her then and knew this case had got her in the same way it got him so many years ago.

'You're in the labyrinth, Jacki. Welcome to the game.'

'So we go to Windsor tomorrow Frank?'

'Yeah. Although I think we're about to hit another dead end.'

'I'll be at the station early.'

'Thanks for the lift.'

He walked past the recycling boxes in his neglected front path. They were stacked with whisky bottles.

As he shut the door and realised he was out of food the frustration of relying on Stone to drive hit him. He was tired and hungry and wanted to sleep.

He opened the fridge: some butter and milk. In the cupboard only a finger of Johnny Walker.

He downed it and went outside and placed it carefully on top of the other bottles making sure it didn't roll off.

Then he walked to the local all night store and bought another bottle, seeing he didn't have enough cash to buy much else. He got some cheese and his change and walked back.

At two a.m. he awoke with a pain in his arm. He was facing the radiator and lying on a plug. He got up, rubbing the feeling back into his arm.

On the coffee table the half-eaten cheese and empty bottle. He staggered to the downstairs loo and started coughing.

Deep crimson gobbets of blood spattered the dirty sink. He looked at himself in the mirror, the tired eyes, the drawn face.

Running the tap only washed some of it away, and he could see there was something else in the blood, something that clung to the porcelain.

He started coughing again, feeling a tearing sensation deep within his chest. Sweat ran down his face stinging his eyes.

When he finally came out it was nearly an hour later.

He fetched a tissue and wiped his mouth, noticing the red smear.

He sat down heavily and then forced himself to get up and made a cup of tea with the remaining milk and staggered with it upstairs, the cup feeling heavy in his hand.

He lay on the bed looking at the street lamp outside the curtainless windows, its light hazing.

He sat up and sipped the tea and felt it burn him. He felt sick and lay there waiting for sleep.

Finally at 7 am he woke and coughed red onto the pillow and walked outside in the clothes he'd slept in.

He got in his car and drove the few miles to the 24 hour Sainsbury's.

He got cash from the wall and bought some food and painkillers and milk and as many bottles of Johnny Walker as he could cram in his basket and still carry.

As he paid he noticed his hands shaking. He dropped his change and knelt on the floor searching for the coins. One had rolled away and he left it, the cashier calling after him.

In the car he chewed two mouthfuls of sandwich, his throat like sandpaper and forced himself to swallow. It took a long time to go down and he started sweating again from the pain.

Then he opened one of the bottles and drank until he stopped shaking.

The pain started to grip him again as he pulled up outside his house and he collapsed in the hallway.

He left the shopping there and lay on the sofa until the coughing woke him again and he made it to the kitchen sink where he stained the metal red.

He ate a bit more of the sandwich and took some painkillers and lay down on his bed.

He realised he'd left the whisky downstairs but felt too weak to move.

Stone was waiting for him at the station when he rang her.

'Jacki.'

'You OK Frank?'

'No. Must be something I ate. I'm gonna have to stay near a bathroom today.'

'Shall I go to the address with Nash?'

'Yeah. Do that.'

'I hope you feel better tomorrow Frank.'

Some time later he went downstairs and put the shopping away and took a bottle of whisky upstairs with him where he lay cradling it like a dying lover.

He slept fitfully and by the afternoon managed to eat something, administering the whisky as if he were on a drip.

Stone briefed Nash and drove there, winding her way out of London, watching the skies clear slightly of the pollution as the sun struggled overhead against the few scattered clouds.

She thought about the range of possibilities behind Alan Maple's disappearance.

Albany road was a dull parade of houses set behind a pleasant belt of green land.

Fletcher hadn't said which side of the road the house was on.

She drove to the end and they got out and walked up the path to the house on the left. She rang the bell.

No answer.

They crossed the street and she rang number 24, hearing chimes from inside, then footsteps.

An attractive woman with light brown hair opened the door. She wore a pink cropped jacket and a black pleated skirt.

'I'm sorry to bother you, madam', Stone said, showing her ID, 'but I'm looking for someone who disappeared two years ago. He was last sighted leaving this address. Were you living here at that time?'

She hesitated.

'Who is it you're looking for?'

'Alan Maple.'

She shook her head.

'Name doesn't mean anything to me.'

'He was sighted leaving this house with another man.'

'It could be anyone. What's this about?'

Stone fished Adam Makepiece's photograph out and showed it to her.

'Do you recognise this man?'

She stared at it for a few seconds and then said 'you better come in.'

The house was immaculate inside and she showed them into the living room. Not an item out of place. The smell of apples and pine.

'Please, sit down', she said, sitting opposite them.

'Do you know the man in the photograph?'

'I do. He's my son.'

'And you are?'

'Kat Norris.'

Nash made a note.

'And your son's name?'

'Elijah.'

Stone remembered Fletcher's mispronunciation of the name.

She tried to suppress the adrenaline rush as she smelt the killer.

'When you last saw him, was he with someone?'

'It was two years ago. He came here for a night with a friend and they left the next morning, I don't remember his name. All I do know is the young man was firmly under my son's sway.'

'How?'

'Elijah was difficult. And forceful. Some people think it was the religious upbringing I gave him. When you've been brought up a Catholic it's hard to shake off, it stays with you. For many years when I was younger I tried to reject it, but you always return to it. I brought him up single-handedly. He never knew his father, maybe that was one of the problems, but he became obsessive about religion, ended up telling me I didn't understand the scriptures. It put me off, really, that level of fanaticism.'

'You think your son's a religious fanatic?'

'He was. I never saw him again after that day. He never called. He never wrote.'

'You have no idea where he went or what happened to him?'

'No.'

'The man he was with was called Alan Maple. You never saw him again?'

'No. But I did have a terrible shock a few days later. Two men, thugs, they looked like bouncers, came bursting into my house looking for Elijah's friend. Threatened me. I don't know what they wanted him for, but I hope for his sake they never caught up with him.'

'Mrs. Norris, do you have any idea where your son could be?', Nash said.

Grief swept over her face as she stared out of the window.

'No I don't.'

She showed them to the door and said 'what is this about? Has Elijah done something?'

Stone looked into her face and saw the deep-etched lines of years of struggle there.

She decided to spare her more pain.

'We're looking for Alan Maple and believe your son may be the last person to have seen him.'

Stone drove back to London, skirting Windsor Forest, thinking of its hunting history and connections to Henry the Eighth. Through the vista of trees she could see stags clashing their antlers.

103

Castle slept that night and woke feeling stronger. The coughing had stopped and he got up and managed to eat breakfast.

He drank some tea with whisky in it and then filled his flask before heading off to the station.

He found Stone and Nash waiting for him.

'Feeling better Frank?', she said, taking in the loss of colour in his face and the slow walk.

'Much.'

They followed him through to his office.

'So?', he said, sitting down.

'We went to the address in Windsor that Fletcher gave us and spoke to the mother of Alan Maple's flat mate.'

'So the lead was good.'

'Everything Fletcher told us pans out. She remembers her son coming there with someone who must be Alan. She remembers a couple of heavies coming round the next morning after they'd left.'

'Do we know where they went?'

'No.'

'She says she's never seen or heard from her son since', Nash said.

'You believe her?'

'For what it's worth yes', Stone said.

'So who is he?'

'Elijah Norris.'

Castle felt a seismic shift in the groundwork of the investigation.

'What do we know about him?'

'His mother said he was trouble. Seemed to have some control over Alan. Very religious. Fanatical.'

Castle narrowed his eyes.

'We have a picture of a guy who's impersonating Adam Makepiece, an assumed name by a man connected to the background of the case who never got the chance to wear the name. The picture is of the librarian.'

'Elijah Norris', Stone said.

'He's our killer.'

'I think so. But he's not the man we've been looking for. He's stolen his identity.'

The frustration at missing out on the interview swept over Castle like fire.

'Jacki, we're going back.'

'To re-interview Mrs Norris?'

'There's more there.'

Stone waited for him as he went to the loo and locked himself in a closet. He took a deep swig from his flask, then got a coffee from the machine and went back into his office where he topped it up with more whisky.

Clouds were building in the sky as she drove there and by the time they reached Windsor the horizon looked black. There was a half-light moving outside the car that gave the events that began to unfold a surreal dreamlike quality.

Castle sat with the window open saying little, sipping from his cup, feeling that this breakthrough was about to bring its resident demons with it. He was right, but nothing could have prepared him for the shock he was about to receive that day.

As Stone drove down Albany road the street suddenly became familiar to Castle, as if he'd known it all his life. He stared at the front door of number 24, feeling some sense of recognition he knew from cases when he was on the killer's turf.

He stepped out and walked up the path, Stone following.

He pressed the bell.

After the chimes had ceased he heard footfalls, then the door opening.

Stone waited for him to speak, but Castle stood there, not saying anything.

Mrs. Norris stared at him, their faces locked together, then she looked away down the street.

'Frank?', Stone said.

He turned round.

She would never forget the expression on his face. Whisky had left its crimson mark on him and used as she was to his ruddy complexion staring back at her over his desk every day, the ashen white face that met her eyes as he turned his head left her reeling.

'You all right?', she said.

He opened his mouth and licked his lips. She could see he had no spittle.

'Can you wait in the car please?'

'Frank?'

'Jacki, that's an order.'

'Why?'

He stared at her without moving until she followed her instinct and left him.

Castle went into the house and stood in the living room. He never sat down.

'Frank?'

'Hello Katlyn.'

'Is this about the young man who disappeared?'

'I've been looking for you.'

She looked away and lit a cigarette.

'Too many years Frank.'

'I couldn't find you.'

'I didn't want you to.'

'How have you been?'

'What kind of question is that?'

'Why didn't you call?'

'Do you remember how I felt living with you, or living with that case? It's still got you. I read the papers. You haven't changed. Still the old Frank.'

'You have a son.'

'Yes.'

'Called Elijah.'

'This about the case? Is that why this Alan's wanted? He a friend of Elijah's? That would be a coincidence wouldn't it? Or is this just some way you've dreamed up to harass me after all these years?'

'Is he mine?'

'I've got nothing to say to you Frank.'

'Is he mine?'

'I brought him up on my own. He doesn't have a father.'

'You were pregnant when you left.'

She looked at him. There was no emotion when she said it.

'He's yours. Genetically only.'

'How much does he know about me?'

'Nothing.'

'How much, Katlyn?'

'He found out about the case. Not until he was in his teens. I tried to bring him up religiously. I had a breakdown after leaving you, Frank. Postpartum depression they call it. Saw psychiatrists, the whole nine yards. That's what marriage to you did to me. I took pills, fistfuls of them for years. Never bonded with Elijah. Couldn't stand the sight of him. No wonder I turned to the Virgin Mary after being married to you.'

'So you never remarried?'

'No.'

'No father figures in Elijah's life?'

'No.'

'So what happened in his teens?'

'Why should I tell you?'

'I could always arrest you.'

'Yeah, I can believe it. Elijah studied the Bible. He knew the scriptures off by heart, but when he started to become a young man he wanted to know about his father, about you, Frank.'

'So why didn't you tell him?'

'Why do you think?'

'Why didn't you tell me?'

'What, and have you screw his life up too?'

'I think you've done that, Katlyn, I think you've done it far more than you realise.'

'I mean, look at us, we haven't seen each other or spoken in twenty-eight years and here we are having another one of our domestics. Just like old times.'

'Tell me about Elijah.'

'What's he done?'

'Just keep reading the papers.'

She took a long drag on her cigarette and looked hard at him.

'He wanted to know about you. I wouldn't tell him. So he became difficult.'

'Difficult how?'

'Started arguing with me, telling me I didn't understand the Bible, telling me that I didn't respect God the father, and then one day, he hit me.'

'He hit you?'

'Yeah.'

She leaned towards him and lifted her hair from her ear. A red scar ran two inches across her scalp.

'He did that?'

'He was ranting and raving about finding his father and he picked up a tea cup and struck me with it.'

'Was this a one off?'

'You bet your life. I had enough shit from you. I threw him out. After that he'd come and go. He was sixteen. He left school, just gave up. Spent hours at the gym. Got into trouble. Small stuff, slap on the wrist time. Then changed. One day he became this calm, never-lose-control guy. He said he'd found the hidden meaning of the scriptures and found his real father.'

'What did he mean by that?'

She shrugged.

'I knew he hadn't found you. He said his father was a monk and he was going to live with him. To be honest with you, I wanted rid of him so I let him go. This was around the time he came here with that young man. He said it was the last time he would ever ask me to put him up, and it was. He didn't cause any trouble, in fact he was very nice, they didn't say much, and they left the next day.'

'You have no idea where he went?'

'None.'

'And he's named Elijah Norris on his birth certificate?'

'I was hardly likely to call him Elijah Castle, was I Frank?'

'My officer says that you described Elijah as a fanatic.'

'Yeah. He was a religious nutter. You know the psychiatrist I saw said that my mental illness was hereditary, that giving birth triggered it and it was likely Elijah would suffer mental health problems too.'

'What did he know about me Katlyn?'

'Shortly before he left home I found a whole bunch of clippings in his room.'

'Clippings?'

'Yeah. Of you. The great detective. The case, you remember the case Frank?'

'Thanks, Katlyn.'

He turned and walked away from the house, down the path and got into the car.

Without looking at Stone he said 'drive'.

She held her hands on the steering wheel and didn't move them.

'Not until you tell me what that was all about, Frank.'

She looked at him and saw his hands were shaking. There was still no colour in his face.

'That was my ex-wife.'

She stared at him, taking in the meaning of his words, absorbing the devastation of their implication for him, and then said: 'while we're breaking police procedure, how about a drink?'

'Why not?'

She drove to the nearest pub.

Frank needed several before he was ready to leave. When she got him in the car she drove him home.

Black gathered his things together as dawn broke on the horizon.

Ice held to the windows in the ancient frames at Rondelo and the corridors felt frozen.

He locked the doors to every room and left by the front, walking down the drive and disappearing at its end.

He carried only a suitcase and a small bag.

104

When Castle drove to the station the next morning he felt as though the familiar streets and signposts of the journey were part of someone else's life, as though the existence he had led had been conducted at some distance from himself and was somehow unreal.

The conversation with Katlyn had wiped the past twenty-eight years and he felt some internal leaking of his soul, as if he had been punctured to his vital core and his life's essence was running away. The case, its resurrection of the past, all of it was an annulment of his life and a bringing to life of the dead.

He needed a distraction and dispelled the idea of whisky this early by switching on the radio. The DJ announced a Wishbone Ash song, triggering a chain of thought in his mind about the killer's favoured tree. The mythological connection it achieved between Heaven and the Underworld seemed more potent than ever to him now. He remembered telling Stone how the roots of the tree were believed to be connected to the Rivers of the Past, the Present and the Future, and he realised in that instant what had happened to time in his universe. Could the ash tree's joint bear the weight of his personal burden? He saw that time for him had died twenty-eight years ago when Katlyn had left him and the case had taken hold of his soul. That the life of his son had been leeching his own, as if Elijah existed like some parasite in his psyche.

He stopped the car and switched the radio off and walked to the nearest shop, past the winos on the shit-stained bench who smiled toothlessly and waved at him in recognition.

He bought a small bottle of Johnny Walker and a bottle of Coke half of which he tipped into the gutter by his car, filling the rest with whisky. He'd stopped coughing blood and was making sure he ate at regular intervals.

He drank some neat and steadied his nerves and aimed the car like a missile at the station and his shame.

Stone was waiting for him.

She'd been up all night debating how to approach him, agonising over what this had done to him. She'd realised during that dark night that Castle was like a father to her, and the impact this would have on his psyche frightened her both professionally and personally.

She set her face into a look of restrained compassion as he walked through the door, wanting to reach him, fearful of patronising him.

He didn't look at her, just marched over to his desk.

'Jacki.'

'Morning Frank.'

He picked up the phone.

'I'm calling Tom, he needs to know. I can't think straight and I need his opinion here.'

'I think that's a good idea Frank. Anything I can do for you?'

'Just a coffee, please.'

'Sure. And if you need to talk.'

She knew how hard it was going to be for him to tell it all to Spinner, so she called him on his mobile and filled him in as he made his way there.

'Are you sure this is Frank's son?'

'Yes.'

'You know what this means don't you?'

'He shouldn't be involved in the case.'

'Right.'

'You gonna tell him that?'

'No.'

'When he tells you act surprised.'

Spinner did and Castle ran through yesterday's events as if he was reading out a list. There was no emotion in his voice and he kept his hands behind his back while he told him.

Stone noticed that his thumbs were interlocked throughout. They were white when he released them and picked up his bottle of Coke.

Spinner shook his head.

'That's unbelievable, Frank, and first of all I must say the impact of this on you is incalculable.'

'Help me solve this case', Castle said.

'I will, but are you all right to go on?'

'I am. I need to end this thing.'

'I know you do. You've needed to end it for years. It felt personal then and it's just got a whole lot more personal now. But I would be unprofessional if I didn't make sure you were mentally fit to carry on.'

'Mentally fit? What the hell does that mean?'

'Nothing. You've just suffered a major trauma, Frank. In fact they don't get much more major than that. Reality check. You've been obsessed by this case for twenty-eight years.

It precipitated a mental breakdown in you which has left a scar in your career. Karl Black played games with you and your superior officer and won. He's still playing. Even your son's name, Elijah, is significant. Your wife gave it to him but do you know what it means?'

'He was a Biblical prophet.'

'According to the Book of Kings, Elijah raised the dead, and he is seen as the harbinger of the Messiah. The case has resurrected itself and I've seen the pressure it's put on you, I've felt it myself. I think you're a first-rate detective, but this thing could explode.'

'Like I don't know that.'

'You're in shock and haven't had time to process what happened yesterday.'

'We haven't got time.'

'I know. But I need to clarify in my mind whether you've registered what this means.'

'What? That my son, the son I didn't know I had is probably the killer, that he's working together with Karl Black?'

'Yes.'

'That the ghost I'm hunting is my own flesh and blood?'

Spinner looked at him.

'That's a start. But consider also that his father now is Karl Black. That whatever happened to him in his mind, you are an enemy and that in effect what this means is that Black's empire extends to your offspring. How much more personal can it get Frank?'

'I've thought all this through. I've thought about all this all night.'

'And have you thought what this will do to your obsession? It will tell your obsession that the reason you never got over the Woodland Killings is that they were personally connected to you, it's your son you're hunting as you say Frank and some piece of you will die if and when you catch him.'

'Yeah. The piece this case has held power over all these years.'

'Also the piece of you that is on this side of crime.'

A white line flashed into Castle's mind and blurred. He took a swig of Coke.

'This case has to end.'

'Yes. My concern is that it will end you.'

'I don't know Elijah. I'm just catching the killer.'

'The killer is your son, Frank. It's your son you need to catch.'

'This is about Black.'

'Oh he's managed to put a rusting hook so deep into your soul he only needs to tap the line and you're twitching.' He saw a veil come over Castle's face, a look of death in his eyes. 'However he and Elijah met, he was gifted an Apostle. And the Apostle is a human being you brought into the world. Your wife deserted you thanks to Black, she bore your child and you didn't even know, what kind of sucker does that make you? You think you're fit to carry on with this case?'

Castle remained in control of himself, knowing the game.

'Yes.'

'So Black took over your son's head having taken over your soul and he turns him into the second Woodlands Killer. The only thing he didn't do is fuck Katlyn.'

'Hey come on Tom', Stone said.

'It's OK', Castle said. 'Tom, I've thought of all of this.'

'And you still want to finish the case?'

'Yes.'

'Black took your son from you and turned him into the ghost you've been haunted by all these years.'

That was when Spinner saw the pain.

'Yes', Castle said, 'yes.'

Spinner looked at him for a while.

'OK', he said. 'We carry on, but we've got a lot we need to talk about.'

'One thing's for sure', Castle said. 'Elijah stole Alan Maple's new identity. He became Adam Makepiece before he got started in his new life away from all his gambling problems, away from the heavies who were after him, before anyone knew what Adam Makepiece looked like. That's him', he said, prodding the picture on his desk. 'So the million dollar question is what happened to Alan Maple?'

'Elijah killed him', Spinner said.

'Right.'

'It's not going to help us find Elijah.'

'No. But say Alan Maple didn't die, say he's part of this whole machine that Black's got going.'

'You mean another cog?'

'Yes.'

'He's not the killer.'

'We need to eliminate him.'

'Well if we're right, and I think we are, then he's dead. We need to find his body.'

'Mike Nash found out that Alan Maple's last job was as a sexton', Stone said.

Spinner looked at her.

'Where?'

'Wimbledon cemetery.'

'We go there then', Castle said.

'And do what?', Spinner said.

'Find out from the records the last burials Alan Maple was involved in. We check that last week before he disappeared and we exhume the graves. Alan Maple's bones are probably lying next to someone else's.'

Spinner looked at Castle with a new respect.

'OK. We eliminate Alan Maple once and for all.'

'What are we waiting for?', Castle said.

'One more thing Frank.'

'What Tom?'

'Say Katlyn filled your son's head with the Bible, priming him for an over-zealous religious father figure. Are you in touch with the fact that he sought Karl Black out, not the other way round? I know Black's good at getting inside people's heads, but only clinical paranoia will tell you that he knew your wife was pregnant and that he sought your son out.'

'Will it?'

'Yes, Frank. So consider this, your son sought Black out deliberately.'

'Yeah, Katlyn screwed his head up with religion.'

'No. What I'm saying is this. He found out you were his father. He found out about the Woodlands Killings. Our profile on Alan Maple still holds good, it's just we were applying it to the wrong person. He reads up about you, it's not hard to do, it's heavily archived. He wants to know about you. But Katlyn's brought him up, she's filled his head with hateful stories about you, and she does hate you Frank. Never telling you about him.'

'After seeing her yesterday you think I don't know that?'

'When Elijah needed his father he wasn't there. He's angry with his mother but he needs her, there's dependency there. He reads how the case took over. Who knows, maybe Katlyn even tells him your obsession with the case drove her away, ruined her life, ruined his.'

'Where are you going with all this Tom?'

'Straight to the body blow you've just been dealt, but I don't think you're feeling yet. And Frank, you need to feel it. If you can do that and then go to the cemetery, then you're OK to carry on. This is the point Frank. Elijah at some point wrote you off. Blamed you, blamed your obsession with the case and transferred onto Black as his father. Like I've been saying, the killer wanted God the father and he sure as hell got him.'

'OK he sought him out.'

'Frank, there's one thing you're feeling that isn't paranoid, and it's that this case is personal.'

'I've always felt that.'

'Well, you may not always have been right, but it is now. Your son has deliberately bonded with your nemesis.'

Castle looked away as he said it.

'I know.'

Spinner and Stone watched him as he tilted the Coke bottle neck up and drank the last dregs.

'Have you figured out what Elijah's motive is?', Spinner said.

'Beyond religion?'

'Revenge, Frank, revenge. He wants to destroy you.'

Stone saw his rage suppress his pain.

'This is a case and I'm gonna solve it', he said. 'I'm gonna focus on Black.'

'OK Frank', Spinner said, 'let's go and dig up the body.'

Stone drove them to Gap road in Wimbledon.

105

Stone parked and they got out and walked the path up to the gatekeeper's office.

Castle had called the cemetery on their way there, and the manager knew the situation and its gravity.

Mr. Morris, the manager, was a small man with a pointed bald head whose eyes sparkled as he spoke.

From time to time he would twitch his nose, and Stone was reminded of a field mouse.

He belonged in a world of dusty books and records and after letting them in proceeded to find the information they wanted.

'We need the records of the last burials Alan Maple was involved in', Castle said.

'Yes, naturally, I understand', he said, bustling about his office. 'Please sit down.'

He pulled out chairs for them, dusting one down and placing it before Stone.

It was obvious this was what he lived and breathed for.

Stone watched as he went through to an inner room of the office. He pulled a cord switching on the single bare bulb and searched for the records among the many box files that lined the walls of the windowless room.

'It's here somewhere', he said, 'Alan Maple, I remember him. What has he done I wonder? Police business, yes, confidential, you don't need to tell me about confidential. Ah, here it is!'

He brought through a sheaf of papers and sat down at his desk and started thumbing through them.

'This is the time period you gave me Chief Inspector Castle. Yes indeed.'

They watched as he licked his index finger, then lovingly turned over page after page with relish and a loud swish of paper.

'Alan Maple carried out two burials during that period, one Edna Jones and Neville Turner.'

He handed Castle the page.

'Thank you. We need to get the coffins out.'

Mr Clarke looked at him and pressed his fingertips close together.

'Exhume the graves?'

'Yes.'

'Oh dear, oh dear me. That is the first time that will have happened at this cemetery to my knowledge.'

'I'm sorry, Sir, but this is a murder inquiry.'

'A murder inquiry? Yes indeed. Well, there's nothing for it. Exhume the graves. I'll need an hour or so, I'll have to close. I'll show you the plots.'

They waited while he checked the papers, then phoned his boss.

Outside it had started to rain and Stone watched as Castle stood in it, water cascading off his jacket, swigging Coke.

Clarke fled down the path under a massive umbrella, looking like a field mouse scurrying away from the elements.

He went about checking there were no visitors, then locking all the gates.

Meanwhile Stone called in a digger. She also called Nash. Then they waited.

They turned up a few hours later after Clarke had given them all tea and biscuits.

He opened the main gate to let them through, directing the digger to the correct area of the cemetery.

Nash joined Stone and Castle as they walked over.

When they got there they found Spinner talking to Clarke.

'We'll have to ask you to leave now, Sir', Castle said.

'Leave?', Clarke said, 'yes, of course, you will be careful, won't you?'

They waited while he scurried away.

'We'll start with Edna Jones', Castle said.

They stood back and watched as the officer removed the earth, depositing it beside the grave in a mound.

It didn't take long.

The officer got out and prised open the lid.

Only the rotten bones of a single corpse, small, shrunken, sad, the brown remnants of what had once been a human life now lost to this indignity and lying there exposed.

They turned away and walked the few metres across the sodden earth while the officer replaced the lid and then put the coffin back in the earth.

No one spoke as they exhumed the grave of Neville Turner. The idea that here too would lie a single corpse was too daunting in a long road of dead ends.

As the coffin was lifted out Castle walked forward. The officer levered off the lid which gave a cracking sound as it gave up all resistance.

There within lay two skeletons, one longer than the other, both sets of bones getting wet in the downfall of rain.

106

Back at the station they knew the case had finally narrowed to that certainty they had sought for so long, and now they were at the destination they'd toiled for but without the taste of victory. They knew who they were looking for and knew his motivation, and Stone dreaded the impact the resolution would have on Castle.

All those years of struggling towards this and the ending so painful. She wished for another conclusion, seeing how brilliantly Black had worked this to his advantage.

The whisky he'd been drinking all day was showing on Castle's face and she looked at him and pitied him. This was not something she wanted to feel for a man she respected so much.

His son the Woodlands Killer.

Castle didn't say much and they wrapped it up fairly quickly.

'Elijah killed Alan and buried him, stealing his identity as Adam Makepiece.'

'He got the perfect cover to carry out what he wanted to do', Spinner said.

'And what Black wanted him to do.'

'He was no one. He was living inside another man. He became the perfect killing machine.'

'So how do we find him?', Nash said.

'The only way is through Black', Castle said. 'They're going to be in contact. What was it you said about the nature of their relationship Tom?'

'A mentor relationship.'

'So they need each other.'

'They most definitely do Frank.'

'So we watch Black.'

'What if we don't have time Frank?', Stone said. 'What if there are more killings?'

'You're right.'

'We need to go back to our list', she said. 'We need to identify which targets he'll strike next, because he's still out there, and only one man knows where.'

They spent the rest of that long day working on the list and Maurice Tweed came out at the top.

His involvement in the government and what was known of his recent machinations against the church primed him as a target.

Castle and Stone put together a special surveillance unit to watch and protect him and made an appointment personally for the next day to meet with him, warn him of the threat he was under and explain the situation.

Outside the window winter was falling with the darkness.

Stone hung up, her reflection in the pane like a lonely shadow in her home.

The house was full of echoes and then silences where her head swam in some river of murders and the hazing of boundaries of who she was, dragged deeper into homicide by the sense of some blackness at the edge of all she knew and recognised as humanity.

She was tired of hearing Don's voicemail. The reassurance his recorded voice offered her of a constant in her fractured world had lost its power to calm her troubled mind.

As if, seeing Castle fall apart, she expected to find one of Black's accomplices lurking in her wardrobe. She knew her betrayal was altogether more mundane.

She thought of how he'd left and looked around her at the house and the papers.

Outside a light sleet flecked the windows.

Adam Makepiece's face swam into her mind, suddenly more real than Don's, and she remembered he was not real as she reached for her husband's picture to steady herself and still the rocking craft she navigated.

That night Tweed was taken from his house in the back of a car where he slept.

Elijah drove slowly, drawing no attention to himself, showing no sign of nerves or hurry.

Tweed would sleep for hours and wake somewhere very different.

He left the town and drove into the countryside.

He had something special planned for Tweed.

Tweed the big shot.

Tweed the supplier of moneys to the government.

Tweed the colleague of Mover.

Tweed who would destroy the churches.

Finally, he stopped by a blackened building and removed the body from the boot, lugging it into the house and down some stairs into a basement.

One light bulb illuminated the bare room, at the end of which stood a tall Cross.

Ten feet high, it was ready for Tweed, who slumped now in a chair to which Elijah strapped him, tying the rope tight.

He looked down at his sleeping captive.

His face glowed handsomely above the fat one below him and he moved stealthily through the nether light and shut the door.

Upstairs he sat and waited.

When Tweed awoke he would go down to him.

Then he would begin to torture him.

Outside the winter night grew colder.

A harsh frost began to settle on the ground.

Tweed stirred in the freezing, blackened basement.

107

While Wilkes remained silent in his cell and Spinner developed his profile on the killer, Castle and Stone drove to their meeting with Tweed.

'We're not going to get him to talk', Castle said.

'Who, Wilkes?'

'Yeah. He's hiding something and he won't let it go until this thing's over.'

'News on Steele?'

'He's gone. Full stages of schizophrenia.'

'How much do we tell Tweed?'

'He'll know the case from the papers. We tell him that we believe he's a target and he needs to go under police protection.'

'That it?'

'You let me do the talking.'

But there was to be no talking.

When they got to his offices, his secretary informed them that Maurice Tweed had not been in and there was no response from his house.

They raced round to Tweed's address. When they got there, his distraught wife showed them the marks on the tiles in the hallway.

'These are drag marks', Castle said. 'Someone's pulled him out of the house.'

Tweed found himself facing his capturer.

He took in the face, handsome and inhuman as a shadow cast by some other order of being broken through into his world.

Tweed had always been able to find the angle, the way into someone, and he looked now for something on which to pin his hopes.

Elijah began to loosen his ties and he thought for a moment he was going to be released, then he felt the pain.

Searing pain as his flesh was stripped away, a good section of his leg hanging from the blade and dripping his blood across his face and head in some baptism.

'What do you want?', he said, the words semi-comprehensible, gobbets of black blood dripping from the wounded mouth.

Elijah looked at him, his eyes as cold as sapphires.

'I want your Crucifixion.'

'How much?'

'Like your friend, you think in terms only of money.'

'What then?'

'I want your Crucifixion.'

He pulled Tweed's head around so that he could see behind him. The Cross loomed down at him.

'Who are you?'

'I am that you seek to destroy.'

'Why are you doing this?'

'You seek the ruination of the churches.'

'No.'

'You are the anti-priest and serve the Filth.'

'It's just taxes.'

'And this is just taxes too.'

'Look, I have a lot of money.'

He stabbed him, piercing the flesh.

Tweed heard the rending of himself in the silent basement, displaced from his own pain like some shadow witness to his execution.

'This is not about money, this is about restoring order to the Earth. The Corrupt like you have destroyed this society and now it is time for you to be brought to book.'

'They'll catch you.'

'They'll never catch me.'

And he brought Blade down and entered him into the Flesh of the man and he removed the man's Flesh and placed it before him as he had done with his colleague, Tweed witnessing this offering of himself like some spectral guest at his own funeral.

And the other listened to Blade singing and the man's cries.

'I'm going to arrest Black', Castle said.

Stone looked at him.

'After the last time?'

'He can try his best shots.'

She drove there in silence.

When they stopped outside Rondelo, they could tell no one was there.

After knocking Castle forced the door with difficulty.

Entering they were struck by the freeze.

'The doors are all locked', Stone said.

Castle managed to find a light and searched for keys.

Then he kicked one in.

Only empty rooms and the old sense that Black was predicting their moves.

She watched him as they returned to the car, his face haunted, somewhere else.

Black entered the small hotel and checked in.

Depositing bags on the bed, he sat and thought.

He switched on the news.

He remained in his room.

'We need to think where he's holding Tweed', Castle said.

He and Stone looked at the map of the basement where they found Mover.

'Any basements, disused buildings within this radius', he said, drawing a circle round it, 'we need checked'.

108

They worked into the night to find out where Tweed was being held captive. Photographs of Black and Elijah went nationwide. Black stayed where he was, a recluse returned to the society he hated. Wilkes remained locked in his cell. Like a monk, he moved in his own world. Any information he held remained locked inside him.

Under section Steele railed about the king and Anne Boleyn, unaware of where he was. He had done what he was assigned to do and he lay within the grip of his psychosis.

A team of police officers scoured the area Castle had designated and went into every basement.

Castle and Stone themselves were part of this hunt, and at the end of two days they returned to the station with nothing.

'He's not going to be where we look', Castle said. 'I know how this goes.'

'The killer would take him somewhere we wouldn't think of', Spinner said.

'So far it's been in the town, so he's likely to have gone outside the city. What kind of buildings are we looking for? We need to think like him.'

'He likes medievalism', Spinner said, 'so let's see what buildings matching that description we can come up with.'

Tweed heard a noise at the door.

He couldn't believe that a man like him could be in this position, and now began to think about Mover.

Elijah entered.

'How long are you going to keep me here?', he said.

'You will not leave.'

'If not money then what?'

He looked at Tweed.

'Do you think everything has a price?'

His eyes bored into Tweed like a drug, removing him from his thoughts and Tweed looked at the face, timeless and not of this century as it moved away in the dim light, the last eyes he would see.

As he looked at him he wondered if his face had changed.

The man looked older and Tweed thought much time must have passed since he came there.

Then the blade was brought forth and Tweed knew it was time.

He said little until the end when he began screaming again, so loudly he shattered one of his own eardrums in the hollow basement.

He was hacked and hewn into pieces and lay all around while still breathing and was hoisted onto the Cross where Elijah placed him and nailed him hard, the blood running down his body and leaving him there.

Tweed looked down at the nails in him.

He felt them tear him as he moved and he stopped.

He saw the basement dim and shadow itself away from him.

In the dim light he saw him writing something on the wall.

The last thing he saw were the words: 'The Whip of Justice Touches their Backs' stretching across the wall like some graffiti at Golgotha.

A chill settled on the grass and the trees outside as another winter night began.

The old carvings on the building were caught by a distant moon and shone with an unearthly light, appearing like some creatures settled on the house.

Elijah came out of the basement and placed some things into a case.

Then he donned the hat and the thick clothes that gave his figure a shapeless look.

The beard had grown and covered his face now, the black hair making him look older.

He left the building and walked across the crisp grass, disappearing into the moonlit landscape.

Black laid the papers on the cheap hotel table.

He studied them, then placed them in his bag.

He looked out of the window down at the street below, the throng full of those he wished to witness his belief.

Then he sat in the room with a single light burning.

'There's a building here', Spinner said.

Castle and Stone turned to look.

'It's a medieval house. Privately owned.'

'Phone number?'

'No.'

Castle looked at the map.

'It's in a deserted part of Essex. I say we go there.'

Stone drove there breaking the speed limit all the way.

They entered a series of country lanes.

'Here', Castle said, seeing a narrow dirt track.

It opened onto some land and at its end was the building.

The front door was unlocked and they walked in.

'It's here', he said, years of waiting coming to this point. 'I can smell him.'

They drew their Glocks.

It didn't take them long to find the cellar door and they descended into the darkness.

Opening the door released the stench that told them they were too late and Stone fumbled for the light. There in the gloom they saw the crucified Tweed and the body parts and the scene of his execution and the hacking of Elijah's Blade.

Castle stood and read the final message and left before Stone who followed him out into the bracing air.

109

They are too late
Now they seek me and I flee
There will be more for them
The Servants of the Corrupt will always be brought to Justice while
the New Jerusalem is being built
Out of their hacked unhallowed Flesh
Served with the spoils of whores and Lies
Their House is sacked and now New Battles will be waged against
the ungodly

Back at the station Castle and Stone sat facing Spinner.

There was an air of failure and doom that hung over the office.

The door opened and Nash walked in.

'What do we do now?', he said.

'We're close', Spinner said.

Castle looked at him, something dying in his eyes.

'Not good enough.'

'We've got to get Elijah', Nash said.

'We're on his tail', Spinner said. 'He targeted Tweed and he killed him. Wilkes is the key. If we can get Black Wilkes might betray him. If we'd got there sooner we would have caught him. I'm convinced we can do so with the next one.'

'While the press finish us off, you mean?', Castle said.

'And what if there isn't a next one?', Stone said.

Spinner looked at her.

'There will be.'

'What if she's right?', Castle said.

'What?'

'Maybe he won't kill again.'

'He will, he has to', Spinner said.

'OK. What if he doesn't kill again for a while?'

'You mean, he goes into hiding? Yes, it's happened before, then I'd say he'll leave the country.'

'I want all airlines searched for tickets bought in the name of Adam Makepiece', Castle said. 'Mike, get everyone on it.'

Elijah moved through the crowd anonymously.

He queued and got his boarding card and waited quietly for the call to board the plane that would take him to his new life.

Black moved like a shadow among the multitude.

He entered the throng and merged with it, at one with those he would see slaughtered on his field of battle. Looking about him, he saw no known faces.

He looked at his watch and seeing the time a sense of deep satisfaction spread across him.

The recruits had been disbanded, some of them returning to the lives they had before they'd joined The Last Brotherhood. Some had prison sentences and would serve these, returning to a world they loathed.

As Stone toiled, Don sat in his office facing her picture.

He picked up the phone. The message he left would give her hope that they could work things out, but she would not get it until later.

It was Castle who got there first.

'A ticket's been bought in the name of Adam Makepiece for the four o'clock flight to Amsterdam', he said.

He'd personally gone through as many airlines as he could and found it.

Heathrow was a mass of heaving bodies and suitcase lugging travellers turning this way and that, getting in Castle's way. He flashed his badge, holding it up in the air as Stone trailed behind him, keeping an eye out for anyone who looked like Elijah, just in case he'd got a tip off and was leaving.

She found it hard to believe at this stage they were going to catch him, the weariness of the case, she told herself.

A young man with a face resembling him only slightly was dragged over to some advertising by Castle. He produced his ID and demanded to know the reason for this and was summarily left by Castle.

They found the queue for Royal Dutch Airlines and checked it: the queue was for another flight and the plane Elijah was on was about to board.

By now police swarmed the building and the airline received the alert to hold the flight.

Castle got the message that all passengers were on the plane and they sealed it off.

'Looks like we got to him just in time', he said to Stone as they ran to the plane.

Cabin crew were about to close the doors as they approached.

'You have a dangerous passenger on board', Castle said, flashing his badge at the flight attendant who retreated red-faced as Castle checked the seat number and headed down the aisle past the turning heads, Stone behind him all the way.

He began to feel a sense of triumph, knowing the case was now over.

They had him.

In the far seat on the aisle sat a man wearing a hat with his head down, obviously shielding himself against their eyes.

Castle raised his Glock, head high, as a startled woman shielded her small son.

He gestured to her to move and she grabbed her child and retreated to the rear of the aircraft.

Stone watched the frozen tableau, Castle with his Glock in the air, the figure unmoving.

'Adam Makepiece, you're under arrest', he said.

It struck her how he used Elijah's assumed name, and then the thought was lost in what followed.

The figure didn't move.

Castle leant into him, his pistol inches from his head.
Then he looked up.
Slowly, he raised his head until his eyes were boring into Castle.
There smiling at him was Karl Black.
'Good afternoon Chief Inspector', he said, 'we meet again.'
Stone looked round, suspecting it was a diversion.
They checked every passenger.
No Elijah on the plane.
They hadn't swapped seats.
Black had boarded as Makepiece, and they led him off cuffed.

110

Elijah landed in Ecuador as Castle and Stone left the airport.

He passed through customs, hailed a taxi and went to his hotel.

Unpacking his case, he looked out of the window: the milling South American life.

Plenty of souls for the Last Brotherhood.

He thought for a moment. He would shave off the beard and get something to eat then it was time to begin the second phase of the War.

Castle sat opposite his nemesis who looked as calm as he always had.

'Where is he?', he said, his voice sounding like crunched gravel.

'Been drinking again, Chief Inspector? Maybe you need a new poison. You know, Jonas provided the congregation with the newly shed blood of Laurence Steele's victims. As they say, that'll put hair on your chest.'

'Where is he?'

'Who are you talking about?'

'You know very well.'

'In search of a son?'

Stone was keeping her eyes glued to Castle and saw him interlock his fingers so tightly his knuckles cracked.

'Ow!', Black said, 'that sounds painful, but then Chief Inspector Castle, you've always been in a lot of pain, haven't you?'

'Why did you board the plane in the name of Adam Makepiece?'

'No doubt an administrative error.'

'You're an accomplice in these murders.'

'Another unfounded statement which you won't be able to prove.

You haven't got a shred of evidence and you'll be made an even bigger laughing stock by this, if that is possible.'

'We'll find him, you know.'

'Your son, Elijah Castle.'

'That's not his name.'

'Yes, Elijah Castle, now let me think.' He fixed his eyes on Castle and as he spoke, some pinpoint of light seemed to sparkle in them. 'He hated you, of course. You do know that? Blamed you for walking out on his mother, leaving them in the lurch. Blamed you for his childhood at her hands, she wasn't nice to him, not nice at all, no, but then you wouldn't know about that, would you, being an absentee father?'

'You will answer the questions I ask you, or I will keep you here until you rot.'

'Let's see what my lawyer has to say about that shall we? He'll be here shortly.'

'What was it? Couldn't do the killings again yourself?'

'You know your son spoke at great length of what he wanted to do to you.'

'Answer my questions.'

Black stared into him.

'He wanted to crucify you.'

'You incited him to kill.'

'Interesting concept.'

'You're going away for a very long time.'

'You would know all about a lifetime's imprisonment.'

'You've run out of manoeuvring space', Stone said.

'Oh? Like you did in your so-called marriage.'

'You might think you've scored some kind of personal triumph over me by involving my son in your sick world, but I never knew him and I never will and much as this may surprise you, to me he is just another killer now, a killer I will have no hesitation arresting.'

'Dear dear, how you delude yourself.'

'Watch me.'

'I am, and what I see is a broken man. You might be convincing yourself right now with your little speech, but even Stone isn't buying it.'

'Let's start with The Last Brotherhood.'

'It no longer exists. Like you.'

'I will catch Elijah, the same way as I've reeled you back in out of the polluted waters you swim in.'

'Unlikely. He's an interesting young man, quite unlike you, but then that happens you know. It's for the best you never knew him because you would have seen how much better than you he is. In every way he is your moral superior, and you would have been in touch with that every day. Your ego wouldn't have coped with it. The same way as your ego can't cope with your failure now.'

'He can't go far.'

'He can. Because he doesn't really exist. Like you. You've been swimming against the tide for years, Castle, fighting that blackness in your soul, slaking its rabid thirst at the fountain of crime and wiping the blood from your lips before anyone notices. Fighting the whisky. And all along there was a piece of you, something that grew in your wife's womb, out there, becoming a re-enactment of the thing that destroyed you all those years ago.'

'Tell us where he is, we can keep you here indefinitely', Stone said.

'He doesn't exist. Who is Adam Makepiece? You've been chasing a chimera. You dwell in the darkness.' Black leant forwards inspecting him. 'Let us say Adam Makepiece is resurrected. Think of the name and its attendant symbolism. Adam. The Garden of Eden. We're living in a Postlapsarian world. You fell years ago in the dark woods Chief Inspector, you've been nursing your bruises ever since. And Elijah. The dead are walking again, Chief Inspector. You understand so little of the nature of what you're involved in. Why did you become a policeman?'

'I'm asking the questions round here.'

'Except you're not answering them. You're a national failure. You sought crime because you are attracted to it, but lack the skill to understand it and catch a criminal. You are already being hounded by the press, think what they'll do when news gets out of another cock-up. What was it, did you expect to gain some intelligence by mixing with criminals?'

'You can't get to me.'

'Drink Frank?'

'I know you. I know you've instructed him to kill again.'

'Except you don't know me. You don't understand much, Chief Inspector.'

'You're sitting in a killer's seat.'

'It's not a crime.'

'Incitement to murder is. What was it? Some sort of Apostle relationship? Acting out the Bible? You think you're Jesus?'

Black looked at him, stilling him in the centre of who he was, holding his world there in that single gaze.

'Do you know what an Apostle is, Chief Inspector? A follower. I have followers and you're one of them. You've been following me for decades now, dragging your tired footsteps through the mud, your life fading to nothing. It's a complex relationship and often the Apostle doesn't know he is one. Your son is mine. And you know what Chief Inspector? So are you.'

Something seemed to fall away from Castle then, some old hope and its attendant fears, and he knew what had kept him alive all these years was the darkness and its shapeless forms. The fear seemed to have been holding him in some conflict with what he dreaded to become and now its absence seemed worse.

The damage Black had wrought had happened many years ago and he'd been fighting that acknowledgement. He knew the worst was over and that knowledge brought only loss.

'If you haven't got any further charges against me, then I will wait for my lawyer', Black said.

He folded his arms and relaxed in his chair.

'I'm not finished with you', Castle said.

'But you haven't got anything on me.'

There was a knock at the door.

Castle found Mike Nash standing in the corridor.

'We've cracked Wilkes', he said.

Castle breathed more deeply than he had in years.

'What's he handed us?'

'He knows we've got Black and he's offered us information. Spinner said that once he felt trapped and saw Black nailed he might turn and boy he did, gave us the lot, the secret meetings with Elijah, Black instructing Elijah to kill. He's even told us where more supplies of the victims' blood are being housed.'

'Excellent Mike.' Castle slapped him on the shoulder. 'Son, you've done a great job, I'm putting a commendation in my report.'

'It's all here', Nash said, handing him Wilkes's statement.

Castle called Stone out of the interview room and they read it together.

'We've got him', she said.

'He's going down for life.'

'And Elijah?'

'Wilkes says he's in Ecuador. We contact the police there, we find him, we get him extradited.'

For the first time Stone saw a glimmer in Castle's eyes.

He went back into the interview room and met Black's gaze.

'We've got you', he said, thumping Wilkes's statement down. He watched Black's eyes drop to the paperwork. 'Now who's lost for words? One of your own, Jonas Wilkes, has turned on the great Karl Black and handed us the nails.' Castle leaned forward until he was inches from Black's face. 'And I'll tell you this, I'm going to drive them so hard into you they will never be removed. The smell of whisky is infinitely preferable to the smell of evil.'

A smile flickered at the corner of Black's face.

'You can waste your words on my lawyer.'

'Wilkes has sold you down the river and I bet it tastes like poison. We have everything we need to put you in prison for the rest of your life. You'll never get out and there are people in jail who won't like you very much, so you better get another Brotherhood together. You've lost. Karl Black, your days will now consist of a cell.'

Black folded his arms and looked away.

Castle was smiling as he left the interview room. Stone saw a veil descend over Black and she walked out into the corridor.

'Drink Frank?'

'Oh yes', he said.

They sat in the Crooked Key and she listened to Don's message on her mobile.

It cheered her and she wondered if she still had a marriage to save.

As she sipped her wine she felt lighter, more hopeful.

Black sat locked in his cell impassive as a monk while they left the pub.

He stared ahead of him, his face blank and devoid of any expression whatsoever.

Castle went home, opened a bottle of whisky and only had a few before going to bed and falling into a deep sleep.

He dreamt he was a young cop again.

When he awoke he could see his son's face. His ice blue eyes pierced his flesh as they tormented him in the semi-darkness of his room.

Castle sat up abruptly, left the house quickly, and made his way to the station.

Rain was falling from the grey polluted skies and he smelt something festering in the downpour.

He drove, white knuckles wrapped around the wheel, a numb sensation in his soul, as if some fisherman were reeling him in and he had forgotten to bleed.

He looked at his face in the rearview mirror and it was the colour of ash.

And behind him there was no road.

Only memory.

And as he drove a private number flashed up on his phone.

He answered.

'Frank Castle.'

'Hello Father, Prepare For Thy Crucifixion.'

If you've enjoyed APOSTLE RISING by Richard Godwin, then why not pick up a copy of THORN IN MY SIDE by Sheila Quigley?

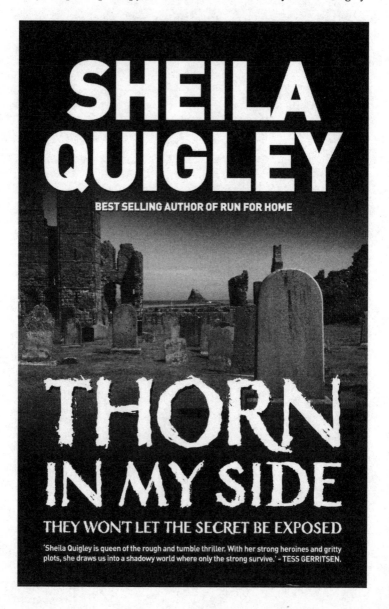

SHEILA QUIGLEY

BEST SELLING AUTHOR OF RUN FOR HOME

THORN
IN MY SIDE

THEY WON'T LET THE SECRET BE EXPOSED

'Sheila Quigley is queen of the rough and tumble thriller. With her strong heroines and gritty plots, she draws us into a shadowy world where only the strong survive.' - TESS GERRITSEN.